In 2004, Jeffery Deaver won the Crime Writers' Association Ian Fleming Steel Dagger Award for his book *Garden of Beasts*. Little did he know that his acceptance speech, where he spoke about his life-long admiration of Fleming's writing, would lead to his being approached to write this James Bond novel.

Deaver is the international number-one best-selling author of two collections of short stories and 28 suspense novels. He is best known for his Lincoln Rhyme thrillers.

Jeffery Deaver lives in North Carolina. Parallels between Bond's and Deaver's lives include their love of fast cars, skiing and whisky.

For further information, visit:
www.jefferydeaver.com and
www.ianfleming.com

CARTE BLANCHE

Fresh from Afghanistan, James Bond has been recruited to a new agency. Conceived in the post-9/11 world, it operates independent of Five, Six and the MoD, its very existence deniable. Its aim: to protect the Realm, by any means necessary. The Night Action alert calls Bond from dinner with a beautiful woman. GCHQ has decrypted an electronic whisper about an attack scheduled for later in the week: casualties estimated in the thousands, British interests adversely affected. And 007 has been given *Carte Blanche* to do whatever it takes to fulfil his mission.

Books by Jeffery Deaver
Published by The House of Ulverscroft:

JEFFERY DEAVER

CARTE BLANCHE
A JAMES BOND NOVEL

Complete and Unabridged

CHARNWOOD
Leicester

First published in Great Britain in 2011 by
Hodder & Stoughton
London

First Charnwood Edition
published 2012
by arrangement with
Hodder & Stoughton
An Hachette UK company
London

British Library CIP Data

Deaver, Jeffery.
　Carte blanche. - - (A James Bond novel)
　1. Bond, James (Fictitious character)- -Fiction.
　2. Intelligence officers- -Great Britain- -Fiction.
　3. Spy stories. 4. Large type books.
　I. Title II. Series
　813.6–dc23

　ISBN 978–1–4448–1154–4

Published by
F. A. Thorpe (Publishing)
Anstey, Leicestershire

Set by Words & Graphics Ltd.
Anstey, Leicestershire
Printed and bound in Great Britain by
T. J. International Ltd., Padstow, Cornwall

*To the man who taught us
we could still believe in heroes,
Ian Fleming*

AUTHOR'S NOTE

This is a work of fiction, although for authenticity I have referred to real places, a few famous historical figures and some well-known brands, such as Audi, Bentley, Inter-continental, iPhone, Mercedes, Maserati and Oakley. Also, with a few exceptions, the intelligence organisations referred to are real. By contrast, all of the characters, their companies and their actions in the book are entirely fictional, and any similarity to any real company or living person is purely coincidental.

The world of intelligence, counter-intelligence and espionage is one of acronyms and shorthand. Since the alphabet soup of security agencies can be a bit daunting, I thought a glossary might prove helpful. It appears at the end of the book.

J.D.

'What is needed is a new organisation to co-ordinate, inspire, control, and assist the nationals of the oppressed countries . . . We need absolute secrecy, a certain fanatical enthusiasm, willingness to work with people of different nationalities and complete political reliability. The organisation should, in my view, be entirely independent of the War Office machinery.'

— Hugh Dalton, Minister of Economic Warfare, describing the formation of Britain's Special Operations Executive espionage and sabotage group at the outbreak of the Second World War.

Sunday
THE RED DANUBE

1

His hand on the dead-man throttle, the driver of the Serbian Rail diesel felt the thrill he always did on this particular stretch of railway, heading north from Belgrade and approaching Novi Sad.

This was the route of the famed Arlberg Orient Express, which ran from Greece through Belgrade and points north from the 1930s until the 1960s. Of course, he was not piloting a glistening Pacific 231 steam locomotive towing elegant mahogany-and-brass dining cars, suites and sleepers, where passengers floated upon vapours of luxury and anticipation. He commanded a battered old thing from America that tugged behind it a string of more or less dependable rolling stock packed snugly with mundane cargo.

But still he felt the thrill of history in every vista that the journey offered, especially as they approached the river, *his* river.

And yet he was ill at ease.

Among the wagons bound for Budapest, containing coal, scrap metal, consumer products and timber, there was one that worried him greatly. It was loaded with drums of MIC — methyl isocyanate — to be used in Hungary in the manufacture of rubber.

The driver — a round, balding man in a well-worn cap and stained overalls — had been briefed at length about this deadly chemical by his supervisor and some idiot from the Serbian Safety and Well-being Transportation Oversight Ministry. Some years ago this substance had killed eight thousand people in Bhopal, India, within a few days of a leak from a manufacturing plant there.

He'd acknowledged the danger his cargo presented but, a veteran railwayman and union member, he'd asked, 'What does that mean for the journey to Budapest . . . specifically?'

The boss and the bureaucrat had regarded each other with the eyes of officialdom and, after a pause, settled for 'Just be very careful.'

The lights of Novi Sad, Serbia's second-largest city, began to coalesce in the distance, and ahead in the encroaching evening the Danube appeared as a pale stripe. In history and in music the river was celebrated. In reality it was brown, undramatic and home to barges and tankers, not candle-lit vessels filled with lovers and Viennese orchestras — or not here, at least. Still, it was the Danube, an icon of Balkan pride, and the railwayman's chest always swelled as he took his train over the bridge.

His river . . .

He peered through the speckled windscreen and inspected the track before him in the headlight of the General Electric diesel. Nothing to be concerned about.

There were eight notch positions on the throttle, number one being the lowest. He was presently at five and he eased back to three to slow the train as it entered a series of turns. The 4,000-horsepower engine grew softer as it cut back the voltage to the traction motors.

As the cars entered the straight section to the bridge the driver shifted up to notch five again and then six. The engine pulsed louder and faster and there came a series of sharp clangs from behind. The sound was, the driver knew, simply the couplings between wagons protesting at the change in speed, a minor cacophony he'd heard a thousand times in his job. But his imagination told him the noise was the metal containers of the deadly chemical in car number three, jostling against each other, at risk of spewing forth their poison.

Nonsense, he told himself and concentrated on keeping the speed steady. Then, for no reason at all, except that it made him feel better, he tugged at the air horn.

2

Lying at the top of a hill, surrounded by obscuring grass, a man of serious face and hunter's demeanour heard the wail of a horn in the distance, miles away. A glance told him that the sound had come from the train approaching from the south. It would arrive here in ten or fifteen minutes. He wondered how it might affect the precarious operation that was about to unfurl.

Shifting position slightly, he studied the diesel locomotive and the lengthy string of wagons behind it through his night-vision monocular.

Judging that the train was of no consequence to himself and his plans, James Bond turned the scope back to the restaurant of the spa and hotel and once again regarded his target through the window. The weathered building was large, yellow stucco with brown trim. Apparently it was a favourite with the locals, from the number of Zastava and Fiat saloons in the car park.

It was eight forty and the Sunday evening was clear here, near Novi Sad, where the Pannonian Plain rose to a landscape that the Serbs called 'mountainous', though Bond guessed the adjective must have been chosen to attract tourists; the rises were mere hills to him, an avid skier. The May air was dry and cool, the surroundings as quiet as an undertaker's chapel of rest.

Bond shifted position again. In his thirties, he

was six foot tall and weighed 170 lb. His black hair was parted on one side and a comma of loose strands fell over one eye. A three-inch scar ran down his right cheek.

This evening he'd taken some care with his outfit. He was wearing a dark green jacket and rainproof trousers from the American company 5.11, which made the best tactical clothing on the market. On his feet were well-worn leather boots that had been made for pursuit and sure footing in a fight.

As night descended, the lights to the north glowed more intensely: the old city of Novi Sad. As lively and charming as it was now, Bond knew the place had a dark past. After the Hungarians had slaughtered thousands of its citizens in January 1942 and flung the bodies into the icy Danube, Novi Sad had become a crucible for partisan resistance. Bond was here tonight to prevent another horror, different in nature but of equal or worse magnitude.

Yesterday, Saturday, an alert had rippled through the British intelligence community. GCHQ, in Cheltenham, had decrypted an electronic whisper about an attack later in the week.

meeting at noah's office, confirm incident friday night, 20th, estimated initial casualties in the thousands, british interests adversely affected, funds transfers as discussed.

Not long after, the government eavesdroppers had also cracked part of a second text message,

7

sent from the same phone, same encryption algorithm, but to a different number.

meet me sunday at restaurant rostilj outside
novi sad, 20:00. i am 6+ foot tall, irish accent.

Then the Irishman — who'd courteously, if inadvertently, supplied his own nickname — had destroyed the phone or flicked out the batteries, as had the other text recipients.

In London the Joint Intelligence Committee and members of COBRA, the crisis management body, met into the night to assess the risk of Incident Twenty, so-called because of Friday's date.

There was no solid information on the origin or nature of the threat but MI6 was of the opinion that it was coming out of the tribal regions in Afghanistan, where al-Qaeda and its affiliates had taken to hiring Western operatives in European countries. Six's agents in Kabul began a major effort to learn more. The Serbian connection had to be pursued, too. And so at ten o'clock last night the rangy tentacles of these events had reached out and clutched Bond, who'd been sitting in an exclusive restaurant off Charing Cross Road with a beautiful woman, whose lengthy description of her life as an under-appreciated painter had grown tiresome. The message on Bond's mobile had read,

NIACT, Call COS.

The Night Action alert meant an immediate response was required, at whatever time it was received.

The call to his chief of staff had blessedly cut the date short and soon he had been en route to Serbia, under a Level 2 project order, authorising him to identify the Irishman, plant trackers and other surveillance devices and follow him. If that proved impossible, the order authorised Bond to conduct an extraordinary rendition of the Irishman and spirit him back to England or to a black site on the Continent for interrogation.

So now Bond lay among white narcissi, taking care to avoid the leaves of that beautiful but poisonous spring flower. He concentrated on peering through the Restoran Roštilj's front window, on the other side of which the Irishman was sitting over an almost untouched plate and talking to his partner, as yet unidentified but Slavic in appearance. Perhaps because he was nervous, the local contact had parked elsewhere and walked here, providing no number plate to scan.

The Irishman had not been so timid. His low-end Mercedes had arrived forty minutes ago. Its plate had revealed that the vehicle had been hired today for cash under a false name, with a fake British driving licence and passport. The man was about Bond's age, perhaps a bit older, six foot two and lean. He'd walked into the restaurant in an ungainly way, his feet turned out. An odd line of blond fringe dipped over a high forehead and his cheekbones angled down to a square-cut chin.

Bond was satisfied that this man was the target. Two hours ago he had gone into the restaurant for a cup of coffee and stuck a listening device inside the front door. A man had arrived at the appointed time and spoken to the head waiter in English — slowly and loudly as foreigners often do when talking to locals. To Bond, listening through an app on his phone from thirty yards away, the accent was clearly mid-Ulster — most likely Belfast or the surrounding area. Unfortunately the meeting between the Irishman and his local contact was taking place out of the bug's range.

Through the tunnel of his monocular, Bond now studied his adversary, taking note of every detail — 'Small clues save you. Small errors kill,' as the instructors at Fort Monckton were wont to remind. He noted that the Irishman's manner was precise and that he made no unnecessary gestures. When the partner drew a diagram the Irishman moved it closer with the rubber of a propelling pencil so that he left no fingerprints. He sat with his back to the window and in front of his partner; the surveillance apps on Bond's mobile could not read either set of lips. Once, the Irishman turned quickly, looking outside, as if triggered by a sixth sense. The pale eyes were devoid of expression. After some time he turned back to the food that apparently didn't interest him.

The meal now seemed to be winding down. Bond eased off the hillock and made his way through widely spaced spruce and pine trees and anaemic undergrowth, with clusters of the ubiquitous white flowers. He passed a faded sign in Serbian, French and English that had amused him when he'd arrived:

He returned to the staging area, behind a decrepit
garden shed that smelt of engine oil, petrol and
piss, near the driveway to the restaurant. His two
'comrades', as he thought of them, were waiting
here.

James Bond preferred to operate alone but the
plan he'd devised required two local agents.
They were with the BIA, the Serbian Security
Information Agency, as benign a name for a spy
outfit as one could imagine. The men, however,
were undercover in the uniform of local police
from Novi Sad, sporting the golden badge of the
Ministry of Internal Affairs.

Faces squat, heads round, perpetually unsmiling, they wore their hair close-cropped beneath
navy-blue brimmed caps. Their woollen uniforms were the same shade. One was around
forty, the other twenty-five. Despite their cover
roles as rural officers, they'd come girded for
battle. They carried heavy Beretta pistols and
swathes of ammunition. In the back seat of their
borrowed police car, a Volkswagen Jetta, there
were two green-camouflaged Kalashnikov machine
guns, an Uzi and a canvas bag of fragmentation

hand grenades — serious ones, Swiss HG 85s.

Bond turned to the older agent, but before he spoke he heard a fierce slapping from behind. His hand moving to his Walther PPS, he whirled round — to see the younger Serb ramming a pack of cigarettes into his palm, a ritual that Bond, a former smoker, had always found absurdly self-conscious and unnecessary.

What was the man *thinking*?

'Quiet,' he whispered coldly. 'And put those away. No smoking.'

Perplexity sidled into the dark eyes. 'My brother, he smokes all time he is out on operations. Looks more normal than *not* smoking in Serbia.' On the drive here the young man had prattled on and on about his brother, a senior agent with the infamous JSO, technically a unit of the state secret service, though Bond knew it was really a black-ops paramilitary group. The young agent had let slip, probably intentionally for he had said it with pride, that big brother had fought with Arkan's Tigers, a ruthless gang that had committed some of the worst atrocities in the fighting in Croatia, Bosnia and Kosovo.

'Maybe on the streets of Belgrade a cigarette won't be noticed,' Bond muttered, 'but this is a tactical operation. Put them away.'

The agent slowly complied. He seemed about to say something to his partner, then thought better of it, perhaps recalling that Bond had a working knowledge of Serbo-Croatian.

Bond looked again into the restaurant and saw that the Irishman was laying some dinars on the metal tray — no traceable credit card, of course.

12

The partner was pulling on a jacket.

'All right. It's time.' Bond reiterated the plan. In the police car they would follow the Irishman's Mercedes out of the drive and along the road until he was a mile or so from the restaurant. The Serbian agents would then pull the car over, telling him it matched a vehicle used in a drug crime in Novi Sad. The Irishman would be asked politely to get out and would be handcuffed. His mobile phone, wallet and identity papers would be placed on the boot of the Mercedes and he'd be led aside and made to sit facing away from the car.

Meanwhile Bond would slip out of the back seat, photograph the documents, download what he could from the phone, look through laptops and luggage, then plant tracking devices.

By then the Irishman would have caught on that this was a shake-down and offered a suitable bribe. He'd be freed, to go on his way.

If the local partner left the restaurant with him, they'd execute essentially the same plan with both men.

'Now, I'm ninety per cent sure he'll believe you,' Bond said. 'But if not, and he engages, remember that under no circumstances is he to be killed. I need him alive. Aim to wound in the arm he favours, near the elbow, not the shoulder.' Despite what one saw in the movies, a shoulder wound was usually as fatal as one to the abdomen or chest.

The Irishman now stepped outside, feet splayed. He looked around, pausing to study the area. Was anything different? he'd be thinking.

13

New cars had arrived since they'd entered; was there anything significant about them? He apparently decided there was no threat and both men climbed into the Mercedes.

'It's the pair of them,' Bond said. 'Same plan.'

'*Da.*'

The Irishman started the engine. The lights flashed on.

Bond oriented his hand on his Walther, snug in the D.M. Bullard leather pancake holster, and climbed into the back seat of the police car, noticing an empty can on the floor. One of his comrades had enjoyed a Jelen Pivo, a Deer Beer, while Bond had been conducting surveillance. The insubordination bothered him less than the carelessness. The Irishman might grow suspicious when stopped by a cop with beer on his breath. Another man's ego and greed can be helpful, Bond believed, but incompetence is simply a useless and inexcusable danger.

The Serbs got into the front. The engine hummed to life. Bond tapped the earpiece of his SRAC, the short-range agent communication device used for cloaked radio transmissions on tactical operations. 'Channel Two,' he reminded them.

'*Da, da.*' The older man sounded bored. They both plugged in earpieces.

And James Bond asked himself yet again: had he planned this properly? Despite the speed with which the operation had been put together, he'd spent hours formulating the tactics. He believed he'd anticipated every possible variation.

Except one, it appeared.

The Irishman did not do what he absolutely had to.

He didn't leave.

The Mercedes turned away from the drive and rolled out of the car park on to the lawn beside the restaurant, on the other side of a tall hedge, unseen by the staff and diners. It was heading for a weed-riddled field to the east.

The younger agent snapped, '*Govno!* What he is doing?' The three men stepped out to get a better view. The older one drew his gun and started after the car.

Bond waved him to a halt. 'No! Wait.'

'He's escaping. He knows about us!'

'No — it's something else.' The Irishman wasn't driving as if he were being pursued. He was moving slowly, the Mercedes easing forward, like a boat in a gentle morning swell. Besides, there was no place to escape *to*. He was hemmed in by cliffs overlooking the Danube, the railway embankment and the forest on the Fruška Gora rise.

Bond watched as the Mercedes arrived at the railtrack, a hundred yards from where they stood. It slowed, made a U-turn and parked, the bonnet facing back towards the restaurant. It was close to a railway work shed and switch rails, where a second track peeled off from the main line. Both men climbed out and the Irishman collected something from the boot.

Your enemy's purpose will dictate your response — Bond silently recited another maxim from the lectures at Fort Monckton's Specialist Training Centre in Gosport. You must find the

15

adversary's intention.

But what *was* his purpose?

Bond pulled out the monocular again, clicked on the night vision and focused. The partner opened a panel mounted on a signal beside the switch rails and began fiddling with the components inside. Bond saw that the second track, leading off to the right, was a rusting, disused spur, ending in a barrier at the top of a hill.

So it was sabotage. They were going to derail the train by shunting it on to the spur. The cars would tumble down the hill into a stream that flowed into the Danube.

But why?

Bond turned the monocular towards the diesel engine and the wagons behind it and saw the answer. The first two cars contained only scrap metal, but behind them, a canvas-covered flatbed was marked *Opasnost-Danger!* He saw, too, a hazardous-materials diamond, the universal warning sign that told emergency rescuers the risks of a particular shipment. Alarmingly this diamond had high numbers for all three categories: health, instability and inflammability. The W at the bottom meant that the substance would react dangerously with water. Whatever was being carried in that car was in the deadliest category short of nuclear materials.

The train was now three-quarters of a mile away from the switch rails, picking up speed to make the gradient to the bridge.

Your enemy's purpose will dictate your response . . .

He didn't know how the sabotage related to

Incident Twenty, if at all, but their immediate goal was clear. As was the response Bond now instinctively formulated. He said to the comrades, 'If they try to leave, block them at the drive and take them. No lethal force.'

He leapt into the driver's seat of the Jetta. He pointed the car towards the fields where he'd been conducting surveillance and jammed down the accelerator as he released the clutch. The light car shot forward, engine and gearbox crying out at the rough treatment, as it crashed over brush, saplings, narcissi and the raspberry bushes that grew everywhere in Serbia. Dogs fled and lights in the tiny cottages nearby flicked on. Residents in their gardens waved their arms angrily in protest.

Bond ignored them and concentrated on maintaining his speed as he drove towards his destination, guided only by scant illumination: a partial moon above and the doomed train's headlight, far brighter and rounder than the lamp of heaven.

3

The impending death weighed on him.

Niall Dunne crouched among weeds, thirty feet from the switch rails. He squinted through the fading light of early evening at the Serbian Rail driver's cab of the freight train as it approached and he again thought: a tragedy.

For one thing, death was usually a waste and Dunne was, first and foremost, a man who disliked waste — it was almost sinful. Diesel engines, hydraulic pumps, drawbridges, electric motors, computers, assembly lines . . . all machines were meant to perform their tasks with as little waste as possible.

Death was efficiency squandered.

Yet there seemed to be no way around it tonight.

He looked south, at the glistening needles of white illumination on the rails from the train's headlight. He glanced round. The Mercedes was out of sight of the train, parked at just the right angle to keep it hidden from the cab. It was yet another of the precise calculations he had incorporated into his blueprint for the evening. He heard, in memory, his boss's voice.

This is Niall. He's brilliant. He's my draughtsman . . .

Dunne believed he could see the shadow of the driver's head in the cab of the diesel.

Death . . . He tried to shrug away the thought.

The train was now four or five hundred yards away.

Aldo Karic joined him.

'The speed?' Dunne asked the middle-aged Serb. 'Is it all right? He seems slow.'

In syrupy English the Serbian said, 'No, is good. Accelerating now — look. You can see. Is good.' Karic, a bearish man, sucked air through his teeth. He'd seemed nervous throughout dinner — not, he'd confessed, because he might be arrested or fired but because of the difficulty in keeping the ten thousand euros secret from everyone, including his wife and two children.

Dunne regarded the train again. He calculated speed, mass, incline. Yes, it *was* good. At this point even if someone tried to wave the train down, even if a Belgrade supervisor happened to notice something was amiss, phoned the driver and ordered him to apply full brakes, it would be physically impossible to stop the train before it hit the switch rails, now configured to betray.

And he reminded himself: sometimes death is necessary.

The train was now three hundred yards away.

It would all be over in ninety seconds. And then —

But what was this? Dunne was suddenly aware of movement in a field nearby, an indistinct shape pounding over the uneven ground making directly for the track. 'Do you see that?' he asked Karic.

The Serbian gasped. 'Yes, I am seeing — It's a car! What is happening?'

It was indeed. In the faint moonlight Dunne

19

could see the small light-coloured saloon, assaulting hillocks and swerving around trees and fragments of fences. How could the driver keep his high speed on such a course? It seemed impossible.

Teenagers, perhaps, playing one of their stupid games. As he stared at the mad transit, he judged velocity, he judged angles. If the car didn't slow it would cross the track with some seconds to spare . . . but the driver would have to vault over the tracks themselves; there was no crossing here. If it were stuck on the rail, the diesel would crush it like a tin of vegetables. Still, that wouldn't affect Dunne's mission here. The tiny car would be pitched aside and the train continue to the deadly spur.

Now — wait — what was *this?* Dunne realised it was a police car. But why no lights or siren? It must have been stolen. A suicide?

But the police car's driver had no intention of stopping on the rail or crossing to the other side. With a final leap into the air from the crest of the hill, the saloon crashed to earth and skidded to a stop, just short of the roadbed, around fifty yards in front of the train. The driver jumped out — a man. He was wearing dark clothing. Dunne couldn't see him clearly but he appeared not to be a policeman. Neither was he trying to flag down the engine driver. He ran into the middle of the track itself and crouched calmly, directly in front of the locomotive, which bore down upon him at fifty or sixty miles an hour.

The frantic blare of the train's horn filled the night and orange streaks of sparks shot from the locked wheels.

With the train feet away from him, the man launched himself from the track and vanished into the ditch.

'What is happening?' Karic whispered.

Just then a yellow-white flash burst from the tracks in front of the diesel and a moment later Dunne heard a crack he recognised: the explosion of a small IED or grenade. A similar blast followed seconds later.

The driver of the police car, it seemed, had a blueprint of his own.

One that trumped Dunne's.

No, he wasn't a policeman or a suicide. He was an operative of some sort, with experience in demolition work. The first explosion had blown out the spikes fixing the rail to the wooden ties, the second had pushed the unsecured track to the side slightly so that the diesel's front left wheels would slip off.

Karic muttered something in Serbian. Dunne ignored him and watched the disc of the diesel's headlight waver. Then, with a rumble and a terrible squeal, the engine and the massive wagons it tugged behind sidled off the track and, spewing a world of dust, pushed forward through the soil and chipped rock of the rail bed.

4

From the ditch, James Bond watched the locomotive and the cars continue their passage, slowing as they dug into the soft earth, peeling up rails and flinging sand, dirt and stones everywhere. Finally he climbed out and assessed the situation. He'd had only minutes to work out how to avert the calamity that would send the deadly substance into the Danube. After braking to a stop, he'd grabbed two of the grenades the Serbians had brought with them, then leapt on to the tracks to plant the devices.

As he had calculated, the locomotive and wagons had stayed upright and hadn't toppled into the stream. He'd orchestrated *his* derailment where the ground was still flat, unlike the intended setting of the Irishman's sabotage. Finally, hissing, groaning and creaking, the train came to a standstill not far from the Irishman and his partner, though Bond could not see them through the dust and smoke.

He spoke into the SRAC radio. 'This is Leader One. Are you there?' Silence. 'Are you there?' he growled. 'Respond.' Bond massaged his shoulder, where a sliver of hot, whistling shrapnel had torn through his jacket and sliced skin.

A crackle. Finally: 'The train is derailed!' It was the older Serbian's voice. 'Did you see? Where are you?'

'Listen to me carefully.'

22

'What has happened?'

'Listen! We don't have much time. I think they'll try to blow up or shoot the haz-mat containers. It's their only way to spill the contents. I'm going to fire towards them and drive them back to their car. Wait till the Mercedes is in that muddy area near the restaurant, then shoot out the tyres and keep them inside it.'

'We should take them now!'

'No. Don't do anything until they're beside the restaurant. They'll have no defensive position inside the Mercedes. They'll have to surrender. Do you understand me?'

The SRAC went dead.

Damn. Bond started forward through the dust towards the place where the third rail car, the one containing the hazardous material, waited to be ripped open.

* * *

Niall Dunne tried to reconstruct what had happened. He'd known he might have to improvise, but this was one thing he had not considered: a pre-emptive strike by an unknown enemy.

He looked out carefully from his vantage-point, a stand of bushes near where the locomotive sat, smoking, clicking and hissing. The assailant was invisible, hidden by the darkness of night, the dust and fumes. Maybe the man had been crushed to death. Or fled. Dunne lifted the rucksack over his shoulder and made his way round the diesel to the far side, where the derailed wagons would give him cover from the intruder — if he was still alive and present.

In a curious way, Dunne found himself relieved of his nagging anxiety. The death had been averted. He'd been fully prepared for it, had steeled himself — anything for his boss, of course — but the other man's intervention had settled the matter.

As he approached the diesel he couldn't help but admire the massive machine. It was an American General Electric Dash 8–40B, old and battered, as you usually saw in the Balkans, but a classic beauty, 4,000 horsepower. He noted the sheets of steel, the wheels, vents, bearings and valves, the springs, hoses and pipes . . . all so beautiful, elegant in simple functionality. Yes, it was such a relief that —

He was startled by a man staggering towards him, begging for help. It was the train driver. Dunne shot him twice in the head.

It was such a relief that he hadn't been forced to cause the death of this wonderful machine, as he'd been dreading. He ran his hand along the side of the locomotive, as a father would stroke the hair of a sick child whose fever had just broken. The diesel would be back in service in a few months' time.

Niall Dunne hitched the rucksack higher on his shoulder and slipped between the wagons to get to work.

5

The two shots James Bond had heard had not hit the hazardous-materials car — he was covering that from thirty yards away. He guessed the engine driver and perhaps his mate had been the victims.

Then, through the dust, he saw the Irishman. Gripping a black pistol, he stood between the two jack-knifed wagons filled with scrap metal directly behind the engine. A rucksack hung from his shoulder. It seemed to be full, which meant that if he intended to blow up the hazardous-material containers, he hadn't set the charges yet.

Bond aimed his pistol and fired two shots close to the Irishman, to drive him back to the Mercedes. The man crouched, startled, then vanished fast.

Bond looked towards the restaurant side of the track, where the Mercedes was parked. His mouth tightened. The Serbian agents hadn't followed his orders. They were now flanking the work shed, having pulled the Irishman's Slavic associate to the ground and slipped nylon restraints around his wrists. The two were now moving closer to the train.

Incompetence . . .

Bond scrabbled to his feet and, keeping low, ran towards them.

The Serbs were pointing at the tracks. The

25

rucksack now sat on the ground, among some tall plants near the engine, obscuring a man. Crouching, the agents moved forward cautiously.

The bag was the Irishman's . . . but, of course, the man behind it was not. The driver's body, probably.

'No,' Bond whispered into the SRAC. 'It's a trick! . . . Are you there?'

But the older agent wasn't listening. He stepped forward, shouting, 'Ne mrdaj! Do not move!'

At that moment the Irishman leant out of the engine's cab and fired a burst from his pistol, hitting him in the head. He dropped hard.

His younger colleague assumed that the man on the ground was firing and emptied his automatic weapon into the dead body of the driver.

Bond shouted, 'Opasnost!'

But it was too late. The Irishman leant out of the cab again and shot the younger agent in the right arm, near the elbow. He dropped his gun and cried out, falling backwards.

As the Irishman leapt from the train, he let go half a dozen rounds towards Bond, who returned fire, aiming for the feet and ankles. But the haze and vapours were thick. He missed. The Irishman holstered his gun, shouldered the rucksack and dragged the younger agent towards the Mercedes. They disappeared.

Bond sprinted back to the Jetta, jumped in and roared off. Five minutes later he soared over a hillock and landed, skidding, in the field behind Restoran Roštilj. The scene was one of complete chaos as diners and staff fled in panic. The Mercedes was gone. Glancing towards the derailed train, he could see that the Irishman had killed not only the older agent but his own associate — the Serbian he'd dined with. He'd shot him as he'd lain on his belly, hands bound.

Bond got out of the Jetta and frisked the body for pocket litter but the Irishman had stripped the man of his wallet and any other material. Bond pulled out his own Oakley sunglasses, wiped them clean, then pressed the dead man's thumb and index finger against the lens. He ran back to the Jetta and sped after the Mercedes, urging the car to seventy miles an hour despite the meandering road and potholes pitting the tarmac.

A few minutes later he glimpsed something light-coloured in a lay-by ahead. He braked hard, barely controlling the fishtailing skid, and stopped, the car engulfed in smoke from its tyres, a few yards from the younger agent. He got out and bent over the man, who was shivering, crying. The wound in his arm was bad and he'd lost a great deal of blood. One shoe was off and a toenail was gone. The Irishman had tortured him.

Bond opened his folding knife, cut the man's shirt with the razor-sharp blade and bound a wool strip round his arm. With a stick he found just off the lay-by he made a tourniquet and applied it. He leant down and wiped sweat from the man's face. 'Where is he going?'

Gasping, his face a mask of agony, he rambled in Serbo-Croatian. Then, realising who Bond was, he said, 'You will call my brother . . . You must take me to the hospital. I will tell you a place to go.'

'I need to know where he went.'

'I didn't say nothing. He tried. But I didn't tell nothing about you.'

The boy had spilt out everything he knew about the operation, of course, but that wasn't the issue now. Bond said, 'Where did he go?'

'The hospital . . . Take me and I will tell you.'

'Tell me or you'll die in five minutes,' Bond said evenly, loosening the tourniquet on his right arm. Blood cascaded.

The young man blinked away tears. 'All right! You bastard! He ask how to get to E Seven-five, the fast road from Highway Twenty-one. That will take him to Hungary. He is going north. Please!'

Bond tightened the tourniquet again. He knew, of course, that the Irishman wasn't going north: the man was a cruel and clever tactician. He didn't need directions. Bond saw his own devotion to tradecraft in the Irishman. Even before he had arrived in Serbia the man would have memorised the geography around Novi Sad. He'd go *south* on Highway 21, the only major road nearby. He'd be making for Belgrade or an evacuation site in the area.

Bond patted the young agent's pockets and pulled out his mobile. He hit the emergency call number, 112. When he heard a woman's voice answer, he propped the phone beside the man's mouth, then ran back to the Jetta. He concentrated on driving as fast as he could over

28

the uneven road surface, losing himself in the choreography of braking and steering.

He took a turn fast and the car skidded, crossing the white line. An oncoming lorry loomed, a big one, with a Cyrillic logo. It veered away and the driver hit the horn angrily. Bond swerved back into his lane, missing a collision by inches, and continued in pursuit of the only lead they had to Noah and the thousands of deaths on Friday.

Five minutes later, approaching Highway 21, Bond slowed. Ahead he saw a flicker of orange and, in the sky, roiling smoke, obscuring the moon and stars. He soon arrived at the accident site. The Irishman had missed a sharp bend and sought refuge in what seemed to be a wide grass shoulder but in fact was not. A line of brush masked a steep drop. The car had gone over and was now upside-down. The engine was on fire.

Bond pulled up, killed the Jetta's motor and got out. Then, drawing the Walther, he half ran, half slid down the hill to where the vehicle lay, scanning for threats and seeing none. As he closed on it he stopped. The Irishman was dead. Still strapped into the seat, he was inverted, arms dangling over his shoulders. Blood covered his face and neck and pooled on the car's ceiling.

Squinting against the fumes, Bond kicked in the driver's window to drag the body out. He would salvage the man's mobile and what pocket litter he could, then wrench open the boot to collect luggage and laptops.

He opened his knife again to cut the seat belt. In the distance: the urgent *wah-ha* of sirens, growing louder. He looked back up the road. The fire engines were still a few miles away but they'd be here soon. Get on with it! The flames from the engine were increasingly energetic. The smoke was vile.

As he began to saw away at the belt, though, he thought suddenly: firefighters? Already?

That made no sense. Police, yes. But not the fire brigade. He gripped the driver's bloodied hair and turned the head.

It was not the Irishman. Bond gazed at the man's jacket: the Cyrillic lettering was the same as on the lorry he'd nearly hit. The Irishman had forced the vehicle to stop. He'd cut the driver's throat, strapped him into the Mercedes and sent it over the cliff here, then called the local fire service in order to slow the traffic and prevent Bond pursuing him.

The Irishman would have taken the rucksack and everything else from the boot, of course. Inside the car, though, on the inverted ceiling, towards the back seat, there were a few scraps of paper. Bond jammed them into his pockets before the flames forced him away. He ran back to the Jetta and sped off towards Highway 21, away from the approaching flashing lights.

He fished out his mobile. It resembled an iPhone, but was a bit larger and featured special optics, audio systems and other hardware. The unit contained multiple phones — one that could be registered to an agent's official or nonofficial cover identity, then a hidden unit, with hundreds of operational apps and encryption packages. (Because the device had been developed by Q Branch it had taken all of a day for some wit in the office to dub them 'iQPhones'.)

He opened an app that gave him a priority link to a GCHQ tracking centre. He recited into the voice-recognition system a description of the yellow Zastava Eurozeta lorry the Irishman was driving. The computer in Cheltenham would automatically recognise Bond's location and determine projected routes for the truck, then train the satellite to look for any nearby vehicle of this sort and track it.

Five minutes later he heard his phone buzz. Excellent. He glanced at the screen.

But the message was not from the snoops; it was from Bill Tanner, chief of staff at Bond's outfit. The subject heading said: CRASH DIVE — shorthand for Emergency.

Eyes flipping from the road to the phone, Bond read on.

GCHQ intercept: Serbian security agent assigned to you in Incident 20 operation died on way to hospital. Reported you abandoned him. Serbs have priority order for your arrest. Evacuate immediately.

Monday
THE RAG-AND-BONE MAN

6

After three and a half hours' sleep James Bond was woken at seven a.m. in his Chelsea flat by the electronic tone of his mobile phone's alarm clock. His eyes focused on the white ceiling of the small bedroom. He blinked twice and, ignoring the pain in his shoulder, head and knees, rolled out of the double bed, prodded by the urge to get on the trail of the Irishman and Noah.

His clothes from the mission to Novi Sad lay on the hardwood floor. He tossed the tactical outfit into a training kitbag, gathered up the rest of his clothes and dropped them into the laundry bin, a courtesy to May, his treasure of a Scottish housekeeper who came three times a week to sort out his domestic life. He would not think of having her pick up his clutter.

Naked, Bond walked into the bathroom, turned on the shower as hot as he could stand it and scrubbed himself hard with unscented soap. Then he turned the temperature down, stood under freezing water until he could tolerate *that* no longer, stepped out and dried himself. He examined his wounds from last night: two large aubergine-coloured bruises on his leg, some scrapes and the slice on his shoulder from the grenade shrapnel. Nothing serious.

He shaved with a heavy, double-bladed safety razor, its handle of light buffalo horn. He used this fine accessory not because it was greener to the environment than the plastic disposables that most men employed but simply because it gave a better shave — and required some skill to wield; James Bond found comfort even in small challenges.

By seven fifteen he was dressed: a navy-blue Canali suit, a white sea island shirt and a burgundy Grenadine tie, the latter items from Turnbull & Asser. He donned black shoes, slip-ons; he never wore laces, except for combat footwear or when trade-craft required him to send silent messages to a fellow agent via prearranged loopings.

Onto his wrist he slipped his steel Rolex Oyster Perpetual, the 34mm model, the date window its only complication; Bond did not need to know the phases of the moon or the exact moment of high tide at Southampton. And he suspected very few people did.

Most days he had breakfast — his favourite meal of the day — at a small hotel nearby in Pont Street. Occasionally he cooked for himself one of the few things he was capable of whipping up in the kitchen: three eggs softly scrambled with Irish butter. The steaming curds were accompanied by bacon and crisp wholemeal toast, with more Irish butter and marmalade.

Today, though, the urgency of Incident Twenty was in full bloom so there was no time for food. Instead he brewed a cup of fiercely strong Jamaica Blue Mountain coffee, which he drank from a china mug as he listened to Radio 4 to learn whether or not the train incident and subsequent deaths had made the international news. They had not.

His wallet and cash were in his pocket, his car key, too. He grabbed the plastic carrier bag of the items he had collected in Serbia and the locked steel box that contained his weapon and ammunition, which he could not carry legally within the UK.

He hurried down the stairs of his flat — formerly two spacious stables. He unlocked the door and stepped into the garage. The cramped space was large enough, just, for the two cars that were inside, plus a few extra tyres and tools. He climbed into the newer of the vehicles, the latest model Bentley Continental GT, its exterior the company's distinctive granite grey, with supple black hide inside.

The turbo W12 engine murmured to life. Tapping the downshift paddle into first gear, he eased into the road, leaving behind his other vehicle, less powerful and more temperamental but just as elegant: a 1960s E-type Jaguar, which had been his father's.

Driving north, Bond manoeuvred through the traffic, with tens of thousands of others who were similarly making their way to offices throughout London at the start of yet another week — although, of course, in Bond's case this mundane image belied the truth.

Exactly the same could be said for his employer itself.

Three years ago, James Bond had been sitting at a grey desk in the monolithic grey Ministry of Defence building in Whitehall, the sky outside not grey at all but the blue of a Highland loch on a bright summer's day. After leaving the Royal Naval Reserve, he had had no desire for a job managing accounts at Saatchi & Saatchi or reviewing balance sheets for NatWest and had telephoned a former Fettes fencing teammate, who had suggested he try Defence Intelligence.

After a stint at DI, writing analyses that were described as both blunt and valuable, he had wondered to his supervisor if there might be a chance to see a little more action.

Not long after that conversation, he had received a mysterious missive, handwritten, not an email, requesting his presence for lunch in Pall Mall, at the Travellers Club.

On the day in question, Bond had been led into the dining room and seated in a corner opposite a solid man in his mid-sixties, identified only as the 'Admiral'. He wore a grey suit that perfectly matched his eyes. His face was jowled and his head crowned with a sparse constellation of birthmarks, evident through the thinning, swept-back brown and grey hair. The Admiral had looked steadily at Bond without challenge or disdain or excessive analysis. Bond had no trouble in returning the gaze — a man who has killed in battle and nearly died himself is not cowed by anyone's stare. He realised, however, that he had absolutely no idea what was going on in the man's mind.

They did not shake hands.

Menus descended. Bond ordered halibut on the bone, steamed, with Hollandaise, boiled potatoes and grilled asparagus. The Admiral selected the grilled kidney and bacon, then asked Bond, 'Wine?'

'Yes, please.'

'You choose.'

'Burgundy, I should think,' Bond said. 'Côte de Beaune? Or a Chablis?'

'The Alex Gambal Puligny, perhaps?' the waiter suggested.

'Perfect.'

The bottle arrived a moment later. The waiter smoothly displayed the label and poured a little into Bond's glass. The wine was the colour of pale butter, earthy and excellent, and exactly the right temperature, not too chilled. Bond sipped, nodded his approval and the glasses were half filled.

When the waiter had departed, the older man said gruffly, 'You're a veteran and so am I. Neither of us has any interest in small-talk. I've asked you here to discuss a career opportunity.'

'I thought as much, sir.' Bond hadn't intended to add the final word, but it had been impossible not to do so.

'You may be familiar with the rule at the Travellers about not exposing business documents. Afraid we'll have to break it.' The older man withdrew from his breast pocket an envelope. He handed it over. 'This is similar to the Official Secrets Act declaration.'

'I've signed one — '

'Of course you have — for Defence Intelligence,' the man said briskly, revealing his impatience at stating the obvious. 'This has a few more teeth. Read it.'

39

Bond did so. More teeth indeed, to put it mildly.

The Admiral said, 'If you're not interested in signing we'll finish our lunch and discuss the recent election or trout fishing in the north or how those damn Kiwis beat us again last week and get back to our offices.' He lifted a bushy eyebrow.

Bond hesitated only a moment, then scrawled his name across the line and handed it back. The document vanished.

A sip of wine. The Admiral asked, 'Have you heard of the Special Operations Executive?'

'I have, yes.' Bond had few idols, but high on the list was Winston Churchill. In his young days as a reporter and soldier in Cuba and Sudan Churchill had formed a great respect for guerrilla operations and later, after the outbreak of the Second World War, he and the minister for economic warfare, Hugh Dalton, had created the SOE to arm partisans behind German lines and to parachute in British spies and saboteurs. Also called Churchill's Secret Army, it had caused immeasurable harm to the Nazis.

'Good outfit,' the Admiral said, then grumbled, 'They closed it down after the war. Inter-agency nonsense, organisational difficulties, in-fighting at MI6 and Whitehall.' He took a sip of the fragrant wine and conversation slowed while they ate. The meal was superb. Bond said so. The Admiral rasped, 'Chef knows what he's about. No aspirations to cook his way on to American television. Are you familiar with how Five and Six got going?'

'Yes, sir — I've read quite a lot about it.'

In 1909, in response to concerns about a German invasion and spies within England (concerns that had been prompted, curiously, by popular thriller novels), the Admiralty and the War Office had formed the Secret Service Bureau. Not long after that, the SSB split into the Directorate of Military Intelligence Section 5, or MI5, to handle domestic security, and Section 6, or MI6, to handle foreign espionage. Six was the oldest continuously operating spy organisation in the world, despite China's claim to the contrary.

The Admiral said, 'What's the one element that stands out about them both?'

Bond couldn't begin to guess.

'Plausible deniability,' the older man muttered. 'Both Five and Six were created as cut-outs so that the Crown, the prime minister, the Cabinet and the War Office didn't have to get their hands dirty with that nasty business of spying. Just as bad now. Lot of scrutiny of what Five and Six do. Sexed-up dossiers, invasion of privacy, political snooping, rumours of illegal targeted killings . . . Everybody's clamouring for *transparency*. Of course, no one seems to care that the face of war is changing, that the other side doesn't play by the rules much any more.' Another sip of wine. 'There's thinking, in some circles, that *we* need to play by a different set of rules too. Especially after Nine-eleven and Seven-seven.'

Bond said, 'So, if I understand correctly, you're talking about starting a new version of the SOE, but one that isn't technically part of Six, Five or the MoD.'

41

The Admiral held Bond's eye. 'I read those reports of your performance in Afghanistan — Royal Naval Reserve, yet still you managed to get yourself attached to forward combat units on the ground. Took some doing.' The cool eyes regarded him closely. 'I understand you also managed some missions behind the lines that weren't quite so official. Thanks to you, some fellows who could have caused quite a lot of mischief never got the chance.'

Bond was about to sip from his glass of Puligny-Montrachet, the highest incarnation of the chardonnay grape. He set the glass down without doing so. How the devil had the old man learnt about *those*?

In a low, even voice the man said, 'There's no shortage of Special Air or Boat Service chaps about who know their way around a knife and sniper rifle. But they don't necessarily fit into other, shall we say *subtler*, situations. And then there are plenty of talented Five and Six fellows who know the difference between . . . ' he glanced at Bond's glass ' . . . a Côte de Beaune and a Côte de Nuits and can speak French as fluently as they can Arabic — but who'd faint at the sight of blood, theirs or anyone else's.' The steel eyes zeroed in. 'You seem to be a rather rare combination of the best of both.'

The Admiral put down his knife and fork on the bone china. 'Your question.'

'My . . . ?'

'About a new version of the Special Operations Executive. The answer is yes. In fact, it already exists. Would you be interested in joining?'

'I would,' Bond said without hesitation. 'Though I should like to ask: what exactly does it do?'

The Admiral thought for a moment, as if polishing burrs off his reply. 'Our mission,' he said, 'is simple. We protect the Realm . . . by any means necessary.'

7

In the sleek, purring Bentley, Bond now approached the headquarters of this very organisation, near Regent's Park, after half an hour of the zigzagging that driving in central London necessitates.

The name of his employer was nearly as vague as that of the Special Operations Executive: the Overseas Development Group. The director-general was the Admiral, known only as M.

Officially the ODG assisted British-based companies in opening or expanding foreign operations and investing abroad. Bond's OC, or official cover, within it was as a security and integrity analyst. His job was to travel the world and assess business risks.

No matter that the moment he landed he assumed an NOC — a *nonofficial* cover — with a fictitious identity, tucked away the Excel spreadsheets, put on his 5.11 tactical outfit and armed himself with a .308 rifle with Nikon Buckmasters scope. Or perhaps he'd slip into a well-cut Savile Row suit to play poker with a Chechnyan arms dealer in a private Kiev club, for the chance to assess his security detail in a run-up to the evening's main event: the man's rendition to a black site in Poland.

Tucked away inconspicuously in the hierarchy of the Foreign and Commonwealth Office, the ODG was housed in a narrow, six-storey Edwardian building on a quiet road, just off Devonshire

Street. It was separated from bustling Marylebone Road by lacklustre — but camouflaging — solicitors' quarters, NGO offices and doctors' surgeries.

Bond now motored to the entrance of the tunnel leading to the car park beneath the building. He glanced into the iris scanner, then was vetted again, this time by a human being. The barrier lowered and he eased the car forward in search of a parking bay.

The lift, too, checked Bond's blue eyes, then took him up to the ground floor. He stepped into the armourer's office, beside the pistol range, and handed the locked steel box to redheaded Freddy Menzies, a former corporal in the SAS and one of the finest firearms men in the business. He would make sure the Walther was cleaned, oiled and checked for damage, the magazines filled with Bond's preferred loads.

'She'll be ready in half an hour,' Menzies said. 'She behave herself, 007?'

Bond had professional affection for certain tools of his trade but he didn't personify them — and, if anything, a .40 calibre Walther, even the compact Police Pistol Short, would definitely be a 'he'. 'Acquitted itself well,' he replied.

He took the lift to the third floor where he stepped out and turned left, walking down a bland, white-painted corridor, the walls a bit scuffed, their monotony broken by prints of London from the era of Cromwell to Victoria's reign and of battlefields aplenty. Someone had brightened up the windowsills with vases of greenery — fake, of course; the real thing would have meant employing external maintenance staff to water and prune.

Bond spotted a young woman in front of a desk at the end of a large open area filled with work stations. Sublime, he had thought, upon meeting her a month ago. Her face was heart-shaped, with high cheekbones, and surrounded by Rossetti red hair that cascaded from her marvellous temples to past her shoulders. A tiny off-centre dimple, which he found completely charming, distressed her chin. Her hazel eyes, golden green, held yours intently, and to Bond, her figure was as a woman's should be: slim and elegant. Her unpainted nails were trimmed short. Today she was in a knee-length black skirt and an apricot shirt, high-necked, yet thin enough to hint at lace beneath, managing to be both tasteful and provocative. Her legs were embraced by nylon the colour of café au lait.

Stockings or tights? Bond couldn't help but wonder.

Ophelia Maidenstone was an intelligence analyst with MI6. She was stationed with the ODG as a liaison officer because the Group was not an intelligence-gathering organisation; it was operational, tactical, largely. Accordingly, like the Cabinet and the prime minister, it was a consumer of 'product', as intelligence was called. And the ODG's main supplier was Six.

Admittedly, Philly's appearance and forthright manner were what had initially caught Bond's attention, just as her tireless efforts and resourcefulness had held it. Equally alluring, though, was her love of driving. Her favourite vehicle was a BSA 1966 Spitfire, the A65, one of the most beautiful motorcycles ever made. It wasn't the most powerful bike in the Birmingham Small Arms' line but it was a true classic and, when properly tuned (which, God bless her, she did herself), it left a broad streak of rubber at the take-off line. She'd told Bond she liked to drive in all weather and had bought an insulated leather jumpsuit that let her take to the roads whenever she fancied. He'd imagined it as an extremely tight-fitting garment and arched an eyebrow. He'd received in return a sardonic smile, which told him that his gesture had ricocheted like a badly placed bullet.

She was, it emerged, engaged to be married. The ring, which he'd noted immediately, was a deceptive ruby.

So, that settled that.

Philly now looked up with an infectious smile. 'James, hello! . . . Why are you looking at me like that?'

'I need you.'

She tucked back a loose strand of hair. 'Delighted to help if I could but I've got something on for John. He's in Sudan. They're about to start shooting.'

The Sudanese had been fighting the British, the Egyptians, other nearby African nations — and themselves — for more than a hundred years. The Eastern Alliance, several Sudanese states near the Red Sea, wanted to secede and form a moderate secular country. The regime in Khartoum, still buffeted by the recent independence movement in the south, was not pleased by this initiative.

Bond said, 'I know. I was the one going originally. I drew Belgrade instead.'

'The food's better,' she said, with studied gravity. 'If you like plums.'

'It's just that I collected some things in Serbia that should be looked into.'

'It's never 'just' with you, James.'

Her mobile buzzed. She frowned, peering at the screen. As she took the call, her piercing hazel eyes swung his way and regarded him with some humour. She said, into the phone, 'I see.' When she had disconnected, she said, 'You pulled in some favours. Or bullied someone.'

'Me? Never.'

'It seems that war in Africa will have to soldier on without me. So to speak.' She went to another work station and handed the Khartoum baton to a fellow spook.

Bond sat down. There seemed to be something different about her space but he couldn't work out what it was. Perhaps she'd tidied it, or rearranged the furniture — as far as anyone could in the tiny area.

When she came back she focused her eyes on him. 'Right, then. I'm all yours. What do we have?'

'Incident Twenty.'

'Ah, that. I wasn't on the hot list so you'd better brief me.'

Like Bond, Ophelia Maidenstone was Developed Vetting Cleared by the Defence Vetting Agency, the FCO and Scotland Yard, which permitted virtually unlimited access to top-secret material, short of the most classified nuclear-arms data. He briefed her on Noah, the Irishman, the threat on Friday and the incident in Serbia. She took careful notes.

'I need you to play detective inspector. This is all we have to go on.' He handed her the carrier bag containing the slips of paper he'd snatched from the burning car outside Novi Sad and his own sunglasses. 'I'll need identification fast — very fast — and anything else you dig up.'

She lifted her phone and requested collection of the materials for analysis at the MI6 laboratory or, if that proved insufficient, Scotland Yard's extensive forensic operation in Specialist Crimes. She rang off. 'Runner's on his way.' She found a pair of tweezers in her handbag and extracted the two slips of paper. One was a bill from a pub near Cambridge, the date recent. It had been settled in cash unfortunately.

The other slip of paper read: *Boots — March. 17. No later than that.* Was it code or merely a reminder from two months ago to pick up something at the chemist?

'And the Oakleys?' She was gazing down into the bag.

'There's a fingerprint in the middle of the right lens. The Irishman's partner. There was no pocket litter.'

She made copies of the two documents, handed him a set, kept one for herself and replaced the originals in the bag with the glasses.

Bond then explained about the hazardous material that the Irishman was trying to spill into the Danube. 'I need to know what it was. And what kind of damage it could have caused. Afraid I've ruffled some feathers among the Serbs. They won't want to co-operate.'

'We'll see about that.'

Just then his mobile buzzed. He looked at the screen, though he knew this distinctive chirp quite well. He answered. 'Moneypenny.'

The woman's low voice said, 'Hello, James. Welcome back.'

'M?' he asked.

'M.'

8

The sign beside the top-floor office read *Director-General.*

Bond stepped into the ante-room, where a woman in her mid-thirties sat at a tidy desk. She wore a pale cream camisole beneath a jacket that was nearly the same shade as Bond's. A long face, handsome and regal, eyes that could flick from stern to compassionate faster than a Formula One gearbox.

'Hello, Moneypenny.'

'It'll just be a moment, James. He's on the line to Whitehall again.'

Her posture was upright, her gestures economical. Not a hair was out of place. He reflected, as he often did, that her military background had left an indelible mark. She'd resigned her commission with the Royal Navy to take her present job with M as his personal assistant.

Just after he'd joined the ODG, Bond had dropped into her office chair and flashed a broad smile. 'Rank of lieutenant, were you, Money-penny?' he'd quipped. 'I'd prefer to picture you *above* me.' Bond had left the service as a commander.

He'd received in reply not the searing rejoinder he deserved but a smooth riposte: 'Oh, but I've found in life, James, that all positions must be earned through experience. And I'm

51

pleased to say I have little doubt that my level of such does not *begin* to approach yours.'

The cleverness and speed of her retort and the use of his first name, along with her radiant smile, instantly and immutably defined their relationship: she'd kept him in his place but opened the avenue of friendship. So it had remained ever since, caring and close but always professional. (Still, he harboured the belief that of all the 00 Section agents she liked him best.)

Moneypenny looked him over and frowned. 'You had quite a time of it over there, I heard.'

'You could say so.'

She glanced at M's closed door and said, 'This Noah situation's a tough one, James. Signals flying everywhere. He left at nine last night, came in at five this morning.' She added, in a whisper, 'He was worried about you. There were some moments last night when you were incommunicado. He was on the phone quite often then.'

They saw a light on her phone extinguish. She hit a button and spoke through a nearly invisible stalk mike. 'It's 007, sir.'

She nodded at the door, towards which Bond now walked, as the do-not-disturb light above it flashed on. This occurred silently, of course, but Bond always imagined the illumination was accompanied by the sound of a deadbolt crashing open to admit a new prisoner to a medieval dungeon.

★ ★ ★

52

'Morning, sir.'

M looked exactly the same as he had at the Travellers Club lunch when they'd met three years ago and might have been wearing the same grey suit. He gestured to one of the two functional chairs facing the large oak desk. Bond sat down.

The office was carpeted and the walls were lined with bookshelves. The building was at the fulcrum where old London became new and M's windows in the corner office bore witness to this. To the west Marylebone High Street's period buildings contrasted sharply with Euston Road's skyscrapers of glass and metal, sculptures of high concept and questionable aesthetics and lift systems cleverer than you were.

These scenes, however, remained dim, even on sunny days, since the window glass was both bomb- and bullet-proof and mirrored to prevent spying by any ingenious enemy hanging from a hot-air balloon over Regent's Park.

M looked up from his notes and scanned Bond. 'No medical report, I gather.'

Nothing escaped him. Ever.

'A scratch or two. Not serious.'

The man's desk held a yellow pad, a complicated console phone, his mobile, an Edwardian brass lamp and a humidor stocked with the narrow black cheroots M sometimes allowed himself on drives to and from Whitehall or during his brief walks through Regent's Park, when he was accompanied by his thoughts and two P Branch guards. Bond knew very little of M's personal life, only that he lived in a Regency

53

manor-house on the edge of Windsor Forest and was a bridge player, a fisherman and a rather accomplished watercolourist of flowers. A personable and talented Navy corporal named Andy Smith drove him about in a well-polished ten-year-old Rolls-Royce.

'Give me your report, 007.'

Bond organised his thoughts. M did not tolerate a muddled narrative or padding. 'Ums' and 'ers' were as unacceptable as stating the obvious. He reiterated what had happened in Novi Sad, then added, 'I found a few things in Serbia that might give us some details. Philly's sorting them now and finding out about the haz-mat on the train.'

'Philly?'

Bond recalled that M disliked the use of nicknames, even though he was referred to exclusively by one throughout the organisation. 'Ophelia Maidenstone,' he explained. 'Our liaison from Six. If there's anything to be found, she'll sniff it out.'

'Your cover in Serbia?'

'I was working false flag. The senior people at BIA in Belgrade know I'm with the ODG and what my mission was, but we told their two field agents I was with a fictional UN peacekeeping outfit. I had to mention Noah and the incident on Friday in case the BIA agents stumbled across something referring to them. But whatever the Irishman got out of the younger man, it wasn't compromising.'

'The Yard and Five are wondering — with the train in Novi Sad, do you think Incident

54

Twenty's about sabotaging a railway line here? Serbia was a dry run?'

'I wondered that too, sir. But it wouldn't be the sort of operation that'd need much rehearsal. Besides, the Irishman's partner rigged the derailment in about three minutes. Our rail systems here must be more sophisticated than a freight line in rural Serbia.'

A bushy eyebrow rose, perhaps disputing that assumption. But M said, 'You're right. It doesn't seem like a prelude to Incident Twenty.'

'Now.' Bond sat forward. 'What I'd like to do, sir, is get back to Station Y immediately. Enter through Hungary and set up a rendition op to track down the Irishman. I'll take a couple of our double-one agents with me. We can trace the lorry he stole. It'll be tricky but — '

M was shaking his head, rocking back in his well-worn throne. 'It seems there's a bit of a flap, 007. It involves you.'

'Whatever Belgrade's saying, the young agent who died — '

M waved a hand impatiently. 'Yes, yes, *of course* what happened was their fault. There was never any question about that. Explanation is a sign of weakness, 007. Don't know why you're doing it now.'

'Sorry, sir.'

'I'm speaking of something else. Last night, Cheltenham managed to get a satellite image of the lorry the Irishman escaped in.'

'Very good, sir.' So, his tracking tactic had apparently succeeded.

But M's scowl suggested Bond's satisfaction

was premature. 'About fifteen miles south of Novi Sad the lorry pulled over and the Irishman got into a helicopter. No registration or ID but GCHQ got a MASINT profile of it.'

Material and Signature Intelligence was the latest in high-tech espionage. If information came from electronic sources like microwave transmissions or radio, it was ELINT; from photographs and satellite images, IMINT; from mobile phones and emails, SIGINT; and from human sources, HUMINT. With MASINT, instruments collected and profiled data such as thermal energy, sound waves, airflow disruption, propeller and helicopter rotor vibrations, exhaust from jet engines, trains and cars, velocity patterns and more.

The director-general continued, 'Last night Five registered a MASINT profile that matched the helicopter he escaped in.'

Bloody hell . . . If MI5 had found the chopper, that meant it was in England. The Irishman — the sole lead to Noah and Incident Twenty — was in the one place where James Bond had no authority to pursue him.

M added, 'The helicopter landed north-east of London at about one a.m. and vanished. They lost all track.' He shook his head. 'I don't see why Whitehall didn't give us more latitude about operating at home when they chartered us. Would have been easy. Hell, what if you'd followed the Irishman to the London Eye or Madame Tussaud's? What should you have done — rung 999? For God's sake, these are the days of globalisation, of the Internet, the EU, yet we can't follow leads in our own country.'

The rationale for this rule, however, was clear. MI5 conducted brilliant investigations. MI6 was a master at foreign intelligence gathering and 'disruptive action', such as destroying a terrorist cell from within by planting misinformation. The Overseas Development Group did rather more, including occasionally, if rarely, ordering its 00 Section agents to lie in wait for enemies of the state and shoot them dead. But to do so within the UK, however morally justifiable or tactically convenient, would play rather badly among bloggers and the Fleet Street scribblers.

Not to mention that the Crown's prosecutors might be counted on to have a say in the matter as well.

But, politics aside, Bond adamantly wanted to pursue Incident Twenty. He'd developed a particular dislike for the Irishman. His words to M were measured: 'I think I'm in the best position to find this man and Noah and to suss out what they're up to. I want to keep on it, sir.'

'I thought as much. And I *want* you to pursue it, 007. I've been on the phone this morning with Five and Specialist Operations at the Yard. They're both willing to let you have a consulting role.'

'Consulting?' Bond said sourly, then realised that M would have done some impressive negotiating to achieve that much. 'Thank you, sir.'

M deflected the words with a jerk of his head. 'You'll be working with someone from Division Three, a fellow named Osborne-Smith.'

Division Three . . . British security and police operations were like human beings: forever being born, marrying, producing progeny, dying and even, Bond had once joked, undergoing sex-change operations. Division Three was one of the more recent offspring. It had some loose affiliation with Five, in much the same way that the ODG had a gossamer thin connection to Six.

Plausible deniability . . .

While Five had broad investigation and surveillance powers, it had no arrest authority or tactical officers. Division Three did. It was a secretive, reclusive group of high-tech wizards, bureaucrats and former SAS and SBS tough boys with serious firepower. Bond had been impressed with its recent successes in taking down terrorist cells in Oldham, Leeds and London.

M regarded him evenly. 'I know you're used to having *carte blanche* to handle the mission as you see fit, 007. You have your independent streak and it's served you well in the past.' A dark look. '*Most* of the time. But at home your authority's limited. Significantly. Do I make myself clear?'

'Yes, sir.'

So, no longer *carte blanche*, Bond reflected angrily, more *carte grise.*

Another dour glance from M. 'Now, a complication. That security conference.'

'Security conference?'

'Haven't read your Whitehall briefing?' M asked petulantly.

These were administrative announcements

58

about internal government matters and, accordingly, no, Bond did not read them. 'Sorry, sir.'

M's jowls tightened. 'We have thirteen security agencies in the UK. Maybe more as of this morning. The heads of Five, Six, SOCA, JTAC, SO Thirteen, DI, the whole lot — myself included — will be holed up in Whitehall for three days later in the week. Oh, the CIA and some chaps from the Continent too. Briefings on Islamabad, Pyongyang, Venezuela, Beijing, Jakarta. And there'll probably be some young analyst in Harry Potter glasses touting his theory that the Chechnyan rebels are responsible for that damned volcano in Iceland. A bloody inconvenience, the whole thing.' He sighed. 'I'll be largely incommunicado. Chief of staff will be running the Incident Twenty operation for the Group.'

'Yes, sir. I'll co-ordinate with him.'

'Get on to it, 007. And remember: you're operating in the UK. Treat it like a country you've never been to. Which means, for God's sake, be diplomatic with the natives.'

9

'It's pretty bad, sir. Are you sure you want to see it?'

To the foreman, the man replied immediately. 'Yes.'

'Right, then. I'll drive you out.'

'Who else knows?'

'Just the shift chief and the lad what found it.' Casting a glance at his boss, the man added, 'They'll keep quiet. If that's what you want.'

Severan Hydt said nothing.

Under an overcast and dusty sky, the two men left the loading bay of the ancient headquarters building and walked to a nearby car park. They climbed into a people-carrier emblazoned with the logo of Green Way International Disposal and Recycling; the company name was printed over a delicate drawing of a verdant leaf. Hydt didn't much care for the design, which struck him as mockingly trendy, but he'd been told that the image had scored well in focus groups and was good for public relations ('Ah, the *public*,' he'd responded with veiled contempt and reluctantly approved it).

He was a tall man — six foot three — and broad-shouldered, his columnar torso encased in a bespoke suit of black wool. His massive head was covered with thick, curly hair, black streaked with white, and he wore a matching beard. His yellowing fingernails extended well past his

60

fingertips, but were carefully filed; they were long by design, not neglect.

Hydt's pallor accentuated his dark nostrils and darker eyes, framed by a long face that appeared younger than his fifty-six years. He was a strong man still, having retained much of his youthful muscularity.

The van started through his company's dishevelled grounds, more than a hundred acres of low buildings, rubbish tips, skips, hovering seagulls, smoke, dust . . .

And decay . . .

As they drove over the rough roads, Hydt's attention momentarily slipped to a construction about half a mile away. A new building was nearing completion. It was identical to two that stood already in the grounds: five-storey boxes from which chimneys rose, the sky above them rippling from the rising heat. The buildings were known as destructors, a Victorian word that Severan Hydt loved. England was the first country in the world to make energy from municipal refuse. In the 1870s the first power plant to do so was built in Nottingham and soon hundreds were operating throughout the country, producing steam to generate electricity.

The destructor now nearing completion in the middle of his disposal and recycling operation was no different in theory from its gloomy Dickensian forebears, save that it used scrubbers and filters to clean the dangerous exhaust and was far more efficient, burning RDF — refuse-derived fuel — as it produced energy that was pumped (for profit, of course) into the London and Home County power grids.

Indeed, Green Way International, plc, was simply the latest in a long British tradition of innovation in refuse disposal and reclamation. Henry IV had decreed that rubbish should be collected and removed from the streets of towns and cities on threat of forfeit. Mudlarks had kept the banks of the Thames clean — for entrepreneurial profit, not government wages — and rag pickers had sold scraps of wool to mills for the production of cheap cloth called shoddy. In London, as early as the nineteenth century, women and girls had been employed to sift through incoming refuse and sort it according to future usefulness. The British Paper Company had been founded to manufacture recycled paper — in 1890.

Green Way was located nearly twenty miles east of London, well past the boxed sets of office buildings on the Isle of Dogs and the sea-mine of the O2, past the ramble of Canning Town and Silvertown, the Docklands. To reach it you turned southeast off the A13 and drove towards the Thames. Soon you were down to a narrow lane, unwelcoming, even forbidding, surrounded by nothing but brush and stalky plants, pale and translucent as a dying patient's skin. The tarmac strip seemed a road to nowhere . . . until it crested a low rise and ahead you could see Green Way's massive complex, forever muted through a haze.

In the middle of this wonderland of rubbish the van now stopped beside a battered skip, six feet high, twenty long. Two workers, somewhere in their forties, wearing tan Green Way overalls, stood uncomfortably beside it. They didn't look any less uneasy now that the owner of the company himself, no less, was present.

'Crikey,' one whispered to the other.

Hydt knew they were also cowed by his black eyes, the tight mass of his beard and his towering frame.

And then there were those fingernails.

He asked, 'In there?'

The workers remained speechless and the foreman, the name *Jack Dennison* stitched on his overalls, said, 'That's right, sir.' Then he snapped to one of the workers, 'Right, sunshine, don't keep Mr Hydt waiting. He hasn't got all day, has he?'

The employee hurried to the side of the skip and, with some effort, pulled the large door open, assisted by a spring. Inside were the ubiquitous mounds of green bin liners and loose junk — bottles, magazines and newspapers — that people had been too lazy to separate for recycling.

And there was another item of discard inside: a human body.

A woman's or teenage boy's, to judge from the stature. There wasn't much else to go on, since, clearly, death had occurred months ago. He bent down and probed with his long fingernails.

This enjoyable examination confirmed the corpse was a woman's.

Staring at the loosening skin, the protruding bones, the insect and animal work on what was left of the flesh, Hydt felt his heart quicken. He said to the two workers, 'You'll keep this to yourselves.'

They'll keep quiet.

'Yes, sir.'

'Of course, sir.'

'Wait over there.'

They trotted away. Hydt glanced at Dennison, who nodded that they'd behave themselves. Hydt didn't doubt it. He ran Green Way more like a military base than a rubbish tip and recycling yard. Security was tight — mobile phones were banned, all outgoing communications monitored — and discipline harsh. But, in compensation, Severan Hydt paid his people very, very well. A lesson of history was that professional soldiers stuck around far longer than amateurs, provided you had the money. And that particular commodity was never in short supply at Green Way. Disposing of what people no longer wanted had always been, and would forever be, a profitable endeavour.

Alone now, Hydt crouched beside the body.

The discovery of human remains here happened with some frequency. Sometimes workers in the construction debris and reclamation division of Green Way would find Victorian bones or desiccated skeletons in building foundations. Or a corpse was that of a homeless person, dead from exposure to the elements, drink or drugs, hurled unceremoniously upon the bin liners. Sometimes it was a murder victim — in which case the killers were usually polite enough to bring the body here directly.

Hydt never reported the deaths. The presence

of the police was the last thing he wanted.

Besides, why should he give up such a treasure?

He eased closer to the body, knees pressing against what was left of the woman's jeans. The smell of decay — like bitter, wet cardboard — would be unpleasant to most people but discard had been Hydt's lifelong profession and he was no more repulsed by it than a garage mechanic is troubled by the scent of grease or an abattoir worker the odour of blood and viscera.

Dennison, the foreman, however, stood back some distance from the perfume.

With one of his jaundiced fingernails, Hydt reached forward and stroked the top of the skull, from which most of the hair was missing, then the jaw, the finger bones, the first to be exposed. Her nails too were long, though not because they had grown after her death, which was a myth; they simply *appeared* longer because the flesh beneath them had shrunk.

He studied his new friend for a long moment, then reluctantly eased back. He looked at his watch. He pulled his iPhone from his pocket and took a dozen pictures of the corpse.

Then he glanced around him. He pointed to a deserted spot between two large mounds over landfills, like barrows holding phalanxes of fallen soldiers. 'Tell the men to bury it there.'

'Yes, sir,' Dennison replied.

As he walked back to the people-carrier, he said, 'Not too deep. And leave a marker. So I'll be able to find it again.'

Half an hour later Hydt was in his office, scrolling through the pictures he'd taken of the corpse, lost in the images, sitting at the three-hundred-year-old gaol door mounted on legs that was his desk. Finally he slipped the phone away and turned his dark eyes to other matters. And there were many. Green Way was one of the world leaders in the disposal, reclamation and recycling of discard.

The office was spacious and dimly lit, located on the top storey of Green Way's headquarters, an old meat-processing factory, dating to 1896, renovated and turned into what interior design magazines might call shabby chic.

On the walls were architectural relics from buildings his company had demolished: scabby painted frames around cracked stained glass, concrete gargoyles, wildlife, effigies, mosaics. St George and the dragon were represented several times. St Joan, too. On one large bas-relief Zeus, operating undercover as a swan, had his way with beautiful Leda.

Hydt's secretary came and went with letters for his signature, reports for him to read, memos to approve, financial statements to consider. Green Way was doing extremely well. At a recycling-industry conference Hydt had once joked that the adage about certainty in life should not be limited to the well-known two. People had to pay taxes, they had to die . . . and they had to have their discard collected and disposed of.

66

His computer chimed and he called up an encrypted email from a colleague out of the country. It was about an important meeting tomorrow, Tuesday, confirming times and locations. The last line stirred him: The number of dead tomorrow will be significant — close to 100. Hope that suits.

It did indeed. And the desire that had arisen within him when he'd first gazed at the body in the skip churned all the hotter.

He glanced up as a slim woman in her mid-sixties entered, wearing a dark trouser suit and black shirt. Her hair was white, cut in a businesswoman's bob. A large, unadorned diamond hung from a platinum chain around her narrow neck, and similar stones, though in more complex arrangements, graced her wrists and several fingers.

'I've approved the proofs.' Jessica Barnes was an American. She'd come from a small town outside Boston; the regional lilt continued, charmingly, to tint her voice. A beauty queen years ago, she'd met Hydt when she was a hostess at a smart New York restaurant. They'd lived together for several years and — to keep her close — he'd hired her to review Green Way's advertisements, another endeavour Hydt had little respect for or interest in. He'd been told, however, that she'd made some good decisions from time to time with regard to the company's marketing efforts.

But as Hydt gazed at her, he saw that something about her was different today.

He found himself studying her face. That was

it. His preference, *insistence*, was that she wore only black and white and kept her face free of make-up; today she had on some very faint blush and perhaps — he couldn't quite be certain — some lipstick. He didn't frown but she saw the direction of his eyes and shifted a bit, breathing a little differently. Her fingers started towards a cheek. She stopped her hand.

But the point had been made. She proffered the ads. 'Do you want to look at them?'

'I'm sure they're fine,' he said.

'I'll send them off.' She left his office, her destination not the marketing department, Hydt knew, but the cloakroom where she would wash her face.

Jessica was not a foolish woman; she'd learned her lesson.

Then she was gone from his thoughts. He stared out of the window at his new destructor. He was very aware of the event coming up on Friday, but at the moment he couldn't get tomorrow out of his head.

The number of dead . . . close to 100.

His gut twisted pleasantly.

It was then that his secretary announced on the intercom, 'Mr Dunne's here, sir.'

'Ah, good.'

A moment later, Niall Dunne entered and swung the door shut so that the two were alone. The cumbersome man's trapezoid face had rarely flickered with emotion in the nine months they'd known each other. Severan Hydt had little use for most people and no interest in social niceties. But Dunne chilled even him.

'Now, what happened over there?' Hydt asked. After the incident in Serbia, Dunne had said they should keep their phone conversations to a minimum.

The man turned his pale blue eyes to Hydt and explained in his Belfast accent that he and Karic, the Serbian contact, had been surprised by several men — at least two BIA Serbian intelligence officers masquerading as police and a Westerner, who'd told the Serbian agent he was with the European Peacekeeping and Monitoring Group.

Hydt frowned. 'It's — '

'There is no such group,' Dunne said calmly. 'It had to be a private operation. There was no back-up, no central communications, no medics. The Westerner probably bribed the intelligence officers to help him. It *is* the Balkans, after all. May have been a competitor.' He added, 'Maybe one of your partners or a worker here let slip something about the plan.'

He was referring to Gehenna, of course. They did everything they could to keep the project secret but a number of people around the world were involved; it wasn't impossible that there'd been a leak and some crime syndicate was interested in learning more about it.

Dunne continued, 'I don't want to minimise the risk — they were pretty clever. But it wasn't a major co-ordinated effort. I'm confident we can go forward.'

Dunne handed Hydt a mobile phone. 'Use this one for our conversations. Better encryption.'

Hydt examined it. 'Did you get a look at the Westerner?'

'No. There was a lot of smoke.'

'And Karic?'

'I killed him.' The blank face registered the same emotion as if he'd said, 'Yes, it's cool outside today.'

Hydt considered what the man had told him. No one was more precise or cautious when it came to analysis than Niall Dunne. If he was convinced this was no problem, then Hydt would accept his judgement.

Dunne continued, 'I'm going up to the facility now. Once I get the last materials up there the team say they can finish in a few hours.'

A fire flared within Hydt, ignited by an image of the woman's body in the skip — and the thought of what awaited up north. 'I'll come with you.'

Dunne said nothing. Finally he asked in a monotone, 'You think that's a good idea? Might be risky.' He offered this as if he'd detected the eagerness in Hydt's voice — Dunne seemed to feel that nothing good could come out of a decision based on emotion.

'I'll chance it.' Hydt tapped his pocket to make certain his phone was there. He hoped there'd be an opportunity to take some more photographs.

10

After leaving M's lair, Bond walked up the corridor. He greeted a smartly dressed Asian woman keyboarding deftly at a large computer and stepped into the doorway behind her.

'You've bought the duty,' he said to the man hunched over a desk as loaded with papers and files as M's was empty.

'I have indeed.' Bill Tanner looked up. 'I'm now the grand overlord of Incident Twenty. Take a pew, James.' He nodded to an empty chair — or, rather, *the* empty chair. The office boasted a number of seats, but the rest were serving as outposts for more files. As Bond sat, the ODG's chief of staff asked, 'So, most important, did you get some decent wine and a gourmet meal on SAS Air last night?'

An Apache helicopter, courtesy of the Special Air Service, had plucked Bond from a field south of the Danube and whisked him to a NATO base in Germany, where a Hercules loaded with van parts completed his journey to London. He said, 'Apparently they forgot to stock the galley.'

Tanner laughed. The retired army officer, a former lieutenant colonel, was a solid man in his fifties, ruddy of complexion and upright — in all senses of the word. He was in his usual uniform: dark trousers and light blue shirt with the sleeves rolled up. Tanner had a tough job, running the ODG's day-to-day operations, and by rights he

71

should have had little sense of humour, though in fact, he had a fine one. He'd been Bond's mentor when the young agent had joined and was now his closest friend within the organisation. Tanner was a devout golfer and every few weeks he and Bond would try to get out to one of the more challenging courses, like Royal Cinque Ports or Royal St George's or, if time was tight, Sunningdale, near Windsor.

Tanner was, of course, generally familiar with Incident Twenty and the hunt for Noah, but Bond now updated him — and explained about his own downsized role in the UK operation.

The chief of staff gave a sympathetic laugh. '*Carte grise*, eh? Must say you're taking it rather well.'

'Hardly have much choice,' Bond allowed. 'Is Whitehall still convinced that the threat's out of Afghanistan?'

'Let's just say they *hope* it's based there,' Tanner said, his voice low. 'For several reasons. You can probably work them out for yourself.'

He meant politics, of course.

Then he nodded towards M's office. 'Did you catch his opinion on that security conference he's been shanghaied to attend this week?'

'Not much room for interpretation,' Bond said. Tanner chuckled.

Bond glanced at his watch and stood up. 'I've got to meet a man from Division Three. Osborne-Smith. You know anything about him?'

'Ah, Percy.' Bill Tanner raised a cryptic eyebrow and smiled. 'Good luck, James,' he said. 'Perhaps it's best just to leave it at that.'

O Branch took up nearly the entire fourth floor.

It was a large open area, ringed with agents' offices. In the centre were work stations for PAs and other support staff. It might have been the sales department of a major supermarket, if not for the fact that every office door had an iris scanner and keypad lock. There were many flatscreen computers in the centre but none of the giant monitors that seemed *de rigueur* in spy outfits on TV and in movies.

Bond strode through this busy area and nodded a greeting to a blonde in her mid twenties, perched forward in her office chair, presiding over an ordered work space. Had Mary Goodnight worked for any other department, Bond might have invited her to dinner and seen where matters led from there. But she wasn't in any other department: she was fifteen feet from his office door and was his human diary, his portcullis and drawbridge, and was capable of repelling the unannounced firmly and, most important in government service, with unimprovable tact. Although none were on view, Goodnight occasionally received — from office mates, friends and dates — cards or souvenirs inspired by the film *Titanic*, so closely did she resemble Kate Winslet.

'Good morning, Goodnight.'

That play on words, and others like it, had long ago moved from flirtatiousness to affection. They had become like an endearment between spouses, almost automatic and never tiresome.

73

Goodnight ran through his appointments for the day but Bond told her to cancel everything. He'd be meeting a man from Division Three, coming over from Thames House, and afterwards he might have to be off at a minute's notice.

'Shall I hold the signals too?' she asked.

Bond considered this. 'I suppose I'll plough through them now. Should probably clear my desk anyway. If I have to be away, I don't want to come back to a week's worth of reading.'

She handed him the top-secret green-striped folders. With approval from the keypad lock and iris scanner beside his door Bond entered his office and turned on the light. The space wasn't small by London office standards, about fifteen by fifteen, but was rather sterile. His government-issue desk was slightly larger than, but the same colour as, his desk at Defence Intelligence. The four wooden bookshelves were filled with volumes and periodicals that had been, or might be, helpful to him and varied in subject from the latest hacking techniques used by the Bulgarians to Thai idioms to a guide for reloading Lapua .338 sniper rounds. There was little of a personal nature to brighten the room. The one object he might have had on display, his Conspicuous Gallantry Cross, awarded for his duty in Afghanistan, was in the bottom drawer of his desk. He'd accepted the honour with good grace, but to Bond, courage was simply another tool in a soldier's kit and he saw no more point in displaying indications of its past use than in hanging a spent cipher pad on the wall.

Bond now sat in his chair and began to read the signals — intelligence reports from Requirements at MI6, suitably buffed and packaged. The first was from the Russia Desk. Their Station R had managed to hack into a government server in Moscow and suck out some classified documents. Bond, who had a natural facility for language and had studied Russian at Fort Monckton, skipped the English synopsis and went to the raw intelligence.

He got one paragraph into the leaden prose when two words stopped him in his tracks. The Russian words for 'Steel Cartridge'.

The phrase pinged deep inside him, just as sonar on a submarine notes a distant but definite target.

Steel Cartridge appeared to be a code name for an 'active measure', the Soviet term describing a tactical operation. It had involved 'some deaths'.

But there was nothing specific on operational details.

Bond sat back, staring at the ceiling. He heard women's voices outside his door and looked up. Philly, holding several files, was chatting with Mary Goodnight. Bond nodded and the Six agent joined him, taking a wooden chair opposite his desk.

'What've you found, Philly?'

She sat forward, crossing her legs, and Bond believed he heard the appealing rustle of nylon. 'First, your photo skills were fine, James, but the light was too low. I couldn't get high enough resolution of the Irishman's face for recognition.

75

And there were no prints on the pub bill or the other note, except for a partial of yours.'

So, the man would have to remain anonymous for the time being.

'But the prints on the glasses were good. The local was Aldo Karic, Serbian. He lived in Belgrade and worked for the national railway.' She pursed her lips in frustration, which emphasised the charming dimple. 'But it's going to take a little longer than I'd hoped to get more details. The same with the haz-mat on the train. Nobody's saying anything. You were right — Belgrade's not in the mood to co-operate.

'Now for the slips of paper you found in the burning car. I got some possible locations.'

Bond noted the printouts she was producing from a folder. They were of maps emblazoned with the cheerful logo of MapQuest, the online directions-finding service. 'Are you having budget problems at Six? I'd be happy to ring the Treasury for you.'

She laughed, a breathy sound. 'I used proxies, of course. Just wanted an idea of where on the pitch we're playing.' She tapped one. 'The receipt? The pub is here.' It was just off the motorway near Cambridge.

Bond stared at the map. Who had eaten there? The Irishman? Noah? Other associates? Or someone who'd hired the car last week and had no connection whatsoever with Incident Twenty?

'And the other piece of paper? With the writing on it?'

Boots — March. 17. No later than that.

She produced a lengthy list. 'I tried to think of

every possible combination of what it could mean. Dates, footwear, geographical locations, the chemist.' Her mouth tightened again. She was displeased that her efforts had fallen short. 'Nothing obvious, I'm afraid.'

He rose and pulled down several Ordnance Survey maps from the shelf. He flipped through one, scanning carefully.

Mary Goodnight appeared in the doorway. 'James, someone downstairs to see you. From Division Three, he says. Percy Osborne-Smith.'

Philly must have caught the sea change in Bond's expression. 'I'll make myself scarce now, James. I'll keep on at the Serbs. They'll crack. I guarantee it.'

'Oh, one more thing, Philly.' He handed her the signal he'd just been reading. 'I need you to catch everything you can about a Soviet or Russian operation called Steel Cartridge. There's a little in here, not much.'

She glanced down at the printout.

He said, 'Sorry it's not translated but you can probably — '

'*Ya govoryu po russki.*'

Bond smiled weakly. 'And with a far better accent than mine.' He told himself never to sell her short again.

Philly examined the printout closely. 'This was hacked from an online source. Who has the original data file?'

'One of your people would. It came out of Station R.'

'I'll contact the Russia Desk,' she said. 'I'll want to look at the metadata coded in the file.

77

That'll have the date it was created, who the author was, maybe cross references to other sources.' She slipped the Russian document into a manila folder and took a pen to tick off one of the boxes on the front. 'How do you want it classified?'

He debated for a moment. 'Our eyes only.'

' "Our"?' she asked. That pronoun was not used in official document classification.

'Yours and mine,' he said softly. 'No one else.'

A brief hesitation and then, in her delicate lettering, she penned at the top: *Eyes only. SIS Agent Maidenstone. ODG Agent James Bond.* 'And priority?' she wondered aloud.

At this question Bond did not hesitate at all. 'Urgent.'

11

Bond was sitting forward at his desk, doing some research of his own in government databases, when he heard footsteps approaching, accompanied by a loud voice.

'I'm fine, just great. You can peel off now, please and thank you — I can do without the sat-nav.'

With that, a man in a close-fitting striped suit strode into Bond's office, having discarded the Section P security officer who'd accompanied him. He'd also bypassed Mary Goodnight, who had risen with a frown as the man stormed past, ignoring her.

He walked up to Bond's desk, thrusting out a fleshy palm. Slim but flabby, unimposing, he nonetheless had assertive eyes and large hands at the end of his long arms. He seemed the sort to deliver a bone-crusher so Bond, darkening his computer screen and standing up, prepared to counter it, shooting his hand in close to deny him leverage.

In fact, Percy Osborne-Smith's clasp was brief and harmless, though unpleasantly damp.

'Bond. James Bond.' He motioned the Division Three officer to the chair Philly had just occupied and reminded himself not to let the man's coiffure — dark blond hair combed and apparently glued to the side of his head — pouting lips and rubbery neck deceive. A

79

weak chin did not mean a weak man, as anyone familiar with Field Marshal Montgomery's career could certify.

'So,' Osborne-Smith said, 'here we are. Excitement galore with Incident Twenty. Who thinks up these names, do you wonder? The Intelligence Committee, I suppose.'

Bond tipped his head noncommittally.

The man's eyes swept around the office, alighted briefly on a plastic gun with an orange muzzle used in close-combat training and returned to Bond. 'Now, from what I hear Defence and Six are firing up the boilers to steam down the Afghan route, looking for baddies in the hinterland. Makes you and me the awkward younger brothers, left behind, stuck with this Serbian connection. But sometimes it's the pawns that win the game, isn't it?'

He dabbed his nose and mouth with a handkerchief. Bond couldn't recall the last time he'd seen anyone under the age of seventy employ this combination of gesture and accessory. 'Heard about you, Bond . . . *James*. Let's go with givens, shall we? My surname's a bit of a mouthful. Crosses to bear. Just like my title — Deputy Senior Director of Field Operations.'

Rather unskilfully inserted, Bond reflected.

'So, it's Percy and James. Sounds like a stand-up act at a Comic Relief show. Anyway, I've heard about you, James. Your reputation precedes you. Not 'exceeds', of course. At least, not from what I hear.'

Oh, God, Bond thought, his patience already worn thin. He pre-empted a continuation of the monologue and explained in detail what had happened in Serbia.

Osborne-Smith took it all in, jotting notes. Then he described what had happened on the British side of the Channel, which wasn't particularly informative. Even enlisting the impressive surveillance skills of MI5's A Branch — known as the Watchers — no one had been able to confirm more than that the helicopter carrying the Irishman had landed somewhere north-east of London. No MASINT or other trace of the chopper had been found since.

'So, our strategy?' Osborne-Smith said, though not as a question. Rather, it was a preface to a directive: 'While Defence and Six and everybody under the sun are prowling the desert looking for Afghans of mass destruction, I want to go all out here, find this Irishman and Noah, wrap them up in tidy ribbons and bring them in.'

'Arrest them?'

'Well, 'detain' might be the happier word.'

'Actually, I'm not sure that's the best approach,' Bond said delicately.

For God's sake, be diplomatic with the natives . . .

'Why not? We don't have time to surveille.' Bond noticed a faint lisp. 'Only to interrogate.'

'If thousands of lives are at risk, the Irishman and Noah can't be operating alone. They might even be pretty low in the food chain. All we know for sure is that there was a meeting at Noah's office. Nothing ever suggested he was in charge of the whole operation. And the Irishman? He's a triggerman. Certainly knows

81

his craft but basically he's muscle. I think we need to identify them and keep them in play until we get more answers.'

Osborne-Smith was nodding agreeably. 'Ah, but you're not familiar with my background, James, my curriculum vitae.' The smile and the smarminess vanished. 'I cut my teeth grilling prisoners. In Northern Ireland. And Belmarsh.'

The infamous so-called 'Terrorists' Prison' in London.

'I've sunned myself in Cuba too,' he continued. 'Guantánamo. Yes, indeed. People end up talking to me, James. After I've been going at them for a few days, they'll hand me the address where their brother's hiding, won't they? Or their son. Or daughter. Oh, people talk when I ask them . . . ever so politely.'

Bond wasn't giving up. 'But if Noah has partners and they learn he's been picked up, they might accelerate whatever's planned for Friday. Or disappear — and we'll lose them until they strike again in six or eight months when all the leads've gone cold. This Irishman would have planned for a contingency like that, I'm sure of it.'

The soft nose wrinkled with regret. 'It's just that, well, if we were on the Continent somewhere or padding about in Red Square, I'd be *delighted* to sit back and watch you bowl leg or off breaks, as you thought best, but, well, it *is* our cricket ground here.'

The whip crack was, of course, inevitable. Bond decided there was no point in arguing. The dandified puppet had a steel spine. He also had

82

ultimate authority and could shut out Bond entirely if he wished to. 'It's your call, of course,' Bond said pleasantly. 'So, I suppose the first step is to find them. Let me show you the leads.' He passed over a copy of the pub receipt and the note: *Boots — March. 17. No later than that.*

Osborne-Smith was frowning as he examined the sheets. 'What do you make of them?' he asked.

'Nothing very sexy,' Bond said. 'The pub's outside Cambridge. The note's a bit of a mystery.'

'March the seventeenth? A reminder to drop in at the chemist?'

'Maybe,' Bond said dubiously. 'I was thinking it might be code.' He pushed forward the MapQuest printout that Philly had provided. 'If you ask me, the pub's probably nothing. I can't find anything distinctive about it — it's not near anywhere important. Off the M11, near Wimpole Road.' He touched the sheet. 'Probably a waste of time. But it ought to be looked into. Why don't I take that? I'll head up there and look around Cambridge. Maybe you could run the March note past the cryptanalysts at Five and see what their computers have to say. That holds the key, I think.'

'I will do. But actually, if you don't mind, James, it's probably best if I handle the pub myself. I know the lie of the land. I was at Cambridge — Magdalene.' The map and the pub receipt vanished into Osborne-Smith's briefcase, with a copy of the March note. Then he produced another sheet of paper. 'Can you get that girl in?'

Bond lifted an eyebrow. 'Which one?'

'The pretty young thing outside. Single, I see.'

'You mean my PA,' Bond said drily. He rose and went to the door. 'Miss Goodnight, would you come in, please?'

She did so, frowning.

'Our friend Percy wants a word with you.'

Osborne-Smith missed the irony in Bond's choice of names and handed the sheet of paper to her. 'Make a copy of this, would you?'

With a glance towards Bond, who nodded, she took the document and went to the copier. Osborne-Smith called after her, 'Double-sided, of course. Waste works to the enemy's advantage, doesn't it?'

Goodnight returned a moment later. Osborne-Smith put the original in his briefcase and handed the copy to Bond. 'You ever get out to the firearms range?'

'From time to time,' Bond told him. He didn't add: six hours a week, religiously, indoor here with small arms, outdoor with full-bore at Bisley. And once a fortnight he trained at Scotland Yard's FATS range — the high-definition computerised firearms training simulator, in which an electrode was mounted against your back; if the terrorist shot you before you shot him, you ended up on your knees in excruciating pain.

'We have to observe the formalities, don't we?' Osborne-Smith gestured at the sheet in Bond's hand. 'Application to become a temporary AFO.'

Only a very few law enforcers — authorised firearms officers — could carry weapons in the UK.

'It's probably not a good idea to use my name on that,' Bond pointed out.

Osborne-Smith seemed not to have thought of this. 'You may be right. Well, use a nonofficial cover, why don't you? John Smith'll do. Just fill it in and do the quiz on the back — gun safety and all that. If you hit a speed bump, give me a shout. I'll walk you through.'

'I'll get right to it.'

'Good man. Glad that's settled. We'll co-ordinate later — after our respective secret missions.' He tapped his briefcase. 'Off to Cambridge.'

He pivoted and strode out as boisterously as he'd arrived.

'What a positively *wretched* man,' Goodnight whispered.

Bond gave a brief laugh. He pulled his jacket off the back of his chair and tugged it on, picked up the Ordnance Survey. 'I'm going down to the armoury to collect my gun and after that I'll be out for three or four hours.'

'What about the firearms form, James?'

'Ah.' He picked it up, tore it into neat strips and slipped them into the map booklet to mark his places. 'Why waste departmental Post-it notes? Works to the enemy's advantage, you know.'

12

An hour and a half later, James Bond was in his Bentley Continental GT, a grey streak speeding north.

He was reflecting on his deception of Percy Osborne-Smith. He'd decided that the lead to the Cambridge pub wasn't, in fact, very promising. Yes, possibly the Incident Twenty principals had eaten there — the bill suggested a meal for two or three. But the date was more than a week ago so it was unlikely that anyone on the staff would remember a man fitting the Irishman's description and his companions. And since the man had proved to be particularly clever, Bond suspected he rotated the places where he dined and shopped; he would not be a regular there.

The lead in Cambridge had to be followed up, of course, but — equally important — Bond needed to keep Osborne-Smith diverted. He could simply not allow the Irishman or Noah to be arrested and hauled into Belmarsh, like a drug dealer or an Islamist who'd been buying excessive fertiliser. They needed to keep both suspects in play to discover the nature of Incident Twenty.

So Bond, a keen poker player, had bluffed. He'd taken inordinate interest in the clue about the pub and had mentioned it was not far from Wimpole Road. To most people this would have meant nothing. But Bond guessed that Osborne-Smith would know that a secret government facility connected to Porton Down, the Ministry of Defence biological weapons research centre in Wiltshire, happened also to be on Wimpole Road. True, it was eight miles to the east, on the other side of Cambridge and nowhere near the pub, but Bond believed that associating the two would encourage the Division Three man to descend on the idea like a seabird spotting a fish head.

This relegated Bond to the apparently fruitless task of wrestling with the cryptic note. *Boots — March. 17. No later than that.*

Which he believed he had deciphered.

Most of Philly's suggestions about its meaning had involved the chemist, Boots, which had shops in every town across the UK. She'd also offered suggestions about footwear and about events that had taken place on 17 March.

But one suggestion, towards the end of her list, had intrigued Bond. She'd noted that 'Boots' and 'March' were linked with a dash and she had found that there was a Boots Road that ran near the town of March, a couple of hours' drive north of London. She had seen, too, the full stop between 'March' and '17'. Given that the last phrase 'no later than that' suggested a deadline, '17' made sense as a date but was possibly 17 *May*, tomorrow.

Clever of her, Bond had thought and in his office, waiting for Osborne-Smith, he had gone into the Golden Wire — a secure fibre-optic network tying together records of all major

British security agencies — to learn what he could about March and Boots Road.

He had found some intriguing facts: traffic reports about road diversions because a large number of lorries were coming and going along Boots Road near an old army base and public notices relating to heavy plant work. References suggested that it had to be completed by midnight on the seventeenth or fines would be levied. He had a hunch that this might be a solid lead to the Irishman and Noah.

And tradecraft dictated that you ignored such intuition at your peril.

So, he was now en route to March, losing himself in the consuming pleasure of driving.

Which meant, of course, driving fast.

Bond had to exercise some restraint, of course, since he wasn't on the N-260 in the Pyrenees, or off the beaten track in the Lake District, but was travelling north along the A1 as it switched identities arbitrarily between motorway and trunk road. Still, the speedometer needle occasionally reached 100 m.p.h., and frequently he'd tap the lever of the silken, millisecond-response Quickshift gearbox to overtake a slow-moving horsebox or Ford Mondeo. He stayed mostly in the right lane, although once or twice he took to the hard shoulder for some exhilarating if illegal overtaking. He enjoyed a few controlled skids on stretches of adverse camber.

The police were not a problem. While the jurisdiction of ODG was limited in the UK — *carte grise*, not *blanche*, Bond now joked to himself — it was often necessary for O Branch agents to get around the country quickly. Bond had phoned in an NDR — a Null Detain Request — and his number plate was ignored by cameras and constables with speed guns.

Ah, the Bentley Continental GT coupé . . . the finest off-the-peg vehicle in the world, Bond believed.

He had always loved the marque; his father had kept hundreds of old newspaper photos of the famed Bentley brothers and their creations leaving Bugattis and the rest of the field in the dust at Le Mans in the 1920s and 1930s. Bond himself had witnessed the astonishing Bentley Speed 8 take the chequered flag at the race in 2003, back in the game after three-quarters of a century. It had always been his goal to own one of the stately yet wickedly fast and clever vehicles. While the E-type Jaguar sitting below his flat had been a legacy from his father, the GT had been an indirect bequest. He'd bought his first Continental some years ago, depleting what remained of the life-insurance payment that had come his way upon his parents' deaths. He'd recently traded up to the new model.

He now came off the motorway and proceeded towards March, in the heart of the Fens. He knew little about the place. He'd heard of the 'March March March', a walk by students from March to Cambridge in, of course, the third month of the year. There was Whitemoor prison. And tourists came to see St Wendreda's Church — Bond would have to trust the tourist office's word that it was spectacular; he hadn't been inside a house of worship, other than for surveillance purposes, in years.

Ahead loomed the old British Army base. He continued in a broad circle to the back, which was surrounded by vicious barbed-wire fencing and signs warning against intrusion. He saw why: it was being demolished. So this was the work he'd learnt of. Half a dozen buildings had already been razed. Only one remained, three storeys high, old red brick. A faded sign announced: *Hospital.*

Several large lorries were present, along with bulldozers, other earth-moving equipment and caravans, which sat on a hill a hundred yards from the building, probably the temporary headquarters for the demolition crew. A black car was parked near the largest caravan, but no one was about. Bond wondered why; today was Monday and not a bank holiday.

He nosed the car into a small copse, where it could not be seen. Climbing out, he surveyed the terrain: complicated waterways, potato and sugarbeet fields and clusters of trees. Bond donned his 5.11 tactical outfit, with the shrapnel tear in the shoulder of the jacket and tainted from the smell of scorching — from rescuing the clue in Serbia that had led him here — then stepped out of his City shoes into low combat boots.

He clipped his Walther and two holsters of ammunition to a canvas web utility belt.

If you hit a speed bump, give me a shout.

He also pocketed his silencer, a torch, tool kit and his folding knife.

90

Then Bond paused, going into that other place, where he went before any tactical operation: dead calm, eyes focused and taking in every detail — branches that might betray with a snap, bushes that could hide the muzzle of a sniper rifle, evidence of wires, sensors and cameras that might report his presence to an enemy.

And preparing to take a life, quickly and efficiently, if he had to. That was part of the other world too.

And he was all the more cautious because of the many questions this assignment had raised.

Fit your response to your enemy's purpose.

But what was Noah's purpose?

Indeed, who the hell was he?

Bond moved through the trees, then cut across the corner of a field dotted with an early growth of sugarbeet. He diverted around a fragrant bog and moved carefully through a tangle of brambles, making his way towards the hospital. Finally he came to the barbed-wire perimeter, posted with warning signs. Eastern Demolition and Scrap was doing the work, they announced. He'd never heard of the company but thought he might have seen their lorries — there was something familiar about the distinctive green-and-yellow colouring.

He scanned the overgrown field in front of the building, the parade grounds behind. He saw nobody, then began to clip his way through the fence with wire cutters, thinking how clever it would be to use the building for secret meetings relevant to Incident Twenty; the place would soon be torn down, which would destroy any evidence of its use.

No workers were nearby but the presence of the black car suggested someone might be inside. He looked for a back door or other unobtrusive entrance. Five minutes later he found one: a depression in the earth, ten feet deep, caused by the collapse of what must have been an underground supply tunnel. He climbed down into the bowl and shone his torch inside. It seemed to lead into the basement of the hospital, about fifty yards away.

He started forward, noting the ancient cracked brick walls and ceiling — just as two bricks dislodged themselves and crashed to the floor. On the ground there were small-gauge rail tracks, rusting and in places covered with mud.

Halfway along the grim passage, pebbles and a stream of damp earth pelted his head. He glanced up and saw that, six feet above, the tunnel ceiling was scored like a cracked eggshell. It looked as if a handclap would bring the whole thing down on him.

Not a great place to be buried alive, Bond reflected.

Then he added wryly to himself, And just where exactly *would* be?

★   ★   ★

'Brilliant job,' Severan Hydt told Niall Dunne.

They were alone in Hydt's site caravan, parked a hundred yards from the dark, brooding British Army hospital outside March. Since the

92

Gehenna team had been under pressure to finish the job by tomorrow, Hydt and Dunne had halted demolition this morning and made sure that the crew stayed away — most of Hydt's employees knew nothing of Gehenna and he had to be very careful when the two operations overlapped.

'I was satisfied,' Dunne said flatly — in the tone with which he responded to nearly everything, be it praise, criticism or dispassionate observation.

The team had left with the device half an hour ago, having assembled it with the materials Dunne had provided. It would be hidden in a safe-house nearby until Friday.

Hydt had spent some time walking around the last building to be razed: the hospital, erected more than eighty years ago.

Demolition made Green Way a huge amount of money. The company profited from people paying to tear down what they no longer wanted, and by extracting from the rubble what other people *did* want: wooden and steel beams, wire, aluminium and copper pipes — beautiful copper, a rag-and-bone man's dream. But Hydt's interest in demolition, of course, went beyond the financial. He now studied the ancient building in a state of tense rapture, as a hunter stares at an unsuspecting animal moments before he fires the fatal shot.

He couldn't help but think of the hospital's former occupants too — the dead and dying.

Hydt had snapped dozens of pictures of the grand old lady as he'd strolled through the rotting halls, the mouldy rooms — particularly the mortuary and autopsy areas — collecting images of decay and decline. His photographic archives included shots of old buildings as well as bodies. He had quite a number, some rather artistic, of places like Northumberland Terrace, Palmers Green on the North Circular Road, the now-vanished Pura oil works on Bow Creek in Canning Town and the Gothic Royal Arsenal and Royal Laboratory in Woolwich. His photos of Lovell's Wharf in Greenwich, a testament to what aggressive neglect could achieve, never failed to move him.

On his mobile, Niall Dunne was giving instructions to the driver of the lorry that had just left, explaining how best to hide the device. They were quite precise details, in accord with his nature and that of the horrific weapon.

Although the Irishman made him uneasy, Hydt was grateful their paths had intersected. He could not have proceeded as quickly, or as safely, on Gehenna without him. Hydt had come to refer to him as 'the man who thinks of everything' and indeed he was. So, Severan Hydt was happy to put up with the eerie silences, the cold stares, the awkward arrangement of robotic steel that was Niall Dunne. The two men made an efficient partnership, if an ironic one: an engineer whose nature was to build, a rag-and-bone man whose passion was destruction.

What a curious package we humans are. Predictable only in death. Faithful only then too, Hydt reflected and then discarded that thought.

Just after Dunne disconnected, there was a

knock on the door. It opened. Eric Janssen, a Green Way security man, who'd driven them up to March, stood in the doorway, his face troubled.

'Mr Hydt, Mr Dunne, someone's gone into the building.'

'What?' Hydt barked, turning his huge equine head the man's way.

'He went in through the tunnel.'

Dunne rattled off a number of questions. Was he alone? Had there been any transmissions that Janssen had monitored? Was his car nearby? Had there been any unusual traffic in the area? Was the man armed?

The answers suggested that he was operating by himself and wasn't with Scotland Yard or the Security Service.

'Did you get a picture or a good look at him?' Dunne asked.

'No, sir.'

Hydt clicked two long nails together. 'The man with the Serbs? From last night?' he asked Dunne. 'The private operator?'

'Not impossible, but I don't know how he could have traced us here.' Dunne gazed out of the caravan's dirt-spattered window as if he wasn't seeing the building. Hydt knew the Irishman was drafting a blueprint in his mind. Or perhaps examining one he'd already prepared in case of such a contingency. For a long moment he was motionless. Finally, drawing his gun, Dunne stepped out of the caravan, gesturing to Janssen to follow.

13

The smells of mould, rot, chemicals, oil and petrol were overwhelming. Bond struggled not to cough and blinked tears from his stinging eyes. Could he detect smoke too?

The hospital's basement here was windowless. Only faint illumination filtered in from where he'd entered the tunnel. Bond splayed light from his torch around him. He was beside a railway turntable, designed to rotate small locomotives after they'd carted in supplies or patients.

His Walther in hand, Bond searched the area, listening for voices, footsteps, the click of a weapon chambering bullets or going off safety. But the place was deserted.

He'd entered through the tunnel at the south end. As he moved farther north and away from the turntable, he came to a sign that prompted a brief laugh: *Mortuary*.

It consisted of three large windowless rooms that had clearly been occupied recently; the floors were dust-free and new cheap work benches were arranged throughout. One of these rooms seemed to be the source of the smoke. Bond saw electricity cables secured to the wall and floor with duct tape, presumably providing power for lights and whatever work had been going on. Perhaps an electrical short had produced the fumes.

He left the mortuary and came to a large open

space, with a double door, to the right, east, opening to the parade ground. Light filtered through the crack between the panels — a possible escape route, he noted, and he memorised its location and the placement of columns that might provide cover in the event he had to make his way to it under fire.

Ancient steel tables, stained brown and black, were bolted to the floor, each with its own drain. For post-mortems, of course.

Bond continued to the north end of the building, which ended in a series of smaller rooms with barred windows. A sign here suggested why: *Mental Health Ward.*

He tried the doors leading up to the ground floor, found them locked and returned to the three rooms next to the turntable. A systematic search finally revealed the source of the smoke. On the floor in the corner of one room there was an improvised hearth. He spotted large curls of ash, on which he could discern writing. The flakes were delicate; he tried to pick one up but it dissolved between his fingers.

Careful, he told himself.

He walked over to one of the wires running up the wall. He pulled off several pieces of the silver duct tape securing the cord and sliced them into six-inch lengths with his knife. He then carefully pressed them on to the grey and black ash curls, slipped them into his pocket and continued his search. In a second room something silvery caught his eye. He hurried to the corner and found tiny splinters of metal littering the floor. He picked them up with another piece of tape, which he also pocketed.

Then Bond froze. The building had begun to vibrate. A moment later the shaking increased considerably. He heard a diesel engine rattling, not far away. That explained why the demolition site had been deserted; the workers must have been at lunch and now they'd returned. He couldn't get to the ground or higher floors without going outside, where he'd surely be spotted. It was time to leave.

He stepped back into the turntable room to leave through the tunnel.

And was saved from a broken skull by a matter of a few decibels.

He didn't see the attacker or hear his breathing or the hiss of whatever he swung, but Bond sensed a faint muting of the diesel's rattle, as the man's clothing absorbed the sound.

Instinctively, he leapt back and the metal pipe missed him by inches.

Bond grabbed it firmly in his left hand and his attacker stumbled, off balance, too surprised to release his weapon. The young blond man wore a cheap dark suit and white shirt, a security man's uniform, Bond assessed. He had no tie; he'd probably removed it in anticipation of the assault. His eyes wide in dismay, he staggered again and nearly fell but righted himself fast and clumsily launched himself into Bond. Together they crashed to the filthy floor of the circular room. He was not, Bond noted, the Irishman.

Bond jumped up and stepped forward, clenching his hands into fists, but it was a feint — he intended to get the muscular fellow to step back and avoid a blow, which he accommodatingly did, giving Bond the chance to draw his weapon. He didn't, however, fire; he needed the man alive.

Covered by Bond's .40-calibre pistol, he froze, although his hand went inside his jacket.

'Leave it,' Bond said coldly. 'Lie down, arms spread.'

Still, the man remained motionless, sweating with nerves, hand hovering over the butt of his gun. A Glock, Bond noted. The man's phone began to hum. He glanced at his jacket pocket.

'Get down now!'

If he drew, Bond would try to wound but he might end up killing the man.

The phone stopped ringing.

'Now.' Bond lowered his aim, focusing on the attacker's right arm, near the elbow.

It appeared the blond man was going to comply. His shoulders drooped and in the shadowy light his eyes widened with fear and uncertainty.

At that moment, though, the bulldozer must have rolled over the ground nearby; bricks and earth rained down from the ceiling. Bond was struck by a large chunk of stone. He winced and stepped back, blinking dust out of his eyes. Had his assailant been more professional — or less panicked — he would have drawn his weapon and fired. But he didn't; he turned and ran down the tunnel.

Bond slipped into his preferred stance, a fencer's, left foot pointing forward and the right perpendicular and behind. Two-handed, he fired

99

a single deafening shot that struck the man in the calf; screaming, he went down hard, about ten yards from the entrance to the tunnel.

Bond raced after him. As he did so, the shaking grew stronger, the rattle louder, and more bricks fell from the walls. Cascades of plaster and dust poured from the ceiling. A cricket ball of concrete landed directly on Bond's shoulder wound and he grunted at the burst of pain.

But he kept moving steadily along the tunnel. The assailant was on the ground, dragging himself towards the fissure where sunlight eased in.

The bulldozer seemed directly overhead now. Move, dammit, Bond told himself. They were probably about to knock the whole bloody place down. As he got closer to the wounded man, the *chug chug chug* of the diesel engine rose in volume. More bricks plummeted to the floor.

Not a great place to be buried alive . . .

Only ten yards to the wounded man. Get a tourniquet on him, get him out of the tunnel and under cover — and start asking questions.

But at a stunning crash, the soft illumination of the spring day at the end of the tunnel dimmed. It was replaced by two burning white eyes, glowing through the dust. They paused and then, as if they belonged to a lion spotting its prey, shifted slightly, turning directly towards Bond. With a fierce cough, the bulldozer ploughed relentlessly forward, pushing a surge of mud and stone before it.

Bond aimed his gun but there was no target — the blade of the machine was high, protecting the operator's cab. The vehicle crawled steadily on, pushing before it a mass of earth, brick and other debris.

'No!' cried the wounded man, as the bulldozer pressed forward. The driver didn't see him. Or if he did, he couldn't have cared less about the man's death.

With a scream, Bond's assailant disappeared under the rocky blanket. A moment later the rattling treads rolled over the spot where he was buried.

Soon the headlights were gone, blocked by debris, and then all was total darkness. Bond clicked his torch on and sprinted back to the turntable room. At the entrance he tripped and fell hard as earth and brick piled up to his ankles, then calves.

A moment later his knees were held fast.

Behind him the bulldozer continued to ram forward, shoving the muddy detritus farther into the room. Bond was now gripped to the waist. Another thirty seconds and his face would be covered.

But the weight of the debris mountain proved too much for the bulldozer or perhaps it had hit the building's foundation. The tide ceased to move forward. Before the operator could manoeuvre for better purchase, Bond dug himself free and scrabbled out of the room. His eyes stung, his lungs were in agony. Spitting dust and grit, he shone the torch back up the tunnel. It was completely plugged.

He hurried back through the three windowless rooms where he'd collected the ash and the bits of metal. He paused beside the door that led to the autopsy chamber; had they sealed the exit

101

to force him into a trap? Were the Irishman and other security people waiting in there? He screwed the silencer on to his Walther.

Inhaling deep breaths, he paused for a moment then pushed the door open fast, dropping into a defensive shooting position, torch pointing forward from his left hand, on which rested his right, clutching the pistol.

The massive empty hall yawned. But the double doors he'd seen earlier, admitting a shaft of light, were sealed; the bulldozer had piled tons of dirt against them too.

Trapped . . .

He sprinted to the smaller rooms on the north side of the basement, the mental health ward. The largest of these — the office, he assumed — had a door but it was securely locked. Bond aimed the Walther and, standing at an oblique angle, fired four wheezing shots into the metal lock plate, then four into the hinges.

This had no effect. Lead, even half-jacketed lead, is no match for steel. He reloaded and slipped the spent magazine into his left pocket, where he always kept the empties.

He was regarding the barred windows when a loud voice made him jump.

'*Attention! Opgelet! Groźba! Nebezpeči!*'

Swinging around, Bond looked for a target.

But the voice came from a loudspeaker on the wall.

'*Attention! Opgelet! Groźba! Nebezpeči! This is the three-minute warning!*' The last sentence, a recording, was repeated in Dutch, Polish and Ukrainian.

Warning?

'*Evacuate immediately! Danger! Explosive charges have been set!*'

Bond shone the torch around the room.

The wires! They weren't to provide electricity for construction — they were attached to explosives. Bond hadn't seen them since the charges were taped to steel joists high in the ceiling. The entire building had been rigged for demolition.

Three minutes . . .

The torch revealed dozens of packets of explosive, enough to turn the stone walls around him to dust — and Bond into vapour. And all the exits had been sealed. His heart rate ratcheting, sweat dotting his forehead, Bond slipped the torch and pistol away and gripped one of the iron bars over a window. He tugged hard, but it held.

In the hazy light trickling through the glass, he looked about, then climbed a nearby girder. He ripped one of the explosive packets down and leapt back to the floor. The charges were an RDX composite, to judge from the smell. With his knife he cut off a large wad and jammed it against the knob and lock on the door. That should be enough to blow the lock without killing himself in the process.

Get on with it!

Bond stepped back about twenty feet, steadied his aim and fired. He hit the explosive dead on.

But, as he'd feared, nothing happened — except that the yellow-grey mass of deadly plastic fell undramatically to the floor with a plop. Composites explode only with a detonator, not with physical impact, even that of a bullet travelling at 2,000 feet per second. He'd hoped this substance might prove the exception.

The two-minute warning resounded through the room.

Bond looked up, to where the detonator he'd pulled from the charge now dangled obscenely. But the only way to set it off was with an electric current.

Electricity . . .

The loudspeakers? No, the voltage was far too low to set off a blasting cap. So was the battery in his torch.

The voice rang out again, giving the one-minute warning.

Bond wiped the sweat from his palms and worked the pistol's slide, ejecting a bullet. With his knife he prised out the lead slug and tossed it aside. He then pressed the cartridge, filled with gunpowder, into the wad of explosive, which he moulded to the door.

He stepped back, aimed carefully at the tiny disc of his cartridge and squeezed off a round. The bullet hit the primer, which set off the powder and in turn the plastic. With a huge flare the explosion blew the lock to pieces.

It also knocked Bond to the floor, amid a shower of wood splinters and smoke. For a few seconds he lay stunned, then struggled to his feet and staggered to the door, which was open, though jammed. The gap was only about eight inches wide. He grabbed the knob and began to slowly wrest the heavy panel open.

'*Attention! Opgelet! Groźba! Nebezpeči!*'

14

In the site caravan, Severan Hydt and Niall Dunne stood beside each other, watching the old British Army hospital, in tense anticipation. Everybody — even the gear-cold Dunne, Hydt speculated — enjoyed watching a controlled explosion bring down a building.

Since Janssen had not answered his phone and Dunne had heard a gunshot from inside, the Irishman had told Hydt he was sure the security man, Eric Janssen, had to be dead. He had sealed the hospital exits, then sprinted back to the caravan, running like an awkward animal, and had told Hydt that he was going to detonate the charges in the building. It was scheduled to come down tomorrow but there was no reason that the demolition couldn't be brought forward.

Dunne had activated the computerised system and pressed two red buttons simultaneously, starting the sequence. An insurance liability policy required that a 180-second recorded warning be broadcast throughout the building in languages representing those spoken by ninety per cent of the workers. It would have taken longer to override the safety measure but if the intruder wasn't buried in the tunnel he was stuck in the mortuary. There was no way he could escape in time.

If, tomorrow or the next day, someone came asking about a missing person Hydt could reply,

'Certainly, we'll check . . . What? Oh, my God, we had no idea! We did all we were supposed to with the fence and the signs. And how could he have missed the recorded warnings? We're sorry — but we're hardly responsible.'

'Fifteen seconds,' Dunne said.

Silence as Hydt mouthed the countdown.

The timer on the wall now hit 0 and the computer sent its prearranged signal to the detonators.

They couldn't see the flash of the explosions at first — the initial ones were internal and low, to take out the main structural beams. But a few seconds later bursts of light flared like paparazzi cameras, followed by the sound of Christmas crackers, then deeper booms. The building seemed to shudder. Then, as if kneeling to offer its neck to an executioner's blade, the hospital slowly dipped and went down, a cloud of dust and smoke rolling outwards fast.

After a few moments, Dunne said, 'People will have heard it. We should go.'

Hydt, though, was mesmerised by the pile of debris, so very different from the elegant if faded structure it had been a few moments ago. What had been something had become naught.

'Severan,' Dunne persisted.

Hydt found himself aroused. He thought of Jessica Barnes, her white hair, her pale, textured skin. She knew nothing about Gehenna so he hadn't brought her today, but he was sorry she wasn't there. Well, he'd ask her to meet him at his office, then drive home.

His belly gave a pleasant tap. A sensation

supercharged by the memory of the body he'd found at Green Way that morning . . . and in anticipation of what would happen tomorrow.

A hundred deaths . . .

'Yes, yes.' Severan Hydt collected his briefcase and stepped outside. He didn't climb into the Audi A8 immediately, though. He turned to study once more the dust and smoke hovering over the destroyed building. He noted that the explosive had been skilfully set. He reminded himself to thank the crew. Rigging charges is a true art. The trick is not to blow up the building but simply to eliminate what keeps it upright, allowing nature — gravity, in this case — to do the job.

Which was, Hydt now reflected, a metaphor for his own role on earth.

15

Early-afternoon zebra bands of sun and shadow rolled over the low rows of sugarbeet in the Fenland field.

James Bond lay on his back, arms and legs splayed, like a child who'd been making angels in snow and didn't want to go home. Surrounded by the sea of low green leaves, he was thirty yards from the pile of rubble that had been the old army hospital . . . the pile of rubble that had very nearly entombed him. He was — temporarily, he prayed — deprived of his hearing, thanks to the shockwaves from the plastic explosive. He'd kept his eyes closed against the flash and shrapnel, but he'd had to use both hands to manage his escape, wrenching open the mental-health ward's door, as the main charges detonated and the building came down behind him.

He now rose slightly — sugar beet in May provided scant cover — and gazed around for signs of a threat.

Nothing. Whoever had been behind the plan — the Irishman, Noah or an associate — wasn't searching for him; they were probably convinced he had died in the collapse.

Breathing hard to clear his lungs of dust and sour chemical smoke, he got to his feet and staggered from the field.

He returned to the car and dropped into the

front seat. He fished a bottle of water from the back and drank some, then leant outside and poured the rest into his eyes.

He fired the massive engine, comforted that he could now hear the bubble of the exhaust, and took a different route out of March, heading east to avoid running into anyone connected with the demolition site, then doubling back west. Soon he was on the A1, heading back to London to decipher whatever cryptic messages about Incident Twenty the scraps of ash he'd collected might hold.

* * *

At close to four that afternoon Bond pulled into the ODG car park beneath the building.

He thought of having a shower but decided he didn't have time. He washed his hands and face, stuck a plaster on a small gash, courtesy of a falling brick, and hurried to Philly. He handed her the pieces of duct tape. 'Can you get these analysed?'

'For God's sake, James, what happened?' She sounded alarmed. The tactical trousers and jacket had taken the bulk of the abuse but some new bruises were already showing in glorious violet.

'Little run-in with a bulldozer and some C4 or Semtex — I'm fine. Find out everything you can about Eastern Demolition and Scrap. And I'd like to know who owns the army base outside March. The MoD? Or have they sold it?'

'I'll get on to it.'

Bond returned to his office and had just sat down when Mary Goodnight buzzed him. 'James. That man is on line two.' Her tone made clear who the caller was.

Bond stabbed the button. 'Percy.'

The slick voice: 'James. Hello! I'm en route back from Cambridge. Thought you and me should have a chinwag. See if we've found any pieces to our puzzle.'

You and *me* . . . Unfortunate pronoun from an Oxbridge man. 'How about *your* excursion?'

'When I got up there, I did some looking around. Turns out the Porton Down folk have a little operation nearby. Stumbled across it. Quite by chance.'

This amused Bond. 'Well, that's interesting. And is there a connection between biochemicals and Noah or Incident Twenty?'

'Can't say. Their CCTVs and visitor logs didn't turn up anything that stood out. But I've got my assistant toiling away.'

'And the pub?'

'Curry was all right. The waitress didn't remember who'd ordered the pie or the ploughman's so long ago but we could hardly expect her to, could we? What about you? Did the mysterious note about the chemist and two days past the Ides of March pan out?'

Bond had prepared for this. 'I tried a long shot. I went to March, Boots Road, and ran across an old military base.'

A pause. 'Ah.' The Division Three man laughed, though the sound seemed devoid of humour. 'So you'd misread the clue when we

110

were chatting earlier. And was the infamous number seventeen *tomorrow*'s date, by any chance?'

Whatever else, Osborne-Smith was sharp. 'Possibly. When I got up there, the place was being demolished.' Bond added evasively, 'It turned up more questions than anything else, I'm afraid. The techies are looking at some finds. A few small things. I'll send over their reports.'

'Do, thanks. I'm peering into all things Islamic here, Afghan connection, spikes in SIGINT, the usual. Should keep me busy for a while.'

Good. Bond couldn't have asked for a better approach to Deputy Senior Director of Field Operations Mr Percy Osborne-Smith.

Keep him busy . . .

They rang off and Bond called Bill Tanner to brief him about what had happened in March. They agreed to do nothing for now about the body of the man who had attacked Bond at the hospital, preferring to keep his cover intact rather than learn anything about the corpse.

Mary Goodnight stuck her head through the door. 'Philly called when you were on the phone. She's found a few things for you. I told her to come up.' His PA was frowning, her eyes turned to one of Bond's dim windows. 'A shame, isn't it? About Philly.'

'What are you talking about?'

'I thought you'd heard? Tim broke it off. He sat her down a few days ago — they even had the church booked, and her hen do was planned. A girls' weekend in Spain. I was going.'

How observant am I? Bond thought. *That's*

111

what was missing from her desk on the third floor. The pictures of her fiancé. Probably the engagement ring had gone MIA too.

'What happened?' he asked.

'I suppose it's always more than one thing, isn't it? They hadn't been getting on well recently, more than a few bad patches — rows about her driving too fast and working all hours. She missed a big family reunion at his parents'. Then, out of the blue, he had the chance of a posting to Singapore or Malaysia. He took it. They'd been together for three years, hadn't they?'

'Sorry to hear that.'

The discussion of the drama ended, though, with the arrival of the person in question.

Not noticing the still atmosphere into which she'd walked, Philly strode past Goodnight with a smile and into Bond's office, where she dropped breezily into a chair. Her sensuous face seemed to have narrowed and her hazel eyes shone with the intensity of a hunter picking up sure track. It made her even more beautiful. A hen party in Spain with the girls? God, he simply could *not* picture that, any more than he could see Philly lugging home two Waitrose carrier bags to assemble a hearty dinner for a man named Tim and their children Matilda and Archie.

Enough! he upbraided himself and concentrated on what she was telling him. 'Our people could read one scrap of the ash. The words were 'the Gehenna plan'. And below that 'Friday, 20 May'.'

'Gehenna? Familiar, but I can't place it.'

'There's a reference to it in the Bible. I'll find out more. I only ran 'Gehenna plan' through the security agencies and criminal databases. It returned negative.'

'What's on the other piece of ash?'

'That was more badly damaged. Our lab could make out the words 'term' and 'five million pounds' but the rest was beyond them. They sent it to Specialist Crime at the Yard, under an eyes-only order. They'll get back to me by this evening.'

''Term' . . . terms of the deal, I'd guess. Payment or down payment of five million for the attack or whatever it's to be. That suggests Noah's doing it for money, not for the sake of politics or ideology.'

She nodded. 'About the Serbian connection: my Hungarian ploy didn't work. The folk in Belgrade are really quite cross with you, James. But I had your I Branch set me up as somebody from the EU — the head of the Directorate of Transportation Safety Investigations.'

'What the hell's that?'

'I made it up. I did a pretty good Swiss-French accent, though I say it myself. The Serbs are dying to do anything they can to keep the European Union happy so they're scurrying to get back to me about haz-mats on the train and more details about Karic.'

Philly was truly golden.

'And Eastern Demolition have headquarters in Slough. They were low bidders for the demolition project at the British Army base in March.'

'Is it a public limited company?'

'Private. And owned by a holding company, also private: Green Way International. It's quite big and operates in half a dozen countries. One man owns all the shares. Severan Hydt.'

'That's really his name?'

She laughed. 'At first I wondered what his parents were thinking. But it seems he changed it by deed poll when he was in his twenties.'

'What was his birth name?'

'Maarten Holt.'

'Holt to Hydt,' Bond mused. 'I don't see the point — though it's hardly remarkable — but Maarten to Severan? Why, in heaven's name?'

She shrugged. 'Green Way is a huge rubbish-collection and recycling operation. You've seen their lorries but probably haven't thought much about them. I couldn't find a great deal because they're not public and Hydt stays clear of the press. Article in *The Times* dubbed him the world's richest rag-and-bone man. The *Guardian* ran a profile of him a few years ago and was fairly complimentary but he gave them only a few generic quotes and that was it. I found out he was Dutch-born, kept dual citizenship for a time and is now just British.'

Philly's body language and the hunter's sheen in her eyes hinted that she hadn't revealed all.

'And?' Bond asked.

She smiled. 'I found some online references to when he was a mature student at the University of Bristol, where he did rather well, by the way.' She explained that Hydt had been active in the university's sailing club, captaining a boat in

114

competitions. 'He not only raced but built his own. It earned him a nickname.'

'And what was it?' Bond asked, though he had a feeling he knew.

'Noah.'

16

The time was now half past five. Since it would be several hours before Philly received the intelligence she was waiting for, Bond suggested they meet for dinner.

She agreed and returned to her work station, while Bond composed an encrypted email to M, copying in Bill Tanner, saying that Noah was Severan Hydt and including a synopsis of his background and what had happened in March. He added that Hydt referred to the attack involved in Incident Twenty as the 'Gehenna plan'. More would be forthcoming.

He received a terse reply:

007 —
Authorised to proceed. Appropriate liaison with
domestic organisations expected.
M

My carte grise . . .

Bond left his office, took the lift to the second floor and entered a large room filled with more computers than an electronics shop. A few men and women laboured at monitors, or at the type of work stations to be found in a university chemistry laboratory. Bond walked to a small, glass-walled office at the far end and tapped on the window.

Sanu Hirani, head of the ODG's Q Branch,

was a slim man of forty or so. His complexion was sallow and his luxuriant black hair framed a face handsome enough to get him roles in Bollywood. A brilliant cricketer, known for his fast bowling, he had degrees in chemistry, electrical engineering and computer science from top universities in the UK and America (where he had been successful in everything except introducing his sport to the Yanks, who could neither grasp the game's subtleties, nor tolerate the length of a Test match).

Q Branch was the technical support enclave within the ODG and Hirani oversaw all aspects of the gadgetry that has always been used in tradecraft. Wizards for departments like Q Branch and the CIA's Science and Technology Division spent their time coming up with hardware and software innovations, like miniature cameras, improbable weapons, concealments, communications devices and surveillance equipment — such as Hirani's latest: a hypersensitive omnidirectional microphone mounted within a dead fly. ('A bug in a bug,' Bond had commented wryly to its creator, who had replied that he was the eighteenth person to make the joke and, by the way, a fly was not, biologically speaking, a bug.)

Since the ODG's *raison d'être* was operational, much of Hirani's work lay in ensuring he had sufficient monoculars, binoculars, camouflage, communications devices, specialised weapons and counter-surveillance gear to hand. In this regard he was like a librarian who made sure the books were checked out appropriately and returned on time.

But Hirani's particular genius was his ability to invent and improvise, coming up with devices like the iQPhone. The ODG was, of all things, the patent holder on dozens of his inventions. When Bond or other O Branch agents were in the field and found themselves in a tight spot, one call to Hirani, at any time of day or night, and he would find a solution. He or his people might put something together in the office and pop it into the FCO diplomatic pouch for overnight delivery. More often, though, time was critical and Hirani would enlist one of his many wily innovators and scroungers around the world to build, find or modify a device in the field.

'James.' The men shook hands. 'You've bought Incident Twenty, I hear.'

'Seems so.'

Bond sat down, noticing a book on Hirani's desk: *The Secret War of Charles Fraser-Smith*. It was one of his own favourites on the history of gadgetry in espionage.

'How serious is it?'

'Rather,' Bond said laconically, not sharing that he'd nearly been killed twice already in pursuing the assignment, which he'd had for less than forty-eight hours.

Sitting beneath pictures of early IBM computers and of Indian cricketers, Hirani asked, 'What do you need?'

Bond lowered his voice so that the closest Q Branch worker, a young woman raptly staring at her screen, could not hear. 'What kind of surveillance kits do you have that one man could put in place? I can't get to the subject's computer or phone but I may be able to plant something in his office, vehicle or home. Disposable. I probably can't retrieve it later.'

'Ah, yes . . . ' Hirani's luminescent eyes dimmed.

'Some problem, Sanu?'

'Well, I must tell you, James. Not ten minutes ago I had a call from upstairs.'

'Bill Tanner?'

'No — farther upstairs.'

M. Dammit, Bond thought. He could see where this was going.

Hirani went on: 'And he said that if anyone from O Branch wished to check out a surveillance kit I was to let him know immediately. A touch coincidental.'

'A touch,' Bond said sourly.

'So,' Hirani said, with a qualified smile, 'shall I tell him that someone from O Branch wishes to check out a surveillance kit?'

'Perhaps you could hold off for a bit.'

'Well, get it sorted,' he said, the gleam in his face restored. 'I have some *wonderful* packages for you to choose from.' He sounded like a car salesman. 'A microphone that's powered by induction. You only have to place it near a power cord, no battery needed. It'll pick up voices from fifty feet away and adjust the volume automatically so there's no distortion. Oh, and another thing we've been having great success with is a two-pound coin — the 'ninety-four tercentenary of the Bank of England commemorative. It's relatively rare so a target tends to keep it for good luck but not so rare that he would sell it.

119

Battery lasts for four months.'

Bond sighed. The off-limits devices sounded so damn perfect. He thanked the man and told him he'd be in touch. He returned to his office, where he found Mary Goodnight at her desk. He saw no reason for her to stay. 'Scoot on home now. Good evening, Goodnight.'

She glanced at his latest injuries and forewent the opportunity for mothering him, which from past experience she knew would be deflected. She settled for 'See to those, James,' then gathered up her handbag and coat.

Sitting back, Bond was suddenly aware of the stench of his sweat and the crescents of brick dust under his nails. He wanted to get home and shower. Have his first drink of the day. Yet there was something he had to sort out first.

He turned to his screen and entered the Golden Wire's general information database, from which he learnt where Severan Hydt's business and home were located, the latter, curiously, in a low-income area of East London known as Canning Town. Green Way's main premises were on the Thames near Rainham, abutting the Wildspace Conservation Park.

Bond peered at satellite maps of Hydt's home and Green Way's operation. It was vitally important to set up surveillance on the man. But there was no legitimate way to conduct it without enlisting Osborne-Smith and the A Branch snoop teams from MI5 — and the instant the Division Three man learnt Hydt's identity he'd move in to 'detain' him and the Irishman. Bond considered the risk again. How realistic was his concern that

120

if the two were pulled in, other co-conspirators would accelerate the carnage, or vanish until they struck again next month or next year?

Evil, James Bond had learnt, can be tirelessly patient.

Surveillance or not?

He debated. After a moment's hesitation, he reluctantly picked up the phone.

17

At half past six, Bond drove to his flat and, in the garage, reversed into the spot beside his racing-green Jaguar. He climbed the stairs to the first floor, unlocked the door, disarmed the alarm and confirmed with a separate security function — a fast-framed video — that only May, his housekeeper, had been there. (Feeling somewhat embarrassed, he'd told her when she'd started working for him that the security camera was a requirement of his government employer's; the flat had to be monitored when he was away, even if she was working there. 'Considering what you must do for the country, being a patriot and all, it's no bother's,' the staunch woman had said, using the fragment of 'sir', a mark of respect reserved for him alone.)

He checked messages on his home phone. He had only one. It was from a friend who lived in Mayfair, Fouad Kharaz, a wily, larger-than-life Jordanian, who had all manner of business dealings, involving vehicles mostly: cars, planes and the most astonishing yachts Bond had ever seen. Kharaz and he were members of the same gaming club in Berkeley Square, the Commodore.

Unlike many such clubs in London, where membership could be had with twenty-four hours' notice and five hundred pounds, the Commodore was a proper establishment, requiring patience and considerable vetting to join. Once you were a member, you were expected to adhere strictly to a number of rules, such as the dress code, and behave impeccably at the tables. It also boasted a fine restaurant and cellar.

Kharaz had called to invite Bond to dine there tonight. 'A problem, James. I have fallen heir to two beautiful women from Saint-Tropez — how it happened is too long, and delicate, a story to leave as a message. But I can't be charming enough for both of them. Will you help?'

Smiling, Bond rang him back and told him he had another engagement. A rain check was arranged.

Then he went through his shower ritual — steaming hot, then icy cold — and dried himself briskly. He ran his fingers over his cheeks and chin and decided to maintain a lifelong prejudice against shaving twice in one day. Then he chided himself: why were you even thinking about it? Philly Maidenstone's pretty and clever and she rides a hell of a fine motorcycle — but she's a colleague. That's all.

The black leather jumpsuit, however, made an unbidden appearance in his mind.

In a towelling robe Bond stepped into the kitchen and poured two fingers of bourbon, Basil Hayden's, into a glass, dropped in one ice cube and drank half, enjoying the sharp nutty flavour. The first sip of the day was invariably the best, especially coming as this one did — after a harrowing excursion against an enemy and ahead of an evening with a beautiful woman . . .

He caught himself again. Stop.

He sat in an old leather chair in the living

room, which was sparsely furnished. The majority of the items in it had been his parents', inherited when they had died and kept in storage near his aunt's in Kent. He'd bought a few things: some lamps, a desk and chairs, a Bose sound system he rarely had a chance to listen to.

On the mantelpiece there were silver-framed photos of his parents and grandparents — on his father's side in Scotland, his mother's in Switzerland. Several showed his aunt Charmian with the young Bond in Kent. On the walls were other photographs, taken by his mother, a freelance photojournalist. Mostly black and white, the photos depicted a variety of images: political gatherings, labour union events, sports competitions, panoramic scenes of exotic locations.

There was also a curious *objet d'art* in the mantelpiece's centre: a bullet. It had nothing to do with Bond's role as an agent in the 00 Section of the ODG's O Branch. Its source was a very different time and place of Bond's life. He walked to the fireplace and turned the solid piece of ammunition in his hand once or twice, finally replacing it and returning to his chair.

Then, despite his protest that he keep affairs with Philly — that he keep *matters* relating to *Agent Maidenstone* purely professional, he couldn't stop thinking of her as a woman.

And one no longer betrothed.

Bond had to admit that what he felt for Philly was more than pure physical lust. And he now asked himself a question that had arisen at other times, about other women, albeit rarely: could something serious develop between them?

Bond's romantic life was more complicated than most. The barriers to his having a partner were to some degree his extensive travelling, the demands of his job and the constant danger that surrounded him. But more fundamental was the tricky matter of admitting who he really was and, more tellingly, his duties within the 00 Section, which some, perhaps most, women would find distasteful, if not abhorrent.

He knew that at some point he would have to admit to at least part of it to any woman who became more than a casual lover. You can keep secrets from those you're close to for only so long. People are far more clever and observant than we think and, between romantic partners, one's fundamental secrets stay hidden only because the other chooses to let them remain so.

Plausible deniability might work in Whitehall but it didn't last between lovers.

Yet with Philly Maidenstone this was not a problem. There would be no confessions about his profession over dinner or amid tousled morning bedclothes; she knew his CV and his remit — knew them intimately.

And she'd suggested a restaurant near her flat.

What sort of message lay in that choice?

James Bond glanced at his watch. It was time to dress and attempt to decipher the code.

18

At eight fifteen the taxi dropped Bond at Antoine's in Bloomsbury and he immediately approved of Philly's choice. He hated crowded, noisy restaurants and bars and on more than one occasion had walked out of upmarket establishments when the decibel level had proved to be too irritating. Upscale pubs were more 'ghastly' than 'gastro', he'd once quipped.

But Antoine's was quiet and dimly lit. An impressive wine selection was visible at the back of the room and the walls were filled with muted portraits from the nineteenth century. Bond asked for a small booth not far from the wall of bottles. He settled into the plush leather, facing the front, as always, and studied the place. Business people and locals, he judged.

'Something to drink?' asked the waiter, a pleasant man in his late thirties, with a shaved head and pierced ears.

Bond decided on a cocktail. 'Crown Royal, on ice, a double, please. Add a half-measure of triple sec, two dashes of bitters and a twist of orange peel.'

'Yes, sir. Interesting drink.'

'Based on an Old Fashioned. My own creation, actually.'

'Does it have a name?'

'Not yet,' he said. 'I've been looking for the right one.'

A few moments later it arrived and he took a sip — it was constructed perfectly and Bond said so. He'd just set the glass down when he saw Philly coming through the door, radiant with a smile. It seemed that her pace quickened when she saw him.

She was in close-fitting black jeans, a brown leather jacket and, under it, a tight dark green sweater, the colour of his Jaguar.

He half rose as she joined him, sitting to his side, rather than across. She was carrying a briefcase.

'You all right?' she said.

He'd half expected something a bit more personal than this rather casual greeting. But then he asked himself sternly, Why?

She had barely taken off her jacket before she'd caught the eye of the waiter, who greeted her with a smile. 'Ophelia.'

'Aaron. I'll have a glass of the Mosel Riesling.'

'On its way.'

Her wine arrived and Bond told Aaron they'd wait to order. Their glasses nodded at one another but did not clink.

'First,' Bond murmured, edging a little closer, 'Hydt. Tell me about him.'

'I checked with Specialist Operations at the Yard, Six, Interpol, NCIC and CIA in America and the AIVD in the Netherlands. I made some discreet enquiries at Five too.' She'd obviously deduced the tension between Bond and Osborne-Smith. 'No criminal records. No watchlists. More Tory than Labour but doesn't have much interest in politics. Not a member of

127

any church. Treats his people well — no labour unrest of any kind. No problems with the Inland Revenue or Health and Safety. He just seems to be a wealthy businessman. Very wealthy. All he's ever done professionally is rubbish collection and recycling.'

The Rag-and-bone Man . . .

'He's fifty-six, never married. Both parents — they were Dutch — are dead now. His father had some money and travelled a lot on business. Hydt was born in Amsterdam, then came here with his mother to live when he was twelve. She had a breakdown so he grew up mostly under the care of the housekeeper, who'd accompanied them from Holland. Then his father lost most of his money and vanished from his son's life. Because she wasn't getting paid, the housekeeper called in Social Services and vanished — after eight years of looking after the boy.' Philly shook her head in sympathy. 'He was fourteen.'

Philly continued, 'He started working as a dustman at fifteen. Then he's off the radar until he's in his twenties. He opened Green Way just as the recycling trend caught on.'

'What happened? Did he inherit some money?'

'No. It's a bit of a mystery. He started penniless, as far as I can tell. When he was older he put himself through university. He read ancient history and archaeology.'

'And Green Way?'

'It handles general rubbish disposal, wheelie-bin collection, removal of construction waste at building sites, scrap metal, demolition, recycling, document shredding, dangerous-materials reclamation and disposal. According to the business press, it's moving into a dozen other countries to start up rubbish tips and recycling centres.' Philly displayed a printout of a company sales brochure.

Bond frowned at the logo. It looked like a green dagger, resting on its side.

'It's not a knife,' Philly said, laughing. 'I thought the same thing. It's a leaf. Global warming, pollution and energy are the sexiest subjects in the *au courant* environmental movement. But rising quickly are planet-friendly rubbish disposal and recycling. And Green Way's one of the big innovators.'

'Any Serbian connection?'

'Through a subsidiary he owns part of a small operation in Belgrade. But, like everybody else in the organisation, nobody there has any criminal past.'

'I just can't work out his game,' Bond said. 'He's not political, has no terrorist leanings. It almost looks like he's been hired to arrange the attack, or whatever it's to be, on Friday. But he hardly needs money.' He sipped his cocktail. 'Right, then, Detective Inspector Maidenstone, tell me about the evidence — that other bit of ash from up in March. Six made out the 'Gehenna plan' and 'Friday, 20 May'. Did Forensics at the Yard find anything else?'

Her voice dropped, which necessitated his leaning closer. He smelt a sweet but undefined scent. Her sweater, cashmere, brushed the back of his hand. 'They did. They think the rest of the words were 'Course is confirmed. Blast radius must be a hundred feet minimum. Ten thirty is the optimal time.''

'So, an explosive device of some kind. Ten thirty Friday — p.m., according to the original intercept. And 'Course' — a shipping route or plane most likely.'

'Now,' she continued, 'the metal you found? It's a titanium-steel laminate. Unique. Nobody in the lab has ever seen anything like it. The pieces were shavings. They'd been machined in the past day or so.'

Was that what Hydt's people had been doing in the basement of the hospital? Were they building a weapon with this metal?

'And Defence still owns the facility but it hasn't been used for three years.'

His eyes swept over her marvellous profile from forehead to breasts as she sipped her wine.

Philly continued, 'As for the Serbs, I practically said I'd force them to take on the euro in place of the dinar if they didn't help me. But they came through. The man working with the Irishman, Aldo Karic, was a load scheduler with the railway.'

'He'd have known exactly which train the haz-mat was on.'

'Yes.' Then she frowned. 'About that, though, James. It's odd. The material was pretty bad. Methyl isocyanate, MIC. It's the chemical that killed all those people in Bhopal.'

'God.'

'But, look, here's the inventory of everything on board the train.' She showed him the list, translated into English. 'The chemical containers are practically bullet-proof. You can drop one from a plane and supposedly it won't break open.'

Bond was confused by this. 'So a train crash wouldn't have produced a spill.'

'Very unlikely. And another thing: the wagon with the chemical contained only about three hundred kilos of MIC. It's really bad stuff, certainly, but at Bhopal, forty-two *thousand* kilos were released. Even if a few of the drums had broken open, the damage would have been negligible.'

But what else would the Irishman have been interested in? Bond looked over the list. Aside from the chemicals, the cargo was harmless: boilers, vehicle parts, motor oil, scrap, girders, timber . . . No weapons, unstable substances, other risky materials.

Maybe the incident had been an elaborate scheme to kill the train driver or someone living at the bottom of the hill below the restaurant. Had the Irishman been going to stage the death to look like an accident? Until they could home in on Noah's purpose, there could be no effective response. Bond could only hope that the surveillance he'd reluctantly put into play earlier in the evening would pay off. He asked, 'Any more on Gehenna?'

'Hell.'

'I'm sorry?'

Her face broke into a smile. 'Gehenna is where the Judaeo-Christian concept of hell came from. The word's a derivation of Gehinnom, or the

131

Valley of Hinnom — a valley in Jerusalem. Ages ago, some people think, it was used as a site to burn rubbish and there may have been natural gas deposits in the rocks that kept the fires going perpetually. In the Bible, Gehenna came to mean a place where sinners and unbelievers would be punished.

'The only recent significant reference — if you can call a hundred and fifty years ago recent — was in a Rudyard Kipling poem.' She'd memorised the verse and recited, ''Down to Gehenna or up to the Throne, / He travels the fastest who travels alone.''

He liked that and repeated it to himself.

She said, 'Now, for my other assignment, Steel Cartridge.'

Relax, Bond told himself. He raised an eyebrow nonchalantly.

Philly said, 'I couldn't see any connection between the Gehenna plan and Steel Cartridge.'

'No, I understand that. I don't think they're related. This is something else — from before I joined the ODG.'

The hazel eyes scanned his face, pausing momentarily on the scar. 'You were Defence Intelligence, weren't you? And before that you were in Afghanistan with the Naval Reserve.'

'That's right.'

'Afghanistan . . . The Russians were there, of course, before we and the Americans decided to pop in for tea. Does it have to do with your assignments there?'

'Could very well. I don't know.'

Philly realised she was asking questions he

132

might not want to answer. 'I got the original Russian data file that our Station R hacked and I went through the metadata. It sent me to other sources and I found out that Steel Cartridge was a targeted killing operation, sanctioned at a high level. That's what the phrase 'some deaths' referred to. I can't find out whether it was KGB or SVR, so we don't know the date yet.'

In 1991 the KGB, the infamous Soviet security and spy apparatus, was redesigned as Russia's FSB, with domestic jurisdiction, and the SVR, with foreign. The consensus among those following the espionage world was that the change was cosmetic only.

Bond considered this. 'Targeted killing.'

'That's right. And one of our clandestine operators — an agent with Six — was in some way involved but I don't know who or how yet. Maybe our man was tracking the Russian assassin. Maybe he wanted to turn him and run him as a double. Or our agent might even have been the target himself. I'm getting more soon — I've opened channels.'

He noticed that he was staring at the tablecloth, brow furrowed. He gave her a fast smile. 'Brilliant, Philly. Thanks.'

On his mobile, Bond typed a synopsis of what Philly had told him about Hydt, Incident Twenty and Green Way International, omitting the information on Operation Steel Cartridge. He sent the message to M and Bill Tanner. Then he said, 'Right. Now it's time for sustenance, after all our hard work. First, wine. Red or white?'

'I'm a girl who doesn't play by the rules.'

Philly let that linger — teasingly, it seemed to Bond. Then she explained: 'I'll do a big red — a Margaux or St Julien — with a mild-mannered fish like sole. And I'll have a Pinot Gris or Albariño with a nice juicy steak.' She relented. 'I'm saying whatever you're in the mood for, James, is fine with me.' She buttered a piece of her roll and ate it, with obvious pleasure, then snatched up the menu and examined the sheet like a little girl trying to decide which Christmas present to open first. Bond was charmed.

A moment later Aaron, the waiter, was beside them. Philly said to Bond, 'You first. I need seven seconds more.'

'I'll start with the pâté. Then I'll have the grilled turbot.'

Philly ordered a rocket and Parmesan salad with pear and, to follow, the poached lobster, with haricots verts and new potatoes.

Bond picked a bottle of an unoaked Chardonnay from Napa, California.

'Good,' she said. 'The Americans have the best chardonnay grapes outside Burgundy but they really must have the courage to throw out some of their damned oak casks.'

Bond's opinion exactly.

The wine arrived and then the food, which proved excellent. He complimented her on her choice of restaurant.

Casual conversation ensued. She asked about his life in London, recent travels, where he'd grown up. Instinctively, he gave her only the broad brush of information that was already in the public domain — his parents' death, his

134

childhood with his aunt Charmian in idyllic Pett Bottom, Kent, his brief tenure at Eton and subsequent attendance at his father's old school in Edinburgh, Fettes.

'Yes, I heard that at Eton you got into a spot of bother — something about a maid?' She let those words linger a bit too. Then smiled. 'I heard the official story — a touch scandalous. But there were other rumours too. That you'd been defending the girl's honour.'

'I think my lips must remain sealed on that.' He offered a smile. 'I'll plead the Official Secrets Act. *Un*-officially.'

'Well, if it's true, you were quite young to play knight errant.'

'I think I'd just read Tolkien's *Sir Gawain*,' Bond told her. And he couldn't help but note that she'd certainly done her research on him.

He asked about her childhood. Philly told him about growing up in Devon, boarding school in Cambridgeshire — where, as a teenager, she'd distinguished herself as a volunteer for human rights organisations — then reading law at the LSE. She loved to travel and talked at length about holidays. She was at her most animated when it came to her BSA motorcycle and her other passion, skiing.

Interesting, Bond thought. Something else in common.

Their eyes met and held for an easy five seconds.

Bond felt the electric sensation with which he was so familiar. His knee brushed against hers, partly by accident, partly not. She ran a hand

135

through her loose red hair.

Philly rubbed her closed eyes with her fingertips. Looking back to Bond, she said, her voice low, 'I must say, this was a brilliant idea. Dinner, I mean. I definitely needed to . . . ' She trailed off, her eyes crinkling with amusement as she couldn't, or didn't want to, explain further. 'I'm not sure I'm ready for the night to be over. Look, it's only half past ten.'

Bond leant forward. Their forearms touched — and this time there was no regrouping.

Philly said, 'I'd like an after-dinner drink. But I don't know exactly what they have here.' Those were her words but what she was actually telling him was that she had some port or brandy in her flat just over the road, a sofa and music too.

And very likely something more awaited.

Codes . . .

His next line was to have been: 'I could use one too. Though maybe not *here*.'

But then Bond happened to notice something, very small, very subtle.

The index finger and the thumb of her right hand were gently rubbing the ring finger of her left. He noted a faint pallor where the tan from a recent holiday was missing; it had been cloaked from the sun by Tim's crimson engagement ring, now absent.

Her radiant golden-green eyes were still fixed on Bond's, her smile intact. He knew that, yes, they could settle the bill and leave and she would take his arm as they walked to her flat. He knew the humorous repartee would continue. He knew the love-making would be consuming

136

— he could tell that from the way her eyes and voice sparkled, from how she'd dived into her food, from the clothes she wore and how she wore them. From her laugh.

And yet he knew, too, that it wasn't right. Not now. When she'd slipped the ring off and handed it back, she'd also returned a piece of her heart. He didn't doubt she was well on the way to recovery — a woman who fishtailed a BSA motorcycle at speed along Peak District byways wouldn't be down for long.

But, he decided, it was better to wait.

If Ophelia Maidenstone was a woman he might let into his life, she would continue to be so in a month or two.

He said, 'I believe I saw an Armagnac on the after-dinner list that intrigued me. I'd like to sample some.'

And Bond knew he'd done the right thing when her face softened, relief and gratitude outweighing the disappointment — though only by a nose. She squeezed his arm and sat back. 'You order for me, James. I'm sure you know what I'd like.'

Tuesday
DEATH IN THE SAND

19

James Bond awoke from a dream he could not recall but that had him sweating fiercely, his heart pounding — and pounding all the faster from the braying of his phone.

His bedside clock told him it was 5:01 a.m. He grabbed the mobile and glanced at the screen, blinking sleep from his eyes. Bless him, he thought.

He hit answer. '*Bonjour, mon ami.*'

'*Et toi aussi!*' said the rich, rasping voice. 'We are encrypted, are we not?'

'*Oui.* Yes, of course.'

'What did we do in the days before encryption?' asked René Mathis, presumably in his office on Boulevard Mortier, in Paris's 20th *arrondissement.*

'There were no days before encryption, René. There were only days before there was an app for it on a touch screen.'

'Well said, James. You are waxing wise, *comme un philosophe.* And so early in the morning.'

The thirty-five-year-old Mathis was an agent for the French secret service, the Direction Générale de la Sécurité Extérieure. He and Bond worked together occasionally, in joint ODG and DGSE operations, most recently wrapping up al-Qaeda and other criminal enterprises in Europe and North Africa. They had also drunk significant quantities of Lillet and Louis

Roederer together and spent some rather ... well, colourful nights in such cities as Bucharest, Tunis and Bari, that free-wheeling gem on Italy's Adriatic coast.

It had been René Mathis whom Bond had called yesterday evening, not Osborne-Smith, to ask his friend to run surveillance on Severan Hydt. He had made the decision reluctantly but he had realised he had to take the politically risky step of circumventing not only Division Three but M himself. He needed surveillance but had to make sure that Hydt and the Irishman remained unaware that the British authorities were on to them.

France, of course, has its own snoop operation, like GCHQ in England, the NSA in America and any other country's intelligence agency with a flush budget. The DGSE was continually listening in to conversations and reading emails of the citizens of other countries, the United Kingdom's included. (Yes, the countries were allies at the moment, but there was that little matter of the history between them.)

So Bond had called in a favour. He'd asked René Mathis to listen to the ELINT and SIGINT from London being hoovered up by the hundred-metre antenna of France's gravity gradient stabilised spy satellite, searching for relevant key words.

Mathis now said, 'I have something for you, James.'

'I'm dressing. I'll put you on speaker.' Bond hit the button and leapt out of bed.

'Does this mean that the beautiful redhead lying beside you will be listening as well?'

Bond chuckled, not least because the Frenchman had happened to pick that particular hair colour. A brief image surfaced of pressing his cheek against Philly's last night on her doorstep as her vibrant hair caressed his shoulder before he returned to his flat.

'I searched for signals tagged 'Severan Hydt' or his nickname 'Noah'. And anything related to Green Way International, the Gehenna plan, Serbia train derailments, or threat-oriented events this coming Friday, and all of those in proximity to any names sounding Irish. But it is very odd, James: the satellite vector was aimed right at Green Way's premises east of London, but there was virtually no SIGINT coming out of the place. It's as if he forbids his workers to have mobiles. Very curious.'

Yes, it was, Bond reflected. He continued dressing fast.

'But there are several things we were able to pick up. Hydt is presently at home and he's leaving the country this morning. Soon, I believe. Going where, I don't know. But he'll be flying. There was a reference to an airport and another to passports. And it will be in a private jet, since his people had spoken to the pilot directly. I'm afraid there was no clue as to which airport. I know there are many in London. We have them targeted . . . for surveillance only, I must add quickly!'

Bond couldn't help but laugh.

'Now, James, we found nothing about this

Gehenna plan. But I have some disturbing information. We decrypted a brief call fifteen minutes ago to a location about ten miles west of Green Way, outside London.'

'Probably Hydt's home.'

Mathis continued, 'A man's voice said, "Severan, it's me." Accented but our algorithms couldn't tell region of origin. There were some pleasantries, then this: "We're confirmed for seven p.m. today. The number of dead will be ninety or so. You must be there no later than six forty-five."'

So Hydt either was part of a plan to murder scores of people or was going to do so himself. 'Who are the victims? And why are they going to die?'

'I don't know, James. But what I found just as troubling was your Mr Hydt's reaction. His voice was like that of *un enfant* offered chocolate. He said, "Oh, such wonderful news! Thank you so much."' His voice dark, Mathis said, 'I've never heard that kind of joy at the prospect of killing. But, even stranger, he then asked, "How close can I get to the bodies?"'

'He said that?'

'Indeed. The man told him he could be very close. And Hydt sounded very pleased at that too. Then the phones went silent and haven't been used again.'

'Seven p.m. Somewhere out of the country. Anything more?'

'I'm afraid not.'

'Thank you, for all this. I'd better get on with the hunt.'

144

'I wish I could keep our satellite online longer but my superiors are already asking questions about why I am so interested in that insignificant little place called London.'

'Next time the Dom is on me, René.'

'But of course. *Au revoir.*'

'*À bientôt, et merci beaucoup.*' Bond hit disconnect.

In his years as a Royal Naval Reserve commander and an agent for ODG, he'd been up against some very bad people: insurgents, terrorists, psychopathic criminals, amoral traitors selling nuclear secrets to men mad enough to use them. But what was Hydt's game?

Purpose . . . response.

Well, even if it wasn't clear what the man's twisted goal might be, at least there was one response Bond could initiate.

Ten minutes later he ran down the stairs, fishing the car key from his pocket. He didn't need to look up Severan Hydt's address. He'd memorised it last night.

20

Thames House, the home of MI5, the Northern Ireland Office and some related security organisations, is less impressive than the residence of MI6, which happens to be nearby, across the river on the South Bank. Six's headquarters look rather like a futuristic enclave from a Ridley Scott film (it's referred to as Babylon-upon-Thames, for its resemblance to a ziggurat, and, less kindly, as Legoland).

But if not as architecturally striking, Thames House is far more intimidating. The ninety-year-old grey stone monolith is the sort of place where, were it a police headquarters in Soviet Russia or East Germany, you would begin answering before questions were asked. On the other hand, the place *does* boast some rather impressive sculpture (Charles Sargeant Jagger's *Britannia* and *St George,* for instance) and every few days tourists from Arkansas or Tokyo stroll up to the front door thinking it's Tate Britain, which is located a short distance away.

In the windowless bowels of Thames House were the offices of Division Three. The organisation conscientiously — for the sake of deniability — rented space and equipment from Five (and nobody has better equipment than MI5), all at arm's length.

In the middle of this fiefdom was a large control room, rather frayed at the edges, the

146

green walls battered and scuffed, the furniture dented, the carpet insulted by too many heels. The requisite government regulatory posters about suspicious parcels, fire drills, health and trade union matters were omnipresent, often tarted up by bureaucrats with nothing better to do.

W E A

R E Y E P R

O T E C

T I O N W H E

N N E C E S

S A R Y

But the computers here were voracious and the dozens of flatscreen monitors big and bright, and Deputy Senior Director of Field Operations Percy Osborne-Smith was standing, arms folded, in front of the biggest and brightest. In brown jacket and mismatched trousers — he'd woken at four a.m. and dressed by five past — Osborne-Smith was with two young men: his assistant and a rumpled technician hovering over a keyboard.

Osborne-Smith bent forward and pressed a button, listened again to the recording that had just been made by the surveillance he'd put in place after the pointless drive up to Cambridge for, as it developed, the sole purpose of eating a meal of chicken curry that had turned on him in the night. The snooping didn't involve the suspect in Incident Twenty, since no one had been courteous enough to share the man's identity, but Osborne-Smith's boys and girls had managed to arrange a productive listen-in. Without informing MI5 that they were doing so, the troops had slapped some microphones on the windows of one of the anonymous evil-doer's co-conspirators: a lad named James Bond, 00 Section, O Branch, Overseas Development Group, Foreign and Commonwealth Office.

And so Osborne-Smith had learnt about Severan Hydt, that he was Noah and that he ran Green Way International. Bond seemed to have neglected to mention that his mission to Boots the road, not Boots the chemist, thank you very much, had resulted in these rather important discoveries.

'Bastard,' said Osborne-Smith's adjutant, a lean young man with an irritating mop of abundant brown hair. 'Bond's playing games with lives.'

'Just calm it now, eh?' Osborne-Smith said to the youngster, whom he referred to as 'Deputy-Deputy', though not in his presence.

'Well, he is. Bastard.'

For his part, Osborne-Smith was rather impressed that Bond had contacted the French secret service. Otherwise, nobody would have learnt that Hydt was about to leave the country and kill ninety-odd people later today, or at least be present at their deaths. This intelligence solidified Osborne-Smith's determination to clap

Severan 'Noah' Hydt in irons, drag him into Belmarsh or Division Three's own interrogation room, which was not much more hospitable than the prison's, and bleed him dry.

He said to Deputy-Deputy, 'Run the whole battery on Hydt. I want to know about his good and his bad, what medicine he takes, the *Independent* or the *Daily Sport*, Arsenal or Chelsea, his dietary preferences, movies that scare him or that make him cry, who he's dallying or who's dallying him. And how. And get an arrest team together. Say, we didn't get Bond's firearms authorisation form, did we?'

'No, sir.'

Now, *this* piqued Osborne-Smith.

'Where's my eye in the sky?' he asked the young technician, sitting at his video-games console.

They had tried to find Hydt's destination the easy way. Since the *espion* in Paris had learnt the man was departing in a private aircraft, they'd searched CAA records for planes registered to Severan Hydt, Green Way, or any subsidiaries. But none could be found. So, it was to be old-fashioned snooping, if one could describe a £3 million drone thus.

'Hold on, hold on,' the technician said, wasting breath. Finally: 'Got Big Bird peeping now.'

Osborne-Smith regarded the screen. The view from two miles overhead was remarkably clear. But then he took in the image and said, 'Are you *sure* that's Hydt's house? Not part of his company?'

149

'Positive. Private residence.'

The home occupied a full square block in Canning Town. It was separated, not surprisingly, from the neighbours in their council houses or dilapidated flats by an imposing wall, glistening at the crest with razor wire. Within the grounds there were neatly tended gardens, in May bloom. The place had apparently been a modest warehouse or factory around a century ago but had been done up recently, it seemed. Four outbuildings and a garage were clustered together.

What was this about? he wondered. Why did such a wealthy man live in Canning Town? It was poor, ethnically complex, prone to violent crime and gangs, but with fiercely loyal residents and activist councillors who worked very, very hard for their constituents. A massive amount of redevelopment was going on, apart from the Olympics construction, which some said was taking the heart out of the place. His father, Osborne-Smith recalled, had seen the Police, Jeff Beck and Depeche Mode perform at some legendary pub in Canning Town decades ago.

'Why does Hydt live there?' he mused aloud.

His assistant called, 'Just had word that Bond left his flat, heading east. He lost our man, though. Bond drives like Michael Schumacher.'

'We *know* where he's going,' Osborne-Smith said. 'Hydt's.' He hated to have to explain the obvious.

As the minutes rolled by without any activity at Hydt's, Osborne-Smith's young assistant gave him updates: an arrest team had been assembled, firearms officers included. 'They want to know their orders, sir.'

Osborne-Smith considered this. 'Get them ready but let's wait and see if Hydt's meeting anybody. I want to scoop up the entire cast and crew.'

The technician said, 'Sir, we have movement.'

Leaning closer to the screen, Osborne-Smith observed that a bulky man in a black suit — bodyguard, he assessed — was wheeling suitcases out of Hydt's house and into the detached garage.

'Sir, Bond's just arrived in Canning Town.' The man teased a joystick and the field of view expanded. 'There.' He pointed. 'That's him. The Bentley.' The subdued grey vehicle slowed and pulled to the kerb.

The assistant whistled. 'A Continental GT. Now, *that*'s a bloody fine automobile. I think they reviewed it on *Top Gear*. You ever watch the show, Percy?'

'Sadly, I'm usually working.' Osborne-Smith cast a mournful gaze towards tousle-haired Deputy-Deputy and decided that if the youngster couldn't muster a bit more humility and respect, he probably wouldn't survive — career wise — much beyond the end of the Incident Twenty assignment.

Bond's car was parked discreetly — if the word could be used to describe a £125,000 car in Canning Town — about fifty yards from Hydt's house, hidden behind several skips.

The assistant: 'The arrest team's on board the chopper.'

Osborne-Smith said, 'Put them in the air. Get them to hover somewhere near the Gherkin.'

The forty-storey Swiss Re office building rising above the City — it looked more like a 1950s spaceship than a pickled cucumber, in Osborne-Smith's view — was centrally located and thus a good place from which to begin the hunt. 'Alert security at all the airports: Heathrow, Gatwick, Luton, Stansted, London City, Southend and Biggin Hill.'

'Right, sir.'

'More subjects,' the technician said.

On the screen, three people were leaving the house. A tall man in a suit, with salt-and-pepper hair and beard, walked next to a gangly blond man whose feet pointed outwards. A slight woman in a black suit, her hair white, followed.

'That's Hydt,' the technician said. 'The one with the beard.'

'Any idea about the woman?'

'No, sir.'

'And the giraffe?' Osborne-Smith asked with a snide inflection. He was really quite irritated that Bond had ignored his firearms form. 'Is he the Irishman everyone's talking about? Get a picture and run with it. Hurry up.'

The trio walked into the garage. A moment later a black Audi A8 sped out through the front gate and pulled into the road, accelerating fast.

'Head count — all three are in the car, along with the bodyguard,' Deputy-Deputy called.

'Lock on it, MASINT. And paint it with a laser for good measure.'

'I'll try,' the technician said.

'You better had.'

They watched Bond in his Bentley, pulling smoothly into traffic and speeding after the Audi.

'Pan out and stay on them,' Osborne-Smith said, with the lisp he was forever trying to slice off, though the affliction had proved a hydra all his life.

The camera latched on to the German car. 'There's a good lad,' he said to the technician.

The Audi speeded up. Bond was following discreetly but never missing a turn. As skilful as the driver of the German car was, Bond was better — anticipating when the chauffeur would try something clever, some aborted turn or unexpected lane change, and counter the measure. The cars zipped through green, amber and red alike.

'Going north. Prince Regent Lane.'

'So London City airport's out.'

The Audi hit Newham Way.

'All right,' Deputy-Deputy enthused, tugging at his eruption of hair. 'It's either Stansted or Luton.'

'Going north on the A406,' another technician, a round blonde woman who had materialised from nowhere, called.

Then, after some impressive fox and hound driving, the competitors, Audi and Bentley, were on the M25 going anti-clockwise.

'It's Luton!' the assistant cried.

More subdued, Osborne-Smith ordered, 'Get the whirly-bird moving.'

'Will do.'

In silence they followed the progress of the

153

Audi. Finally it sped into the short-term car park at Luton airport. Bond wasn't far behind. The car parked carefully out of view of Hydt's.

'Chopper's setting down on the anti-terror pad at the airport. Our people'll deploy towards the car park.'

No one got out of the Audi. Osborne-Smith smiled. 'I knew it! Hydt's waiting to meet associates. We'll get them all. Tell our people to stay under cover until I give the word. And get all the eyes at Luton online.'

He reflected that the CCTV cameras on the ground might make it possible for them to see Bond's shocked reaction when the Division Three teams descended like hawks and arrested Hydt and the Irishman. That hadn't been Osborne-Smith's goal in ordering the video, of course . . . but it would be a very nice bonus.

21

Hans Groelle sat behind the wheel of Severan Hydt's sleek, black Audi A8. The thickly built, blond Dutch Army veteran had done some motocross and other racing in his younger days and he was pleased Mr Hydt had asked him to put his driving skills to use this morning. Relishing the memory of the frantic drive from Canning Town to Luton airport, Groelle listened absently to the three-way conversation of the man and woman in the back seat and the passenger in the front.

They were laughing about the excitement of the race. The driver of the Bentley was extremely competent but, more important, intuitive. He couldn't have known where Groelle was going so he'd had to anticipate the turns, many of them utterly random. It was as if the pursuing driver had had some sixth sense that told him when Groelle was going to turn, to slow, to speed forward.

A natural driver.

But who was he?

Well, they'd soon find out. No one in the Audi had been able to get a description of the driver — he was that clever — but they'd pieced together the number plate. Groelle had called an associate in the Green Way headquarters, who was using some contacts at the Driver and Vehicle Licensing Agency in Swansea to find out who owned the car.

But whatever the threat, Hans Groelle would be ready. A Colt 1911 .45 sat snug and warm in his left armpit.

He glanced once more at the sliver of the Bentley's grey wing and said to the man in the back seat, 'It worked, Harry. We tricked them. Call Mr Hydt.'

The two passengers in the back and the man sitting beside Groelle were Green Way workers involved in Gehenna. They resembled Mr Hydt, Ms Barnes and Niall Dunne, who were currently en route to an entirely different airport, Gatwick, where a private jet was waiting to fly them out of the country.

The deception had been Dunne's idea, of course. He was a cold fish, but that didn't dull his brain. There'd been trouble up in March — somebody had killed Eric Janssen, one of Groelle's fellow security men. The killer was dead, but Dunne had assumed there might be others, watching the factory or the house, perhaps both. So he had found three employees close enough in appearance to deceive watchers and had driven them to Canning Town very early that morning. Groelle had then carted suitcases out to the garage, followed by Mr Hydt, Ms Barnes and the Irishman. Groelle and the decoys, who'd been waiting in the Audi, then sped towards Luton. Ten minutes later the real entourage got into the back of an unmarked Green Way International lorry and drove to Gatwick.

Now the decoys would remain in the Audi as

156

long as possible to keep whoever was in the Bentley occupied long enough for Mr Hydt and the others to get out of UK airspace.

Groelle said, 'We have a bit of a wait.' He gestured at the radio with a glance toward the Green Way workers. 'What'll it be?'

They voted and Radio 2 took the majority.

⋆ ⋆ ⋆

'Ah, ah. It was a bloody decoy,' Osborne-Smith said. His voice was as calm as always but the expletive, if that was what it was nowadays, indicated that he was livid.

A CCTV camera in the Luton car park was now beaming an image on to the big screen in Division Three and the reality show presently airing was not felicitous. The angular view into the Audi wasn't the best in the world but it was clear that the couple in the back seats were not Severan Hydt and his female companion. And the passenger in the front, whom he'd taken to be the Irishman, was not the gawky blond man he'd seen earlier, plodding to the garage.

Decoys.

'They have to be going to *some* London airport,' Deputy-Deputy pointed out. 'Let's split up the team.'

'Unless they decided to cruise up to Manchester or Leeds-Bradford.'

'Oh. Right.'

'Send all the Watchers in A Branch Hydt's picture. Without delay.'

'Yes, sir.'

Osborne-Smith squinted as he looked at the image broadcast from the CCTV. He could see a bit of the wing of James Bond's Bentley parked twenty-five yards from the Audi.

If there was any consolation to the flap, it was that at least Bond had fallen for the ruse too. Combined with his lack of co-operation, his questionable use of the French secret service and his holier-than-thou attitude, the lapse might just signal a significant downsizing of his career.

22

The fifteen-foot lorry, leased to Green Way International but unmarked, pulled up to the kerb at the executive flight services terminal at Gatwick airport. The door slid open and Severan Hydt, an older woman and the Irishman climbed out and collected their suitcases.

Thirty feet away, in the car park, sat a black-and-red Mini Cooper, whose interior décor included a yellow rose in a plastic vase wedged into the cup holder. Behind the wheel, James Bond was watching the trio of passengers deploy to the pavement. The Irishman, naturally, was looking around carefully. He never seemed to drop his guard.

'What do you think of it?' Bond asked, into the hands-free connected to his mobile.

'It?'

'The Bentley.'

'"It"? Honestly, James, a car like this simply *demands* a name,' Philly Maidenstone chided. She was sitting in his Bentley Continental GT, at Luton airport, having chased Hydt's Audi all the way from Canning Town.

'I never got into the habit of naming my cars.' Any more than I'd give my gun a gender, he reflected. And kept his eyes on the threesome not far away.

Bond had been convinced that after the incidents in Serbia and March, Hydt — or the Irishman, more likely — would suspect he might be tailed in London. He was also concerned that Osborne-Smith had arranged to follow Bond himself. So, after he had talked to René Mathis, he'd left his flat and sped to a covered car park in the City, where he'd met Philly to swap cars. She was to trail Hydt's Audi, which Bond was sure would be a decoy, in his Bentley, while he, in her Mini, would wait for the man's true departure, which came just ten minutes after the German car had sped away from Hydt's Canning Town home.

Bond now watched Hydt, head down, making a phone call. Beside him stood the woman. In her early to mid-sixties, Bond guessed, she had attractive features, though her face was pale and gaunt, an image accentuated by her black overcoat. Too little sleep, perhaps.

His lover? Bond wondered. Or a long-time assistant? From her expression as she looked at Hydt, he decided the former.

Also, the Irishman. Bond hadn't seen him clearly in Serbia but there was no doubt; the gawky stride, feet turned out, bad posture, the odd blond fringe.

Bond supposed he was the man in the bulldozer in March — who had so ruthlessly crushed his security man to death. He also pictured the dead in Serbia — the agents, the train and lorry drivers, as well as the man's own associate — and he let the anger rising in him crest and dissolve.

Philly said, 'In answer to your question, I liked it very much. A lot of engines have horses

160

nowadays; you can get AMG Mercedes estate cars to take the kids to school, for God's sake — but how many pounds torque does the Bentley have? I've never felt anything like it.'

'A touch over five hundred.'

'Oh, my God,' Philly whispered, either impressed or envious, perhaps both. 'And I'm in love with the all-wheel drive. How's it distributed?'

'Sixty-forty rear to front.'

'Brilliant.'

'Yours isn't bad either,' he told her, of the Mini. 'You added a supercharger.'

'I did indeed.'

'Whose?'

'Autorotor. The Swedish outfit. Nearly doubled the horsepower. Close to three hundred now.'

'I thought as much.' Bond was himself impressed. 'I must get the name of your mechanic. I have an old Jaguar that needs work.'

'Oh, tell me it's an E-type. That's the sexiest car in the history of motoring.'

Yet one more thing in common. Bond wrapped this thought up and put it quickly away. 'I'll leave you in suspense. Hold on. Hydt's on the move.' Bond climbed out of the Mini and hid Philly's key in the wheel arch. He grabbed his suitcase and laptop bag, slipped on a new pair of tortoiseshell sunglasses and eased into a crowd to follow Hydt, the Irishman and the woman to Gatwick's private jet terminal.

'You there?' he asked, into the hands-free.

'I am,' Philly replied.

'What's happening with the decoys?'

'They're just sitting in the Audi.'

161

'They'll be waiting until Hydt takes off and the plane's out of UK airspace. Then they'll turn round to lead you — and probably Mr Osborne-Smith — back to London.'

'You think Ozzy's watching?'

Bond had to smile. 'You've got a drone hovering about ten thousand feet over you, I'm sure. They're walking into the terminal now. I should go, Philly.'

'I don't get out of the office enough, James. Thanks for the chance to play Formula One.'

Impulsively he said, 'Here's an idea. Maybe we'll take it out into the country together, do some serious driving.'

'James!' she said crossly. He wondered if he'd crossed a line. 'You simply can't keep referring to this magnificent machine as 'it'. I shall rack my brains and think up a proper name for *her*. And, yes, a trip out to the country sounds divine, provided you let me drive for exactly half the time. And we put in a null-detain request. I already have a few points on my driving licence.'

They rang off and Bond discreetly followed his prey. The threesome paused at a gate in a chain-link fence and presented passports to the guard. Bond saw that the woman's was blue. American? The uniformed man jotted on a clipboard and gestured the three through. As Bond got to the fence he caught a glimpse of them climbing the stairs to a white private jet, a large one, seven round windows on each side of the fuselage, running lights already on. The door closed.

Bond hit speed-dial.

'Flanagan. Hello, James.'

'Maurice,' he said to the head of T Branch, the group within the ODG that handled all things vehicular. 'I need a destination for a private plane, departing just about now from Gatwick.' He read off the five-letter registration painted on the engine.

'Give me a minute.'

The aircraft moved forward. Dammit, he thought angrily. Slow down. He was all too aware that, if René Mathis's information was correct, Hydt was on his way to oversee the murder of at least ninety people that evening.

Maurice Flanagan said, 'I have it. Nice bird, Grumman Five-fifty. State-of-the-art and damned expensive. That one's owned by a Dutch company in the business of waste and recycling.'

One of Hydt's, of course.

'The flight plan's filed for Dubai.'

Dubai? Was that where the deaths were going to happen? 'Where will it stop for refuelling?'

Flanagan laughed. 'James, the range is over six and a half thousand miles. Flies at Mach point eight eight.'

Bond watched the plane taxiing to the runway. Dubai was about 3,500 miles from London. With the time difference the Grumman would land at three or four p.m.

'I need to beat that plane to Dubai, Maurice. What can you cobble together for me? I have passports, credit cards and three grand in cash. Whatever you can do. Oh, I have my weapon — you'll need to take that into account.'

Bond kept staring at the sleek white jet,

163

wingtips turned up. It looked less like a bird than a dragon, though that might have been because he knew who the occupants were and what they had planned.

Ninety dead . . .

Several tense moments passed as Bond watched the jet edge closer to the runway.

Then Flanagan said, 'Sorry, James. The best I can do is get you on a commercial flight out of Heathrow in a few hours. Puts you in Dubai around six twenty.'

'Won't do, Maurice. Military? Government?'

'Nothing available. Absolutely nothing.'

Damn. At least he could have Philly or Bill Tanner arrange with someone at Six's UAE desk to have a watcher meet the flight at Dubai airport and tail Hydt and Dunne to their destination.

He sighed. 'Put me on the commercial flight.'

'Will do. Sorry.'

Bond glanced at his watch.

Nine hours until the deaths . . .

He could always hope for a delay to Hydt's flight.

Just then he saw the Grumman turn on to the main runway and, without pause, accelerate fast, lifting effortlessly from the concrete, then shrinking to a dot as the dragon shot higher into the sky, speeding directly away from him.

* * *

Percy Osborne-Smith was leaning towards the large, flatscreen monitor, split into six rectangles.

Twenty minutes ago, they'd had a CCTV hit on the number plate of a lorry registered to Severan Hydt's company at the Redhill and Reigate exit from the A23, which led to Gatwick. He and his underlings were now scanning every camera in and around the airport for the vehicle.

The second technician to join them finished securing her blonde hair with an elastic band and pointed a pudgy finger to one of the screens. 'There. That's it.'

It seemed that fifteen minutes ago, according to the time stamp, the lorry had paused at the kerb near the private aviation terminal and several people had got out. Yes, it was the trio.

'Why didn't Hydt's face get read when he arrived? We can find hooligans from Rio before they get into Old Trafford but we can't spot a mass murderer in broad daylight. My God, does that say something about Whitehall's priorities? Don't repeat that, anyone. Scan the tarmac.'

The technician manipulated the controls. There was an image of Hydt and the others walking to a private jet.

'Bring up the registration number. Run it.'

To his credit Deputy-Deputy already had. 'Owned by a Dutch company that does recycling. Okay, got the flight plan. He's headed for Dubai. They've already taken off.'

'Where are they now? *Where?*'

'Checking . . . ' The assistant sighed. 'Just passing out of UK airspace.'

Teeth clenched, Osborne-Smith stared at the still video image of the plane. He mused, 'Wonder what it would take to scramble some

Harriers and force them down?' Then he looked up to note everyone staring at him. 'I'm not serious, people.'

Though he had been, just a little.

'Look at that,' the male technician interrupted.

'Look at bloody *what*?'

Deputy-Deputy said, 'Yes, somebody *else* is watching them.'

The screen was showing the entrance to the private jet terminal at Gatwick. A man was standing at the wire fence, staring at Hydt's plane.

My God — it was *Bond*.

So, the bloody clever ODG agent, with a fancy car and without permission to carry a firearm in the UK, had tailed Hydt after all. Osborne-Smith wondered briefly who'd been in the Bentley. The ruse, he knew, had been not only to fool Hydt but to fool Division Three.

With considerable contentment he watched Bond turn from the fence and head back to the car park, head down and speaking into his mobile, undoubtedly enduring a verbal lashing from his boss for having let the fox slip away.

23

Usually we never hear the sound that wakes us. Perhaps we might, if it repeats: an alarm or an urgent voice. But a once-only noise rouses without registering in our consciousness.

James Bond didn't know what lifted him from his dreamless sleep. He glanced at his watch.

It was just after one p.m.

Then he smelt a delicious aroma: a combination of floral perfume — jasmine, he believed — and the ripe, rich scent of vintage champagne. Above him he saw the heavenly form of a beautiful Middle Eastern woman, wearing a sleek burgundy skirt and long-sleeved golden shirt over her voluptuous figure. Her collar was secured with a pearl, which was different from the lower buttons. He found the tiny cream dot particularly appealing. Her hair was as blue-black as crow feathers, pinned up, though a teasing strand fell loose, cupping one side of her face, which was subtly and meticulously made-up.

He said to her, '*Salam alaikum.*'

'*Wa alaikum salam*,' she replied. She set the crystal flute on the tray table in front of him, along with the elegant bottle of the king of Moëts, Dom Pérignon. 'I'm sorry, Mr Bond, I've woken you. I'm afraid the cork popped more loudly than I'd hoped. I was just going to leave the glass and not disturb you.'

'*Shukran*,' he said, as he took the glass. 'And don't worry. My second favourite way to wake up is to the sound of champagne opening.'

She responded to this with a subtle smile. 'I can arrange some lunch for you too.'

'That would be lovely, if it's not too much trouble.'

She returned to the galley.

Bond sipped his champagne and looked out of the private jet's spacious window, the twin Rolls-Royce engines pulsing smoothly as it flew towards Dubai at 42,000 feet, doing more than 600 miles an hour. The aircraft was, Bond reflected with amusement, a Grumman, like Severan Hydt's, but Bond was in a Grumman *650*, the faster model, with a greater range than the Rag-and-bone Man's.

Bond had started the chase hours ago, with the modern equivalent of a scene from an old American police movie, in which the detective leaps into a taxi and orders, 'Follow that car.' He'd decided that the commercial flight would get him to Dubai too late to stop the killings so he'd placed a call to his Commodore Club friend, Fouad Kharaz, who had instantly put a private jet at his disposal. 'My friend, you know I owe you,' the Arab assured him.

A year ago he had approached Bond awkwardly for help, suspecting he did something that involved government security. On his way home from school, Kharaz's teenage son had become the target of some hooded thugs, nineteen or twenty years old, who flaunted their anti-social behaviour orders like insignias of

168

rank. The police were sympathetic but had little time for the drama. Worried sick about his son, Kharaz asked if there was anything Bond could recommend. In a moment of weakness, the knight errant within Bond had prevailed and he had trailed the boy home from school one day when nothing much was going on at the ODG. When the tormentors had moved in, so had Bond.

With a few effortless martial arts manoeuvres he had gently laid two of them out on the pavement and pinned the third, the ringleader, to a wall. He had taken their names from their driving licences and whispered coldly that if the Kharaz boy was ever troubled again, the hoodies' next visit from Bond would not end so civilly. The boys had strode off defiantly, but the son was never troubled again; his status at school had soared.

So, Bond had become Fouad Kharaz's 'best friend of all best friends'. He'd decided to call in the favour and borrow one of the man's jets.

According to the digital map on the bulkhead, beneath the airspeed and altitude indicators, they were over Iran. Two hours to go until they touched down in Dubai.

Just after takeoff, Bond had called Bill Tanner and told him of his destination and about the ninety or so deaths planned for seven o'clock that evening, presumably in Dubai, but perhaps anywhere in the United Arab Emirates.

'Why's Hydt going to kill them?' the chief of staff had asked.

'I'm not sure he is, but all those people are

169

going to die and he'll be there.'

'I'll go through diplomatic channels, tell the embassies there's some threat but we don't have anything concrete. They'll leak word to the Dubai security apparatus too, through back channels.'

'Don't mention Hydt's name. He needs to get into the country undisturbed. He can't suspect anything. I have to find out what he's up to.'

'I agree. We'll handle it on the sly.'

He'd asked Tanner to check the Golden Wire about Hydt's affiliation with the Emirates, hoping there was a specific place he might be headed for. A moment later the chief of staff was back. 'No offices, residences or business affiliations anywhere in the area. And I've just done a data-mining search. No hotel reservations in his name.'

Bond wasn't pleased. As soon as Hydt landed, he would disappear into the sprawling emirate of two and a half million people. It would be impossible to find him before the attack.

Just as he disconnected, the flight attendant appeared. 'We have many different dishes but I saw you look at the Dom with appreciation so I decided you would like the best we have aboard. Mr Kharaz said you were to be treated like a king.' She set the silver tray on the table beside his champagne flute, which she refilled for him. 'I've brought you Iranian caviar — beluga, of course — with toast, not blinis, crème fraîche and capers.' The capers were the large ones, so large she had sliced them. 'The grated onions are Vidalia, from America, the sweetest in the world.'

170

She added, 'They are kind to the breath too. We call them 'lovers' onions'. To follow, there is duck in aspic, with minted yogurt and dates. I can also cook you a steak.'

He laughed. 'No, no. This is more than enough.'

She left him to eat. When he had finished, he had two small cups of cardamom-flavoured Arabic coffee, as he read the intelligence that Philly Maidenstone had provided about Hydt and Green Way. He was struck by two things: the man's care in steering clear of organised crime and his almost fanatical efforts to expand the company throughout the world. She had discovered recently filed applications to do business in South Korea, China, India, Argentina and half a dozen smaller countries. He was disappointed that he could find no clue in any of the material as to the Irishman's identity. Philly had run the man's picture, along with that of the older woman, through databases, but found no matches. And Bill Tanner had reported that the MI5 agents, SOCA and Specialist Crime officers who'd descended on Gatwick had been told that, unfortunately, records about the passengers on the Grumman 'seem to have vanished'.

It was then that he received more troubling news. An encrypted email from Philly. Someone, it seemed, had been unofficially checking with Six about Bond's whereabouts and planned itinerary.

The 'someone', Bond supposed, had to be his dear friend Percy Osborne-Smith. Technically he'd be out of the Division Three man's jurisdiction, in Dubai, but that didn't mean the man couldn't make a great deal of trouble for him and even blow his cover.

Bond had no relation with Six's people in Dubai. He'd have to assume, though, that Osborne-Smith might. Which meant Bond couldn't have local ops or assets meet Hydt's flight, after all. Indeed, he decided he couldn't have anything to do with *any* of his countrymen — a particular shame because the consul general in Dubai was clever and savvy . . . and a friend of Bond's. He texted Bill Tanner and told him to hold off setting up a liaison with Six.

Bond called the pilot on the intercom to learn the status of the jet they were pursuing. It seemed that air-traffic control had slowed their own plane, though not Hydt's, and they would not be able to overtake him. They would land half an hour, at least, after Hydt did.

Damn. That thirty minutes could mean the difference between life and death for at least ninety people. He stared out of the window at the Persian Gulf. Pulling out his mobile, he was thinking again of the great espionage balance sheet as he scrolled through his extensive phone book to find a number. I'm beginning to feel a bit like Lehman Brothers, he thought. My debts vastly outweigh my assets.

Bond placed a call.

24

The limousine bearing Severan Hydt, Jessica Barnes and Niall Dunne pulled up at the Intercontinental Hotel, situated on broad, peaceful Dubai Creek. The solid, stern driver was a local man they'd used before. Like Hans Groelle in England, he doubled as a bodyguard (and did a bit more than that from time to time).

They remained in the car while Dunne read a text or an email. He logged off his iPhone, looked up and said to Hydt, 'Hans has found out about the driver of the Bentley. It's interesting.'

Groelle had told someone at Green Way to check the number-plate. Hydt tapped his long fingernails together.

Dunne avoided looking at them. He said, 'And there's a connection to March.'

'Is there?' Hydt tried to read Dunne's eyes. As usual, they remained utterly cryptic.

The Irishman said nothing more — not with Jessica present. Hydt nodded. 'We'll check in now.'

Hydt lifted the cuff of his elegant suit jacket and regarded his watch. Two and a half hours to go.

The number of dead will be ninety or so.

Dunne stepped out first; his keen eyes made their usual scan for threats. 'All right,' came the Irishman's slight brogue. 'It's clear.'

Hydt and Jessica climbed out into the astonishing heat and headed quickly into the chill of

173

the Intercontinental lobby, which was dominated by a stunning ten-foot-high assembly of exotic flowers. On a nearby wall hung portraits of the United Arab Emirates' ruling families, gazing down sternly and confidently.

Jessica signed for the room, which they'd taken in her name, another of Dunne's ideas. Though they would not be staying long — their onward flight was this evening — it was helpful to have somewhere to leave the bags and get some rest. They handed the luggage to the bell captain to have it taken to the room.

Leaving Jessica beside the flowers, Hydt nodded Dunne aside. 'The Bentley? Who was it?'

'Registered to a company in Manchester — same address as Midlands Disposal.'

Midlands was connected to one of the bigger organised-crime syndicates operating out of south Manchester. In America the Mob had traditionally been heavily involved in waste management, and in Naples, where the Camorra crime syndicate ruled, refuse collection was known as Il Re del Crimine. In Britain organised crime was less interested in the business, but occasionally some local underworld boss tried to bluster his way into the market, like a heavy in a Guy Ritchie film.

'And this morning,' Dunne continued, 'the coppers came round to the army base site, showing pictures of somebody who'd been spotted in the area the day before. There's a warrant on him for grievous bodily harm. He worked for Midlands. The police said he's gone missing.'

As will happen, Hydt reflected, when one's

body is commencing to rot beneath a thousand tons of wrecked hospital. 'What would he have been doing up there?' Hydt asked.

Dunne considered this. 'Probably planning to sabotage the demolition job. Something goes wrong, you get bad publicity and Midlands moves in to pick up some of your business.'

'So whoever was in the Bentley only wanted to find out what happened to his mate yesterday.'

'Right.'

Hydt was vastly relieved. The incident had nothing to do with Gehenna. And, more important, the intruder wasn't the police or Security Service. Merely one more instance of the underbelly of the discard business. 'Good. We'll deal with Midlands later.'

Hydt and Dunne returned to Jessica. 'Niall and I have some things to take care of. I'll be back for dinner.'

'I think I'll go for a walk,' she said.

Hydt frowned. 'In this heat? It might not be good for you.' He didn't like her to stray too far afield. He wasn't worried that she'd let slip anything she shouldn't — he had kept all aspects of Gehenna from her. And what she knew of the rest of his darker life, well, that was potentially embarrassing but not illegal. It was just that when he wanted her, he wanted her and Severan Hydt was a man whose belief in the inevitable power of decay had taught him that life is far too short and precarious to deny yourself anything at any time.

'I can judge that,' she said, but spoke timidly.

'Of course, of course. Only . . . a woman

175

alone?' Hydt continued. 'The men, you know how they can be.'

'You mean Arab men?' Jessica asked. 'It's not Tehran or Jeddah. They don't even leer. In Dubai they're more respectful than they are in Paris.'

Hydt smiled his gentle smile. That was amusing. And true. 'But still . . . don't you think it would be best just to be safe? Anyway, the hotel has a wonderful spa. It will be perfect for you. And the pool is partly Plexiglas. You can look down and see the ground forty feet below. The view of the Burj Khalifa is quite impressive.'

'I suppose.'

It was then that Hydt noticed a new configuration of wrinkles around her eyes, as she peered up at the towering floral arrangement.

He thought, too, of the body of the woman found in the Green Way skip yesterday, her grave now subtly marked, according to the foreman, Jack Dennison. And Hydt felt that subtle unravelling within him, a spring loosening.

'As long as you're happy,' he said to her softly and brushed her face, near the wrinkles, with one of his long nails. She'd stopped recoiling long ago, not that her reactions had ever affected him one bit.

Hydt was suddenly aware of Dunne's crystalline blue eyes turning his way. The younger man stiffened, ever so slightly, then recovered and looked elsewhere. Hydt was irritated. What business was it of his what Hydt found alluring? He wondered, as he often had, if perhaps Dunne's distaste for his brands of lust stemmed not from the fact that they were unconventional but from his disdain for *any* sexuality. In the months he'd known him, the Irishman hadn't so much as glanced at a woman or man, with bedroom eyes.

Hydt lowered his hand and looked again at Jessica, at the lines radiating from her resigned eyes. He gauged the timing. They would fly out tonight and the plane boasted no private suites. He couldn't imagine making love to her when Dunne was nearby, even if the man was asleep.

He debated. Was there time now to get to the room, lay Jessica on the bed, pull the curtains wide so that the low sun streamed across the soft flesh, illuminating the topography of her body . . .

. . . and run his nails over her skin?

The way he felt at the moment, absorbed with her and thinking of the spectacle at seven o'clock tonight, the liaison wouldn't take long.

'Severan,' Dunne said crisply. 'We don't know what al-Fulan has for us. We probably should go.'

Hydt appeared to ponder the words but it was not serious consideration. He said, 'It's been a long flight. I feel like a change of clothes.' He glanced down at Jessica's weary eyes. 'And you might like a nap, my dear.' He directed her firmly to the lift.

25

At around four forty-five on Tuesday afternoon Fouad Kharaz's private jet eased to a stop. James Bond unbuckled his seatbelt and collected his luggage. He thanked the pilots and the flight attendant, gripping her hand warmly and resisting the urge to kiss her cheek; they were now in the Middle East.

The immigration officer lethargically stamped his passport, slid it back and gestured him into the country. Bond strode through the 'Nothing to Declare' lane at Customs with a suitcase containing its deadly contraband, and was soon outside in the piquant heat, feeling as if a huge burden had been lifted.

He was in his element once more, the mission his and his alone to pursue. He was on foreign soil, his *carte blanche* restored.

The short ride from the airport to his destination at Festival City took Bond through a nondescript part of the town — drives to and from airports were similar throughout the world and this route was little different from the A4 just west of London, or the toll road to Dulles in Washington, D.C., although it was decorated with far more sand and dust. And, as most of the emirate, was immaculately clean.

On the way Bond gazed out over the sprawling city, looking north towards the Persian Gulf. In the late-afternoon, heat-shimmering light, the needle of the Burj Khalifa glowed, soaring above the geometrically complex skyline of Sheikh Zayed Road. It was presently the tallest building on earth. That distinction seemed to change monthly but this tower would surely hold that honour for a long time to come.

He noted one other ubiquitous characteristic of the city — the construction cranes, white and yellow and orange. They were everywhere and busy once again. On his last trip there had been just as many of these looming stalks but most were sitting idle, like toys discarded by a child who'd lost interest in playing with them. The emirate had been hit hard in the recent economic downturn. For his official cover Bond had to keep up on world finance and he found himself impatient with the criticism ladled upon places like Dubai, which often originated in London or New York; yet weren't the City and Wall Street the more enthusiastic co-conspirators in causing the economic woe?

Yes, there had been excess here and many ambitious projects might never be finished — like the artificial archipelago in the shape of a map of the world, composed of small sand islands offshore. Yet the reputation for swelling luxury was but a small aspect of Dubai — and, in truth, no different from Singapore, California, Monaco and hundreds of other places where the wealthy worked and played. To Bond, in any event, Dubai was not about unfettered business or real estate but about its exotic ways, a place where new and old blended, where many cultures and religions coexisted respectfully. He particularly enjoyed the vast, empty landscape of red sand, populated by camels and Range Rovers, as different from his boyhood vistas of Kent as one could imagine. He wondered if his mission today would take him to the Empty Quarter.

They drove on, past small brown, white and yellow one-storey buildings whose names and services were disclosed in modest green Arabic lettering. No gaudy billboards, no neon lights, except for a few announcements of forthcoming events. The minarets of mosques rose above the low residences and businesses, persistent spikes of faith throughout the hazy distance. The intrusion of the ubiquitous desert was every-where and date palm, neem and eucalyptus trees formed gallant outposts against the encroaching, endless sand.

The taxi driver dropped Bond, as directed, at a shopping centre. He handed over some ten-dirham notes and climbed out. The mall was packed with locals — it was between *Asir* and *Maghrib* prayer times — as well as many foreigners, all carting carrier bags and crowding the shops, which were doing brisk business. The country was often referred to as 'Do buy', he recalled.

Bond lost himself in the crowd, looking around, as if he were trying to find a companion he'd agreed to meet. In fact, he was searching for someone else: the man who'd been following him from the airport, probably with hostile intent. Twice now he'd seen a man in sunglasses and a blue shirt or jacket: at the airport and then in a dusty black Toyota behind Bond's taxi. For the drive he had donned a plain black cap but, from the set of his head and shoulders and the shape of his glasses, Bond knew he was the man he'd seen at the airport. The same Toyota had just now eased past the shopping centre — driving slowly for no apparent reason — and vanished behind a nearby hotel.

This was no coincidence.

Bond had considered sending the taxi on a diversionary route but, in truth, he wasn't sure he wanted to lose the tail. More often than not it's better to trap your pursuer and see what he has to say for himself.

Who was he? Had he been waiting in Dubai for Bond? Or somehow followed him from London? Or did he not even know who Bond was, but had chosen merely to keep an eye on a stranger in town?

Bond bought a newspaper. Today it was hot, searingly so, but he shunned the air-conditioned interior of the café he had selected and sat outside where he could observe all the entrances and exits to and from the area. He looked around occasionally for the tail but saw nothing specific.

As he sent and received several text messages, a waiter came to him. Bond glanced at the faded menu on the table and ordered Turkish coffee and sparkling water. As the man walked away, Bond looked at his watch. Five p.m.

Only two hours until more than ninety people died somewhere in this elegant city of sand and heat.

Half a block away from the shopping centre, a solidly built man in a blue jacket slipped a Dubai traffic warden several hundred dirhams and told him in English that he'd only be a short while. He'd certainly be gone before the crowds returned after sunset prayer.

The warden wandered off as if the conversation about the dusty black Toyota, parked illegally at the kerb, had never occurred.

The man, who went by the name Nick, lit a cigarette and lifted his backpack over his shoulder. He eased into the shadows of the shopping centre where his target was nonchalantly sipping espresso or Turkish coffee and reading the paper as if he hadn't a care in the world.

That was how he thought of the man: target. Not bastard, not enemy. Nick knew that in an operation like this you had to be utterly dispassionate, as difficult as that might be. This man was no more of a person than the black dot of a bull's-eye.

A target.

He supposed the man was talented but he'd been pretty damn careless leaving the airport. Nick had easily followed him. This gave him confidence at what he was about to do.

Face obscured by a baseball cap with a long brim and sunglasses, Nick moved closer to his target, dodging from shadow to shadow. Unlike in other places, the disguise did not draw attention to him; in Dubai everyone wore head coverings and sunglasses.

182

One thing that was a bit different was the long-sleeved blue jacket, which few local people wore, given the heat. But there was no other way to hide the pistol that was tucked into his waistband.

Nick's gold earring, too, might have earned him some curious glances but this area of Dubai Creek, with its shopping malls and amusement park, was filled with tourists and as long as people didn't drink alcohol or kiss each other in public, the locals forgave unusual dress.

He inhaled deeply on his cigarette, then dropped and crushed it, easing closer to his target.

A hawker appeared suddenly and asked, in English, if he wanted to buy rugs. 'Very cheap, very cheap. Many knots! Thousands upon thousands of knots!' One look from Nick shut his mouth and he vanished.

Nick considered his plan. There would be some logistical problems, of course — in this country everyone watched everyone else. He would have to get his target out of sight, into the car park or, better, the basement of the shopping centre, perhaps during prayer time, when the crowds thinned. Probably the simplest approach was the best. Nick could slip up behind him, shove the gun into his back and 'escort' him downstairs.

Then the knife work would begin.

Oh, the target — all right, maybe I will think of him as a bastard — would have many things to say when the blade began its leisurely journey across his skin.

Nick reached under his jacket and pushed up the safety lever of his pistol, moving smoothly from shadow to shadow.

26

James Bond had his coffee and water in front of him as he sat with the *National* newspaper, published out of Abu Dhabi. He considered it the best newspaper in the Middle East. You could find every sort of story imaginable, from a scandal about Mumbai firemen's inefficient uniforms to pieces about women's rights in the Arab world to a half-page exposé on a Cypriot gangster stealing the body of the island's former president from his grave.

Excellent Formula One coverage too — important to Bond.

Now, however, he was paying no attention to the paper but was using it as a prop . . . though not with the cliché of an eyehole torn from the gutter between ads for Dubai's Lulu Hypermarkets and the local news. The paper sat flat in front of him and his head was down. His eyes, however, were up, scanning.

It was at that moment that he heard a brief rasp of shoe leather behind him and was aware of someone moving quickly towards his table.

Bond remained completely still.

Then a large hand — pale and freckled — gripped the chair beside him and yanked it back.

A man dropped heavily into it.

'Howdy, James.' The voice was thick with a Texas accent. 'Welcome to Dubai.'

Du-bah . . .

Bond turned to his friend with a grin. They shook hands warmly.

A few years older than Bond, Felix Leiter was tall and had a lanky frame, on which his suit hung loose. The pale complexion and mop of straw-coloured hair largely precluded most undercover work in the Middle East unless he was playing exactly who he was: a brash, savvy *guy* from the American South, who'd ridden into town for business, with no small amount of pleasure thrown in. His slow manners and easy-going speech were deceptive; he could react like a spring knife when the occasion demanded . . . as Bond had seen first hand.

When the pilot of Fouad Kharaz's Grumman had reported that they weren't going to beat Hydt's to Dubai, it was Felix Leiter whom Bond had rung, calling in his Lehman Brothers favour. While Bond was uneasy using the MI6 connections here, because of Osborne-Smith's inquiries earlier, he had no such reservations about enlisting the CIA, which had an extensive operation throughout the United Arab Emirates. Asking Leiter, a senior agent in the Agency's National Clandestine Service, to help out was risky politically. Using a sister agency without clearance from the top might result in serious diplomatic repercussions and Bond had already done so once with René Mathis. He was certainly putting his newly reinstated *carte blanche* to the test.

Felix Leiter was more than willing to meet Hydt's plane and follow the trio to their destination, which had turned out to be the

Intercontinental Hotel — it was connected to the shopping centre where the two men now sat.

Bond had briefed him about Hydt, the Irishman and, ten minutes ago via text, about the man in the Toyota. Leiter had remained in surveillance positions at the shopping centre for a time to — literally — watch Bond's back.

'So, do I have a friend hanging about?'

'Spotted him moving in, about forty yards to the south,' said Leiter, smiling as if counter-surveillance was the last thing on his mind. 'He was by the entrance, thataway. But the son-of-a-bitch vanished.'

'Whoever he is, he's good.'

'You got that right.' Gazing around, Leiter now asked, 'You believe the shopping here?' He gestured at the patrons. 'You have malls in England, James?'

'Yes indeed. Televisions too. And running water. We're hoping to get computers some day.'

'Ha. I'll come visit some time. Soon as you learn how to refrigerate beer.'

Leiter flagged down the waiter and ordered coffee. He whispered to Bond, 'I'd say 'Americano', but then people might guess my nationality, which'd blow my cover all to hell.'

He tugged at his ear — a signal, it seemed, for a slightly built Arab man, dressed like a local, appeared. Bond had no idea where he'd been stationed. The man looked as if he might have been piloting one of the abra boat taxis that plied Dubai Creek.

'Yusuf Nasad,' Leiter introduced him. 'This is Mr Smith.'

186

Bond assumed that Nasad was not the Arab's real name either. He would be a local asset and, because Leiter was running him, he'd be a damn good one too. Felix Leiter was a master handler. It was Nasad who'd helped him track Hydt from the airport, the American explained.

Nasad sat down. Leiter asked, 'Our friend?'

'Gone. He saw you, I am thinking.'

'I stand out too damn much.' Leiter laughed. 'Don't know why Langley sent me here. If I was undercover in Alabama, nobody'd notice me.'

Bond said, 'I didn't get much of a view. Dark hair, blue shirt.'

'A tough boy,' Nasad said, in what Bond thought of as American TV English. 'Athletic. Hair's cut very short. And he has a gold earring. No beard. I tried to get a picture. But he was gone too fast.'

'Besides,' Leiter filled in, 'all we've got is crap to take pictures with. You still have that fellow giving you folks neat toys? What's his name again — Q Somebody? Quentin? Quigley?'

'Q's the branch, not a person. Stands for Quartermaster.'

'And it was a jacket he was wearing,' Nasad added, 'not a shirt. Like a windbreaker.'

'In this heat?' Bond asked. 'So he was carrying. You see what type of weapon?'

'No.'

'Any idea who he might be?'

Nasad offered, 'Definitely not Arab. Could have been a *katsa*.'

'Why the hell would a Mossad field officer be interested in me?'

Leiter said, 'Only you can answer that, boy.'

Bond shook his head. 'Maybe somebody recruited by the secret police here?'

'Naw, doubt it. The Amn al-Dawla don't tail you. They just invite you to their four-star accommodations in the Deira, where you spill everything they want to know. And I mean everything.'

Nasad's quick eyes took in the café and surrounding area and apparently noted no threats. Bond had observed him doing this since his arrival.

Leiter asked Bond, 'You think it was somebody working for Hydt?'

'Possibly. But if so I doubt they know who I am.' Bond explained that before he'd left London he'd been concerned that Hydt and the Irishman would get too suspicious that he was on their trail, especially after the flap in Serbia. He'd had T Branch adjust the records of his Bentley to link the number plate to a disposal company in Manchester with possible under-world ties. Then Bill Tanner had sent agents posing as Scotland Yard officers to the March demolition site with a story about one of Midlands Disposal's security men going missing in the area.

'It'll put Hydt and the Irishman off the scent at least for a few days,' Bond said. 'Now, have you heard any chatter here?'

The American's otherwise cheerful face tightened. 'No relevant ELINT or SIGINT. Not that I care much about eavesdropping.'

Felix Leiter, a former marine whom Bond had

met in the service, was a HUMINT spy. He vastly preferred the role of handler — running local assets, like Yusuf Nasad. 'I pulled in a lot of favours and talked to all my key assets. Whatever Hydt and his local contacts're up to, they're keeping the lid on really tight. I can't find any leads. Nobody's been moving any mysterious shipments of nasty stuff into Dubai. Nobody's been telling friends and family to avoid this mosque or that shopping centre around seven tonight. No bad actors're slipping in from across the Gulf.'

'That's the Irishman's doing — keeping the wraps on everything. I don't know exactly what he does for Hydt but he's bloody clever, always thinking about security. It's as if he can anticipate whatever we're going to do and think up a way to counter it.'

They fell silent as they casually surveyed the shopping centre. No sign of the blue-jacketed tail. No sign of Hydt or the Irishman.

Bond asked Leiter, 'You still a scribbler?'

'Sure am,' the Texan confirmed.

Leiter's cover was as a freelance journalist and blogger, specialising in music, particularly the blues, R&B and Afro-Caribbean. Journalism is a commonly used cover for intelligence agents; it gives credence to their frequent travelling, often to hotspots and the less-savoury places of the world. Leiter was fortunate in that the best covers are those that mirror an agent's actual interests, since an assignment may require the operative to be undercover for weeks or months at a time. The filmmaker Alexander Korda

189

— recruited by the famed British spymaster Sir Claude Dansey — reportedly used location scouting expeditions as a cover to photograph off-limits areas in the run-up to the Second World War. Bond's bland official cover, a security and integrity analyst for the Overseas Development Group, subjected him to excruciatingly boring stints when he was on assignment. On a particularly bad day he would long for an official cover as a skiing or SCUBA instructor.

Bond sat forward and Leiter followed his gaze. They watched two men come out of the front door of the Intercontinental and walk towards a black Lincoln Town Car.

'It's Hydt. And the Irishman.'

Leiter sent Nasad to fetch his vehicle, then pointed to a dusty old Alfa Romeo in a nearby car park, whispering to Bond, 'Over there. My wheels. Let's go.'

27

The Lincoln carrying Severan Hydt and Niall Dunne eased east through the haze and heat, paralleling the massive power lines conducting electricity to the outer regions of the city-state. Nearby was the Persian Gulf, the rich blue muted nearly to beige by the dust in the air and the glare of the low but unrelenting sun.

They were taking a convoluted route through Dubai, cruising past the indoor ski complex, the striking Burj Al-Arab hotel, which resembled a sail and was nearly as tall as the Eiffel Tower, and the luxurious Palm Jumeirah — the sculpted development of shops, homes and hotels extending far into the Gulf and fashioned, as the name suggested, in the likeness of an indigenous tree. These areas of glistening beauty upset Severan Hydt: the new, the unblemished. He felt much more comfortable when the vehicle slipped into the older Satwa neighbourhood, densely populated by thousands upon thousands of working-class folk — mostly immigrants.

The time was nearly five thirty. An hour and a half before the event. It was also, Hydt had noted, with irony, an hour and a half until sunset.

Curious coincidence, he reflected. A good sign. His ancestors — his spiritual, if not necessarily genetic forebears — had believed in omens and portents and he allowed himself to do so as well;

yes, he was a practical, hard-headed businessman . . . but he had his *other* side.

He thought again about tonight.

They continued to cruise along the roads in a complicated fashion. The purpose of this dizzying tour wasn't to sightsee. No, taking the roundabout route to get to a spot merely five miles from the Intercontinental had been Dunne's idea of security.

But the driver — a mercenary with experience in Afghanistan and Syria — reported, 'I thought we were being followed, an Alfa and possibly a Ford. But if so, we've lost them, I'm sure.'

Dunne looked back, then said, 'Good. Go to the works.'

They circled back to the city. In ten minutes they were at an industrial complex in the Deira, the cluttered and colourful area in the centre of town nestled along Dubai Creek and the Gulf. This was another place in which Hydt felt immediately comfortable. To enter the neighbourhood was to take a step back in time: its uneven houses, traditional markets and the rustic port along the Creek, whose docks teemed with dhows and other small vessels, might have been the backdrop to a 1930s adventure film. The ships were piled impossibly high with stacks of cargo lashed into place. The driver found the destination, a good-sized factory and warehouse, with attached offices, one storey, the shabby beige paint peeling. Razor wire, rare in low-crime Dubai, topped the chain-link fence surrounding the place. The driver pulled up to an intercom and spoke in Arabic. The gate slowly swung open. The Town Car eased into the car park and stopped.

The two men climbed out. With an hour and fifteen minutes to sunset, the air was cooling, even as the ground radiated heat banked during the day.

Hydt heard a voice, carried on the dusty wind. 'Please! My friend, please come in!' The man waving his hand was in a white *dishdasha* robe — in the uniquely Emirates style — and had no head covering. He was in his mid-fifties, Hydt knew, although, like many Arab men, he looked younger. A studious face, smart glasses, Western shoes. His longish hair was swept back.

Mahdi al-Fulan strode over sprays of red sand, which drifted along the tarmac and sloped against the kerb, the walkways and the sides of buildings. The Arab's eyes were bright, as if he were a schoolboy about to show off a treasured project. Which wasn't far from the truth, Hydt reflected. A black beard framed his smile; Hydt had been amused to learn that, while hair colouring was not a good product to market in a land where both male and female heads were usually covered, beard dye was a bestseller.

Hands were gripped. 'My friend.' Hydt didn't try to offer an Arabic greeting. He had no talent for languages and believed it a weakness to attempt anything you were not skilled at.

Niall Dunne stepped forward, his shoulders bouncing as they always did in his gangling walk, and also greeted the man, but the pale eyes were gazing past the Arab. For once, they were not searching for threats. He was staring raptly at the

193

bounty that the warehouse held, which could be seen through the open door: perhaps fifty or so machines, in every shape a geometrician could name, made of raw and painted steel, iron, aluminium, carbon fibre . . . who knew what else? Pipes protruded, wires, control panels, lights, switches, chutes and belts. If robots had pleasant dreams, they would be set in this room.

They entered the warehouse, which was devoid of workers. Dunne paused to study and occasionally even caress some device or other.

Mahdi al-Fulan was an industrial product designer, MIT educated. He shunned the kind of high-profile entrepreneurship that gets you on the cover of business magazines — and often into the bankruptcy court — and specialised instead in designing functional industrial equipment and control systems for which there was a consistent market. He was one of Severan Hydt's main suppliers. Hydt had met him at a recycling-equipment conference. Once he'd learnt about certain trips the Arab took abroad and about the dangerous men to whom he sold his wares, they'd become partners. Al-Fulan was a clever scientist, an innovative engineer, a man with ideas and inventions important to Gehenna.

And with other connections too.

Ninety dead . . .

At that thought, Hydt involuntarily consulted his watch. Nearly six.

'Follow me, please, Severan, Niall.' Al-Fulan had caught Hydt's glance. The Arab led them through the various rooms, dim and still. Dunne again slowed his step to examine some machinery or a

194

control panel. He'd nod approvingly or frown, perhaps trying to understand how a system worked.

Leaving behind the machines with their scent of oil, paint and the unique metallic, almost blood-like odour of high-powered electrical systems, they entered the offices. At the end of a dim corridor al-Fulan used a computer key to open an unmarked door and they stepped into a work area, which was large and cluttered with thousands of sheets of paper, blueprints and other documents on which were words, graphs and diagrams, many of them incomprehensible to Hydt.

The atmosphere was eerie, to say the least, both because of the dimness and the clutter . . . and because of what decorated the walls.

Images of eyes.

Eyes of all sorts — human, fish, canine, feline and insect — photos, computerised three-dimensional renderings, medical drawings from the 1800s. Particularly unsettling was a fanciful, detailed blueprint of a human eye, as if a modern-day Dr Frankenstein had used current engineering techniques to construct his monster.

In front of one of the dozens of large computer monitors sat an attractive woman, a brunette, in her late twenties. She stood up, strode to Hydt and shook his hand vigorously. 'Stella Kirkpatrick. I'm Mahdi's research assistant.' She greeted Dunne too.

Hydt had been to Dubai several times but had not met her before. The woman's accent was American. Hydt supposed she was clever, hard-headed and typical of a common phenomenon

195

in this part of the world, one that went back hundreds of years: the Westerner in love with Arab culture.

Al-Fulan said, 'Stella worked up most of the algorithms.'

'Did you now?' Hydt asked, with a smile.

She blushed, the ruddy colour stemming from her affection for her mentor, whom she glanced at quickly, a supplication for approval, which al-Fulan provided in the form of a seductive smile; Hydt was not a participant in this exchange.

As the decorations on the walls suggested, al-Fulan's speciality was optics. His goal in life was to invent an artificial eye for the blind that would work as well as those 'Allah — praise be to Him — created for us'. But until that happened he would make a great deal of money designing industrial machinery. He had come up with most of the specialised safety, control and inspection systems for Green Way's sorters and document-destruction devices.

Hydt had recently commissioned him to create yet another device for the company and had come here today with Dunne to see the prototype.

'A demonstration?' the Arab said.

'Please,' Hydt replied.

They all walked back into the garden of machines. Al-Fulan led them to a complicated device, weighing several tons, sitting in the loading bay beside two large industrial refuse compactors.

The Arab hit buttons and, with a growl, the machine slowly warmed up. It was about twenty feet long, six high and six wide. At the front end a metal conveyor-belt led into a mouth about a yard square. Inside all was blackness, although Hydt could just make out horizontal cylinders, covered with spikes, like a combine harvester. At the rear, half a dozen chutes led to bins, each containing a thick grey plastic liner, open at the top to catch whatever the machine disgorged.

Hydt studied it carefully. He and Green Way made a lot of money from destroying documents securely, but the world was changing. Most data resided on computer and flash drives nowadays and this would be increasingly the case in the future. Hydt had decided to expand his empire by offering a new approach to destroying computer data storage devices.

A number of companies did this, as did Green Way, but the new approach would be different, thanks to al-Fulan's invention. At the moment, to destroy data effectively, computers had to be dismantled by hand and hard drives had to be wiped of data with magnetic degaussing units, then crushed. Other steps were required to separate the other components of the old computer — many of them dangerous e-waste.

This machine, however, did everything automatically. You simply tossed the old computer on to the belt and the device did the rest, breaking it apart while al-Fulan's optical systems identified the components and sent them to appropriate bins. Hydt's sales people could assure his customers that this machine would make certain not only that the sensitive information on the hard drive was destroyed but that all the other components were identified and disposed of

197

according to local environmental regulations.

At a nod from her boss, Stella picked up an old laptop and set it on the ribbed conveyor-belt. It vanished into the dim recesses of the device.

They heard a series of sharp cracks and thuds and finally a loud grinding noise. Al-Fulan directed his guests to the rear, where after five or six minutes they watched the machine spit the various sorted bits of scrap into different bins — metal, plastic, circuit boards and the like. In the bin liner marked 'Media Storage' they saw fine metal and silicon dust, all that was left of the hard drive. The dangerous e-waste, like the batteries and heavy metals, was deposited in a receptacle marked with warning labels and the benign components were dropped into recycling bins.

Al-Fulan then directed Hydt and Dunne to a monitor, on which a report about the machine's efforts scrolled past.

Dunne's icy façade had slipped. He seemed almost excited.

Hydt, too, was pleased, very pleased. He began to ask a question. But then he looked at a clock on the wall. It was six thirty. He could concentrate on the machinery no longer.

28

James Bond, Felix Leiter and Yusuf Nasad were fifty feet from the factory, crouching beside a large skip, observing Hydt, the Irishman, an Arab in a traditional white robe and an attractive dark-haired woman through a loading-bay window.

With Bond and Leiter in the American's Alfa, and Nasad in his Ford bringing up the rear, they'd started to follow the Lincoln Town Car from the Intercontinental but both agents immediately recognised that the Arab driver was starting evasion techniques. Worried that they'd be spotted, Bond used an app in his mobile to paint the car with a MASINT profile and took its co-ordinates with a laser, then uploaded the data to the GCHQ tracking centre. Leiter eased off the accelerator and let the satellites follow the vehicle, beaming the results to Bond's mobile.

'Damn,' Leiter had drawled, looking at the phone in Bond's hand. 'I want one of them.'

Bond had followed the Town Car's progress on his map and directed Leiter, with Nasad following, in the general direction that Hydt was going, which was proving to be a very circuitous route. Finally the Lincoln headed back to the Deira, the old part of town. A few minutes later Bond, Leiter and his asset arrived, left the cars in an alleyway between two dusty warehouses and sliced their way through the chain-link fence for a closer view of what Hydt and the Irishman were up to. The driver of the Lincoln had remained in the car park.

Bond plugged in an earpiece and trained his phone's camera eye on the foursome, eavesdropping with an app that Sanu Hirani had developed. The Vibra-Mike reconstructed conversation observed through windows or transparent doors by reading vibrations on glass or other nearby smooth surfaces. It combined what it detected sonically with visual input of lip and cheek movement, eye expression and body language. In circumstances like this it could reconstruct conversations with about 85 per cent accuracy.

After listening to the conversation, Bond told the others, 'They're talking about equipment for the Green Way facilities, his legitimate company. Dammit.'

'Look at the bastard,' the American whispered. 'He knows that around ninety people are going to die in a half-hour and it's like he's talking to a store clerk about pixels on big-screen TVs.'

Nasad's phone buzzed. He took the call, speaking in staccato Arabic, some of which Bond could decipher. He was getting information about the factory. He disconnected and explained to the agents that the place was owned by a Dubai citizen, Mahdi al-Fulan. A picture confirmed he was the man Hydt and the Irishman were with. He was not suspected of having any terrorist ties, had never been to Afghanistan and seemed to be merely an engineer and businessman. He did, however, design and sell his products to, among others, warlords and arms dealers. He had recently developed an optical scanner on a land mine that could differentiate between enemies' and friendlies' uniforms or badges.

Bond recalled notes he'd found up in March: *blast radius* . . .

As conversation in the warehouse resumed, Bond cocked his head and listened once more. Hydt was saying to the Irishman, 'I want to leave for the . . . event. Mahdi and I will go there now.' He turned to his Arab associate with eerie, almost hungry, eyes. 'It's not far, is it?'

'No, we can walk.'

Hydt said to his Irish partner, 'Maybe you and Stella could work out some of the technical details.'

The Irishman turned to the woman as Hydt and the Arab vanished into the warehouse.

Bond closed down the app and glanced at Leiter. 'Hydt and al-Fulan are going to the site where the attack is to take place. They're walking. I'll follow them. See if you can find out anything more here. The woman and the Irishman are going to stay. Get closer if you can. I'll call you when I find out what's going on.'

'You bet,' the Texan said.

Bay-at . . .

Nasad nodded.

Bond checked his Walther and slipped it back into the holster.

'Wait, James,' Leiter said. 'You know, saving these people, the ninety or whatever, well, it could tip your hand. If he thinks you're on to him, Hydt could rabbit — he'll disappear — and you'll never find him, until he comes up with a

201

new Incident Twenty. And he'll be a lot more careful about keeping it secret then. If you let him go ahead with whatever he's about to do here, he'll stay in the dark about you.'

'Sacrifice them, you mean?'

The American held Bond's eyes. 'It's a tough call. I don't know that I could do it. But it's something to think about.'

'I already have. And, no, they're not dying.'

He spotted the two men making their way out of the compound.

Crouching, Leiter ran to the building and hauled himself through a small window, disappearing silently on the other side. He reappeared and gestured. Nasad joined him.

Bond slipped back through the breach in the fence and made his way after his two targets. After several blocks of meandering through industrial alleys, Hydt and al-Fulan entered the Deira Covered Souk: hundreds of outdoor stalls, as well as more conventional shops, where you could buy gold, spices, shoes, TV sets, CDs, videos, Mars bars, souvenirs, toys, Middle Eastern and Western clothing . . . virtually anything imaginable. Only a portion of the population here seemed to be Emirates-born; Bond heard bits of conversation in Tamil, Malayalam, Urdu and Tagalog, but relatively little Arabic. Shoppers were everywhere, hundreds of them. Intense negotiations were going on at every stall and in every shop, hands gesticulating feverishly, brows furrowed, clipped words flying back and forth.

Do Buy . . .

Bond was following at a discreet distance, looking for any sign of their target: the people who were going to die in twenty-five minutes.

What could the Rag-and-bone Man possibly have in mind? A trial run in anticipation of the carnage on Friday, which would be ten or twenty times as bad? Or was this unrelated? Perhaps Hydt was using his role as an international businessman as a cover. Were he and the Irishman just hired killers? State-of-the-art hitmen?

Bond dodged through the log-jam of merchants, shoppers, tourists and dock workers loading the dhows with cargo. It was very crowded now, just before *Maghrib*, the sunset prayer. Were the markets to be the site of the attack?

Then Hydt and al-Fulan left the souk and continued to walk for half a block. They stopped and gazed up at a modern structure, three storeys high, with large glass windows, overlooking Dubai Creek. It was a public building, filled with men, women and children. Bond moved closer and saw a sign in Arabic and English. *The Museum of the Emirates.*

So this was the target. And it was a damn good one. Bond scanned it. At least a hundred people meandered through the ground floor alone and there would surely be many more on the floors above. The building was close to the Creek with only a narrow road in front, which meant that emergency vehicles would have a difficult time getting close to the scene of the carnage.

Al-Fulan looked around uneasily but Hydt

203

pushed through the front door. They vanished into the crowd.

I'm not letting those people die. Bond plugged his earpiece in and called up the eavesdropping app on his phone. He followed the two men inside, paid a small admission fee and eased closer to his targets, blending with a group of Western tourists.

He couldn't help but think about what Felix Leiter had said. Saving these people might indeed alert Hydt that someone was on to him.

What would M do under these circumstances?

He supposed the old man would sacrifice the ninety to save thousands. He'd been an active-duty admiral in the Royal Navy. Officers at that level had to make hard decisions like this all the time.

But, dammit, Bond thought, I have to do something. He saw children scampering around, saw men and women gazing at and talking animatedly about the exhibits, people laughing, people nodding with rapt interest as a tour guide lectured.

Hydt and al-Fulan moved further into the building. What were they doing? Had they planned to leave an explosive device? Perhaps it was what had been constructed in the hospital basement in March.

Or perhaps the industrial designer al-Fulan had made something else for Hydt.

Bond circled through the large marble lobby, filled with Arabic art and antiquities. A massive chandelier, in gold, dominated the room. Bond casually pointed the microphone towards the men. He caught dozens of scraps of conversation from others but none between Hydt and al-Fulan. Angry with himself, he adjusted his aim more carefully and finally heard Hydt's voice: 'I've been looking forward to this for a long time. I must thank you again for making it happen.'

Al-Fulan: 'I am pleased to do what I can. It is good we are in business together.'

Distracted, Hydt whispered, 'I would like to take pictures of the bodies.'

'Yes, yes, of course. Anything you want, Severan.'

How close can I get to the bodies?

Hydt then said, 'It's almost seven. Are we ready?'

What should I do? Bond thought desperately. People are about to die.

Your enemy's purpose will dictate your response . . .

On the wall, he noted a fire alarm. He could pull it, evacuate the building. But he also saw CCTVs and security guards. He'd be identified immediately as the man who'd pulled the lever and, though he'd try to flee, the guards and police might stop him, find his weapon. Hydt might see him. He'd easily deduce what had happened. The mission would collapse.

Was there any better response?

He couldn't think of one and edged close to the fire-alarm panel.

Six fifty-five.

Hydt and al-Fulan were walking quickly to a door at the rear of the lobby. Bond was at the alarm now. He was in full view of three security cameras.

205

And a guard was no more than twenty feet away. He had noticed Bond now and perhaps registered that his behaviour wasn't quite what you'd expect of a casual Western tourist in an arcane museum of this sort. The man bent his head and spoke into a microphone attached to his shoulder.

In front of Bond a family stood before a diorama of a camel race. The little boy and his father were laughing at the comical models.

Six fifty-six.

The squat guard turned towards Bond. He wore a pistol. And the protective flap covering it had been unsnapped.

Six fifty-seven.

The guard started forward, his hand near his gun.

Still, with Hydt and al-Fulan merely twenty feet away, Bond reached for the fire-alarm lever.

29

At that moment an announcement in Arabic came over the public-address system.

Bond paused to listen. He understood most of it. The English translation a moment later confirmed his take on the words.

'Gentlemen. Will ticket holders for the seven o'clock show now proceed through the North Wing door.'

That was the entrance Hydt and al-Fulan were now approaching, at the back of the main hall. They weren't leaving the museum; if this was the location where the people would die, why weren't the two men fleeing?

Bond left the alarm panel and stepped to the door. The guard eyed him once more, then turned away, fixing his holster flap.

Hydt and his colleague stood at the entrance to a special show the museum was hosting. Bond exhaled slowly as he understood at last. The title of the exhibition was 'Death in the Sand'. A notice at the entrance explained that last autumn archaeologists had discovered a mass grave dating back a thousand years, located near Abu Dhabi's Liwa oasis, about a hundred kilometres inland from the Persian Gulf. An entire nomadic Arab tribe, ninety-two people, had been attacked and slaughtered. Just after the battle, a sandstorm had buried the bodies. When the village had been discovered last year the remains were found perfectly preserved in the hot dry sands.

The exhibition was of the desiccated bodies laid out exactly as they were found, in a re-creation of the village. For the general public, it seemed, the bodies were modestly covered. The special exhibition tonight, at seven — which included only men — was for scientists, doctors and professors. The corpses were not covered. Al-Fulan had apparently managed to get Hydt a ticket.

Bond nearly laughed out loud, and relief flooded over him. Misunderstandings — and even outright errors — are not uncommon in the nuanced business of espionage, where operatives have to make plans and execute them with only fragments of information at their disposal. Often the results of such mistakes are disastrous; Bond couldn't recall an instance in which the opposite was true, as here, when a looming tragedy turned into an evening's innocuous cultural excursion. His first thought was that he'd enjoy telling Philly Maidenstone the story.

His amusement dimmed, however, as he reflected soberly: he'd almost destroyed the mission for the sake of ninety people who had been dead for nearly a millennium.

Then his mood grew more sombre yet as he looked into the large exhibition room and caught glimpses of the panorama of death: the bodies, some retaining much of the skin, like leather. Others were mostly skeletons. Hands reaching out, perhaps in a last plea for mercy. Emaciated forms of mothers cradling their children. Eye sockets empty, fingers mere twigs and more than a few mouths twisted into horrific smiles by the ravages of time and decay.

Bond looked at Hydt's face as the Rag-and-bone Man stared down at the victims. He was enraptured; an almost sexual lust glowed in his eyes. Even al-Fulan seemed troubled at the pleasure his business associate was displaying.

I've never heard that kind of joy at the prospect of killing . . .

Hydt was taking picture after picture, the repeated flash from his mobile bathing the corpses in brilliant light and making them all the more supernatural and horrific.

What a bloody waste of time, Bond reflected. All he'd learnt from the trip was that Hydt had some fancy new machinery for his recycling operations and that he got a sick high from images of dead bodies. Was Incident Twenty, whatever it might be, a similar misreading of the intercept? He thought back to the phrasing of the original message and concluded that whatever was planned for Friday was a real threat.

. . . estimated initial casualties in the thousands, british interests adversely affected, funds transfers as discussed.

That clearly described an attack.

Hydt and al-Fulan were moving deeper into the exhibition hall and, without a special ticket, Bond couldn't pursue them further. But Hydt was speaking again. Bond lifted the phone.

'I do hope you understand about that girl of

209

yours. What's her name again?'

'Stella,' al-Fulan said. 'No, we don't have any choice. When she finds out I'm not leaving my wife she'll be a risk. She knows too much. And, frankly,' he added, 'she's been quite a nuisance lately.'

Hydt continued, 'My associate's handling everything. He'll take her out to the desert, make her disappear. Whatever he does, though, will be efficient. He's quite amazing at planning . . . well, everything.'

That was why the Irishman had remained at the warehouse.

If he was going to kill Stella, there *was* something more to this trip than legitimate business. He'd have to assume it involved Incident Twenty. Bond hurried from the museum, calling Felix Leiter. They had to save the woman and learn what she knew.

Leiter's mobile, however, rang four times, then stepped into voicemail. Bond tried again. Why the hell wasn't the American picking up? Were he and Nasad trying to save Stella at this moment, perhaps fighting with the Irishman or the chauffeur? Or both of them?

Another call. Voicemail again. Bond broke into a run, weaving through the souks as haunting voices calling the faithful to prayer filled the sunset sky.

Sweating hard, gasping, he arrived at al-Fulan's warehouse five minutes later. Hydt's Town Car was gone. Bond slipped through the hole they'd cut earlier in the fence. The window Leiter had climbed through was now closed. Bond ran to

210

the warehouse and used a lock pick to open a side door. He slipped inside, drawing the Walther.

The place seemed to be deserted, though he could hear the loud whining of machinery from somewhere nearby.

No sign of the girl.

And where were Leiter and Nasad?

Just a few seconds later Bond learnt the answer to that question, part of it, at least. In the room Leiter had entered, he found bloodstains on the floor, fresh. There were signs of a struggle, with several tools lying nearby . . . along with Leiter's pistol and phone.

Bond summoned a scenario of what might have happened. Leiter and Nasad had separated, with the American hiding here. He must have been watching the Irishman and Stella when the Arab chauffeur had slipped up behind and hit him with a spanner or pipe. Had Leiter been dragged off, thrown into the boot of the Town Car and taken to the desert with the girl?

Gun in his hand, Bond headed for the doorway where he heard the sound of the machine.

He froze at what he saw ahead of him.

The man in the blue jacket — his tail from earlier — was rolling the barely conscious form of Felix Leiter into one of the massive rubbish-compacting machines. The CIA agent lay sprawled, feet first, on the conveyor-belt, which wasn't moving, though the machine itself was running; in the centre two huge metal plates on either side of the belt pressed forward, nearly meeting, then withdrawing to accept a new batch of junk.

Leiter's legs were a mere two yards from them.

The assailant glanced up and, scowling, stared at the intruder.

Bond steadied his weapon's sights on the man and shouted, 'Hands out to your sides!'

The man did so but suddenly lunged to his right and slapped a button on the machine, then sprinted away, vanishing from sight.

The conveyor-belt began rolling steadily forward, with Leiter easing towards the thick steel plates, which came within six inches of each other then shot back to allow more refuse into their path.

Bond sped to the unit and slapped the red OFF button, then started after the attacker. But the heavy-duty motor didn't stop immediately; the belt continued to carry his friend towards the deadly plates, pulsing relentlessly back and forth.

Oh, God! . . . Bond holstered his Walther and turned back. He grabbed Leiter and struggled to pull him out of the machinery. But the conveyor-belt was dotted with pointed teeth, to improve its grip, and Leiter's clothing was caught.

Head lolling, blood streaming into his eyes, he continued to be drawn towards the compactor mechanism.

Eighteen inches away, sixteen . . . twelve.

Bond leapt on to the belt and jammed a foot against the frame, then wound Leiter's jacket around his hands and gripped furiously hard. The momentum slowed but the massive motor continued to drive the belt relentlessly under the faces of the plates shooting back and forth.

Leiter was eight inches, then six, from the plates that would turn his feet and ankles to pulp.

His arm and leg muscles in fiery agony, Bond tugged harder, groaning at the effort.

Three inches . . .

Finally the belt stopped and, with a hydraulic gasp, so did the plates.

Struggling for breath, Bond reached in and untangled the American's trousers from the teeth on the belt and pulled him out, easing him to the floor. He ran to the loading bay, drawing his weapon, but there was no sign of the man in blue. Then, scanning for other threats, Bond returned to the CIA agent, who was coming round. He sat up slowly, Bond helping, and oriented himself.

'Can't leave you alone for five minutes, can I?' Bond asked, masking the horror he'd felt at his friend's near fate, as he examined the wound in the man's head and mopped it with a rag he'd found nearby.

Leiter gazed at the machine. Shook his head. Then his familiar grin spread across his lean face. 'You Brits're always barging in at the wrong time. I had him just where I wanted him.'

'Hospital?' Bond asked. His heart pounded from the effort of the rescue and relief at the outcome.

'Naw.' The American examined the rag. It was bloody but Leiter seemed more angry than injured. 'Hell, James, we're past the deadline! The ninety people?'

Bond explained about the exhibition.

213

Leiter barked a harsh laugh. 'What a screw-up! Brother, did we misread that one. So Hydt gets off on dead bodies. And he wanted *pictures* of them? Man's got a whole new idea of porn.'

Bond collected Leiter's phone and weapon and returned them to him. 'What happened, Felix?'

Leiter's eyes stilled. 'The driver of the Town Car came into the warehouse right after you left. I could see him and that Irishman talking, looking at the girl. I knew something was going down, and that meant she'd know something. I was going to finesse it somehow and save her. Claim we were safety inspectors or something. Before I could move, they grabbed the girl and taped her up, dragged her toward the office. I sent Yusuf around to the other side and started toward them but that bastard nailed me before I got ten feet — the guy from the shopping centre, your tail.'

'I know. I spotted him.'

'Man, the SOB knows some martial-arts crap, I'll tell you that. He clocked me good and I was down for the count.'

'Did he say anything?'

'Grunted a lot. When he hit me.'

'Was he working with the Irishman or al-Fulan?'

'Couldn't tell. I didn't see them together.'

'And the girl? We've got to find her if we can.'

'They're probably on their way out to the desert. If we're lucky, Yusuf's following them. Probably tried to call when I was out.' With Bond helping, the agent struggled to his feet. He

214

took his phone and hit speed dial.

And from nearby came the chirp of a ringtone, a cheerful electronic tune. But muted.

Both men looked around.

Then Leiter turned to Bond. 'Oh, no,' the American whispered, closing his eyes briefly. They hurried to the back of the compactor. The sound was coming from inside a large, filled bin liner, which the machine had automatically sealed with wire and then disgorged on to the loading-bay platform to be carted off for disposal.

Bond, too, had realised what had happened. 'I'll look,' he said.

'No,' Leiter said firmly. 'It's my job.' He unwound the wire, took a deep breath and looked inside the bag. Bond joined him.

The dense jigsaw of sharp metal pieces, wires and nuts, bolts and screws were entwined with a mass of gore and bloody cloth, bits of human organs, bone.

The glazed eyes in Yusuf Nasad's crushed, distorted face stared directly between the two men.

★ ★ ★

Without a word, they returned to the Alfa and checked the satellite tracking system, which reported that Hydt's limo had returned to the Intercontinental. It had made two brief stops on the way — presumably to transfer the girl to another car, for her last trip out to the desert, and to collect Hydt from the museum.

Fifteen minutes later Bond piloted the Alfa past the hotel and into the car park.

'Do you want to get a room?' Bond asked. 'Take care of that?' He gestured at Leiter's head.

'Naw, I need a goddamn drink. I'll just wash up. Meet you in the bar.'

They parked and Bond opened the boot. He collected his laptop bag, leaving the suitcase inside. Leiter pulled his own small bag over his shoulder and found a cap — branded, so to speak, with the logo of the University of Texas Longhorns gridiron team. He pulled it gingerly over his wound and stuffed his straw-coloured hair underneath. They took the side entrance into the hotel.

Inside, Leiter went to wash and Bond, making sure none of the Hydt entourage was in the lobby, passed through it and stepped outside. He assessed a group of limo drivers standing in a cluster and talking busily. Bond saw that none of them was Hydt's driver. He gestured to the smallest of the lot and the man walked over eagerly.

'You have a card?' Bond asked.

'Indeed, yes, I do, sir.' And offered one. Bond glanced at and pocketed it. 'What would like, sir? A dune bashing trip? No, I know, the gold souk! For your lady. You will bring her something from Dubai and be her hero.'

'The man who hired that limo?' Bond's gaze swept quickly over Hydt's Lincoln.

The driver's eyes went still. Bond wasn't worried; he knew when somebody was for sale. He tried once more. 'You know him, don't you?'

216

'Not especially, sir.'

'But you drivers always talk among yourselves. You know everything that goes on here. Especially regarding a curious fellow like Mr Hydt.'

He slipped the man five hundred dirhams.

'Yes, sir, yes, sir. I may have heard something . . . Let me think. Yes, perhaps.'

'And what might that have been?'

'I believe he and his friends have gone to the restaurant. They will be there for two hours or so. It's a very good restaurant. Meals are leisurely.'

'Any idea where they're going from here?'

A nod. But no accompanying words.

Another five hundred dirhams joined their friends.

The man laughed softly and cynically. 'People are careless around us. We are simply people to shepherd folks around. We are camels. Beasts of burden. I'm referring to the fact that people think we don't exist. Therefore whatever they say in front of us they believe we do not hear, however sensitive it might be. However *valuable*.'

Bond held up more cash, then returned it to his pocket.

The driver glanced about briefly then said, 'He's flying to Cape Town tonight. A private jet, leaving in about three hours. As I told you, the restaurant downstairs is known for its sumptuous and leisurely dining experience.' A fake pout. 'But your questions tell me you probably do not want me to have an associate book a table. I understand. Perhaps on your next trip to Dubai.'

217

Now Bond handed over the rest of the money. He then withdrew the man's business card and, flicking it with his thumb, asked, 'My associate? The man who came in with me? Did you see him?'

'Tough one?'

'Very tough. I will be leaving Dubai soon but he will be staying. He most sincerely hopes your information about Mr Hydt is accurate.'

The smile blew away like sand. 'Yes, yes, sir, it is completely accurate, I swear to Allah. Praise be to Him.'

30

Bond went into the bar and took a table on the outdoor terrace overlooking Dubai Creek, a peaceful mirror dotted with swaying reflections of coloured light, which utterly belied the horror he had witnessed at al-Fulan's works.

The waiter approached and asked what he would like. American bourbon was Bond's favourite spirit, but he believed vodka was medicinal, if not curative, when served bitingly cold. He now ordered a double Stolichnaya martini, medium dry, and asked that it be shaken very well, which not only chilled the vodka better than stirring but bruised — aerated — it too, improving the flavour considerably.

'Lemon peel only.'

When the drink arrived, suitably opaque — evidence of a proper shaking — he drank half immediately and felt the oxymoronic burning chill flow from throat to face. It helped dull the frustration that he hadn't been able to save either the young woman or Yusuf Nasad.

It did nothing, however, to mitigate the memory of Hydt's eerie expression as he gazed, lusting, at the petrified bodies.

He sipped again, staring absently at the television above the bar, on whose screen the beautiful Bahraini singer Ahlam was swirling through a video edited in the jerky style fashionable on Arab and Indian TV. Her infectious, trilling voice floated from the speakers.

He drained the glass, then called Bill Tanner. He explained about the false alarm at the history museum and the deaths and added that Hydt would head for Cape Town that night. Could T Branch arrange a ride for Bond? He could no longer hitch-hike on his friend's Grumman, which had gone back to London.

'I'll see what I can do, James. Probably have to be commercial. I don't know if I can get you there ahead of Hydt, though.'

'I just need a watcher to meet the flight and see where he goes. What's the Six situation down there?'

'Station Z's got a covert operator on the Cape. Gregory Lamb. Let me check his status.' Bond heard typing. 'He's up in Eritrea at the moment — that sabre-rattling on the Sudanese border's got worse. But, James, we don't want to get Lamb involved if we can avoid it. He doesn't have an entirely irreproachable record. He went native, like some character out of a Graham Greene novel. I think Six have been meaning to hand him a redundancy package but haven't got round to it. I'll find somebody local for you. I'd recommend SAPS, the police service, rather than National Intelligence — NIA's been in the news lately and not in a good way. I'll make some calls and let you know.'

'Thanks, Bill. Can you patch me to Q?'

'Will do. Good luck.'

A thoughtful voice was soon on the line: 'Q Branch. Hirani.'

'It's 007, Sanu. I'm in Dubai. I need something fast.'

After Bond had explained, Hirani seemed disappointed at the simplicity of the assignment. 'Where are you?' he asked.

'Intercontinental, Festival City.'

Bond heard typing.

'All right. Thirty minutes. Just remember: flowers.'

They rang off, as Leiter arrived, sat down and ordered a Jim Beam, neat. 'That means no ice, no water, no fruit salad, no nothing. But it does mean a double. And I could live with a triple.'

Bond ordered another martini. When the waiter left he asked, 'How's the head?'

'It's nothing,' Leiter murmured. He didn't seem badly injured and Bond knew that his subdued mood was due to the loss of Nasad. 'You find out anything about Hydt?'

'They're leaving tonight. A couple of hours. Going to Cape Town.'

'What's down there?'

'No idea. That's what I have to find out.'

And find out within three days, Bond reminded himself, if he wanted to save those thousands of people.

They fell silent as the waiter brought their drinks. Both agents scanned the large room as they sipped. There was no sign of the dark-haired man with the earring, or of watchers paying too much attention — or not enough — to the men in the corner.

Neither man raised a toast to the memory of the asset who'd just died. As tempted as you were, you never did that.

'Nasad?' Bond asked. 'His body?' The thought

221

of an ally going to such an ignominious grave was hard.

Leiter's lips tightened. 'If Hydt and the Irishman were involved and I called in a team, they'd know we were on to them. I'm not risking our cover at this point. Yusuf knew what he was getting into.'

Bond nodded. It was the right way to handle it, though that didn't make the decision any easier.

Leiter inhaled the fumes of his whiskey, then drank again. 'You know, in this business, it's choices like that that're the hard ones — not pulling out your six-shooter and playing Butch Cassidy. That, you just do without thinking.'

Bond's mobile buzzed. T Branch had booked him an overnight flight on Air Emirates to Cape Town. It left in three hours. Bond was pleased with the choice of carrier. The airline had studiously avoided becoming just another mass market operation and treated its passengers to what he guessed was the quality service that typified the golden age of air travel fifty or sixty years ago. He told Leiter of his departure arrangements. He added, 'Let's get some food.'

The American waved over a waiter and asked for a *mezze* platter. 'And then bring us a grilled hammour. Bone it, if y'all'd be so kind.'

'Yes, sir.'

Bond ordered a bottle of a good *premier cru* Chablis, which arrived a moment later. They sipped from the chilled glasses silently until the first course arrived: *kofta*, olives, hummus, cheese, aubergine, nuts and the best flatbread

Bond had ever had. Both men began to eat. After the waiter had cleared away the remnants, he brought the main course. The simple white fish lay steaming on a bed of green lentils. It was very good, delicate yet with a faint meatiness. Bond had eaten only a few mouthfuls when his phone hummed again. Caller ID showed only the code for a British government number. Thinking Philly might be ringing from a different office, Bond answered.

He immediately regretted doing so.

31

'James! James! James! Guess who? Percy here. Long time no speak!'

Bond's heart sank.

Leiter frowned at the glower on Bond's face.

'Percy . . . yes.'

Division Three's Osborne-Smith enquired, 'You well? No altercations requiring anything more than a plaster, I trust.'

'I'm fine.'

'Delighted to hear it. Now, things are proceeding apace here. Your boss has briefed everyone about the Gehenna plan. You were perhaps too busy fleeing the jurisdiction to be in touch.' He let that hang for a moment, then said, 'Aha. Just winding you up, James. Fact is, I'm calling for several reasons and the first is to apologise.'

'Really?' Bond asked, suspicious.

The Division Three man's voice grew serious. 'In London this morning, I'll admit I had a tac team ready to grab Hydt at the airport, bring him in for some tea and conversation. But it turns out you were right. The Watchers picked up a scrap and managed to decrypt it. Hold on — I quote from the record. Here we go: something garbled, then 'Severan has three main partners . . . any one of them can push the button if he's not available.' So you see, James, arresting him *would* have been a disaster, just as

224

you said. The others would have scurried down the rabbit hole and we'd've lost any chance to find out what Gehenna was about and stop it.' He paused for breath. 'I was a touch whingey when we met and I'm sorry about that too. I want to work with you on this, James. Apologies accepted? Bygones turned to bygones with a swipe of Hermione's magic wand?'

In the intelligence world, Bond had learnt, your allies sought forgiveness for their transgressions against you about as often as your enemies did. He supposed that some of Osborne-Smith's contrition was based on staying in the game for part of the glory, but that was all right with Bond. All he cared about was learning what the Gehenna plan was and preventing thousands of deaths.

'I suppose.'

'Good. Now, your boss sent us a signal about what you found up in March and I'm following it up. The 'blast radius' is pretty obvious — an IED — so we're tracking down any reports of stray explosives. And we know that one of the 'terms' of the deal involves five million quid. I've called in some favours at the Bank of England to check SFT activity.'

Bond too had thought of calling the Bank with a request to flag suspect financial transactions. But nowadays five million pounds was such small change that he'd believed there would be far too many responses to plough through. Still, it couldn't hurt for Osborne-Smith to go ahead.

The Division Three man added, 'As for the reference to the 'course' being confirmed, well, until we know more, there're no aircraft or ships to monitor. But I've put the aviation and port chaps on alert to move fast if we need to.'

'Good,' Bond said, without adding that he'd asked Bill Tanner to do much the same. 'I've just found out that Hydt, his lady friend and the Irishman are on their way to Cape Town.'

'Cape Town? Now that's worth chewing over. I've been peering into Hydt's recesses, so to speak.'

This was, Bond supposed, what passed for a comradely joke with Percy Osborne-Smith.

'South Africa is one of Green Way's biggest operations. His home from home. I bet Gehenna must have some connection with it — Lord knows, there're plenty of British interests there.'

Bond told him about al-Fulan and the girl's death. 'All we learnt specifically is that Hydt gets a kick out of pictures of dead bodies. And the Arab's company probably has something to do with Gehenna. He's supplied equipment to arms dealers and warlords in the past.'

'Really? Interesting. Which reminds me. Take a look at the photo I'm uploading. You should have it now.'

Bond minimised the active-call screen on his mobile and opened a secure attachment. The picture was of the Irishman. 'That's him,' he told Osborne-Smith.

'Thought it might be. His name's Niall Dunne.' He spelt it out.

'How did you find him?'

'Footage from the CCTVs at Gatwick. He's not in the databases but I had my indefatigable

226

staff compare the pic with street cameras in London. There were some close hits of a man with that weird fringe inspecting tunnels that Green Way's building near the Victoria Embankment. It's the latest thing — underground rubbish transfer and collection. Keeps the roads clear and the tourists happy. A few of our boys pretended they were from Public Works, flashed his picture and got his real name. I've sent his file to Five, the Yard and your chief of staff.'

'What's Dunne's story?' Bond asked. In front of him the fish cooled but he'd lost interest in it.

'It's curious. He was born in Belfast, studied architecture and engineering, came top of his year. Then he became a sapper in the Army.'

Sappers were combat engineers, the soldiers who built bridges, airports and bomb shelters for the troops, as well as laid and cleared minefields. They were known for their improvisational skills, building defensive or offensive machinery and bulwarks with whatever supplies were available and under less-than-ideal conditions.

The ODG's Lieutenant Colonel Bill Tanner had been a sapper and the soft-spoken, golf-loving chief of staff was one of the cleverest and most dangerous men Bond had ever met.

Osborne-Smith continued, 'After he left the service he became a freelance engineering inspector. I didn't know that any such line of work existed but it turns out that in constructing a building, ship or plane, the project has to be inspected at hundreds of stages. Dunne would look over the work and say yea or nay. He was apparently at the top of his game — he could find flaws that nobody else could. But suddenly he quit and became a consultant, according to Inland Revenue records. He's a damn good one, too — he makes about two hundred grand a year . . . and doesn't have a company logo or cute mascots like Wenlock and Mandeville.'

Bond found that, since the apology, he felt less impatient with Osborne-Smith's wit, such as it was. 'That's probably how they met. Dunne inspected something for Green Way and Hydt hired him.'

Osborne-Smith continued, 'Data mining's placed Dunne going to and from Cape Town over the past four years. He's got a flat there and one in London, which we've been through, by the way, and found nothing of interest. The travel records also show he's been in India, Indonesia, the Caribbean and a few other places where trouble's brewing. Working on new outposts for his boss, I'd guess.' He added, 'Whitehall's still looking at Afghanistan, but I don't give a toss about their theories. I'm sure you're on the money, James.'

'Thanks, Percy. You've been very helpful.'

'Delighted to be of service.' The words that Bond would have found condescending yesterday now sounded sincere.

They rang off and Bond told Felix Leiter what Osborne-Smith had turned up.

'So that scarecrow Dunne's an engineer? We call 'em geeks in the states.'

A hawker had entered the restaurant and was moving from table to table selling roses.

Leiter saw the direction of Bond's gaze.

228

'Listen up, James, I've had a wonderful dinner but if you're thinking of sealing the deal with a bouquet, it ain't gonna happen.'

Bond smiled.

The hawker stepped up to the table next to Bond's and extended a flower to a young couple seated there. 'Please,' he said to the wife, 'the lovely lady will have this for free, with my compliments.' He moved on.

After a moment Bond lifted his napkin and opened the envelope he'd casually removed from the man's pocket in a perfect brush pass.

Remember: flowers . . .

Discreetly he examined the forgery of a South African firearms permit, suitably franked and signed. 'We should go,' he said, noting the time. He didn't want to run into Hydt, Dunne and the woman on the way out of the hotel.

'We'll put this on Uncle Sam,' Leiter said and settled the bill. They left the bar and slipped out by a side door, heading for the car park.

Within half an hour they were at the airport.

The men gripped hands and Leiter offered in a low voice, 'Yusuf was a great asset, sure. But more than that, he was a friend. You run across that son-of-a-bitch in the blue jacket again and you have a shot, James, take it.'

Wednesday
KILLING FIELDS

32

As the Air Emirates Boeing taxied smoothly over the tarmac towards the gate in Cape Town, James Bond stretched, then slipped his shoes back on. He felt refreshed. Soon after take-off in Dubai he'd administered to himself two Jim Beams with a little water. The nightcap had done the trick famously and he'd had nearly seven hours of blessedly uninterrupted sleep. He was now reviewing texts from Bill Tanner.

> Contact: Capt. Jordaan, Crime Combating & Investigation, SA Police Service. Jordaan to meet you landside @ airport. Surveillance active on Hydt.

A second followed.

> MI6's Gregory Lamb reportedly still in Eritrea. Opinion here all around, avoid him if possible.

There was a final one.

> Happy to hear you and Osborne-Smith have kissed and made up. When's the stag do?

Bond had to smile.

The plane eased to a stop at the gate and the purser ran through the liturgy of landing with which Bond was all too familiar. 'Cabin crew,

233

doors to manual, and crosscheck. Ladies and gentlemen, please take care when opening the overhead lockers; the contents may have shifted during the flight.'

Bless you, my child, for Fate has decided to bring you safely back to earth . . . at least for a little longer.

Bond pulled down his laptop bag — he'd checked in his suitcase, which contained his weapon — and proceeded to Immigration in the busy hall. He received a pro forma stamp in his passport. Then he went into the Customs hall. To a stocky, unsmiling officer he displayed the firearms permit so he could collect his suitcase. The man stared at him intently. Bond tensed and wondered if there was going to be a problem.

'Okay, okay,' the man said, his broad, glistening face inflated with the power of small officialdom. 'Now you will tell me the truth.'

'The truth?' Bond asked calmly.

'Yes . . . How do you get close enough to a kudu or springbok to use a handgun when you hunt?'

'That's the challenge,' Bond replied.

'I must say it would be.'

Then Bond frowned. 'But I never hunt springbok.'

'No? It makes the best biltong.'

'Perhaps so, but shooting a springbok would be very bad luck for England on the rugby pitch.'

The Customs agent laughed hard, shook Bond's hand and nodded him to the exit.

The arrivals hall was packed. Most people were in Western clothing, though some wore traditional African garb: men's *dashikis* and brocade sets and, for the women, *kente* kaftans and head wraps, all brightly coloured. Muslim robes and scarves were present as well and a few saris.

As Bond made his way through the passenger meeting point he detected several distinct languages and many more dialects. He had always been fascinated by the clicking in African languages; in some words, the mouth and tongue create that very sound for consonants. Khoisan — spoken by the original inhabitants of this part of Africa — made the most use of it, although Zulus and Xhosas also clicked. Bond had tried and found the sound impossible to replicate.

When his contact, Captain Jordaan, did not immediately appear he went into a café, dropped on to a stool at the counter and ordered a double espresso. He drank it down, paid and stepped outside, eyeing a beautiful businesswoman. She was in her mid-thirties, he guessed, with exotically high cheekbones. Her thick, wavy black hair contained a few strands of premature grey, which added to her sensuality. Her dark-red suit, over a black shirt, was cut close and revealed a figure that was full yet tautly athletic.

I believe I shall enjoy South Africa, he thought, and smiled as he let her pass in front of him on her way to the exit. Like most attractive women in transitory worlds like airports, she ignored him.

He stood for several moments in the centre of Arrivals, then decided that perhaps Jordaan was waiting for him to approach. He texted Tanner to ask for a photograph. But just after he hit send he spotted the police officer: a large, bearded redhead in a light-brown suit — a bear of a man — glanced at Bond once, with a hint of reaction, but he turned away rather quickly and went to a kiosk to buy cigarettes.

Tradecraft is all about subtext: cover identities masking who you really are, dull conversations filled with code words to convey shocking facts, innocent objects used for concealment or as weapons.

Jordaan's sudden diversion to buy cigarettes was a message. He hadn't approached Bond because hostiles were present.

Glancing behind him, he saw no immediate sign of a threat. Instinctively he followed prescribed procedure. When an agent waves you off, you circle casually out of the immediate area as inconspicuously as possible and contact a third-party intermediary who co-ordinates a new rendezvous in a safer location. Bill Tanner would be the cut-out.

Bond started to move towards an exit.

Too late.

As he saw Jordaan slipping into the Gents, pocketing cigarettes he would probably never smoke, he heard an ominous voice close to his ear, 'Do not turn around.' The English was coated with a smooth layer of a native accent. He sensed that the man was lean and tall. From the corner of his eye, Bond was aware of at least one partner, shorter but stockier. This man moved in quickly and relieved him of his laptop bag and the suitcase containing his useless Walther.

The first assailant said, 'Walk straight out of the hall — now.'

There was nothing for it but to comply. He turned and went where the man had told him, down a deserted corridor.

Bond assessed the situation. From the echo of the footsteps Bond knew the tall man's partner was far enough away that his initial move could only neutralise one of them instantly. The shorter man would have to shed Bond's suitcase and laptop bag, which would give Bond a few seconds to get to him but he would still have a chance to draw his weapon. The man could be taken down but not before shots were fired.

No, Bond reflected, too many innocents. It was best to wait until they were outside.

'Through the door on your left. I said you are not to look back.'

They walked out into stark sunlight. Here it was autumn, the temperature crisp, the sky a stunning azure. As they approached the kerb in a deserted construction site, a battered black Range Rover sped forward and squealed to a stop.

More hostiles, but no one as yet was getting out of the vehicle.

Purpose . . . response.

Their purpose was to kidnap him. His response would be textbook protocol in an attempted rendition: disorient and then attack. Casually working his Rolex over his fingers to act as a knuckleduster, he turned abruptly to confront the pair with a disdainful smile. They were young, deadly serious men, their skin contrasting sharply with the brilliant white of their starched shirts. They wore suits — one brown, the other navy — and narrow dark ties. They were probably armed, but overconfidence, perhaps, had led them to keep their weapons holstered.

As the Range Rover door swung open behind him, Bond stepped aside so that he couldn't be attacked from behind and judged angles. He decided to break the jaw of the tallest first and use his body as a shield as he pushed forward towards the shorter man. He looked calmly into the man's eyes and laughed. 'I think I'll report you to the tourist bureau. I've heard a lot about the friendliness of South Africans. I was expecting rather more in the way of hospitality.'

Just before he lunged, he heard from behind him, inside the vehicle, a woman's flinty voice: 'And we would have offered some if you hadn't made yourself so obvious a target by enjoying a leisurely coffee in plain view with a hostile loose in the airport.'

Bond relaxed his fist and turned. He looked into the vehicle and tried unsuccessfully to mask his surprise. The beautiful woman he'd seen just moments ago in Arrivals was sitting in the back seat.

'I'm Captain Bheka Jordaan, SAPS, Crime Combating and Investigation Division.'

'Ah.' Bond looked at her full lips, untouched by cosmetics, and her dark eyes. She wasn't smiling.

His mobile buzzed. The screen showed he had a message from Bill Tanner, along with, of course, an MMS picture of the woman in front of him.

The tall abductor said, 'Commander Bond, I am SAPS Warrant Officer Kwalene Nkosi.' He reached out his hand and their palms met in the traditional South African way — an initial grip, as in the West, followed by a vertical clasp and back to the original. Bond knew it was considered impolite to let go too quickly. Apparently he timed the gesture right; Nkosi grinned warmly, then nodded to the shorter man, who was taking Bond's suitcase and laptop bag to the rear of the Range Rover. 'And that is Sergeant Mbalula.'

The stocky man nodded unsmilingly and, after stowing Bond's belongings, vanished fast, presumably to his own vehicle.

'You will please forgive our brusqueness, Commander,' Nkosi said. 'We thought it best to get you out of the airport as quickly as possible, rather than spend the time to explain.'

'We should not waste more time on pleasantries, Warrant Officer,' Bheka Jordaan muttered impatiently.

Bond eased himself into the back beside her. Nkosi got into the passenger seat in the front. A moment later Sergeant Mbalula's black saloon, also unmarked, pulled up behind them.

'Let's go,' Jordaan barked. 'Quickly.'

The Range Rover peeled away from the kerb and skidded brazenly into the traffic, earning the driver a series of energetic hoots and lethargic curses, and accelerated to more than ninety k.p.h. in a zone marked forty.

Bond pulled his mobile off his belt. He typed into the keyboard, read the responses.

'Warrant Officer?' Jordaan asked Nkosi. 'Anything?'

He had been staring into the wing mirror and answered in what seemed to be Zulu or Xhosa. Bond did not speak either language but it was clear from the tone of the answer, and the woman's reaction, that there was no tail. When they were outside the airport grounds and making their way towards a cluster of low but impressive mountains in the distance, the vehicle slowed somewhat.

Jordaan thrust her hand forward. Bond reached out to shake it, smiling, then stopped. She was holding a mobile phone. 'If you don't mind,' she said sternly, 'you will touch the screen here.'

So much for warming international relations.

He took the phone, pressed his thumb into the centre of the screen and handed it back. She read the message that appeared. 'James Bond. Overseas Development Group, Foreign and Commonwealth Office. Now, you'll want to confirm my identity.' She held out her hand, fingers splayed. 'You have an app that can take my prints too, I assume.'

'There's no need.'

'Why?' she asked coolly. 'Because I'm what passes for a beautiful woman in your mind and you have no need to check further? I could be an assassin. I could be an al-Qaeda terrorist wearing a bomb vest.'

He decided not to mention that his earlier

perusal of her figure had revealed no evidence of explosives. He answered, perhaps a bit glibly, 'I don't need your prints because, in addition to the photo of you that my office just sent me, my mobile read your iris a few minutes ago and confirmed to me that you are indeed Captain Bheka Jordaan, Crime Combating and Investigation Division, South African Police Service. You've worked for them for eight years. You live in Leeuwen Street in Cape Town. Last year you received a Gold Cross for bravery. Congratulations.'

He had also learnt her age, thirty-two, her salary and that she was divorced.

Warrant Officer Nkosi twisted round in his seat, glanced at the mobile and said, with a broad smile, 'Commander Bond, that is a nice toy. Without doubt.'

Jordaan snapped, 'Kwalene!'

The young man's smile vanished. He turned back to his wing mirror sentry duty.

She glanced with disdain at Bond's phone. 'We will go to my headquarters and consider how to approach the situation with Severan Hydt. I worked with your Lieutenant Colonel Tanner when he was with MI6 so I agreed to help you. He is intelligent and very devoted to his job. Quite a gentleman too.'

The implication being that Bond himself probably was not. He was irritated that she'd taken such umbrage at what had been an innocent — *relatively* innocent — smile in the arrivals hall. She was attractive and he couldn't have been the first man to lob a flirt her way. 'Is

241

Hydt in his office?' he asked.

'That's correct,' Nkosi said. 'He and Niall Dunne are both in Cape Town. Sergeant Mbalula and I followed them from the airport. There was a woman with them too.'

'You have surveillance on them?'

'That's right,' the lean man said. 'We based our CCTV plan on London's so there are cameras everywhere downtown. He is in his office and being monitored from a central location. We can track him anywhere if he leaves. We ourselves are not completely free of toys, Commander.'

Bond smiled at him, then said to Jordaan, 'You mentioned a hostile at the airport.'

'We learnt from Immigration that a man arrived from Abu Dhabi around the time you did. He was travelling on a fake British passport. We discovered this only after he cleared Customs and disappeared.'

The bearish man he'd mistaken for Jordaan? Or the man in the blue jacket at the shopping centre on Dubai Creek? He described them.

'I don't know,' Jordaan offered curtly. 'As I said, our only information was documentary. Because he was unaccounted for, I thought it best not to meet you in person in the arrivals hall. I sent my officers instead.' She leant forward suddenly and asked Nkosi, 'Anyone now?'

'No, Captain. We are not being followed.'

Bond said to her, 'You seem concerned about surveillance.'

'South Africa is like Russia,' she said. 'The old

regime has fallen and it is a whole new world here. This draws people who wish to make money and involve themselves in politics and all manner of affairs. Sometimes legally, sometimes not.'

Nkosi said, 'We have a saying. 'With many opportunities come many operatives.' We keep that always in mind at the SAPS and look over our shoulder often. You would be wise to do the same, Commander Bond. Without doubt.'

33

The central police station in Buitenkant Street, central Cape Town, resembled a pleasant hotel more than a government building. Two storeys high, with walls of scrubbed red brick and a red-tiled roof, it overlooked the wide, clean avenue, which was dotted with palms and jacaranda.

The driver paused at the front to let them out. Jordaan and Nkosi stepped on to the pavement and looked around. When they saw no signs of surveillance or threat the warrant officer gestured Bond out. He went to the back for his laptop bag and suitcase, then followed the officers inside.

As they entered the building Bond blinked in surprise at what he saw. There was a plaque that read '*Servamus et Servimus*', the motto of the SAPS, he assumed. 'We protect and we serve.'

What gave him pause, though, was that the two principal words were eerie, and ironic, echoes of Severan Hydt's first name.

Without waiting for the lift, Jordaan climbed the stairs to the first floor. Her modest office was lined with books and professional journals, present-day maps of Cape Town and the Western Cape, and a framed 120-year-old map of the eastern coast of South Africa, showing the region of Natal, with the port of D'Urban and the town of Ladysmith mysteriously circled in ancient fading ink. Zululand and Swaziland were depicted to the north.

There were framed photographs on Jordaan's desk. A blond man and a dark-skinned woman held hands in one — they appeared in several others. The woman bore a vague resemblance to Jordaan, and Bond assumed they were her parents. Prominent also were pictures of an elderly woman in traditional African clothing and several featuring children. Bond decided that they weren't Jordaan's. There were no shots of her with a partner.

Divorced, he recalled.

Her desktop was graced with fifty or so case folders. The world of policing, like espionage, involves far more paperwork than firearms and gadgets.

Despite the late autumn season in South Africa, the weather was temperate and her office warm. After a moment of debate, Jordaan removed her red jacket and hung it up. Her black blouse was short sleeved and he saw a large swath of make-up along the inside of her right forearm. She didn't seem like the tattoo sort but perhaps she was concealing one. Then he decided that, no, the cream covered a lengthy and wide scar.

Gold Cross for Bravery . . .

Bond sat across from her, beside Nkosi, who unbuttoned his jacket and remained stiffly upright. Bond asked them both, 'Did Colonel Tanner tell you about my mission here?'

'Just that you were investigating Severan Hydt on a matter of national security.'

Bond ran through what they knew of Incident Twenty — a.k.a. Gehenna — and the impending deaths on Friday.

245

Nkosi frowned ridges into his high forehead. Jordaan took in the information with still eyes. She pressed her hands together — modest rings encircled the middle fingers of both hands. 'I see. And the evidence is credible?'

'It is. Does that surprise you?'

She said evenly, 'Severan Hydt is an unlikely evil. We are aware of him, of course. He opened Green Way International here two years ago and has contracts for much of the refuse collection and recycling in the major cities in South Africa — Pretoria, Durban, Port Elizabeth, Joburg and, of course, throughout the west here. He's done many good things for our nation. Ours is a country in transition, as you know, and our past has led to problems with the environment. Gold and diamond mining, poverty and lack of infrastructure have taken their toll. Refuse collection was a serious problem in the townships and squatters' settlements. To make up for the displacement caused by the Group Areas Act under apartheid, the government built residences — *lokasies*, or locations, they are called — for the people to live in instead of shacks. But even there the population was so high that refuse collection could not be performed efficiently, or sometimes at all. Disease was a problem. Severan Hydt has reversed much of that. He also donates to AIDS and hunger-relief charities.'

Most serious criminal enterprises have public-relations specialists on board, Bond reflected; being an 'unlikely evil' did not exempt you from diligent investigation.

Jordaan seemed to note his scepticism. She

246

continued, 'I'm simply saying that he does not much fit the profile of a terrorist or master criminal. But if he is, my department stands ready to do all it can to help.'

'Thank you. Now, do you know anything about his associate, Niall Dunne?'

She said, 'I had never heard the name until this morning. I've looked into him. He comes and goes here on a legitimate British passport and has been doing so for several years. We've never had any problem with him. He's not on any watchlists.'

'What do you know of the woman with them?'

Nkosi consulted a file. 'American passport. Jessica Barnes. She's a cipher to us, I'd say. No police record. No criminal activity. Nothing. We have some photos.'

'That's not her,' Bond said, looking at the images of a young, truly beautiful blonde.

'Ah, I am sorry, I should have said. These are old shots. I got them off the Internet.' Nkosi turned the picture over. 'This was from the '70s. She was Miss Massachusetts and competed in the Miss America contest. She is now sixty-four years old.'

Bond could see the resemblance, now that he knew the truth. Then he asked, 'Where is the Green Way office?'

'There are two,' Nkosi said. 'One nearby and one about twenty miles north of here — Hydt's major refuse disposal and recycling plant.'

'I need to get inside them, find out what he's up to.'

'Of course,' Bheka Jordaan said. There came a

lengthy pause. 'But you are speaking of legal means, correct?'

' 'Legal means'?'

'You can follow him on the street, you can observe him in public. But I cannot get a warrant for you to place a bug in his home or office. As I said, Severan Hydt has done nothing wrong here.'

Bond nearly smiled. 'In my job I don't generally ask for warrants.'

'Well, I do. Of course.'

'Captain, this man has twice tried to kill me, in Serbia and the UK, and yesterday he engineered the death of a young woman and possibly a CIA asset in Dubai.'

She frowned, sympathy evident in her face. 'That's very unfortunate. But those crimes did not happen on South African soil. If I'm presented with extradition orders from those jurisdictions, approved by a magistrate here, I will be happy to execute them. But barring that . . . ' She lifted her palms.

'We don't want him arrested,' Bond said, with exasperation. 'We don't want evidence for trial. The point of my coming here is to find out what he has planned for Friday and stop it. I intend to do that.'

'And you may, provided you do so legally. If you're thinking of breaking into his home or office, that would be trespass, subjecting *you* to a criminal complaint.' She turned her eyes, like black granite, towards him, and Bond had absolutely no doubt that she would enjoy ratcheting the shackles on to his wrists.

34

'He has to die.'

Sitting in his office at the Green Way International building in the centre of Cape Town, Severan Hydt was holding his phone tightly as he listened to Niall Dunne's chilly words. No, he reflected, that wasn't accurate. There was neither chill nor heat. His comment had been completely neutral.

Which was chilling in its own way.

'Explain,' Hydt said, absently tracing a triangle on the desktop with a long, yellowing fingernail.

Dunne told him that a Green Way worker had very likely learnt something about Gehenna. He was one of the legitimate workers in the Cape Town disposal plant to the north of the city, who had known nothing of Hydt's clandestine activities. He'd accidentally got into a restricted area in the main building and might have seen some emails about the project. 'He wouldn't know what they meant at this point but when the incident makes the news later in the week — which it's going to, of course — he might realise we were behind it and tell the police.'

'So what do you suggest?'

'I'm looking into it now.'

'But if you kill him, won't the police ask questions? Since he's an employee?'

'I'll take care of him where he lives — a squatters' camp. There won't be many police,

249

probably none at all. The taxis'll look into it, most likely, and they won't cause us any problems.'

In the townships, squatters' settlements and even the new *lokasies*, the minibus companies were more than just transport providers. They had taken on the role of vigilante judge and jury, hearing cases and tracking down and punishing criminals.

'All right. Let's move fast, though.'

'Tonight, after he gets home.'

Dunne disconnected and Hydt returned to his work. He'd spent all morning since their arrival making arrangements for the manufacture of Mahdi al-Fulan's new hard-drive destruction machines and for Green Way's sales people to start hawking them to clients.

But his mind wandered and he kept imagining the body of the young woman, Stella, now in a grave somewhere beneath the restless sands of the Empty Quarter south of Dubai. While her beauty in life hadn't aroused him, the picture in his mind's eye of her in a few months or years certainly did. And in a thousand, she'd be just like the bodies he'd viewed at the museum last night.

He rose, slipped his suit jacket on to a hanger and returned to his desk. He took and placed a string of phone calls, all relating to Green Way's legitimate business. None was particularly engaging . . . until the company's head of sales for South Africa, who was on the floor just below Hydt's, called.

'Severan, I've got some Afrikaner from

Durban on the line. He wants to talk to you about a disposal project.'

'Send him a brochure and tell him I'll be tied up till next week.' Gehenna was the priority and Hydt had no interest in taking on new accounts at the moment.

'He doesn't want to hire us. He's talking about some arrangement between Green Way and his company.'

'Joint venture?' Hydt asked cynically. Entrepreneurs always emerged when you started to enjoy success, and got publicity, in your chosen field. 'Too much going on now. I'm not interested. Thank him, though.'

'All right. Oh, but I was supposed to mention one thing. Something odd. He said to tell you that the problem he's got is the same as at Isandlwana in the 1870s.'

Hydt looked away from the documents on his desk. A moment later he realised he was gripping the phone hard. 'You're sure that's what he said?'

'Yes. 'The same as at Isandlwana'. No idea what he meant.'

'He's in Durban?'

'His company's headquarters are there. He's at his Cape Town office for the day.'

'See if he's free to come in.'

'When?' the sales manager asked.

A fractional pause, then Hydt said, 'Now.'

★ ★ ★

In January 1879, the war between Great Britain and the Zulu Kingdom kicked off in earnest with

251

a stunning defeat for the British. At Isandlwana, overwhelming forces (twenty thousand Zulus versus fewer than two thousand British and colonial troops) and some bad tactical decisions resulted in a complete rout. It was there that the Zulus broke the British Square, the famous defensive formation in which one line of soldiers fired while another, directly behind, reloaded, offering the enemy a nearly unremitting volley of bullets — in that instance, with the deadly Martini-Henry breech-loading rifles.

But the tactic hadn't worked; thirteen hundred British soldiers and allied forces died.

The 'disposal' problem that the Afrikaner had referred to could mean only one thing. The battle had occurred in January, the fiercely hot dog days of summer in the region of what was now KwaZulu-Natal; removing the bodies quickly was a necessity . . . and a major logistical issue.

The disposal of remains was also one of the major problems that Gehenna would present in future projects and Hydt and Dunne had been discussing it over the past month.

Why on earth would a businessman from Durban have a problem along these lines that required Hydt's assistance?

Ten lengthy minutes later his secretary stepped into his doorway. 'A Mr Theron is here, sir. From Durban.'

'Good, good. Show him in. Please.'

She vanished and returned a moment later with a tough-looking, edgy man, who glanced around Hydt's office cautiously, yet with an air of challenge. He was dressed in the business outfit common to South Africa: a suit and smart shirt, but no tie. Whatever his line he must have been successful; a heavy gold bracelet encircled his right wrist and his watch was a flashy Breitling. A gold initial ring too, which was a touch brash, Hydt thought.

'Morning.' The man shook Hydt's hand. He noticed the long yellowing fingernails but did not recoil, as had happened on more than one occasion. 'Gene Theron,' he said.

'Severan Hydt.'

They exchanged business cards.

Eugene J. Theron
President, EJT Services, Ltd
Durban, Cape Town and Kinshasa

Hydt reflected: an office in the capital of Congo, one of the most dangerous cities in Africa. This was interesting.

The man glanced at the door, which was open. Hydt rose and closed it, returned to his desk. 'You're from Durban, Mr Theron?'

'Yes, and my main office is there. But I travel a lot. And you?' The faint accent was melodious.

'London, Holland and here. I get to the Far East and India too. Wherever business takes me. Now, 'Theron'. The name's Huguenot, isn't it?'

'Yes.'

'We forget Afrikaners are not always Dutch.'

Theron lifted an eyebrow as if he'd heard such comments since he was a child and was tired of them.

Hydt's phone trilled. He looked at the screen. It was Niall Dunne. 'Excuse me a moment,' he said to Theron, who nodded. Then: 'Yes?' Hydt asked, pressing the phone close to his ear.

'Theron's legit. South African passport. Lives in Durban and has a security company with headquarters there, with branches here and in Kinshasa. Father's Afrikaner, mother's British. Grew up mostly in Kenya.'

Dunne continued, 'He's been suspected of supplying troops and arms to conflict regions in Africa, South East Asia and Pakistan. No active investigations. The Cambodians detained him in a human trafficking and mercenary investigation because of what he'd been up to in Shan, Myanmar, but let him go. Nothing in Interpol. And he's pretty successful, from what I can tell.'

Hydt had deduced that himself; the man's Breitling was worth around five thousand pounds.

'I just texted a picture to you,' Dunne added.

It appeared on Hydt's screen and showed the man in front of him. Dunne went on, 'But . . . whatever he's proposing, are you sure you want to think about it now?'

Hydt thought he sounded jealous — perhaps that the mercenary might have a project that would deflect attention from Dunne's plans for Gehenna. He said, 'Those sales figures are better than I thought. Thank you.' He disconnected. Then he asked Theron, 'How did you hear about me?'

Although they were alone Theron lowered his voice as he turned hard, knowing eyes on Hydt:

254

'Cambodia. I was doing some work there. Some people told me of you.'

Ah. Hydt understood now and the realisation gave him a thrill. Last year on business in the Far East he'd stopped to visit several gravesites of the infamous Killing Fields, where the Khmer Rouge had slaughtered millions of Cambodians in the 1970s. At the memorial at Choeung Ek, where nearly nine thousand bodies had been buried in mass graves, Hydt had spoken to several veterans about the slaughter and taken hundreds of pictures for his collection. One of the locals must have mentioned his name to Theron.

'You had business there, you say?' Hydt asked, thinking of what Dunne had learnt.

'Nearby,' Theron replied with a suitable brush of evasion.

Hydt was intensely curious but, a businessman first and foremost, he tried not to appear too enthusiastic. 'And what do Isandlwana and Cambodia have to do with me?'

'They are places where there was a great loss of life. Many bodies were interred where they fell in battle.'

Choeung Ek was genocide, not a battle, but Hydt did not correct him.

'They've become sacred areas. And that's good, I suppose. Except . . . ' The Afrikaner paused. 'I'll tell you about a problem I have become aware of and about a solution that has occurred to me. Then you can tell me if that solution is possible and if you have an interest in helping me achieve it.'

'Go on.'

Theron said, 'I have many connections to governments and companies in various parts of Africa.' He paused. 'Darfur, Congo, Central African Republic, Mozambique, Zimbabwe, a few others.'

Conflict regions, Hydt observed.

'And these groups are concerned about the consequences that arise after, say, a terrible natural disaster — like drought or famine or storms — or, frankly, anywhere that a major loss of life has occurred and bodies have been buried. As in Cambodia or Isandlwana.'

Hydt said innocently, 'Such cases have serious health implications. Water supply contamination, disease.'

'No,' Theron said bluntly. 'I mean something else. Superstition.'

'Superstition?'

'Say, for instance, because of a lack of money or resources, bodies have been left in mass graves. A shame, but it happens.'

'Indeed it does.'

'Now, if a government or a charity wishes to build something for the good of the people — a hospital, a housing development or a road in that area — they would be reluctant to do so. The land is perfectly good, there is money to build and workers who wish to be employed but many people would fear ghosts or spirits and be afraid to go to that hospital or move into those houses. It's absurd to me, and to you too, I'm sure. But that's how many people feel.' Theron shrugged. 'How sad for the citizens of those areas if their

256

health and safety were to suffer because of such foolish ideas.'

Hydt was riveted. He was tapping his nails on the desk. He forced himself to stop.

'So. Here is my idea: I am thinking of offering a service to, well, those government agencies to remove the human remains.' His face brightened. 'This will allow more building of factories, hospitals, roads, farms, schools, and it will help the poor, the unfortunate.'

'Yes,' Hydt said. 'Rebury the bodies somewhere else.'

Theron laid his hands on the desk. The gold initial ring glittered in a shaft of sunlight. 'That's one possibility. But it would be very expensive. And the problem might arise later at the new location.'

'True. But are there other alternatives?' Hydt asked.

'Your speciality.'

'Which is?'

In a whisper Theron said, 'Perhaps . . . recycling.'

Hydt saw the scenario clearly. Gene Theron, a mercenary and obviously a very successful one, had supplied troops and weapons to various armies and warlords throughout Africa, men who'd secretly massacred hundreds or thousands of people and hidden the bodies in mass graves. Now they were growing worried that legitimate governments, peacekeeping forces, the press or human-rights groups would discover the corpses.

Theron had made money by providing the means of destruction. Now he wanted to make money by removing the evidence of their use.

'It seemed to me an interesting solution,' Theron continued. 'But I wouldn't know how to go about it. Your . . . interests in Cambodia and your recycling business here told me that perhaps this is something you had thought of, too. Or would be willing to consider.' His cold eyes regarded Hydt. 'I was thinking maybe concrete or plaster. Or fertiliser?'

Turning the bodies into products that ensured they couldn't be recognised as human remains! Hydt could hardly contain himself. Utterly brilliant. Why, there must be hundreds of opportunities like this throughout the world — Somalia, the former Yugoslavia, Latin America . . . and there were killing fields aplenty in Africa. Thousands. His chest pounded.

'So, that's my idea. A fifty-fifty partnership. I provide the refuse and you recycle it.' Theron seemed to find this rather amusing.

'I think we may be able to do business.' Hydt offered his hand to the Afrikaner.

35

The worst risk of James Bond assuming the NOC — nonofficial cover — of Gene Theron was that Niall Dunne had perhaps got a look at him in Serbia or the Fens, or had been given his description in Dubai — if the blue-jacketed man who'd been tailing him was in fact working for Hydt.

In which case when Bond walked brazenly into the Green Way office in Cape Town and sought to hire Hydt to dispose of bodies hidden in secret graves throughout Africa, Dunne would either kill him on the spot or spirit him to their own personal killing field, where the job would be done with cold efficiency.

But now, having shaken hands with an intrigued Severan Hydt, Bond believed his cover was holding. So far. Hydt had been suspicious at first, of course, but he had been willing to give Theron the benefit of the doubt. Why? Because Bond had tempted him with a dangle, a lure he couldn't resist: death and decay.

That morning, at SAPS headquarters, Bond had contacted Philly Maidenstone and Osborne-Smith — his new ally — and they had data-mined Hydt's and Green Way's credit cards. They'd learnt that he'd not only travelled to the Killing Fields in Cambodia but to Krakow, Poland, where he'd taken several tours of Auschwitz. Among his purchases at the time

259

were double-A batteries and a second flash chip for a camera.

Man's got a whole new idea about porn . . .

Bond decided that to work his way into Hydt's life he would offer a chance to satisfy that lust: access to secret killing fields throughout Africa and a proposal to recycle human remains.

For the past three hours Bond had struggled, under the tutelage of Bheka Jordaan, to become an Afrikaner mercenary from Durban. Gene Theron would have a slightly unusual background: he'd had Huguenot rather than Dutch forebears and his parents favoured English and French in the household of his youth, which explained why he didn't speak much Afrikaans. A British education in Kenya would cover his accent. She had, however, made Bond learn something of the dialect; if Leonardo DiCaprio and Matt Damon had mastered the subtle intonation for recent films — and they were American, for heaven's sake — he could do so too.

While she'd coached him on facts that a South African mercenary might know, Sergeant Mbalula had gone to the evidence locker and found an incarcerated drug dealer's gaudy Breitling watch, to replace Bond's tasteful Rolex, and gold bracelet for the successful mercenary to wear. He'd then sped to a jeweller in the Gardens Shopping Centre in Mill Street, where he'd bought a gold signet ring and had it engraved with the initials *EJT*.

Meanwhile, Warrant Officer Kwalene Nkosi had worked feverishly with the ODG's I Branch in London to create the fictional Gene Theron, uploading to the Internet biographical information about the hard-boiled mercenary, with Photoshopped pictures and details about his fictional company.

A series of lectures on cover identities at Fort Monckton could be summarised in the instructor's introductory sentence: 'If you don't have a web presence, you're not real.'

Nkosi had also printed business cards for EJT Services Ltd, and MI6 in Pretoria pulled in some favours to get the company registered in record time, the documents backdated. Jordaan was not happy about this — it was, to her, a breach of the sacred rule of law — but since she and SAPS were not involved, she let it go. I Branch also created a fake criminal investigation in Cambodia about Theron's questionable behaviour in Myanmar, which mentioned shady activities in other countries too.

The *faux* Afrikaner was over the first hurdle. The second — and most dangerous — was close. Hydt was on the phone summoning Niall Dunne to meet 'a businessman from Durban'.

After he'd hung up, Hydt said casually, 'One question. Would you happen to have pictures of the fields? The graves?'

'That can be arranged,' Bond said.

'Good.' Hydt smiled like a schoolboy. He rubbed the back of his hand on his beard.

Bond heard the door behind him open. 'Ah, here is my associate, Niall Dunne . . . Niall, this is Gene Theron. From Durban.'

Now for it. Was he about to be shot? Bond

rose, turned and went up to the Irishman, looking straight into his eyes and offering the stiff smile of one businessman meeting another for the first time. As they shook hands, Dunne stared at him, a knife slash from the chill blue eyes.

There was, however, no suspicion in the gaze. Bond was confident he had not been recognised.

Closing the door behind him, the Irishman shot a quizzical glance at his boss, who handed him the EJT Services business card. The men sat down. 'Mr Theron has a proposition,' Hydt said enthusiastically. He ran through the plan in general terms.

Bond could see that Dunne, too, was intrigued. 'Yes,' he said. 'This could be good. Some logistics to consider, of course.'

Hydt continued, 'Mr Theron's going to arrange for us to see pictures of the locations. Give us a better idea of what would be involved.'

Dunne shot him a troubled glance — the Irishman wasn't suspicious, but seemed put off by this. He reminded Hydt, 'We have to be at the plant by fifteen thirty. That meeting?' He turned his eyes on Bond again. 'Your office is just round the corner.' He'd memorised the address at a glance, Bond noted. 'Why don't you get them now? Those pictures?'

'Well ... I suppose I could,' Bond said, stalling.

Dunne eyed him levelly. 'Good.' As he opened the door for Bond, his jacket swung open, revealing the Beretta pistol on his belt, probably the one he'd used to murder the men in Serbia.

Was it a message? A warning?

Bond pretended not to see it. He nodded to both men. 'I'll be back in thirty minutes.'

★ ★ ★

But Gene Theron had been gone only five when Dunne said, 'Let's go.'

'Where to?' Hydt frowned.

'To Theron's office. Now.'

Hydt noted that the gangly man had one of *those* expressions on his face, challenging, petulant.

That bizarre jealousy again. What went on in Dunne's soul?

'Why, don't you trust him?'

'It's not a bad idea, mind,' Dunne said off-handedly. 'We've been talking about disposal of the bodies. But it doesn't matter for Friday. It just seems a bit dodgy to me that he shows up out of the blue. Makes me nervous.'

As if such an emotion would ever register with the icy sapper.

Hydt relented. He needed somebody to keep his feet on the ground and it was true that he'd been seduced by Theron's proposition. 'You're right, of course.'

They picked up their jackets and left the office. Dunne directed them up the street, to the address printed on the man's business card.

The Irishman *was* right, but Severan Hydt prayed that Theron was legitimate. The bodies, the acres of bones. He wanted to see them so badly, to breathe in the air surrounding them.

263

And he wanted the pictures too.

They came to the office building where Theron's Cape Town branch was located. It was typical of the city's business district, functional metal and stone. This particular structure seemed half deserted. There was no guard in the lobby, which was curious. The men took the lift to the fourth floor and found the office door, number 403.

'There's no company name,' Hydt observed. 'Just the number. That's odd.'

'This doesn't look right,' Dunne said. He listened. 'I don't hear anything.'

'Try it.'

He did so. 'Locked.'

Hydt was fiercely disappointed, wondering if he'd given anything away to Theron, anything incriminating. He didn't think so.

Dunne said, 'We should get some of our security people together. When Theron comes back, if he does, we'll take him down to the basement. I'll find out what he's about.'

They were about to leave when Hydt, desperate to believe Theron was legitimate, said, 'Knock — see if anybody's in there.'

Dunne hesitated, then drew aside his jacket, exposing the Beretta's grip. The man's large knuckles rapped on the wooden door.

Nothing.

They turned to the lift.

Just then the door swung open.

Gene Theron blinked in surprise. 'Hydt . . . Dunne. What are you doing here?'

36

The Afrikaner hesitated for a moment then bluntly gestured the two men inside. They entered. There had been no sign outside but here on the wall was a modest plaque: *EJT Services Ltd, Durban, Cape Town, Kinshasa*.

The office was small and staffed with only three employees, their desks covered with files and the paperwork that is the mainstay of such entrepreneurial dens throughout the world, however noble or dark their products or services.

Dunne said, 'We thought we'd save you the trouble.'

'Did you now?' Theron responded.

Hydt knew that the mercenary understood that they had made their surprise visit because they didn't trust him completely. On the other hand, Theron was in a line of work where trust was as dangerous as unstable explosives, so his displeasure was minimal. After all, Theron must have done much the same, checking out Hydt's credentials with the Cambodians and elsewhere before coming to him with his proposal. That was how business worked.

Scuffed walls and windows offering a bleak view of a courtyard reminded Hydt that even illegal activity such as Theron plied was not necessarily as lucrative as the movies and news portrayed it. The biggest office, at the back, was Theron's but even that was modest.

One employee, a tall young African, was scrolling through an online catalogue of automatic weapons. Some were flagged with bold stars, indicating a 10 per cent discount. Another employee was typing urgently on a computer keyboard, using only his index fingers. Both men were in white shirts and narrow ties.

A secretary sat at a desk outside Theron's office. Hydt saw she was attractive but she was young and therefore of no interest to him.

Theron glanced at her. 'My secretary was just printing out some of the files we were talking about.' A moment later pictures of mass graves began easing from the colour printer.

Yes, these are good, Hydt thought, staring down at them. Very good indeed. The first images had been taken not long after the killings. Men, women and children had been gunned down or hacked to death. Some had suffered earlier amputations — hands or arms above the elbow — a popular technique used by warlords and dictators in Africa to punish and control the people. About forty or so lay in a ditch. The setting was sub-Saharan but it was impossible to say exactly where. Sierra Leone, Liberia, Ivory Coast, Central African Republic. There were so many possibilities on this troubled continent.

Other pictures followed, showing different stages of decay. Hydt lingered on those particularly.

'LRA?' Dunne asked, looking them over clinically.

It was the tall, skinny employee who answered. 'Mr Theron does *not* work with the Lord's Resistance Army.'

266

The rebel group, operating out of Uganda, the Central African Republic and parts of Congo and Sudan, had as its philosophy, if you could call it that, religious and mystical extremism — a violent Christian militia of sorts. It had committed untallied atrocities and was known, among other things, for employing child soldiers.

'There's plenty of other work,' Theron said.

Hydt was amused by his sense of morality.

Another half-dozen pictures rolled from the printer. The last few showed a large field from which protruded bones and partial bodies with desiccated skin.

Hydt showed the pictures to Dunne. 'What do you think?' He turned to Theron. 'Niall is an engineer.'

The Irishman studied them for a few minutes. 'The graves look shallow. It's easy to get the bodies out. The trick is to cover up the fact that they were there in the first place. Depending on how long they've been in the ground, once we remove them there'd be measurable differences in the soil temperature. That lasts for many months. It's detectable with the right equipment.'

'Months?' Theron asked, frowning. 'I had no idea.' He glanced at Dunne, then said to Hydt, 'He's good.'

'I call him the man who thinks of everything.'

Dunne said thoughtfully, 'Fast-growing vegetation could work. And there are some sprays that will eliminate DNA residue too. There's a lot to consider but nothing seems impossible.'

The technical issues fell away and Hydt

focused again on the images. 'May I keep these?'

'Of course. Do you want digital copies too? They'd be sharper.'

Hydt gave him a smile. 'Thank you.'

Theron put them on a flash drive and handed it to Hydt, who looked at his watch. 'I'd like to discuss this further. Are you free later?'

'I can be.'

But Dunne was frowning. 'You're at the meeting this afternoon and there's the fundraiser tonight.'

Hydt scowled. 'One of the charities I donate to is having an event. I have to be present. But . . . if you're free why don't you meet me there?'

'Do I have to give money?' Theron asked.

Hydt couldn't tell if he was joking. 'Not necessarily. You'll have to listen to a few speeches and drink some wine.'

'All right. Where is it?'

Hydt looked at Dunne, who said, 'At the Lodge Club. Nineteen hundred hours.'

Hydt added, 'You should wear a jacket but don't bother with a tie.'

'See you then.' Theron shook their hands.

They left his offices and made their way outside.

'He's legitimate,' Hydt said, half to himself.

They were en route to the Green Way office when Dunne took a phone call. After a few minutes he rang off and said, 'That was about Stephan Dlamini.'

'Who?'

'The worker we need to eliminate in the maintenance department. He's the one who might've seen the emails about Friday.'

'Oh. Right.'

'Our people found his shanty in Primrose Gardens, east of town.'

'How are you going to handle it?'

'It seems that his teenage daughter complained about a local drug dealer. He threatened to kill her. We'll set it up to make it seem that he's behind Dlamini's death. He's firebombed people before.'

'So Dlamini has a family.'

'A wife and five children,' Dunne explained. 'We'll have to kill them too. He could have told his wife what he saw. And if he's in a shanty town, the family will live in only one or two rooms, so anybody could have heard. We'll use grenades before the firebomb. I think suppertime is best — everybody will be in one room together.' Dunne shot a glance toward the tall man. 'They'll die fast.'

Hydt replied, 'I wasn't worried about them suffering.'

'I wasn't either. I just meant that it'll be a pretty easy way to kill them all quickly. Convenient, you know.'

★   ★   ★

After the men had left, Warrant Officer Kwalene Nkosi rose from the desk where he'd been scrolling through price lists for automatic weapons and nodded at the screen. 'It is truly amazing what you can buy online, isn't it, Commander Bond?'

269

'I suppose so.'

'If we buy nine machine guns, we can get one for free,' he joked to Sergeant Mbalula, the relentless two-finger typist.

'Thanks for that fast thinking about the LRA, Warrant Officer,' Bond said. He hadn't recognised the abbreviation for the Lord's Resistance Army — a group that any mercenary in Africa would have been familiar with. The operation might have ended there and then in disaster.

Bond's 'secretary', Bheka Jordaan, peered out of the window. 'They're heading away. I don't see any other security people.'

'We fooled them, I think,' said Sergeant Mbalula.

The trick indeed seemed to have been successful. Bond had been convinced that one of the men — the quick-minded Dunne, most likely — would want to see his branch in Cape Town. He believed that a good, solid set — a cover location — would be critical in seducing Hydt into believing he was an Afrikaner troubleshooter with a great many bodies to dispose of.

While Bond had telephoned Hydt to talk his way into Green Way, Jordaan had found a small government office leased by the Ministry of Culture but presently unused. Nkosi had printed some business cards with the address, and before Bond had gone to meet Hydt and Dunne, the SAPS officers had moved in.

'You'll be my partner,' Bond had told Jordaan, with a smile. 'It'll be a good cover for me to have a clever — and attractive — associate.'

She had bristled. 'To be credible, an office like

270

this needs a secretary and she must be a woman.'

'If you like.'

'I don't,' she had said stiffly. 'But that's how it must be.'

Bond had anticipated the men's visit but not that Hydt would want to see pictures of the killing fields, though he supposed he should have. The minute he'd left Hydt's office, he'd called Jordaan and told her to find photos of mass graves in Africa from military and law enforcement archives. Sadly, it had been all too easy and she'd downloaded a dozen by the time he'd returned from Hydt's office.

'Can you keep some people here for a day or two?' Bond asked. 'In case Dunne comes back.'

'I can spare one officer,' she said. 'Sergeant Mbalula, you will stay for the time being.'

'Yes, Captain.'

'I'll brief a patrolman on the situation and he will replace you.' She turned back to Bond. 'Do you think Dunne will return?'

'No, but it's possible. Hydt's the boss but he gets distracted. Dunne is more focused and suspicious. To my mind, that makes him more dangerous.'

'Commander.' Nkosi opened a battered briefcase. 'This came for you at Headquarters.' He produced a thick envelope. Bond ripped it open. Inside he found ten thousand rand in used banknotes, a fake South African passport, credit cards and a debit card, all in the name of Eugene J. Theron. I Branch had worked its magic once more.

There was also a note: *Reservation for open*

271

stay at Table Mountain Hotel, waterfront room.

Bond pocketed everything. 'Now, the Lodge Club, where I'm meeting Hydt tonight. What's it like?'

'Too expensive for me,' Nkosi said.

'It's a restaurant and venue for events,' Jordaan told him. 'I've never been either. It used to be a private hunting club. White men only. Then after the elections in 'ninety-four, when the ANC came to power, the owners chose to dissolve the club and sell the building rather than open up membership. The board wasn't concerned about admitting black or coloured men but they didn't want women. I'm sure you have no clubs like that at home, James, do you?'

He didn't admit that there were indeed such establishments in the UK. 'At my favourite club in London, you'll see pure democracy at work. Anyone at all is free to join . . . and lose money at the gaming tables. Just like I do. With some frequency, I might add.'

Nkosi laughed.

'If you're ever in London, I'd be delighted to show it to you,' he added to Jordaan.

She seemed to view this as yet more shameless flirting because she icily ignored the comment.

'I will drive you to your hotel.' The tall police officer's face wore a serious look. 'I think I shall quit the SAPS and see if you can get me a job in England, Commander.'

To work for the ODG or MI6, you had to be a British citizen and the child of at least one citizen or someone with substantial ties to the UK. There was also a residency requirement.

'After my great undercover work' — Nkosi's arm swept around the room — 'I now know I am quite the actor. I will come to London and work in the West End. That's where the famous theatres are — correct?'

'Well, yes.' Though Bond had not been to one voluntarily in years.

The young man said, 'I'm sure I will be quite successful. I'm partial to Shakespeare. David Mamet is quite good too. Without doubt.'

Bond supposed that, working for a boss like Bheka Jordaan, Nkosi did not get much of a chance to exercise his sense of humour.

37

The hotel was near Table Bay in the fashionable Green Point area of Cape Town. It was an older building, six storeys, in classic Cape style, and could not quite disguise its colonial roots — though it didn't try very hard; you could see them clearly in the meticulous landscaping presently being tended by a number of diligent workers, the delicate but firm reminder on placards about the dining-room dress code, the spotless white uniforms of the demure, ever-present staff, the rattan furniture on the sweeping veranda overlooking the bay.

Another clue was the enquiry as to whether Mr Theron would like a personal butler for his stay. He politely declined.

The Table Mountain Hotel — referred to everywhere as 'TM' in scrolling letters, from the marble floor to embossed napkins — was just the place where a well-heeled Afrikaner businessman from Durban would stay, whether a legitimate computer salesman or a mercenary with ten thousand bodies to hide.

After checking in, Bond started towards the lift, but something outside caught his eye. He popped into the gift shop for shaving foam he didn't need. Then he circled back to Reception to help himself to some complimentary fruit juice from a large glass tank surrounded by an arrangement of purple jacaranda and red and white roses.

He wasn't certain but someone might have been conducting surveillance. When he'd turned abruptly to get the juice, a shadow had vanished equally abruptly.

With many opportunities come many operatives . . .

Bond waited for a moment but the apparition didn't reappear.

Of course, operational life sows the seeds of paranoia and sometimes a passer-by is just a passer-by, a curious gaze signifies nothing more than a curious mind. Besides, you can't protect yourself from every risk in this business; if somebody wants you dead badly enough, they'll get their wish. Mentally Bond shrugged off the tail and took the lift to the first floor, where the rooms were accessed from an open balcony that overlooked the lobby. He stepped inside, closed and chained the door.

He tossed the suitcase on to one of the beds, strode to the window and closed the curtains. He slipped everything that identified him as James Bond into a large carbon-fibre envelope with an electronic lock on the flap and sealed it. With his shoulder he tipped a chest of drawers and pushed the pouch underneath. It might be found and stolen, of course, but any attempt to open it without his thumbprint on the lock would send an encrypted message to the ODG's C Branch, and Bill Tanner would send a *Crash Dive* text to alert him that his cover had been compromised.

He rang room service and ordered a club sandwich and a Gilroy's dark ale. Then he showered. By the time he'd dressed in a pair of battleship grey trousers and a black polo shirt, the food was at the door. He ran a comb through his damp hair, checked the peephole and let the waiter in.

The tray was placed on the small table, the bill signed as *E. J. Theron* — in Bond's own handwriting; that was one thing you never tried to fake, however deep your cover. The waiter pocketed his tip with overt gratitude. When Bond stepped back to the door to see the young man out and refix the chain, he automatically scanned the balcony and the lobby below.

He squinted, gazing down, then shut the door fast.

Damn.

Glancing with regret at the sandwich — and even more regretfully at the beer — he stepped into his shoes and flung open his suitcase. He screwed the Gemtech silencer on to the muzzle of his Walther and, although he'd done so recently at SAPS headquarters, eased the slide of the pistol back a few millimetres to verify that a round was in the chamber.

The gun went into the folds of today's edition of the *Cape Times*, which Bond then set on the tray between his sandwich and the beer. He lifted it one-handed over his shoulder and left the room, the tray obscuring his face. He was not dressed in a waiter's uniform but he moved briskly, head down, and might have been mistaken by a casual observer for a harried member of staff.

At the end of the corridor, he went through the fire doors of the stairwell, put the tray down and picked up the newspaper with its deadly contents. Then he descended a flight of stairs, quietly, to the ground floor.

Looking out through a porthole in the swing door, he spotted his target, sitting in an armchair in the shadows of a far corner of the lobby, nearly invisible. Facing away from Bond, he was scanning from his newspaper to the lobby to the first-floor balcony. Apparently he had missed Bond's escape.

Bond gauged distances and angles, the location and number of guests, staff and security guards. He waited while a porter wheeled a cart of suitcases past, a waiter carried a tray bearing a silver coffee pot to another guest at the far end of the lobby, and a cluster of Japanese tourists moved *en masse* out of the door, taking with them his target's attention.

Bond thought clinically: now.

He pushed out of the stairwell and walked fast towards the back of an armchair over which the crown of his target's head could just be seen. He circled around it and dropped into the chair just opposite, smiling as if he'd run into an old friend. He kept his finger off the trigger of the Walther, which Corporal Menzies had fine-tuned to a feather-light pull.

The freckled ruddy face glanced up. The man's eyes flashed wide in surprise that he'd been duped. In recognition too. The look said, no, it wasn't a coincidence. He *had* been conducting surveillance on Bond.

He was the man Bond had seen at the airport that morning, whom he'd originally taken for Captain Jordaan.

'Fancy seeing you here!' Bond said cheerfully, to allay the suspicions of anybody witnessing the rendezvous. He lifted the curled newspaper so that the muzzle of the silencer was focused on the bulky chest.

But, curiously, the surprise in the milky green eyes was replaced not by fear or desperation but amusement. 'Ah, Mr . . . Theron, is it? Is that who we are at the moment?' The accent was Mancunian. His pudgy hands swung up, palms out.

Bond cocked his head to one side. 'These rounds are nearly subsonic. With this suppressor, you'll be dead and I'll be gone long before anybody notices.'

'Oh, but you don't want to kill me. That would go down rather badly.'

Bond had heard plenty of monologues at moments like this when he'd got the draw on an opponent. Usually the *bons mots* were to buy time or for distraction as the target prepared himself for a desperate assault. Bond knew to ignore what the man was saying and watch his hands and body language.

Still, he could hardly dismiss the next lines issuing from the flabby lips. 'After all, what would M say if he heard you'd gunned down one of the Crown's star agents? And in *such* a beautiful setting.'

38

His name was Gregory Lamb, confirmed by the iris and fingerprint scan app — MI6's man on the ground in Cape Town. The agent Bill Tanner had told him to avoid.

They were in Bond's room, *sans* beer and sandwich; to his consternation, the tray containing his lunch had been whisked out of the stairwell by an efficient hotel employee by the time he and Lamb had returned to the first floor.

'You could've got yourself killed,' Bond muttered.

'I wasn't in any real danger. Your outfit doesn't give out those double noughts to trigger-happy fools . . . Now, now, my friend, don't get all ruffled. Some of us know what your Overseas Development outfit *really* does.'

'How did you know I was in town?'

'Put it together, didn't I? Heard about some goings-on and got in touch with friends at Lambeth.'

One of the disadvantages in having to use Six or DI for intelligence was that more people knew about your affairs than you might prefer. 'Why didn't you just contact me through secure channels?' Bond snapped.

'I was going to, but just as I got here I saw somebody playing shadow.'

Now Bond paid attention. 'Male, slim, blue jacket? Gold earring?'

'Well, now, didn't see the earring, did I? Eyes aren't what they used to be. But you've got the general kit right. Hovered about for a while, then vanished like the Tablecloth when the sun comes out. You know what I mean: the fog on Table Mountain.'

Bond was in no mood for travelogues. Dammit, the man who killed Yusuf Nasad and who had nearly done the same to Felix Leiter had learned he was here. He was probably the man Jordaan had told him about, the one who'd slipped into the country that morning from Abu Dhabi on a fake British passport.

Who the hell was he?

'Did you get a picture?' Bond asked.

'Drat no. The man was fast as a waterbug.'

'Spot anything else about him, type of mobile, possible weapons, vehicle?'

'None. Gone. Waterbug.' A shrug of the broad shoulders, which Bond supposed were as freckled and red as the face.

Bond said, 'You were at the airport when I landed. Why did you turn away?'

'I saw Captain Jordaan. She never took to me, for some reason. Maybe she thinks I'm the great white hunter colonist here to steal back her country. She gave me a bloody tongue lashing a few months ago, didn't she?'

'My chief of staff said you were in Eritrea,' Bond said.

'I was indeed — there and across the border in Sudan for the past week. Looks like their hearts're set on war so I tooled on up to make sure my covers would survive the gunplay. I got

280

that sorted and heard about an ODG operation.' His eyes dimmed. 'Surprised nobody gave me a bell about it.'

'The thinking was that you were involved in a rather serious op. Delicate,' Bond said judiciously.

'Ah.' Lamb seemed to believe this. 'Well, anyway, I thought I'd better race here to help out. You see, the Cape's tricky. It looks neat and clean and touristy but there's a lot more to it. I hate to blow my own trumpet, my friend, but you need somebody like me to weasel under the surface, tell you what's really going on. I'm *connected*. You know any other Six agent who's finagled local-government-development-fund money to finance his covers? I made the Crown a tidy profit last year.'

'All went to Treasury coffers, did it?'

Lamb shrugged. 'I've got a role to play, haven't I? To the world I'm a successful businessman. If you don't live your cover for all it's worth, well, a bit of sand gets into the works and the next thing you know there's a big pearl yelling, 'I'm a spy!' . . . Say, you mind if we hit that minibar of yours?'

Bond waved at it. 'Go ahead.' Lamb helped himself to a miniature of Bombay Sapphire gin, then another. He poured them into a glass. 'No ice? Pity. Well, never mind.' He sloshed in a bit of tonic.

'What *is* your cover?'

'Mostly I arrange cargo ship charters. Brilliant idea, if I say so myself. Gives me a chance to hobnob with the bad boys on the docks. I also do a spot of gold and aluminium exploration and road and infrastructure construction.'

'And you still have time to spy?'

'Good one, my friend!' For some reason Lamb started telling Bond his life story. He was a British citizen, as was his mother, and his father was South African. He'd come down here with his parents and decided he liked it better than life in Manchester. After training at Fort Monckton he'd asked to be sent back. Station Z was the only one he'd ever worked for . . . and the only one he'd ever cared to. He spent most of his time in the Western Cape but travelled frequently around Africa, attending to his NOC operations.

When he noticed Bond was not listening, he swigged at his drink and said, 'So what exactly are you working on? Something about this Severan Hydt? Now there's a name to conjure with. And Incident Twenty. Love it. Sounds rather like something from DI Fifty-five — you know, the characters looking into UFOs over the Midlands.'

Exasperated, Bond said, 'I was attached to Defence Intelligence. Division Fifty-five was about missiles or planes breaching British airspace, not UFOs.'

'Ah, yes, yes, I'm sure it was . . . Of course, that *would* be the line they'd give the public, wouldn't it?'

Bond was close to throwing him out. Still, it might just be worth picking his brain. 'You heard about Incident Twenty, then. Any thoughts on how it could relate to South Africa?'

'I did get the signals,' Lamb conceded, 'but I didn't pay much attention since the intercept said the attack was going to be on British soil.'

Bond reminded him of the exact wording, which gave no location but said merely that British interests would be 'adversely affected'.

'Could be anywhere, then. I didn't think of that.'

Or you didn't read it very carefully.

'And now the cyclone has touched down on my pitch. Odd how fate can strike, isn't it?'

The app on Bond's mobile that had verified Lamb's identity had also indicated his security clearance, which was higher than Bond would have guessed. Now he felt more or less comfortable in talking about the Gehenna plan, Hydt and Dunne. He asked again, 'So, have you any thoughts on a connection here? Thousands of people at risk, British interests threatened, the plan hatched in Severan Hydt's office.'

Eyes on his glass, Lamb said thoughtfully, 'The fact is, I don't know what kind of attack here would fit the bill. We've got plenty of British ex-pats and tourists and a lot of business interests with connections to London. But killing that many people in one fell swoop? Sounds like it'd have to be civil unrest. And I don't see that happening in South Africa. We've got our troubles here, there's no denying it — Zimbabwe asylum seekers, trade union unrest, corruption, AIDS . . . but we're still the most stable country on the continent.'

For once the man had provided Bond with some real insight, slight though it was. This reinforced his idea that, while buttons might be pushed in South Africa, Friday's deaths could likely occur elsewhere.

The man had finished most of his gin. 'You're not drinking?' When Bond didn't answer, he added, 'We miss the old days, don't we, my friend?'

Bond didn't know what the old days were and decided it was unlikely he would miss them, whatever they had been. He also decided too that he quite disliked the phrase 'my friend'. 'You said you didn't get on with Bheka Jordaan.'

Lamb grunted.

'What do you know about her?'

'She's damn good at her job, I'll give her that. She was the officer who ran that investigation of the NIA — the South African National Intelligence Agency — for conducting illegal surveillance on politicians here.' Lamb chuckled darkly. 'Not that that'd ever happen in *our* country, would it?'

Bond recalled that Bill Tanner had chosen to use an SAPS liaison rather than National Intelligence.

Lamb continued, 'They gave her the job hoping she'd fumble. But not Captain Jordaan. Oh no. That would *never* do.' His eyes gleamed perversely. 'She started to make headway in the case and everybody at the top got scared. Her boss at SAPS told her to lose the evidence against the NIA agents.'

'So she arrested him?'

'And *his* boss too!' Lamb roared with laughter and knocked back the last of his drink. 'She earned herself a big commendation.'

The Gold Cross for Bravery? 'Did she get roughed up in the investigation?'

'Roughed up?'

He mentioned her scarred arm.

'In a way. Afterwards she was promoted. Had to happen — politically. You know how *that* works. Well some of the SAPS men who were passed over didn't take too kindly to it. She got threats — women shouldn't be taking men's jobs, that sort of thing. Somebody chucked a Molotov cocktail under her squad car. She'd gone into the station, but there was a prisoner in the back seat, drunk and sleeping it off. None of the attackers saw him. She ran outside and saved him but got burnt in the process. They never found out who did it — the perpetrators were masked. But everybody knows it was people she was working with. Maybe still is.'

'God.' Now Bond believed he understood Jordaan's attitude towards him — perhaps she'd thought his flirtatious glance at the airport had meant he, too, didn't take a woman seriously as a police officer.

He explained to Lamb his next step: meeting Hydt tonight.

'Oh, the Lodge Club. It's all right. Used to be exclusive but now they let in everybody . . . Hey, I saw that look. I didn't mean what you think. I just have a low opinion of the general public. I do more business with blacks and coloureds than whites . . . There's that look again!'

' "Coloureds'?' Bond said sourly.

'It just means mixed-race and it's perfectly

285

acceptable here. No one would take offence.'

Bond's experience, however, was that people using such terms weren't the ones likely to be offended by them. But he wasn't going to debate politics with Gregory Lamb. Bond looked at the Breitling. 'Thanks for your thoughts,' he said, without much enthusiasm. 'Now, I've got work to do before my meeting with Hydt.' Jordaan had sent him some material on Afrikaners, South African culture and conflict regions that Gene Theron might have been active in.

Lamb rose and hovered awkwardly. 'Well, I stand ready to assist. I'm at your service. Really, anything you need.' He seemed painfully sincere.

'Thanks.' Bond felt the urge, absurdly, to slip him twenty rand.

Before he left, Lamb returned to the minibar and relieved it of two miniatures of vodka. 'You don't mind, do you? M's got a positively massive budget; everyone knows that.'

Bond saw him out.

Good riddance, he thought, as the door closed. Percy Osborne-Smith was a charmer by comparison with this fellow.

39

Bond sat at the expansive desk in the hotel suite, booted up his computer, logged on via his iris and fingerprint and scrolled through the information Bheka Jordaan had uploaded. He was ploughing through it when an encrypted email arrived.

James:
For your eyes only.
Have confirmed Steel Cartridge was a major active measure by KGB/SVR to assassinate clandestine MI6 and CIA agents and local assets, so that the extent of Russian infiltration would not be learnt, in attempt to promote détente during fall of Soviet Union and improve relations with the West.
The last Steel Cartridge targeted killings occurred late '80s or early '90s. Found only one incident so far: the victim was a private contractor working for MI6. Deep cover. No other details, except that the active measures agent made the death appear to be an accident.
Actual steel cartridges were sometimes left at the scenes of the deaths as warning to other agents to keep quiet.
    Am continuing investigation.
    Your other eyes,
    Philly

Bond slouched back in the chair, staring at the ceiling. Well, what do I do with *this*? he asked himself.

He read the message again, then sent a brief email thanking Philly. He rocked back and, in the mirror across the room, caught a glimpse of his eyes, hard and set like a predator's.

He reflected: so, the KGB active measures agent killed the MI6 contract op in the late eighties, early nineties.

James Bond's father had died during that period.

It had happened in December, not long after his eleventh birthday. Andrew and Monique Bond had dropped young James off with his aunt Charmian in Pett Bottom, Kent, leaving behind the promise that they would return in plenty of time for Christmas festivities. They had then flown to Switzerland and driven to Mont Blanc for five days of skiing and rock and ice climbing.

His parents' assurance, however, had been hollow. Two days later they were dead, having fallen from one of the astonishingly beautiful cliff faces of the Aiguilles Rouges, near Chamonix.

Beautiful cliffs, yes, impressive . . . but not excessively dangerous, not where they had been climbing. As an adult, Bond had looked into the circumstances of the accident. He'd learnt that the slope they'd fallen from did not require advanced climbing techniques; indeed, no one had ever been injured, let alone died, there. But, of course, mountains are notoriously fickle and Bond had taken at face value the story the gendarme had told his aunt: that his parents had fallen because a rope frayed at the same time as a large boulder had given way.

'*Mademoiselle, je suis désolé de vous dire . . .*'

When he was young, James Bond had enjoyed travelling with his parents to the foreign countries where Andrew Bond's company sent him. He'd enjoyed living in hotel suites. He'd enjoyed the local cuisines, very different from that served in the pubs and restaurants in England and Scotland. He'd been captivated with the exotic cultures — the dress, the music, the language.

He also enjoyed spending time with his father. His mother would hand James over to carers and friends when one of her freelance photojournalism assignments arose, but his father would occasionally take him to business meetings in restaurants or hotel lobbies. The boy would perch nearby, with a volume of Tolkien or an American detective novel, while his father talked to unsmiling men named Sam or Micah or Juan.

James was happy to be included — what son doesn't like to tag along with his dad? He had always been curious, though, as to why sometimes Andrew insisted that he join him while at others he said no quite firmly.

Bond had thought nothing more of this . . . until the training sessions at Fort Monckton.

It was there, in the lessons on clandestine operations, that one instructor had said something that caught his attention. The round, bespectacled man from MI6's tradecraft training section had told the group, 'In most clandestine situations, it's not advisable for an agent or an asset to be married or have children. If they happen to, it's best to make sure the family is kept far removed from the agent's operational life. However, there's one instance in which it's advantageous to have a quote 'typical' life. These agents will be operating in deepest cover and handling the most critical assignments, where the intelligence to be gathered is vital. In these cases a family life is important to remove the enemy's suspicions that they're operatives. Typically their official cover will be working for a company or organisation that interests enemy agents: infrastructure, information, armaments, aerospace or government. They will be posted to different locations every few years and take their families with them.'

James Bond's father had worked for a major British armaments company. He had been posted to a number of international capitals. His wife and son had accompanied him.

The instructor had continued, 'And in certain circumstances, on the most critical assignments — whether a brush pass or a face-to-face meeting — it's useful for the operative to take his child with him. Nothing proclaims innocence more than having a youngster with you. Seeing this, the enemy will almost always believe that you're the real deal — no parent would want to endanger his or her child.' He regarded the agents sitting before him in the classroom, their faces registering varying reactions at his passionless message. 'Combating evil sometimes requires a suspension of accepted values.'

Bond had thought: his father a spy?

Impossible. Absurd.

Still, after he had left Fort Monckton he spent some time looking into his father's past, but found no evidence of a clandestine life. The only evidence was a series of payments made to his aunt for her and James's benefit, over and above the proceeds from his parents' insurance policy. These were made annually until James had turned eighteen by a company that must have had some affiliation with Andrew's employer, though he could never find out exactly where it was based or what the nature of the payments had been.

Eventually he convinced himself that whole idea was mad and forgot about it.

Until the Russian signal about Steel Cartridge.

Because one other aspect of his parents' death had been largely overlooked.

In the accident report that the gendarmes had prepared, it was mentioned that a steel rifle cartridge, 7.62mm, had been found near his father's body.

Young James had received it among his parents' effects and, since Andrew had been an executive with an arms company, it was assumed that the bullet had been a sample of his wares to show to customers.

On Monday, two days ago, after he had read the Russian report, Bond had gone into the online archives of his father's company. He'd learnt that it did not manufacture ammunition. Neither had it ever sold any weapons that fired a 7.62mm round.

This was the bullet that sat now in a

conspicuous place on the mantelpiece of his London flat.

Had it been dropped accidentally by a hunter? Or left intentionally as a warning?

The KGB's reference to Operation Steel Cartridge had solidified within Bond the desire to learn whether or not his father had been a secret agent. He had to. He did not need to reconcile himself to the possibility that his father had lied to him. All parents deceive their children. In most cases, though, it's for the sake of expedience or through laziness or thoughtlessness; if *his* father had lied it was because the Official Secrets Act had compelled him to.

Neither did he need to know the truth so that he could — as a TV psychiatrist might suggest — revisit his youthful loss and mourn somehow more authentically. What nonsense.

No, he wanted to know the truth for a much simpler reason, one that fitted him like a Savile Row bespoke suit: the person who had killed his parents might still be at large in the world, enjoying the sun, sitting down to a pleasant meal or even conspiring to take other lives. If such were the case, Bond knew he would make certain that his parents' assassin met the same fate as they had, and he would do so efficiently and in accordance with his official remit: by any means necessary.

40

At close to five p.m. on Wednesday, Bond's mobile emitted the ringtone reserved for emergency messages. He hurried from the bathroom, where he'd just showered, and read the encrypted email. It was from GCHQ, reporting that Bond's attempt to bug Severan Hydt had been somewhat successful. Unknown to Captain Bheka Jordaan, the flash drive that Bond had given Hydt, holding digital pictures of the killing fields in Africa, also contained a small microphone and transmitter. What it lacked in audio resolution and battery life, it made up for in range. The signal was picked up by a satellite, amplified and beamed down to one of the massive receiving antennae at Menwith Hill in the beautiful Yorkshire countryside.

The device had transmitted fragments of a conversation Hydt and Dunne had had just after they'd left the fictional EJT Services office in downtown Cape Town. The words had finally made their way through the decryption queue and been read by an analyst, who had flagged them as critical and shot the missive to Bond.

He now read the CX — the raw intelligence — and the analysed product. It seemed that Dunne was planning to kill one of Hydt's workers, Stephan Dlamini, and his family, because the employee had seen something in a secure part of Green Way that he shouldn't have, perhaps information that related to Gehenna. Bond's goal was clear: save him at all costs.

Purpose . . . response.

The man lived outside Cape Town. The death would be made to look like a gang attack. Grenades and firebombs would be used. And the attack would occur at suppertime.

After that, though, the battery died and the device had stopped transmitting.

At suppertime. Perhaps any moment now.

Bond hadn't managed to rescue the woman in Dubai. He wasn't going to let this family die now. He needed to find out what Dlamini had learnt.

But he could hardly contact Bheka Jordaan and tell her what he'd found out via illegal surveillance. He picked up the phone and called the concierge.

'Yes, sir?'

'I have a question for you,' Bond said casually. 'I had a problem with my car today and a local fellow helped me out. I didn't have much cash with me and I wanted to give him something for his trouble. How would I go about finding his address? I have his name and the town he lives in, but nothing more.'

'What's the town?'

'Primrose Gardens.'

There was silence. Then the concierge said, 'It's a township.'

A squatters' camp, Bond recalled, from the briefing material Bheka Jordaan had given him. The shacks rarely had standard postal addresses.

'Well, could I go there, ask if anyone knew him?'

294

Another pause. 'Well, sir, it might not be very safe.'

'I'm not too worried about that.'

'I think it would not be practical, either.'

'Why is that?'

'The population of Primrose Gardens is around fifty thousand.'

★ ★ ★

At 17:30 hours, as autumn dusk descended, Niall Dunne watched Severan Hydt leave the Green Way office in Cape Town, striding tall and with a certain elegance to his limousine.

Hydt's feet didn't splay, *his* posture wasn't hunched, *his* arms didn't swing from side to side. ('Oi, lookit the tosser! Niall's a bleedin' giraffe!')

Hydt was on his way home, where he would change, then take Jessica to the fundraiser at the Lodge Club.

Dunne was standing in the Green Way lobby, staring out of the window. His eyes lingered on Hydt as he vanished down the street, accompanied by one of his Green Way guards.

Watching him leave, en route to his home and his companion, Dunne felt a pang.

Don't be so bloody ridiculous, he told himself. Concentrate on the job. All hell's going to break loose on Friday and it'll be your fault if a single cog or gear malfunctions.

Concentrate.

So he did.

Dunne left Green Way, collected his car and

295

drove out of Cape Town towards Primrose Gardens. He would meet up with a security man from the company and proceed with the plan, which he now ran through his mind: the timing, the approach, the number of grenades, the firebomb, the escape.

He reviewed the blueprint with precision and patience. The way he did everything.

This is Niall. He's brilliant. He's my draughtsman . . .

But other thoughts intruded and his sloping shoulders slumped even more as he pictured his boss at the fundraising gala later that night. The pang stabbed him again.

Dunne supposed people wondered why he was alone, why he didn't have a partner. They assumed the answer was that he lacked the ability to feel. That he was a machine. They didn't understand that, according to the concept of classical mechanics, there were *simple* machines — like screws and levers and pulleys — and *complex* machines, like engines, which by definition transferred energy into motion.

Well, he reasoned logically, calories were turned into energy, which moved the human body. So, yes, he *was* a machine. But so were we all, every creature on earth. That didn't preclude the capacity for love.

No, the explanation of his solitude was simply that the object of his desire didn't, in turn, desire him.

How embarrassingly mundane, how common.

And bloody unfair, of course. God, it was unfair. No draughtsman would design a machine in which the two parts necessary to create harmonious movement didn't work perfectly, each needing the other and in turn satisfying the reciprocal need. But that was exactly the situation in which he found himself: he and his boss were mismatched parts.

Besides, he thought bitterly, the laws of attraction were far riskier than the laws of mechanics. Relationships were messy, dangerous and plagued with waste and while you could keep an engine humming for hundreds of thousands of hours, love between human beings often sputtered and seized just after it caught.

It betrayed you too, far more often than machinery did.

Bollocks, he told himself with what passed for anger within Niall Dunne. Forget all this. You have a job to do tonight. He ran through his blueprint again and then once more.

As the traffic thinned he drove quickly east of the city, heading towards the township along dark roads gritty and damp as a riverside dock.

He pulled into a shopping-centre car park and killed the engine. A moment later a battered van stopped behind him. Dunne climbed from his car and got into the other vehicle, nodding to the security man, very large, wearing military fatigues. Without saying a word, they set off at once and, in ten minutes, were driving through the unmarked streets of Primrose Gardens. Dunne climbed into the back of the van, where there were no windows. He was, of course, distinctive here, with his height, his hair. More significant, he was white and would be extremely conspicuous in a South African township after dark. It was possible that the drug dealer who was threatening Dlamini's daughter was white or had whites who worked for him, but Dunne decided it was better to stay hidden — at least until the time to throw the grenades and fire bombs through the windows of the shanty.

They drove along the endless paths that served as roads in the shanty town, past packs of running children, skinny dogs, men sitting on doorsteps.

'No GPS,' the huge security man said, his first words. He wasn't smiling and Dunne didn't know if he was making a joke. The man had spent two hours that afternoon tracking down Dlamini's shack. 'There it is.'

They parked across the road. The place was tiny, one storey, as were all the shacks in Primrose Gardens, and the walls were constructed of mismatched panels of plywood and corrugated metal, painted bold red, blue, yellow, as if in defiance of the squalor. A clothes-line hung in the yard to the side, festooned with laundry for a family ranging in age, it seemed, from five or six to adulthood.

This was an efficient location for a kill. The shack was opposite a patch of empty ground so there would be few witnesses. Not that it mattered — the van had no number plate, and white vehicles of this sort were as common in the Western Cape as sea gulls at Green Way.

They sat in silence for ten minutes, just on the verge of attracting attention. Then the security man said, 'There he is.'

Stephan Dlamini was walking down the dusty road, a tall, thin man with greying hair, wearing a faded jacket, orange T-shirt and brown jeans. Beside him was one of his sons. The boy, who was about eleven, carried a mud-streaked football, and wore a Springboks rugby shirt, without a jacket, despite the autumn chill.

Dlamini and the boy paused outside to kick the ball back and forth for a moment or two. Then they entered their home. Dunne nodded to the security man. They pulled on ski masks. Dunne surveyed the shanty. It was larger than most, but the explosives and incendiary were sufficient. The curtains were drawn across the windows, the cheap fabric glowing with light from inside.

For some reason Dunne found himself thinking again about his boss, at the event that night. He put the image away.

He gave it five minutes more, to make sure that Dlamini had used the toilet — if there was one in the shack — and that the family was seated at the dinner table.

'Let's go,' Dunne said. The security guard nodded. They stepped out of the van, each holding a powerful grenade, filled with deadly copper shot. The street was largely deserted.

Seven family members, Dunne reflected. 'Now,' he whispered. They pulled the pins on the grenades and flung them through each of the two windows. In the five seconds of silence that followed, Dunne grabbed the firebomb — a petrol can with a small detonator — and readied it. When stunning explosions shook the ground

299

and blew out the remaining glass, he threw the incendiary through the window and the two men leapt into the van. The security man started the engine and they sped off.

Exactly five seconds later, flames erupted from the windows and, spectacularly, a stream of fire from the cooking stove chimney rose straight into the air twenty feet, reminding Dunne of the fireworks displays he'd so enjoyed as a boy in Belfast.

41

'*Hayi! Hayi!*'

The woman's wail filled the night, as she stared at the fiery shack, her home, tears lensing her eyes.

She and her five children were clustered behind the inferno. The back door was open, providing a wrenching view of the rampaging flames destroying all of the family's possessions. She struggled to run inside and rescue what she could but her husband, Stephan Dlamini, gripped her hard. He spoke to her in a language James Bond took to be Xhosa.

A large crowd was gathering and an informal fire brigade had assembled, passing buckets of water in a futile attempt to extinguish the raging flames.

'We have to leave,' Bond said to the tall man standing beside him, next to an unmarked SAPS van.

'Without doubt,' said Kwalene Nkosi.

Bond meant that they should get the family out of the township before Dunne realised they were still alive.

Nkosi, though, had a different concern. The warrant officer had been eyeing the growing crowd, who were staring at the white man; the collective gaze was not friendly.

'Display your badge,' Bond told him.

Nkosi's eyes widened. 'No, no, Commander,

301

that is not a wise idea. Let us leave. Now.'

They shepherded Stephan Dlamini and his family into the van. Bond got in with them and Nkosi climbed behind the wheel, gunned the engine and steered them away into the night.

They left behind the angry, confused crowd and the tumultuous flames . . . but not a single injury.

It had been a true race to the finish line to save the family.

After he'd learned that Dlamini was going to be targeted by Dunne and that he lived virtually anonymously in a huge township, Bond had struggled to come up with a way to locate him. GCHQ and MI6 could find no mobile in his name or any personal records in South African census or trade-union records. He had taken a chance and called Kwalene Nkosi. 'I'm going to tell you something, Warrant Officer, and I hope I can rely on you to keep it to yourself. From *everyone*.'

There'd been a pause and the young man had said cautiously, 'Go on.'

Bond had laid out the problem, including the fact that the surveillance had been illegal.

'Your signal is breaking up, Commander. I missed that last part.'

Bond had laughed. 'But we have to find where this Stephan Dlamini lives. Now.'

Nkosi had sighed. 'It is going to be difficult. Primrose Gardens is huge. But I have an idea.' The minibus taxi operations, it seemed, knew far more about the shanty towns and *lokasies* than the local government did. The warrant officer would begin calling them. He and Bond had met, then driven fast to Primrose Gardens, Nkosi continuing his search for the family's shack via his mobile. At close to six p.m. they'd been cruising through the township when a taxi driver had reported that he knew where Dlamini lived. He'd directed Bond and Nkosi there.

As they'd approached, they'd seen another van at the front, a white face glancing out.

'Dunne,' Nkosi had said.

He and Bond had veered away and parked behind the shanty. They'd pushed through the back door and the family had panicked, but Nkosi had told them, in their own language, that the men had come to save them. They had to get out immediately. Stephan Dlamini was not at home yet, but soon would be.

A few minutes later he'd come through the door with his young son, and Bond, knowing the attack was imminent, had had no choice but to draw his gun and force them out of the back door. Nkosi had just finished explaining Bond's purpose and the danger, when the grenades went off, followed by the petrol bomb.

Now they were on the N1, cruising west. Dlamini gripped Bond's hand and shook it. Then he leant forward to the front passenger seat and hugged him. Tears stood in his eyes. His wife huddled in the back with her children, studying Bond suspiciously as the agent told him who'd been behind the attack.

Finally, after hearing the story, Dlamini asked in dismay, 'Mr Hydt? But how can that be? He is best boss. He treat all of us good. Very good. I

303

am not understanding this.'

Bond explained. It seemed that Dlamini had learnt something about illegal activities Hydt and Dunne were engaged in.

His eyes flashed. 'I know what you are speaking of.' His head bobbed up and down. He told Bond that he was a maintenance man at the Green Way plant north of town. That morning he'd found the door to the company's Research and Development office left open for deliveries. The two employees inside were at the back of the room. Dlamini had seen an overflowing bin inside. The rubbish there was supposed to be handled by somebody else but he decided to empty it anyway. 'I just was trying to do good job. That's all.' He shook his head. 'I go inside and start to empty this bin when one of the workers sees me and starts screaming at me. What did I see? What was I looking at? I said, 'Nothing.' He ordered me out.'

'And *did* you see anything that might've upset them?'

'I don't think so. On the computer beside the bin there was a message, an email, I think. I saw 'Serbia' in English. But I paid no more attention.'

'Anything else?'

'No, sir.'

Serbia . . .

So, some of the secrets to Gehenna lay beyond the door to Research and Development.

Bond said to Nkosi, 'We have to get the family away. If I give them money, is there a hotel where they can stay until the weekend?'

'I can find some rooms for them.'

Bond gave them fifteen hundred rand. The man blinked as he stared at the sum. Nkosi explained to Dlamini that he would have to stay in hiding for a short while.

'And have him call other family members and close friends. He should tell them that he and his family are all right but that they have to play dead for a few days. Can you plant a story in the media about their deaths?'

'I think so.' The warrant officer was hesitating. 'But I'm wondering if . . . ' His voice faded.

'We'll keep this between ourselves. Captain Jordaan does not need to know.'

'Without doubt, that is best.'

As the glorious vista of Cape Town rose before them, Bond glanced at his watch. It was time for the second assignment of the night — one that would require him to enlist a very different set of tradecraft skills from dodging grenades and firebombs, though he suspected that this job would be no less challenging.

42

Bond wasn't impressed by the Lodge Club.

Perhaps back in the day, when it was the enclave of hunters in jodhpurs and jackets embellished with loops to hold ammunition for their big-five game rifles, it had been more posh but the atmosphere now was that of a function room hosting simultaneous wedding receptions. Bond wasn't even sure if the Cape buffalo head, staring down at him angrily from near the front door, was real or had been manufactured in China.

He gave the name Gene Theron to one of the attractive young women at the door. She happened to be blonde and voluptuous and wearing a tight-fitting crimson dress with a lazy neckline. The other hostess was of Zulu or Xhosa ancestry but equally built and clad. Bond suspected that whoever ran the fundraising organisation knew how to tactically appeal to what was, of whatever race, predominantly a male donor pool. He added, 'Guest of Mr Hydt.'

'Ah, yes,' the golden-haired woman said and let him into the low-lit room where fifty or so people milled about. Still wine, champagne and soft drinks were on offer and Bond went for the sparkling.

Bond had followed Hydt's suggestions on dress and the Durban mercenary was in light grey trousers, a black sports jacket and a light blue shirt, no tie.

Holding his champagne flute, Bond looked around the plush hall. The group behind the event was the International Organisation Against Hunger, based in Cape Town. Pictures on easels showed workers handing out large sacks to happy recipients, women mostly, Hercules planes being unloaded and boats laden with sacks of rice or wheat. There were no pictures of starving emaciated children. A tasteful compromise all around. You wanted donors to feel slightly, but not too, uneasy. Bond guessed that the world of altruism had to be as carefully navigated as Whitehall politics.

From speakers in the ceiling, the harmonies of Ladysmith Black Mambazo and the inspirational songs of the Cape Town singer Verity provided an appealing soundtrack to the evening.

The event was a silent auction — tables were filled with all sorts of items donated by supporters of the group: a football signed by players from Bafana Bafana, the South African national football team, a whale-watching cruise, a weekend getaway in Stellenbosch, a Zulu sculpture, a pair of diamond earrings and much more. The guests would circulate and write their bids for each item on a sheet of paper; the one who'd put down the highest amount when the auction closed would win the article. Severan Hydt had donated a dinner for four, worth eight thousand rand — about seven hundred pounds, Bond calculated — at a first-class restaurant.

The wine flowed generously and waiters circulated with silver trays of elaborate canapés.

Ten minutes after Bond had arrived, Severan

Hydt appeared with his female companion on his arm. Niall Dunne was nowhere to be seen. He nodded to Hydt, who was in a nicely cut navy-blue suit, probably American, if he read the sloping shoulders right. The woman — her name, he recalled, was Jessica Barnes — was in a simple black dress and heavily bejewelled, all diamonds and platinum. Her stockings were pure white. Not a hint of colour was to be found on her; she didn't even wear a touch of lipstick. His earlier impression held: how gaunt she was, despite her attractive figure and face. Her austerity aged her considerably, giving her a ghostly look. Bond was curious; every other woman here of Jessica's age had clearly spent hours dolling herself up.

'Ah, Theron,' Hydt boomed and marched forward, detaching himself from Jessica, who followed. As Bond shook his hand, the woman regarded him with a noncommittal smile. He turned to her. Tradecraft requires constant, often exhausting effort. You must maintain an expression of faint curiosity when meeting a person you're familiar with only through surveillance. Lives have been lost because of a simple slip: 'Ah, good to see you again,' when in fact you've never met face to face.

Bond kept his eyes neutral as Hydt introduced her. 'This is Jessica.' He turned to her. 'Gene Theron. We're doing business together.'

The woman nodded and, though she held his eye, took his hand tentatively. It was a sign of insecurity, Bond concluded. Another indication of this was her handbag, which she kept over her shoulder and pinned tight between arm and ribcage.

Small-talk ensued, Bond reciting snippets from Jordaan's lessons about the country, taking care to be accurate, assuming that Jessica might report their conversation to Hydt. In a low voice he offered that the South African government should busy itself with more important things than renaming Pretoria Tshwane. He was glad the trade union situation was calming. Yes, he enjoyed life on the east coast. The beaches near his home in Durban were particularly nice, especially now that the shark nets were up, though he'd never had any problems with the Great Whites, which occasionally took bites out of people. They talked then about wildlife. Jessica had visited the famed Kruger game reserve again recently and seen two adolescent elephants tear up trees and bushes. It had reminded her of the gangs in Somerville, Massachusetts, just north of Boston — teenagers vandalising public parks. Oh, yes, he'd thought her accent was American.

'Have you ever been there, Mr Theron?'

'Call me, Gene, please,' Bond said, scrolling mentally through the biography written by Bheka Jordaan and I Branch. 'No,' he said. 'But I hope to some day.'

Bond looked at Hydt. His body language had shifted; he was giving out signs of impatience. A glance at Jessica suggested he wished her to leave them. Bond thought of the abuse Bheka Jordaan had endured at the hands of her co-workers. This was different only in degree. A moment later the woman excused herself to 'powder her nose', an expression Bond had not heard in years. He thought it ironic that she used the term, considering that she probably wouldn't be doing so.

When they were alone, Hydt said to him, 'I've thought more about your proposal and I'd like to move forward.'

'Good.' They took refills of champagne from an attractive young Afrikaner woman. Bond said, '*Dankie*,' and reminded himself not to overdo his act.

He and Hydt retired to a corner of the room, the older man waving to and shaking hands with people on the way. When the men were alone, beneath the mounted head of a gazelle or antelope, Hydt peppered Bond with questions about the number of graves, the acreage, the countries they were in, and how close the authorities were to discovering some of the killing fields. As Bond ad-libbed the answers, he couldn't help but be impressed with the man's thoroughness. It seemed he'd spent all afternoon thinking about the project. He was careful to remember what he told Hydt and made a mental note to write it down later so that he would be consistent in the future.

After fifteen minutes Bond said, 'Now, there are things I would like to know. First, your operation here. I'd like to see it.'

'I think you should.'

When he didn't suggest a time, Bond said, 'How about tomorrow?'

'That might be difficult, with my big project on Friday.'

Bond nodded. 'Some of my clients are eager to

310

move forward. You are my first choice but if there'll be delays I'll have to . . . '

'No, no. Please. Tomorrow will be fine.'

Bond began to probe more but just then the lights dimmed and a woman ascended the raised platform near where Hydt and Bond were standing. 'Good evening,' she called out, her low voice glazed with a South African accent. 'Welcome, everyone. Thank you for coming to our event.'

She was the managing director of the organisation and Bond was amused by her name: Felicity Willing.

She wasn't, to Bond's eye, cover-girl beautiful, as was Philly Maidenstone. However, her face was intense, striking. Expertly made up, it exuded a feline quality. Her eyes were a deep green, like late summer leaves caught in the sun, and her hair dark blonde, pulled back severely and pinned up, accentuating the determined angles of her nose and chin. She wore a close-fitting navy-blue cocktail dress that was cut low at the front and lower still at the back. Her silver shoes sported thin straps and precarious heels. Faintly pink pearls shone at her throat and she wore one ring, also a pearl, on her right index finger. Her nails were short and uncoloured.

She scanned the audience with a penetrating, almost challenging gaze and said, 'I must warn you all . . . ' Tension swelled. 'At university I was known as Felicity *Wilful* — an appropriate name, as you'll find out later when I make the rounds. I advise you all, for your own safety, to

311

keep your chequebooks at the ready.' A smile replaced the fierce visage.

As the laughter died down, Felicity began to talk about the problems of hunger. 'Africa must import twenty-five per cent of its food . . . While the population has soared, crop yields today are no higher than they were in 1980 . . . In places like the Central African Republic, nearly a third of all households are food insecure . . . In Africa iodine deficiency is the number-one cause of brain damage, vitamin A deficiency is the number-one cause of blindness . . . Nearly three hundred million people in Africa do not have enough to eat — that number equals the entire population of the United States . . . '

Africa, of course, was not alone in the need for food aid, she continued, and her organisation was attacking the plague on all fronts. Thanks to the generosity of donors, including many here, the group had recently expanded its charter from being a purely South African charity to an international one, opening offices in Jakarta, Port-au-Prince and Mumbai, with others planned.

And, she added, the biggest shipment of maize, sorghum, milk powder and other high-nutrient staples ever to arrive in Africa was soon to be delivered in Cape Town for distribution across the continent.

Felicity acknowledged the applause. Then her smile vanished and she gazed at the crowd with piercing eyes once more, speaking in a low, even menacing, voice about the need to make poorer countries independent of Western 'agropolies'. She railed against the prevailing approach of

America and Europe to end hunger: foreign-owned megafarms forcing their way into third-world nations and squeezing out the local farmers — the people who knew how to get the best yield from the land. Those enterprises were using Africa and other nations as laboratories to test untried methods and products, like synthetic fertilisers and genetically engineered seeds.

'The vast majority of international agribusiness cares only about profit, not about relieving the suffering of the people. And this is simply not acceptable.'

Finally, having delivered her assault, Felicity smiled and singled out the donors, Hydt among them. He responded to the applause with a wave. He was smiling too, but his whisper to Bond told a different story: 'If you want adulation, just give away money. The more desperate they are, the more they love you.' He clearly didn't want to be here.

Felicity stepped off the platform to circulate as the guests continued their silent bidding.

Bond said to Hydt, 'I don't know if you have plans but I was thinking we could go for some dinner. On me?'

'I'm sorry, Theron, but I have to meet an associate who's just arrived in town for that project I mentioned.'

Gehenna . . . Bond certainly wanted to meet whoever this man was. 'I'd be happy to take everyone out, your associate too.'

'Tonight's no good, I'm afraid,' Hydt said absently, pulling his iPhone out and scrolling through messages or missed calls. He glanced up

313

and spotted Jessica standing by herself awkwardly in front of a table on which items were being offered for auction. When she looked at him he beckoned her over impatiently.

Bond tried to think of some other way to conjure an invitation but decided to back off before Hydt became suspicious. Seduction in tradecraft is like seduction in love; it works best if you make the object of your desire come to you. Nothing ruins your efforts faster than desperate pursuit.

'Tomorrow then,' Bond said, seemingly distracted and glancing at his own phone.

'Yes — good.' Hydt looked up. 'Felicity!'

With a smile, the charity's managing director detached herself from a fat, balding man in a dusty dinner jacket. He'd been gripping her hand for far longer than courtesy dictated. She joined Hydt, Jessica and Bond.

'Severan. Jessica.' They brushed cheeks.

'And an associate, Gene Theron. He's from Durban, in town for a few days.'

Felicity gripped Bond's hand. He asked obvious questions about her organisation and the shipments of food arriving soon, hoping Hydt would change his mind about dinner.

But the man looked once more at his iPhone and said, 'I'm afraid we have to be going.'

'Severan,' Felicity said, 'I don't think my remarks really conveyed our gratitude. You've introduced some important donors to us. I really can't thank you enough.'

Bond took note of this. So she knew the names of some of Hydt's associates. He wondered how

314

best to exploit this connection.

Hydt said, 'I'm delighted to help. I've been lucky in life. I want to share that good fortune.' He turned to Bond. 'See you tomorrow, Theron. Around noon, if that's convenient. Wear old clothes and shoes.' He brushed his curly beard with an index finger whose nail reflected a streak of jaundiced light. 'You'll be taking a tour of hell.'

After Hydt and Jessica had left, Bond turned to Felicity Willing. 'Those statistics were disturbing. I might be interested in helping.' Standing close, he was aware of her perfume, a musky scent.

'Might be interested?' she asked.

He nodded.

Felicity kept a smile on her face but it didn't reach her eyes. 'Well, Mr Theron, for every donor who actually writes a cheque, two others say they're 'interested' but I never see a rand. I'd rather somebody told me up front they don't want to give anything. Then I can get on with my business. Forgive me if I'm blunt, but I'm fighting a war here.'

'And you don't take prisoners.'

'No,' she said, smiling sincerely now. 'I don't.'

Felicity Wilful . . .

'Then I'll most certainly help,' Bond said, wondering what A Branch would say when they encountered a donation on his expense account back in London. 'I'm not sure I'm able to rise to Severan's level of generosity.'

'One rand donated is one rand closer to solving the problem,' she said.

He paused a judicious moment, then said, 'Just had a thought: Severan and Jessica couldn't make it for dinner and I'm alone in town. Would you care to join me after the auction?'

Felicity considered this. 'I don't see why not. You look reasonably fit.' And turned away, a lioness preparing to descend on a herd of gazelles.

43

At the conclusion of the event, which raised the equivalent of £30,000 — including a modest donation on the credit card of Gene Theron — Bond and Felicity Willing walked to the car park behind the Lodge Club.

They approached a large van, beside which were dozens of large cardboard cartons. She tugged up her hem, bent down, like a stevedore on a dock, and muscled a heavy box through the open side door of the vehicle.

The reference to his physical well-being was suddenly clear. 'Let me,' he said.

'We'll both do it.'

Together they began to transfer the cartons, which smelt of food. 'Left-overs,' he said.

'Didn't you think it was rather ironic that we were serving gourmet finger food at a campaign to raise money for the hungry?' Felicity asked.

'I did, yes.'

'If I'd offered tinned biscuits and processed cheese, they'd have devoured the lot. But with fancier stuff — I extorted some three-star restaurants to donate it — they didn't dare take more than a bite or two. I wanted to make sure there was plenty left over.'

'Where are we delivering the excess?'

'A food bank not far away. It's one of the outlets my organisation works with.'

When they had finished loading, they got into

the van. Felicity climbed into the driver's seat and slipped off her shoes to drive barefoot. Then they sped into the night, bounding assertively over the uneven tarmac as she tormented the clutch and gearbox.

In fifteen minutes they were at the Cape Town Interdenominational Food Bank Centre. Her shoes back on, Felicity opened the side door and together they offloaded the scampi, crab cakes and Jamaican chicken, which the staff carried inside the shelter.

When the van was empty, Felicity gestured to a large man in khaki slacks and T-shirt. He seemed impervious to the May chill. He hesitated, then joined them, eyeing Bond curiously. Then he said, 'Yes, Miss Willing? Thank you, Miss Willing. Lot of good food for everyone tonight. Did you see inside the shelter? It's crowded.'

She ignored his questions, which to Bond had sounded like diversionary chatter. 'Joso, last week a shipment disappeared. Fifty kilos. Who took it?'

'I didn't hear anything — '

'I didn't ask whether you heard anything. I asked who took it.'

His face was a mask, but then it sagged. 'Why you asking me, Miss Willing? I didn't do nothing.'

'Joso, do you know how many people fifty kilos of rice will feed?'

'I — '

'Tell me. How many people.' He towered over her but Felicity held her ground. Bond wondered

318

if *this* was what she had meant with her assessment of his fitness — she had wanted someone to back her up. But her eyes revealed that, to her, Bond wasn't even present. This was between Felicity and a transgressor who'd stolen food from those she'd pledged to protect, and she was entirely capable of taking him on alone. Her eyes reminded him of his when he confronted an enemy. 'How many people?' she repeated.

Miserably, he lapsed into Zulu or Xhosa.

'No,' she corrected. 'It will feed more than that, many more.'

'It was an accident,' he protested. 'I forgot to close the door. It was late. I was working — '

'It was no accident. Someone saw you unlock the door before you left. Who has the rice?'

'No, no you must believe me.'

'Who?' she persisted coolly.

He was defeated. 'A man from the Flats. In a gang. Oh, please, Miss Willing, if you tell the SAPS, he'll find out it was me. He'll know I told you. He will come for me and he will come for my family.'

Her jaw tightened and Bond couldn't dislodge the impression he'd had earlier, of a feline — now about to strike. There was no sympathy in her voice as she said, 'I won't go to the police. Not this time. But you'll tell the director what you did. And he'll decide whether to keep you on or not.'

'This is my only job,' he protested. 'I have a family. My only job.'

'Which you were happy to endanger,' she

responded. 'Now, go and tell Reverend van Groot. And if he keeps you on and another theft occurs, I *will* tell the police.'

'It will not happen again, Miss Willing.' He turned and vanished inside.

Bond couldn't help but be impressed with her cool, efficient handling of the incident. He noted too it made her all the more attractive.

She caught Bond's eye and her face softened. 'The war I'm fighting? Sometimes you're never quite sure who the enemy is. They might even be on your side.'

How well do I know that? thought Bond.

They returned to the van. Felicity bent down to remove her shoes again but Bond said quickly, 'I'll drive. Save you unstrapping.'

She laughed. They got in and set off. 'Dinner?' she asked.

He almost felt guilty, after all he'd heard about hunger. 'If you're still up for it.'

'Oh, I most certainly am.'

As they drove, Bond asked, 'Would he really have been killed if you'd gone to the police?'

'The SAPS would have laughed at the idea of investigating fifty kilos of stolen rice. But the Cape Flats *are* dangerous, that's true, and if anyone there thought Joso betrayed them, he very likely would be killed. Let's hope he's learnt his lesson.' Her voice grew cool again as she added, 'Leniency can win you allies. It can also be a cobra.'

Felicity guided him back to Green Point. Since the restaurant she'd suggested was near the Table Mountain Hotel, he left the van there and they walked on. Several times, Bond noted, Felicity glanced behind her, her face alert, shoulders tensed. The road was deserted. What did she feel threatened by?

She relaxed once they were in the front lobby of the restaurant, which was decorated with tapestry, the fixtures dark wood and brass. The large windows overlooked the water, which danced with lights. Much of the illumination inside came from hundreds of cream-coloured candles. As they were escorted to the table, Bond noticed that her clinging dress glistened in the light and seemed to change colour with every step, from navy to azure to cerulean. Her skin glowed.

The waiter greeted her by name, then smiled at Bond. She ordered a Cosmopolitan, and Bond, in the mood for a cocktail, ordered the drink he had had with Philly Maidenstone. 'Crown Royal whisky, a double, on ice. Half a measure of triple sec, two dashes of Angostura. Twist of orange peel, not a slice.'

When the waiter left, Felicity said, 'I've never heard of that before.'

'My own invention.'

'Have you named it?'

Bond smiled to himself, recalling that the waiter at Antoine's in London had wondered about the drink too. 'Not yet.' He had a flash of inspiration from his conversation with M several days earlier. 'Though I think I will now. I'll call it the Carte Blanche. In your honour.'

'Why?' she asked, her narrow brow furrowed.

'Because if your donors drink enough of them,

321

they'll give you complete freedom to take their money.'

She laughed and squeezed his arm, then picked up the menu.

Sitting closer to her now, Bond could see how expertly she'd applied her make-up, accentuating the feline eyes and the thrust of her cheeks and jaw. A thought came to him. Philly Maidenstone was perhaps more classically attractive, but hers was a passive beauty. Felicity's was far more assertive, forceful.

He upbraided himself for dwelling on the comparison, reached for the menu and began to study it. Scanning the extensive card he learnt that the restaurant, Celsius, was famed for its special grill, which reached 950 degrees centigrade.

Felicity said, 'You order for us. Anything to start but I must have a steak for my main course. There's nothing like the grilled meat at Celsius. My God, Gene, you're not a vegan, are you?'

'Hardly.'

When the waiter arrived Bond ordered fresh grilled sardines to be followed by a large rib-eye steak for two. He asked if the chef could grill it with the bone in — known in America as the 'cowboy cut'.

The waiter mentioned that the steaks were typically served with exotic sauces: Argentinian Chimichurri, Indonesian Coffee, Madagascan Peppercorn, Spanish Madeira or Peruvian Anticuchos. But Bond declined them all. He believed that steaks had flavour enough of their own and should be eaten with only salt and pepper.

Felicity nodded that she was in agreement.

Bond then selected a bottle of South African red wine, the Rustenberg Peter Barlow Cabernet 2005.

The wine came and was as good as he'd expected. They clinked glasses and sipped.

The waiter brought the first course and they ate. Bond, deprived of his lunch by Gregory Lamb, was starving.

'What do you do for a living, Gene? Severan didn't say.'

'Security work.'

'Ah.' A faint chill descended. Felicity was obviously a tough, worldly businesswoman and recognised the euphemism. She would guess he was in some way involved with the many conflicts in Africa. War, she'd said during her speech, was one of the main causes for the plague of hunger.

He said, 'I have companies that install security systems and provide guards.'

She seemed to believe this was at least partly true. 'I was born in South Africa and have been living here now for four or five years. I've seen it change. Crime is less of a problem than it used to be, but security staff are still needed. We have a number of them at the organisation. We must. Charitable work doesn't exempt us from risk.' She added darkly, 'I'm happy to give food away. I won't have it stolen from me.'

To divert her from asking more questions about him Bond enquired about her life.

She'd grown up in the bush, in the Western Cape, the only child of English parents, her father a mining company executive. The family had moved back to London when she was thirteen. She was an outsider at boarding school, she confessed. 'I might have fitted in a bit better if I'd kept my mouth shut about how to field-dress gazelles — especially in the dining hall.'

Then it had been the London Business School and a stint at a major City investment bank, where she'd done 'all right'; her dismissive modesty suggested she'd done extremely well.

But the work had proved ultimately unsatisfying. 'It was too easy for me, Gene. There was no challenge. I needed a steeper mountain. Well, four or five years ago I decided to reassess my life. I took a month off and spent some time back here. I saw how pervasive hunger was. And I decided to do something about it. Everybody told me not to bother. It was impossible to make a difference. Well, that was like waving a red flag at a bull.'

'Felicity Wilful.'

She smiled. 'So, here I am, bullying donors to give us money and taking on the American and European megafarms.'

'"Agropoly". Clever term.'

'I coined it,' she said, then burst out, 'They're destroying the continent. I'm not going to let them get away with it.'

The serious discussion was cut short when the waiter appeared with the steak sizzling on an iron platter. It was charred on the outside and succulent within. They ate in silence for a time. At one point he sliced off a crusty piece of meat, but took a sip of wine before he put it into his mouth. When he returned to his plate the morsel was gone and Felicity was chewing mischievously. 'Sorry. I tend to go after things that appeal to me.'

Bond laughed. 'Very clever, stealing from under the nose of a security expert.' He waved to the sommelier, and a second bottle of the cabernet appeared. Bond steered the conversation to Severan Hydt.

He was disappointed to find that she didn't seem to know much about the man that might be helpful to his mission. She mentioned the names of several of his partners who'd donated money to her group and he memorised them. She had not met Niall Dunne but she knew Hydt had some brilliant assistant who performed all sorts of technical wizardry. She lifted an eyebrow and said, 'I just realised — you're the one he uses.'

'Sorry?'

'For his security at the Green Way operation north of town. I've never been but one of my assistants collected a donation from him. All those metal detectors and scanners. You can't get inside the place with a paperclip, let alone a mobile phone. You have to check everything at the door. Like in those old American westerns — you leave your guns outside when you go into the bar.'

'He awarded that contract to somebody else. I do other jobs.' This intelligence worried Bond; he'd intended to get into the Green Way building with far more than a paperclip and a mobile phone, despite Bheka Jordaan's disdain for illegal surveillance. He'd have to consider the implications.

The meal wound down and they finished the wine. They were the last patrons in the restaurant. Bond called for the bill and settled it. 'The second of my donations,' he said.

They returned to the entrance, where he collected her black cashmere coat and draped it over her shoulders. They started down the pavement, the narrow heels of her shoes tapping on the concrete. Again she surveyed the streets. Then, relaxing, she took his arm and held it tightly. He was keenly aware of her perfume and of the occasional pressure of her breast against his arm.

They approached his hotel, Bond fishing the van key from his pocket. Felicity slowed. The night sky was clear above them, encrusted with a plenitude of stars.

'A very nice evening,' Felicity said. 'And thank you for your help in delivering the leftovers. You're even fitter than I thought.'

Bond found himself asking, 'Another glass of wine?'

The green eyes were looking up and into his own. 'Would *you* like one?'

'Yes,' he said firmly.

In ten minutes they were in his room in the Table Mountain Hotel sitting on the sofa, which they had turned and slid close to the window. Glasses of a Stellenbosch pinotage were in their hands.

They looked out over the flickering lights in

the bay, muted yellow and white, like benign insects hovering in anticipation.

Felicity turned to him, perhaps to say something, perhaps not, and he bent forward and pressed his lips gently to hers. Then he eased back a little, gauging her reaction, and moved forward and kissed her again, harder, losing himself in the contact, the taste, the heat. Her breath on his cheek, Felicity's arms snaked around his shoulders as her mouth held his. Then she kissed his neck and teasingly bit the base where it met his firm shoulder. Her tongue slid along a scar that arced down to his upper arm.

Bond's fingers slipped up her neck into her hair and pulled her closer. He was lost in the pungent musk of her perfume.

A parallel to this moment is skiing: when you pause on the ridge atop a beautiful but perilous downhill run. You have a choice to go or not. You can always snap free the bindings and walk down the mountain. But in fact, for Bond, there never was such a choice; once on the edge, it was impossible not to give in to the seduction of gravity and speed. The only true choice left is how to control the accelerating descent.

The same now, here.

Bond whisked her dress off, the insubstantial blue cloth spilling leisurely to the floor. Felicity then eased back, pulling him with her, until they were lying on the couch, she beneath him. She began tugging at his lower lip with her teeth. He cupped her neck again and pulled her face to his, while her hands rested on the small of his back, kneading hard. Felicity shuddered and inhaled sharply and he understood that, for whatever reason, she liked touching him there. He knew too that she wanted his hands to curl firmly behind her waist. Such is the way lovers communicate, and he would remember that place, the delicate bones of her spine.

For his part, Bond found rapture throughout her body, all its aspects: her hungry lips, her strong, flawless thighs, breasts encased in taut black silk, her delicate neck and throat, from which a whispered moan issued, the dense hair framing her face, the softer strands elsewhere.

They kissed endlessly and then she broke away and locked onto his fierce eyes with her own, whose lids, dusted with faint green luminescence, halfway lowered. Mutual surrender, mutual victory.

Bond lifted her easily. Their lips met once more, briefly, and he carried her to the bed.

Thursday
DISAPPEARANCE ROW

44

He awoke with a start from a nightmare he could not remember. Curiously James Bond's first thought was of Philly Maidenstone. He felt — absurdly — that he'd been unfaithful, yet his most intimate contact with her had been a brief brush of cheeks that had lasted half a second.

He rolled over. The other side of the bed was empty. He looked at the clock. It was half past seven. He could smell Felicity's perfume on the sheets and pillows.

The previous evening had begun as an exercise in learning about his enemy and his enemy's purpose but had become something more. He had felt a strong empathy with Felicity Willing, a tough woman who'd conquered the City and was now turning her resources to a nobler battle. He reflected that, in their own ways, they were both knights errant.

And he wanted to see her again.

But first things first. He got out of bed and pulled on a towelling dressing-gown. He hesitated for a moment then told himself: has to be done.

He went to his laptop in the suite's living area. The device had been modified by Q Branch to incorporate a motion-activated, low-light camera. Bond booted up the machine and looked over the replay. It had been pointed only at the front door and the chair, where Bond had tossed his jacket and trousers, containing his wallet, passport and mobile. At around five thirty a.m., according to the time stamp, Felicity, dressed, had walked past his clothing, showing no interest in his phone, pockets or the laptop. She paused and looked back towards the bed. With a smile? He believed so but couldn't be sure. She put something on the table by the door and let herself out.

He stood up and strode to the table. Her business card lay next to a lamp. She had penned a mobile number underneath her organisation's main phone line. He slipped the card into his wallet.

He cleaned his teeth, showered and shaved, then dressed in blue jeans and a loose black Lacoste shirt, chosen to conceal his Walther. Laughing to himself, he donned the gaudy bracelet and watch and slipped on his finger the initial ring, *EJT*.

Checking his texts and emails, he found one from Percy Osborne-Smith. The man was staying true to his reformed ways and gave a succinct update on the investigation in Britain, though little headway had been made. He concluded:

Our friends in Whitehall are positively obsessed with Afghanistan. I say, all the better for us, James. Looking forward to sharing a George Cross with you, when we see Hydt in shackles.

While he had breakfast in his room, he considered his impending trip to Hydt's Green Way plant, thinking back to last night, to all he'd seen and heard, especially about the super-tight security. When he finished, he called Q Branch and got through to Sanu Hirani. He could hear children's voices in the background and supposed he had been patched through to the branch director's mobile at home. Hirani had six children. They all played cricket, and his eldest daughter was a star batswoman.

Bond told him of his communications and weapons needs. Hirani had some ideas but was uncertain that he could come up quickly with a solution. 'What's your time frame, James?'

'Two hours.'

There followed a thoughtful exhalation from down the line seven thousand miles away. Then: 'I'll need a cut-out in Cape Town. Somebody with knowledge of the area and top clearance. Oh, and a solid NOC. Do you know anybody who fits the bill?'

'I'm afraid I do.'

             ★   ★   ★

At ten thirty a.m. Bond, in a grey windcheater, made his way to the central police station and was escorted to the Crime Combating and Investigation Division office.

'Morning, Commander,' Kwalene Nkosi said, smiling.

'Warrant Officer.' Bond nodded. Their eyes met conspiratorially.

'You see the news this morning?' Nkosi asked, tapping the *Cape Times*. 'Tragic story. A family was killed in a firebombing in Primrose Gardens

333

township last night.' He frowned rather obviously.

'How terrible,' Bond said, reflecting that, despite his West End ambitions, Nkosi was not a very good actor.

'Without doubt.'

He glanced into Bheka Jordaan's office and she waved him inside. 'Morning,' he said, spotting a pair of well-worn trainers in the corner of the office. He hadn't noticed them yesterday. 'You run much?'

'Now and then. It's important to stay in shape for my job.'

When he was in London, Bond spent at least an hour a day exercising and running, using the ODG's gym and jogging along the paths in Regent's Park. 'I enjoy it too. Maybe if time permits you could show me some running trails. There must be some beautiful ones in town.'

'I'm sure the hotel will have a map,' she said dismissively. 'Was your meeting at the Lodge Club successful?'

Bond gave her a rundown of what had happened at the fundraiser.

Jordaan then asked, 'And afterwards? Ms Willing proved . . . useful to you?'

Bond lifted an eyebrow. 'I thought you didn't believe in unlawful surveillance.'

'Making certain someone is safe on the public sidewalks and streets is hardly illegal. Warrant Officer Nkosi told you of our CCTV cameras in the centre of town.'

'Well, in answer to your question, yes, she *was* helpful. She gave me some information about the

334

enhanced security at Green Way.' He added stiffly, 'I was lucky she did. No one else seemed to be aware of it. Otherwise my trip there today might have been disastrous.'

'That's fortunate, then,' Jordaan said.

Bond told her the names of the three donors Felicity had mentioned last night — the men Hydt had introduced her to.

Jordaan knew of two as successful legitimate businessmen. Nkosi conducted a search and learnt that neither they nor the third had any criminal record. In any event, all three were out of town. Bond assessed they would not be of any immediate help.

Bond was looking at the policewoman. 'You don't like Felicity Willing?'

'You think I'm jealous?' Her face said: just what a man would believe.

Nkosi turned away. Bond glanced toward him but he was offering no allegiance to Britain in this international dispute.

'That idea couldn't have been further from my mind. Your eyes told me you don't like her. Why?'

'I've never met her. She's probably a perfectly nice woman — I don't like what she represents.'

'Which is?'

'A foreigner who comes here to pat us on the head and dispense alms. It's twenty-first-century imperialism. People used to exploit Africa for diamonds and slaves. Now it's exploited for its ability to purge the guilt of wealthy Westerners.'

'It seems to me,' Bond said evenly, 'that no one can progress when they're hungry. It doesn't matter where the food comes from, does it?'

'Charity undermines. You need to fight your way out of oppression and deprivation. We can do it ourselves. Perhaps more slowly but we will do it.'

'You have no problem when Britain or America imposes arms embargoes on warlords. Hunger's as dangerous as rocket-propelled grenades and land mines. Why shouldn't we help stop that too?'

'It's different. Obviously.'

'I don't see how,' he said coolly. 'Besides, Felicity might be more on your side than you give her credit for. She's made some enemies among the big corporations in Europe, America and Asia. She thinks they're meddling in African affairs and that more should be left to the people here.' He remembered her ill ease on the short walk to the restaurant last night. 'My take is that she's put herself at quite some risk saying so. If you're interested.'

But Jordaan clearly wasn't. How *completely* irritating this woman was.

Bond looked at his huge Breitling watch. 'I should leave for Green Way soon. I need a car. Can someone arrange a hire in Theron's name?'

Nkosi nodded enthusiastically. 'Without doubt. You like to drive, Commander.'

'I do,' Bond said. 'How did you know?'

'On the way from the airport yesterday you looked with some interest at a Maserati, a Moto Guzzi and a left-hand-drive Mustang from America.'

'You notice things, Warrant Officer.'

'I try to. That Ford — it was a very nice set of

wheels. Some day I will own a Jaguar. It is my goal.'

Then a loud voice was calling a greeting from the corridor. 'Hallo, hallo!'

Bond wasn't surprised it belonged to Gregory Lamb. The MI6 agent strode into the office, waving to everyone. It was obvious that Bheka Jordaan didn't care for him, as Lamb had admitted yesterday, though he and Nkosi seemed to get on well. They had a brief conversation about a recent football match.

Casting a cautious glance at Jordaan, the big, ruddy man turned to Bond. 'Came through for you, my friend. Got a signal from Vauxhall Cross to help you out.'

Lamb was the cut-out whom Bond had reluctantly mentioned to Hirani earlier that morning. He couldn't think of anybody else to use on such short notice and at least the man had been vetted.

'Leapt into the fray, even missed breakfast, my friend, I'll have you know. Talked to that chap in your office's Q Branch. Is he always so bloody cheerful that early in the morning?'

'Actually he is,' said Bond.

'Got talking to him. I'm having some navigation problems on my ship charters. Pirates've been jamming signals. Whatever happened to the eye patches and peg legs, hmm? Well, this Hirani says there are devices that will jam the jammers. He wouldn't ship me any, though. Any chance you could put in a word?'

'You know our outfit doesn't officially exist, Lamb.'

'We're all part of the same team,' he said huffily. 'I've got a huge charter coming up in a day or so. Massive.'

Helping Lamb's lucrative cover career was the last thing on Bond's mind at the moment. He asked sternly, 'And your assignment today?'

'Ah, yes.' Lamb handed Bond the black satchel he was carrying as if it contained the Crown Jewels. 'Must say in all modesty the morning's been a smashing success. Positively brilliant. I've been running hither and yon. Had to tip rather heavily. You'll reimburse me, of course?'

'I'm sure it'll get sorted.' Bond opened the satchel and regarded the contents. He examined one item closely. It was a small plastic tube labelled, 'Re-Leef. For Congestion Problems Caused by Asthma'.

Hirani was a genius.

'An inhaler. You have lung problems?' Nkosi asked. 'My brother too. He is a gold miner.'

'Not really.' Bond pocketed it, along with the other items Lamb had delivered.

Nkosi took a call. When he hung up he said, 'I have a nice car for you, Commander. Subaru. All-wheel drive.'

A Subaru, thought Bond, sceptical. A suburban estate wagon. But Nkosi was beaming so he said graciously, 'Thank you, Warrant Officer. I'll look forward to driving it.'

'The petrol mileage is very good,' Nkosi said enthusiastically.

'I'm sure it is.' He started out of the door.

Gregory Lamb stopped him. 'Bond,' he said softly. 'Sometimes I'm not sure the powers that

338

be in London take me all that seriously. I was exaggerating a bit yesterday — about the Cape, I mean. Fact is, the worst that happens down here is a warlord coming in from Congo to take the waters. Or a Hamas chap in transit at the airport. Just want to thank you for including me, my friend. I — '

Bond interrupted, 'You're welcome, Lamb. But how's this: let's just assume I'm your friend. Then you won't have to keep repeating it. How's that?'

'Fair enough, my . . . fair enough.' A grin spread over the fat face.

Then Bond was out the door, thinking: next stop, hell.

45

James Bond enjoyed Kwalene Nkosi's little joke.

Yes, the car he'd procured for the agent's use was a small Japanese import. It wasn't, however, a staid family saloon but a metallic blue Subaru Impreza WRX, the STI model, which boasted a turbocharged 305-horsepower engine, six gears and a high spoiler. The jaunty little vehicle would be far more at home on rally courses than in some Asda car park and, settling into the driver's seat, Bond couldn't restrain himself. He laid twin streaks of rubber as he sped up Buitenkant Street, heading for the motorway.

For the next half-hour he made his way north of Cape Town proper, guided by sat-nav, and finally skidded the taut little Subaru off the N7 and proceeded east along an increasingly deserted road, past a vast bottomless quarry and then into a grubby landscape of low hills, some green, some brown with autumn tint. Sporadic stands of trees broke the monotony.

The May sky was overcast and the air was humid but dust rose from the road, churned up by the Green Way lorries carting their refuse in the direction Bond was going. In addition to the typical dustcarts, there were much larger ones, painted with the Green Way name and distinctive green leaf — or dagger — logo. Signs on the sides indicated that they came from company operations throughout South Africa. Bond was surprised to see one lorry was from a branch in Pretoria, the administrative capital of the country, many miles away — why would Hydt go to the expense of bringing rubbish to Cape Town when he could open a recycling depot where it was needed?

Bond changed down and blew past a series of the lorries at speed. He was enjoying this sprightly vehicle very much. He'd have to tell Philly Maidenstone about it.

A large road sign, stark in black and white, flashed past.

Gevaar!!!
Danger!!!

Privaat Eiendom
Private Property

He'd been off the N7 for several miles when the road divided, with the lorries going to the right. Bond steered down the left fork, with an arrowed sign:

Hoofkantoor
Main Office

Motoring fast through a dense grove of trees — they were tall but looked recently planted — he came to a rise and shot over it, ignoring the posted limit of forty k.p.h., and braked hard as Green Way International loomed. The rapid stop wasn't because of obstruction or a sharp curve but the unnerving sight that greeted him.

341

An endless expanse of the waste facility filled his view and disappeared into a smoky, dusty haze in the distance. The orange fires of some burn-off operation could been seen from at least a mile away.

Hell indeed.

In front of him, beyond a crowded car park, was the headquarters building. It was eerie, too, in its own way. Though not large, the structure was stark and bleakly imposing. The unpainted concrete bunker, one storey high, had only a few windows, small ones — sealed, it seemed. The entire grounds were enclosed by two ten-foot metal fences, both topped with wicked razor wire, which glinted even in the muted light. The barriers were thirty feet apart, reminding Bond of a similar perimeter: the shoot-to-kill zone surrounding the North Korean prison from which he'd successfully rescued a local MI6 asset last year.

Bond scowled at the fences. One of his plans was ruined. He knew from what Felicity had told him that there'd be metal detectors and scanners and, most likely, an imposing security fence. But he'd assumed a single barrier. He'd planned to slip some of the equipment Hirani had provided — a weatherproof miniature communications device and weapon — through the fence into grass or bushes on the other side for him to retrieve once he had entered. That wasn't going to work with two fences and a great distance between them.

As he drove forward again, he saw that the entrance was barred by a thick steel gate, on top of which was a sign.

The Green Way anthem chilled Bond. Not the words themselves but the configuration: a crescent of stark black metal letters. It reminded him of the sign over the entrance to the Nazi death camp Auschwitz, the horrifically ironic assurance that work would set the prisoners free: ARBEIT MACHT FREI.

Bond parked. He climbed out, keeping his Walther and mobile with him so that he could find out how effective the security really was. He also had in his pocket the asthma inhaler Hirani had provided; he had hidden under the front seat the other items Lamb had delivered that morning: the weapon and com device.

He approached the first guardhouse at the outer fence. A large man in uniform greeted him with a reserved nod. Bond gave his cover name. The man made a call and a moment later an equally large, equally stern fellow in a dark business suit came up and said, 'Mr Theron, this way, please.'

Bond followed him through the no man's land between the two fences. They entered a room where three armed guards sat about, watching a football match. They stood up immediately.

The security man turned to Bond. 'Now, Mr Theron, we have very strict rules here. Mr Hydt and his associates do most of the research and development work for his companies on these premises. We must guard our trade secrets carefully. We don't allow any mobiles or radios of any kind in with you. No cameras or pagers

343

either. You'll have to hand them in.'

Bond was looking at a large rack, like the cubbyholes for keys behind the front desk in old-fashioned hotels. There were hundreds and most of them had phones in them. The guard noticed. 'The rule applies to all our employees too.'

Bond recalled that René Mathis had told him the same thing about Hydt's London operation — that there was virtually no SIGINT going into or coming out of the company. 'Well, you have landlines I can use, I assume. I'll have to check my messages.'

'There are some, but all the lines go through a central switchboard in the security department. A guard could make the call for you but you wouldn't have any privacy. Most visitors wait until after they leave. The same is true for email and Internet access. If you wish to keep anything metal on you, we'll have to X-ray it.'

'I should tell you I'm armed.'

'Yes.' As if many people coming to visit Green Way were. 'Of course — '

'I'll have to hand in my weapon too?'

'That's right.'

Bond silently thanked Felicity Willing for filling him in on Hydt's security. Otherwise he would have been caught with one of Q Branch's standard-issue video or still surveillance cameras in a pen or jacket button, which would have shattered his credibility . . . and probably led to a full-on fight.

Playing the tough mercenary, he scoffed at the inconvenience, but handed over his gun and phone, programmed to reveal only information about his Gene Theron cover identity, should anyone try to crack it. Then he stripped off his belt and watch, placed them and his keys in a tray for the X-ray.

He strode through quickly and was reunited with his possessions — after the guard had checked that the watch, keys and belt held no cameras, weapons or recording devices.

'Wait here, please, sir,' the security man said. Bond sat where indicated.

The inhaler was still in his pocket. If they had frisked him, found and dismantled the device, they would have discovered it was in fact a sensitive camera, constructed without a single metal part. One of Sanu Hirani's contacts in Cape Town had managed to find or assemble the device that morning. The shutter was carbon fibre, as were the springs operating it.

The image-storage medium was quite interesting — unique nowadays: old-fashioned microfilm, the sort spies had used during the Cold War. The camera had a fixed-focus lens and Bond could snap a picture by pressing the base, then twisting it to advance the film. It could take thirty pictures. In this digital age, the cobwebbed past occasionally offered an advantage.

Bond looked for a sign to Research and Development, which he knew from Stephan Dlamini contained at least some information about Gehenna, but there was none. He sat for five minutes before Severan Hydt appeared, in silhouette but unmistakable: the tall stature, the massive head framed with curly hair and beard, the well-tailored suit. He paused, looming, in the doorway. 'Theron.' His black eyes bored into Bond's.

They shook hands and Bond tried to ignore the grotesque sensation he experienced as Hydt's long nails slid across his palm and wrist.

'Come with me,' Hydt said and led him into the main office building, which was much less austere than the outside suggested. Indeed, the place was rather nicely appointed, with expensive furniture, art, antiques, and comfortable work spaces for the staff. It seemed like a typical medium-sized company. The front lobby was furnished with the obligatory sofa and chairs, a table with trade magazines and a Cape Town newspaper. On the walls there were pictures of forests, rolling fields of grain and flowers, streams and oceans.

And everywhere, that eerie logo — the leaf that looked like a knife.

As they walked along the corridors, Bond kept an eye open for the Research and Development department. Finally, towards the rear of the building, he saw a sign pointing to it and he memorised the location.

But Hydt turned the other way. 'Come along. We're going for the fifty-rand tour.'

At the back of the building Bond was handed a dark-green hard hat. Hydt donned one too. They walked to a rear door, where Bond was surprised to see a second security post. Curiously, workers coming *into* the building from the rubbish yard were checked. Hydt and he stepped outside on to a patio overlooking scores of low buildings. Lorries and forklift trucks moved in and out of each one like bees at a hive. Workers in hard hats and uniforms were everywhere.

The sheds, in neat rows like barracks, reminded Bond again of a prison or concentration camp.

ARBEIT MACHT FREI . . .

'This way,' Hydt called loudly, striding through a landscape cluttered with earth-moving equipment, skips, oil drums, pallets holding bales of paper and cardboard. Low rumblings filled the air, and the ground seemed to quiver, as if huge underground furnaces or machines were at work, a counterpoint to the high-pitched shrieks of the seagulls that swooped in to pick up scraps in the wake of the lorries entering through a gate a quartermile to the east. 'I'll give you a brief lesson in the business,' he offered.

Bond nodded. 'Please.'

'There are four ways to rid ourselves of discard. Dump it somewhere out of the way — in tips or landfill now mostly, but the ocean's still popular. Did you know that the Pacific has four times as much plastic in it as zooplankton? The biggest rubbish tip in the world is the Great Pacific Garbage Patch, circulating between Japan and North America. It's at least twice the size of Texas and could be as big as the entire United States. Nobody actually knows. But one thing *is* certain: it's getting bigger.

'The second way is to burn discard, which is very expensive and can produce dangerous ash. Third, you can recycle it — that's Green Way's area of expertise. Finally, there's minimising, which means making sure that fewer disposable materials are created and sold. You're familiar with plastic water bottles?'

'Of course.'

'They're a lot thinner now than they used to be.'

Bond took his word for it.

'It's called 'lightweighting'. Much easier to compact. You see, generally the products themselves aren't the problem when it comes to discard. It's *packaging* that causes most of the volume. Discard was easily handled until we shifted to a consumer manufacturing society and started to mass-produce goods. How to get the products into the hands of the people? Encase it in polystyrene foam, put that in a cardboard box and then, for God's sake, put *that* in a plastic carrier bag to take home with you. Ah, and if it's a present, let's wrap it up in coloured paper and ribbon! Christmas is an absolute hurricane of discard.'

Standing tall, looking over his empire, Hydt continued, 'Most waste plants extend over fifty to seventy-five acres. Ours here is a hundred. I have three others in South Africa and dozens of transfer stations, where the carters — the lorries you see on the streets — take all the discard for compacting and shipment to treatment depots. I was the first to set up transfer stations in the South African squatters' camps. In six months the countryside was sixty to seventy per cent cleaner. Plastic carrier bags used to be called 'South Africa's national flower'. Not any more.

I've dealt with that.'

'I saw the lorries bringing rubbish from Pretoria and Port Elizabeth to the yard here. Why from so far away?'

'Specialised material,' Hydt said dismissively.

Were those substances particularly dangerous? Bond wondered.

His host continued, 'But you must get your vocabulary right, Theron. We call wet discard 'garbage' — left-over food, for instance. 'Trash' means dry materials, like cardboard and dust and tins. What the bin collectors pick up from in front of homes and offices is 'municipal solid waste', or 'MSW'. That's also called 'refuse' or 'rubbish'. 'C and D' is construction and demolition debris. Institutional, commercial and industrial waste is 'ICI'. The most inclusive term is 'waste' but I prefer 'discard'.'

He pointed east to the rear of the plant. 'Everything that's not recyclable goes there, to the working face of the landfill, where it's buried in layers of plastic lining to keep bacteria and pollution from leaching into the ground. You can spot it by looking for the birds.'

Bond followed his gaze towards the swooping gulls.

'We call the landfill 'Disappearance Row'.'

Hydt led Bond to the doorway of a long building. Unlike the other work sheds here, this one had imposing doors, which were sealed. Bond peered through the windows. Workers were disassembling computers, hard drives, TVs, radios, pagers, mobile phones and printers. There were bins overflowing with batteries, light

349

bulbs, computer hard drives, printed circuit boards, wires and chips. The staff were wearing more protective clothing than any other employees — respirators, heavy gloves and goggles or full face masks.

'Our e-waste department. We call this area 'Silicon Row'. E-waste accounts for more than ten per cent of the deadly substances on earth. Heavy metals, lithium from batteries. Take computers and mobiles. They have a life expectancy of two or three years at most, so people just throw them out. Have you ever read the warning booklet that comes with your laptop or phone, 'Dispose of properly'?'

'Not really.'

'Of course not. No one does. But pound for pound computers and phones are the most deadly waste on earth. In China, they just bury or burn them. They're killing their population by doing that. I'm starting a new operation to address this situation — separating the components of computers at my clients' companies and then disposing of them properly.' He smiled. 'In a few years that will be my most lucrative operation.'

Bond recalled the device he'd seen demonstrated at al-Fulan's, the one near to the compactor that had taken Yusuf Nasad's life.

Hydt pointed, with a long, yellow fingernail. 'And at the back of this building there is the Dangerous-materials Recovery department. One of our biggest money-making services. We handle everything from paint to motor oil to arsenic to polonium.'

350

'Polonium?' Bond gave a cool laugh. This was the radioactive material that had been used to kill the Russian spy Alexander Litvinenko, an expatriate in London, a few years ago. It was one of the most toxic substances on earth. 'It's just thrown out? That has to be illegal.'

'Ah, but that's the thing about discard, Theron. People throw away an innocent-looking anti-static machine . . . that just happens to contain polonium. But nobody knows that.'

He led Bond past a car park where several lorries stood, each about twenty feet long. On the side was the company name and logo, along with the words *Secure Document Destruction Services*.

Hydt followed Bond's gaze and said, 'Another of our specialities. We lease shredders to companies and government offices, but smaller outfits would rather hire us to do it for them. Did you know that when the Iranian students took over the American embassy in the 1970s, they were able to reassemble classified CIA documents that had been shredded? They learnt the identities of most of the covert agents there. Local weavers did the work.'

Everyone in the intelligence community knew this but Bond feigned surprise.

'At Green Way we perform DIN industrial-standard level-six shredding. Basically our machines turn the documents to dust. Even the most secret government installations hire us.'

He then led Bond to the largest building on the plant, three storeys high and two hundred yards long. A continuous string of lorries rolled

351

in through one door and came out through another. 'The main recycling facility. We call *this* area 'Resurrection Row'.'

They stepped inside. Three huge devices were being fed an endless stream of paper, cardboard, plastic bottles, polystyrene, scrap metal, wood and hundreds of other items. 'The sorters,' Hydt shouted. The noise was deafening. At the far end the separated materials were being packed into lorries for onward shipment — tins, glass, plastic, paper and other materials.

'Recycling's a curious business,' Hydt yelled. 'Only a few products — metals and glass mostly — can be recycled indefinitely. Everything else breaks down after a while and has to be burnt or go to landfill. Aluminium's the only consistently profitable recyclable. Most products are far cheaper, cleaner and easier to make from raw materials than recycled ones. The extra lorries for transporting recycling materials and the recycling process itself add to fossil fuel pollution. And remanufacturing uses *more* power than the initial production, which is a drain on resources.'

He laughed. 'But it's politically correct to recycle . . . so people come to me.'

Bond followed his tour guide outside and noticed Niall Dunne approaching on his long legs, his gait clumsy and feet turned outward. The fringe of blond hair hung down above his blue eyes, which were as still as pebbles. Putting aside the memory of Dunne's cruel treatment of the men in Serbia and his murder of al-Fulan's assistant in Dubai, Bond smiled amiably and

352

shook his wide hand.

'Theron.' Dunne nodded, his own visage not particularly welcoming. He looked at Hydt. 'We should go.' He seemed impatient.

Hydt motioned for Bond to get into a nearby Range Rover. He did so, sitting in the front passenger seat. He was aware of a sense of anticipation in the two men, as if some plan had been made and was now about to unfurl. His sixth sense told him something had perhaps gone awry. Had they discovered his identity? Had he given something away?

As the other men climbed in, with the unsmiling Dunne taking the driver's seat, Bond reflected that if ever there was a place to dispose of a body clandestinely, this was it.

Disappearance Row . . .

46

The Range Rover bounded east along a wide dirt road, passing squat lorries with massive ribbed wheels, carrying bales or containers of refuse. It passed a wide chasm, at least eighty feet deep.

Bond looked down. The lorries were dropping their loads, and bulldozers were compacting them against the face of the landfill site. The bottom of the pit was lined with thick dark sheets. Hydt had been right about the seagulls. They were everywhere, thousands of them. The sheer number, the screams, the frenzy were unsettling and Bond felt a shiver trickle up his spine.

As they drove on, Hydt pointed to the flames Bond had seen earlier. Here, much closer, they were giant spheres of fire — he could feel their heat. 'The landfill produces methane,' he said. 'We drill down and extract it to power the generators, though there's usually too much gas and we have to burn some off. If we didn't, the entire landfill site could blow up. That happened in America not too long ago. Hundreds of people were injured.'

After fifteen minutes, they passed through a dense row of trees and a gate. Bond barked an involuntary laugh. The wasteland of the rubbish tips had vanished. Surrounding them now was an astonishingly beautiful scene: trees, flowers, rock formations, paths, ponds, forest. The

354

meticulously landscaped grounds extended for several miles.

'We call it Elysian Fields. Paradise . . . after our time in hell. And yet it's a landfill too. Underneath us there is nearly a hundred feet of discard. We've reclaimed the land. In a year or so I'll open it to the public. My gift to South Africans. Decay resurrected into beauty.'

Bond was not an aficionado of botany — his customary reaction to the Chelsea Flower Show was irritation at the traffic problems it caused around his home — but he had to admit that these gardens were impressive. He found himself squinting at some tree roots.

Hydt noticed. 'Do they seem a little odd?'

They were metal tubes, painted to look like roots.

'Those pipes transport the methane generated under here to be burnt off or to the power plants.'

He supposed this detail had been thought up by Hydt's star engineer.

They drove on into a grove of trees and parked. A blue crane, the South African national bird, stood regally in a pond nearby, perfectly balanced on one leg.

'Come on, Theron. Let's talk business.'

Why here? Bond wondered, as he followed Hydt down a path, along which small signs identified the plants. Again he wondered if the men had plans for him and he looked, futilely, for possible weapons and escape routes.

Hydt stopped and looked back. Bond did too — and felt a jolt of alarm. Dunne was approaching, carrying a rifle.

Bond outwardly remained calm. ('You wear your cover to the grave,' the lecturers at Fort Monckton would tell their students.)

'You shoot long guns?' Dunne displayed the hunting rifle, with its black plastic or carbon-fibre stock, brushed steel receiver and barrel.

'I do, yes.' Bond had been captain of the shooting team at Fettes and had won competitions in both small and full bore. He'd won the Queen's Medal for Shooting Excellence when in the Royal Naval Reserve — the only shooting medal that can be worn in uniform. He glanced down at what Dunne held. 'Winchester .270.'

'Good gun, wouldn't you agree?'

'It is. I prefer that calibre to the .30–06. Flatter trajectory.'

Hydt asked, 'Do you shoot game, Theron?'

'Never had much opportunity.'

Hydt laughed. 'I don't hunt either . . . except for one species.' The smile faded. 'Niall and I have been discussing you.'

'Have you now?' Bond asked, his tone blasé.

'We've decided you might be a valuable addition to certain *other* projects we're working on. But we need a show of faith.'

'Money?' Bond was stalling; he believed he understood his enemy's purpose here and needed a response. Fast.

'No,' Hydt said softly, his huge head tilting Bond's way. 'That's not what I mean.'

Dunne stepped forward, the Winchester on his hip, muzzle skyward. 'All right. Bring him out.'

Two workers in security uniforms led a skinny

356

man in a T-shirt and shabby khaki trousers from behind a thick stand of jacaranda. The man's face was a mask of terror.

Hydt regarded him with contempt. He said to Bond, 'This man broke into our property and was trying to steal mobile phones from the e-waste operation. When he was approached he pulled a gun and shot at a guard. He missed and was overpowered. I've checked his records and he's an escaped convict. In prison for rape and murder. I could turn him over to the authorities, but his appearance here today has given me — and you — an opportunity.'

'What are you talking about?'

'You are being given a chance to make your first kill as a hunter. If you shoot this man — '

'No!' the captive cried.

'If you kill him, that's all the down-payment I need. We'll proceed with your project and I'll hire you to help me with others. If you choose not to kill him, which I would certainly understand, Niall will drive you back to the front gate and we will part ways. As tempting as your offer is, to cleanse the killing fields, I'll have to decline.'

'Shoot a man in cold blood?'

Dunne said, 'The decision's yours. Don't shoot him. Leave.' The brogue seemed harsher.

But what a chance this was to get into the inner sanctum of Severan Hydt! Bond could learn everything about Gehenna. One life versus thousands.

And how many more would die if, as seemed likely, the event on Friday was the first of other such projects?

He stared at the criminal's dark face, eyes wide, hands shaking at his sides.

Bond glanced at Dunne. He strode forward and took the rifle.

'No, please!' the man cried.

The guards shoved him on to his knees and stepped away. The man stared at Bond, who realised for the first time that, in firing squads, the blindfold wasn't for the condemned's benefit; it was for the *executioners*, so they didn't have to look into the prisoner's eyes.

'Please, no, sir!' he cried.

'There's a round in the chamber,' Dunne called. 'Safety's on.'

Had they slipped a blank in to test him? Or had Dunne not loaded the rifle at all? The thief clearly wasn't wearing a bulletproof vest under the thin T-shirt. Bond hefted the gun, which had open sights only, not telescopic. He assessed the thief, forty feet away, and aimed at him. The man raised his hands to cover his face. 'No! Please!'

'You want to move closer?' Hydt asked.

'No. But I don't want him to suffer,' Bond said matter-of-factly. 'Does the rifle shoot high or low at this range?'

'I couldn't tell you,' Dunne said.

Bond aimed towards the right, at a leaf that was about the same distance as the captive. He squeezed the trigger. There was a sharp crack and a hole appeared in the centre of the leaf, just where he was aiming. Bond worked the bolt, ejecting the spent shell and chambering another. Still, he hesitated.

'What's it to be, Theron?' Hydt whispered.

Bond lifted the gun, aiming steadily at the victim once again.

There was a moment's pause. He pulled the trigger. Another stunning crack and a red dot blossomed in the middle of the man's T-shirt as he fell backwards into the dust.

47

'So,' Bond snapped, opening the rifle's bolt and tossing the weapon to Dunne. 'Are you satisfied?'

The Irishman easily caught the weapon in his large hands. He remained as impassive as ever. He said nothing.

Hydt, however, seemed pleased.

He said, 'Good. Now let us go to the office and have a drink to celebrate our partnership . . . and to allow me to apologise to you.'

'For forcing me to kill a man.'

'No, for forcing you to *believe* you were killing a man.'

'What?'

'William!'

The man Bond had shot leapt to his feet with a big grin on his face.

Bond spun towards Hydt. 'I — '

'Wax bullets,' Dunne called. 'Police use them in training, filmmakers use them in action scenes.'

'It was a goddamn test?'

'Which our friend Niall here devised. It was a good one and you passed.'

'You think I'm a schoolboy? Go to hell.' Bond turned and stormed towards the garden's gate.

'Wait — wait.' Hydt was walking after him, frowning. 'We're business people. This is what we do. We must make certain.'

Bond spat an obscenity and continued down the path, his fists clenching and unclenching.

Urgently Hydt said, 'You can keep going. But please know, Theron, you're walking away not only from me but from one million dollars, which will be yours tomorrow if you stay. And there will be much more.' Bond stopped. He turned.

'Let us go back to the office and talk. Let us be professional.' Bond looked at the man he'd shot, who was still grinning happily. Then he asked Hydt, 'A million?'

Hydt nodded. 'Yours tomorrow.'

Bond remained where he was for a moment, staring across the gardens, which were truly magnificent. He walked back to Hydt, casting a cool glance at Niall Dunne, who was unloading the rifle and cleaning it carefully, caressing the metal parts.

Bond tried to keep an indignant look on his face, playing the role of offended party.

And fiction it was, for he'd figured out about the wax bullets. Nobody who's fired a gun with a normal load of gunpowder and a lead bullet would be fooled by a wax round, which produces far less recoil than a real slug (giving a blank round to a soldier in a firing squad is absurd; he clearly knows his bullet is not real the minute he shoots). A few moments ago Bond had been given the clue when the 'thief' covered his eyes. People about to be shot don't shield anything with their hands. So, Bond had reflected, he's afraid of being blinded, not killed. That suggested that the bullets were blank or wax.

He'd fired into the foliage to judge the recoil and learnt from the very light kick that these were non-lethal rounds.

He guessed that the man would earn hazard pay for his efforts. Hydt seemed to take care of his employees, whatever else one could say about him. This was confirmed now. Hydt peeled off some rand and gave them to the man, who walked up to Bond and pumped his hand. 'Hey, mister, sir! You a good shot. You got me in a blessed spot. Look, right here!' He tapped his chest. 'One man shot me down below, you know where. He was bastard. Oh, that hurt and hurt for days. An' my lady, she complain much.'

In the Range Rover once more, the three men drove in silence back to the plant, the beautiful gardens giving way to harrowing Disappearance Row, the cacophony of the gulls, the fumes.

Gehenna . . .

Dunne parked at the main building, nodded to Bond and told Hydt, 'Our associates? I'll meet the flights. They're arriving around nineteen hundred hours. I'll get them settled and then come back.'

So, Dunne and Hydt would be working into the night. Did that bode well or badly for any future reconnaissance at Green Way? One thing was clear: Bond had to get inside Research and Development now.

Dunne strode away, while Hydt and Bond continued to the building. 'You going to give me a tour here?' Bond asked Hydt. 'It's warmer . . . and there aren't as many seagulls.'

Hydt laughed. 'There isn't much to see. We'll

362

just go to my office.' He didn't, however, spare his new partner the procedures at the back-door security post — though the guards missed the inhaler again. As they stepped into the main corridor, Bond noted again the sign to Research and Development. He lowered his voice. 'Well, I wouldn't mind a tour of the toilet.'

'That way.' Hydt pointed, then pulled out his mobile to make a call. Bond walked quickly down the corridor. He entered the empty men's room, grabbed a large handful of paper towels and tossed them into one of the toilets. When he flushed, the paper jammed in the drain. He went to the door and looked towards where Hydt was waiting. The man's head was down and he was concentrating on his call. There was no CCTV, Bond saw, so he walked away from Hydt, planning his cover story.

Oh, one cubicle was occupied and the other was jammed so I went for another one. Didn't want to bother you when you were on the phone.

Plausible deniability . . .

Bond remembered where he'd seen the sign when he'd entered. He now hurried down a deserted hallway.

RESEARCH AND DEVELOPMENT. RESTRICTED

The metal security door was operated by a number pad, in conjunction with a key card reader. Bond palmed the inhaler and took several pictures, including close-ups of the pad.

Come on, he urged an unsuspecting confederate inside the room — someone must be

363

thinking about a visit to the loo or fetching some coffee from the canteen.

But no one co-operated. The door remained shut and Bond decided he had to get back to Hydt. He turned on his heel and hurried down the corridor again. Thank God, Hydt was still on his mobile. He looked up when Bond was past the bathroom door; to Hydt's mind he had just exited.

He disconnected. 'Come this way, Theron.'

He led Bond down a corridor and into a large room that seemed to serve as both an office and living quarters. A huge desk faced a picture window, with a view of Hydt's wasteland empire. A bedroom, curiously, was off to the side. Bond noticed that the bed was unmade. Hydt diverted him away from it and closed the door. He gestured Bond to a sofa and coffee-table in a corner.

'Drink?'

'Whisky. Scotch. Not a blend.' 'Auchentoshan?'

Bond knew the distillery, outside Glasgow. 'Good. A drop of water.'

Hydt tipped a generous quantity into a glass, added the water and handed it to him. He poured himself a glass of South African Constantia. Bond knew the honey-sweet wine, a recently revived version of Napoleon's favourite drink. The deposed emperor had had hundreds of gallons shipped to St Helena, where he spent his last years in exile. He had sipped it on his deathbed.

The gloomy room was filled with antiques.

Mary Goodnight was forever reporting excitedly on bargains she'd found in London's Portobello Road market, but none of the items in Hydt's office looked as if they'd fetch much money there; they were scuffed, battered, lopsided. Old photographs, paintings and bas-reliefs hung on the walls. Slabs of stone showed fading images of Greek and Roman gods and goddesses, though Bond couldn't tell who they were supposed to be.

Hydt sat and they tipped their glasses towards one another. Hydt gazed affectionately at the walls. 'Most of these have come from buildings my companies demolished. To me, they're like relics from the bodies of saints. Which also interest me, by the way. I own several — though that is a fact no one in Rome is aware of.' He caressed the wineglass. 'Whatever is old or discarded gives me comfort. I couldn't tell you why. Nor do I care to know. I think, Theron, most people waste far too much time wondering why they are as they are. Accept your nature and satisfy it. I love decay, decline . . . the things others shun.' He paused, then asked, 'Would you like to know how I got started in this business? It's an informative story.'

'Yes, please.'

'I had some difficult times in my youth. Ah, who didn't, of course? But I was forced to start work young. It happened to be at a rubbish collection company. I was a London binman. One day my mates and I were having tea, taking a break, when the driver pointed to a flat over the road. He said, 'That's where one of those

365

blokes with the Clerkenwell crowd lives.' '

Clerkenwell: perhaps the biggest and most successful organised-crime syndicate in British history. It was now largely dismantled but for twenty years its members had brutally ruled their turf around Islington. They were reportedly responsible for twenty-five murders.

Hydt continued, his dark eyes sparkling, 'I was intrigued. After tea we continued on our rounds, but without the others knowing I hid the rubbish from *that* flat nearby. I went back at night and collected the bag, brought it home and went through it. I did that for weeks. I examined every letter, every tin, every bill, every condom wrapper. Most of it was useless. But I found one thing that was interesting. A note with an address in East London. 'Here,' was all it said. But I had an idea what it meant. Now, in those days I was supplementing my income as a detectorist. You know about them? Those folks who walk along the beach at Brighton or Eastbourne and find coins and rings in the sand after the tourists have gone for the day. I had a good metal detector and so the next weekend I went to the property mentioned in the note. As I'd expected, it was a vacant lot.' Hydt was animated, enjoying himself. 'It took me ten minutes to find the buried gun. I bought a fingerprint kit and, though I was no expert, it seemed that the prints on the gun and the note matched. I didn't know exactly what the gun had been used for but — '

'But why bury it if it hadn't been used to murder somebody?'

'Exactly. I went to see the Clerkenwell man. I told him that my solicitor had the gun and the note — there was no solicitor, of course, but I bluffed well. I said if I didn't call him in an hour he would send everything to Scotland Yard. Was it a gamble? Of course. But a calculated one. The man blanched and immediately asked me what I wanted. I named a figure. He paid in cash. I was on my way to opening a small collection company of my own. It eventually became Green Way.'

'That gives a whole new meaning to the word 'recycling', doesn't it?'

'Indeed.' Hydt seemed amused by the comment. He sipped his wine and gazed out at the grounds, the spheres of the burn-off flames glowing in the distance. 'Did you know that there were three man-made phenomena you could see from outer space? The Great Wall of China, the Pyramids . . . and the old Fresh Kills landfill in New Jersey.'

Bond did not.

'To me discard is more than a business,' Hydt said, 'It's a window on to our society . . . and into our souls.' He sat forward. 'You see, we may *acquire* something in life unintentionally — through a gift, neglect, inheritance, fate, error, greed, laziness — but when we discard something, it's almost always with cold intent.'

He took a judicious sip of wine. 'Theron, do you know what entropy is?'

'No, I don't.'

'Entropy,' said Hydt, clicking his long, yellow nails, 'is the essential truth of nature. It's the tendency towards decay and disorder — in

physics, in society, in art, in living creatures
. . . in everything. It's the path to anarchy.' He
smiled. 'That sounds pessimistic, but it isn't. It's
the most wonderful thing in the world. You can
never go wrong by embracing the truth. And
truth it is.'

His eyes settled on a bas-relief. 'I changed my
name, you know.'

'I didn't,' Bond said, thinking: Maarten Holt.

'I changed it because my surname was my
father's and my given name was selected by him.
I wished to have no more connection with him.'
A cool smile. 'That childhood I mentioned. I
chose 'Hydt' because it echoed the dark side of
the protagonist in *Dr Jekyll and Mr Hyde*, which
I'd read at school and enjoyed. You see, I believe
we all have a public side and a dark side. The
book confirmed that.'

'And 'Severan'? It's unusual.'

'You wouldn't think so if you'd lived in Rome
in the second and third centuries AD.'

'No?'

'I read history and archaeology at university.
Mention ancient Rome, Theron, and most
people think of what? The Julio-Claudian line of
emperors. Augustus, Tiberius, Caligula, Claudius
and Nero. At least they think so if they read *I,
Claudius* or saw Derek Jacobi in brilliant form
on the BBC. But that whole line lasted a
pathetically short time — slightly over a hundred
years. Yes, yes, *mare nostrum*, Praetorian guards,
films staring Russell Crowe . . . all very decadent
and dramatic. 'My God, Caligula, that's your
sister!' But for me, the truth of Rome was

368

revealed much later in a different family line, the Severan emperors, founded by Septimius Severus many years after Nero killed himself. You see, they presided over the *decay* of the Empire. Their reign culminated in what historians called the Period of Anarchy.'

'Entropy,' Bond said.

'*Exactly*.' Hydt beamed. 'I'd seen a statue of Septimius Severus and I look a bit like him so I took his family name.' He focused on Bond. 'Are you feeling uneasy, Theron? Don't worry. You haven't signed on with Ahab. I'm not mad.'

Bond laughed. 'I wasn't thinking you were. Honestly. I was thinking about the million dollars you mentioned.'

'Of course.' He studied Bond closely. 'Tomorrow the first of a number of projects I'm engaged in will come to fruition. My main partners will be here. You will come too. Then you'll see what we're about.'

'For a million, what do you want me to do?' He frowned. 'Shoot somebody with *real* bullets?'

Hydt fondled his beard again. He did indeed resemble a Roman emperor. 'You don't need to do anything tomorrow. That project is finished. We'll just be watching the results. And celebrating, I hope. We'll call your million a signature bonus. After that, you'll be very busy.'

Bond forced himself to smile. 'I'm pleased to be included.'

Just then Hydt's mobile rang. He looked at the screen, rose and turned away. Bond guessed there was some difficulty. Hydt didn't get angry but his stillness indicated he wasn't happy. He

369

disconnected. 'I'm sorry. A problem in Paris. Inspectors. Trade unions. It's a Green Way issue, nothing to do with tomorrow's project.'

Bond didn't want to make the man suspicious so he backed off. 'All right. What time do you want me?'

'Ten a.m.'

Recalling the original intercept that GCHQ had decrypted and the clues he'd found up in March about the time the attack would take place, Bond understood he would have about twelve hours to find out what Gehenna was about and stop it.

A figure appeared in the doorway. It was Jessica Barnes. She wore what seemed to be her typical garb — a black skirt and modest white shirt. Bond had never liked women to wear excessive make-up but he wondered again why she didn't use even the minimum.

'Jessica, this is Gene Theron,' Hydt said absently. He'd forgotten they'd met last night.

The woman didn't remind him.

Bond took her hand. She returned a timid nod. Then she said to Hydt, 'The ad proofs didn't come in. They won't be here till tomorrow.'

'You can review them then, can't you?'

'Yes, but there's nothing more to do here. I was thinking I'd like to go back to Cape Town.'

'Something's come up. I'll be a few hours, maybe more. You can wait . . . ' His eyes strayed to the door behind which Bond had seen the bed.

She hesitated. 'All right.' A sigh.

370

Bond said, 'I'm going back into town. I can drive you if you like.'

'Really? It's not too much trouble?' Her question, however, was not directed towards Bond but to Hydt.

The man was scrolling through his mobile. He looked up. 'Good of you, Theron. I'll see you tomorrow.'

They shook hands.

'*Totsiens.*' Bond gave the Afrikaans farewell, which he knew courtesy of the Captain Bheka Jordaan School of Language.

'What time will you be home, Severan?' Jessica asked Hydt.

'When I get there,' he responded absently, punching a number into his phone.

Five minutes later Jessica and Bond were at the front security post, where he again passed through the metal detector. But before he was reunited with his gun and mobile, a guard walked up and said, 'What is that, sir? I see something in your pocket.'

The inhaler. How the hell had he spotted the slight bulge in the windcheater? 'It's nothing.'

'I'll see it, please.'

'I'm not stealing anything from a junkyard,' he snapped, 'if that's what you're thinking.'

Patiently the man said, 'Our rules are very clear, sir. I'll see it or I have to call Mr Dunne or Mr Hydt.'

Follow your cover to the grave . . .

With a steady hand Bond withdrew the black plastic tube and displayed it. 'It's medicine.'

'Is it now?' The man took the device and

371

examined it closely. The camera lens was recessed but, to Bond, seemed all too obvious. The guard was about to hand it back but then changed his mind. He lifted the hinged cap, exposed the plunger and put his thumb on it.

Bond eyed his Walther, sitting in one of the cubbyholes. It was ten feet away and separated from him by the two other guards, both armed.

The guard pressed the plunger . . . and released a fine mist of denatured alcohol into the air near his face.

Sanu Hirani, of course, had created the toy with typical forethought. The spray mechanism was real, even if the chemical inside was not; the camera was located in the *lower* part of the base. The smell of the alcohol was strong. The guard wrinkled his nose and his eyes were watering as he handed back the device. 'Thank you, sir. I hope you need not take that medicine often. It seems quite unpleasant.'

Without replying, Bond pocketed the inhaler and received his weapon and phone.

He headed towards the front door, which opened on to the no man's land between the two fences. He was almost outside when an alarm klaxon blared fiercely and lights began to flash.

48

Bond was a split second away from spinning around, dropping into a combat shooting stance and drawing down on priority targets.

But instinct told him to hold back.

It was a good thing he did. The guards weren't even looking at him. They had gone back to watching the TV.

Bond glanced casually around. The alarm had gone off because Jessica, exempt from security procedures, had come through the metal detector with her handbag and jewellery. A guard casually flicked a switch to reset the unit.

His heartbeat returning to normal, Bond and Jessica continued outside, through the next security post and out into the car park, filled with curled brown leaves blowing in the light wind. Bond opened the passenger door of the Subaru for her, then got into the driver's seat and started the engine. They drove along the dusty road towards the N7, amid the ever-present Green Way lorries.

For a while Bond said nothing, but then, subtly, he went to work. He started with innocuous questions, easing her into talking to him. Did she like to travel? Which were her favourite restaurants here? What was her job at Green Way?

Then he asked, 'I'm curious — how did you two meet?'

'You really want to know?'

'Tell me.'

'I was a beauty queen when I was young.'

'Really? I've never met one before.' He smiled.

'I didn't do too badly. I was in the Miss America Pageant once. But what really . . . ' She blushed. 'No, it's silly.'

'Please. Go on.'

'Well, once I was competing in New York, at the Waldorf-Astoria. It was before the pageant and a lot of us girls were in the lobby. Jackie Kennedy saw me and she came up to me and said how pretty she thought I was.' She glowed with a pride he had not seen in her face. 'That was one of the high points of my life. She was my idol when I was a little girl.' The smile tempered. 'You don't really want to know this, do you?'

'I asked.'

'Well, you can only go on for so long, of course, in the pageant world. After I stopped the circuit, I did some commercials and then infomercials. Then, well, those jobs dried up too. A few years later my mother passed away — I was very close to her — and I went through a rough time. I got a job as a hostess in a restaurant in New York. Severan was doing some business nearby and he'd come in to meet clients. We got to talking. He was so fascinating. He loves history and he's travelled everywhere. We talked about a thousand different things.

'We had such a connection. It was very . . . refreshing. In the pageants, I used to joke that life isn't even skin deep; it's *makeup* deep. That's all people see. Make-up and clothes.

374

Severan saw some depth in me, I guess. We hit it off. He asked for my number and kept calling. Well, I wasn't a stupid woman. I was fifty-seven years old, no family, very little money. And here was a handsome man . . . a *vital* man.'

Bond wondered if that meant what he suspected it might.

Sat-nav instructed him to leave the highway. He drove carefully along a congested road. The minibus taxis were everywhere. Tow trucks waited at intersections, apparently to be the first at the site of an accident. People sold drinks by the roadside; impromptu businesses operated from the backs of lorries and vans. Several were doing a booming trade selling batteries and performing alternator repairs. Why did that malady plague South African vehicles in particular?

Now that he had broken yet more ice, Bond asked casually about the meeting tomorrow, but she said she knew nothing about it and he believed her. Frustratingly to Bond, it seemed that Hydt kept her in the dark about Gehenna and any other illegal activities he, Dunne or the company were involved in.

They were five minutes from their destination, the sat-nav reported, when Bond said, 'I have to be honest. It's odd.'

'What is?'

'Just how he surrounds himself with it all.'

'All of what?' Jessica asked, her eyes on him closely.

'Decay, destruction.'

'Well, it's his business.'

'I don't mean his work with Green Way. That I understand. I'm speaking of his *personal* interest with the old, the used . . . the discarded.'

Jessica said nothing for a moment. She pointed ahead to a large wooden private residence, surrounded by an imposing stone fence. 'That's it, the house. That's — '

Her voice choked and she began to cry.

Bond pulled to the kerb. 'Jessica, what's the matter?'

'I . . . ' Her breathing was coming fast.

'Are you all right?' He reached down and pulled the adjustment lever, moving the seat back, so he could turn to face her.

'It's nothing, oh, nothing. How embarrassing is this?'

Bond took her handbag and dug around inside for a tissue. He found one and handed it to her.

'Thank you.' She tried to speak, then surrendered to her sobs. When she had calmed, she tilted the rear-view mirror towards herself. 'He doesn't let me wear make-up — so at least my mascara hasn't run and turned me into a clown.'

'Doesn't let you . . . What do you mean?'

The confession died on her lips. 'Nothing,' Jessica whispered.

'Was it something I said? I'm sorry if I've upset you. I was just making conversation.'

'No, no, it's nothing you've done, Gene.'

'Tell me what's wrong.' His eyes locked with hers.

She debated a moment. 'I wasn't being honest with you. I put on a good show but it's all a

376

façade. We don't have a connection. We never have. He wants me . . . ' She raised her hand. 'Oh, you don't want to hear this.'

Bond touched her arm. 'Please, I'm responsible in some way. I was just blundering along. I feel the fool. Tell me.'

'Yes, he loves the old . . . the used, the discarded. *Me*.'

'My God, no. I didn't mean — '

'I know you didn't. But that *is* what Severan wants me for — because I'm part of the downward spiral too. I'm his laboratory for fading, for ageing, for decay.

'That's all I mean to him. He hardly talks to me, ever. I've got almost no idea what goes on in that mind of his and he has no interest in finding out who I am. He gives me credit cards, takes me nice places, provides for me. In return he . . . well, he watches me age. I'll catch him staring at me, a new wrinkle here, an age-spot there. That's why I can't wear make-up. He leaves the lights on when . . . you know what I mean. Do you know how humiliating that is for me? He knows it too. Because humiliation is another form of decay.'

She laughed bitterly, dabbing her eyes with the tissue. 'And the irony, Gene? The goddamn irony? When I was young I lived for beauty pageants. Nobody cared about who I was inside, the judges, my fellow contestants . . . even my mother. Now I'm old and Severan doesn't care about who I am inside either. There are times when I hate being with him. But what can I do? I'm powerless.'

Bond applied a bit more pressure to her arm. 'That's not true. You're not powerless at all. Being older is strength. It's experience, judgement, discernment, knowing your resources. Youth is mistake and impulse. Believe me, I know that quite well.'

'But without him what could I do — where would I go?'

'Anywhere. You could do whatever you wanted. You're obviously clever. You must have some money.'

'Some. But it's not about money. It's about finding someone at my age.'

'Why do you need someone?'

'Spoken like a young man.'

'And *that's* spoken like someone who believes what she's been told, rather than thinking for herself.'

Jessica gave a faint smile. '*Touché*, Gene.' She patted his hand. 'You've been very kind and I can't believe I had a meltdown with a total stranger. Please, I've got to get inside. He'll be calling to check up on me.' She gestured at the house.

Bond drove forward and pulled up to the gate, under the watchful eye of a security guard — which put to rest his plan to get inside the house and see what secrets lay there.

Jessica gripped his hand in both of hers, then climbed out.

'I will see you tomorrow?' he asked. 'At the plant?'

A faint smile. 'Yes, I'll be there. My leash is pretty short.' She turned and walked quickly through the opening gate.

Then Bond shoved the car into first and skidded away, Jessica Barnes vanishing instantly from his thoughts. His attention was on his next destination and what would greet him there.

Friend or foe?

In his chosen profession, though, James Bond had learnt that those two categories were not mutually exclusive.

49

All Thursday morning, all afternoon there had been talk of threats.

Threats from the North Koreans, threats from the Taliban, threats from al-Qaeda, the Chechnyans, the Islamic Jihad Brotherhood, eastern Malaysia, Sudan, Indonesia. There'd been a brief discussion about the Iranians; despite the surreal rhetoric issuing from their presidential palace, nobody took them too seriously. M almost felt sorry for the poor regime in Tehran. Persia had once been such a great empire.

Threats . . .

But the actual assault, he thought wryly, was occurring only now, during a tea break at the security conference. M disconnected from Moneypenny and sat back stiffly in the well-worn, gilt drawing room of a building in Richmond Terrace, between Whitehall and the Victoria Embankment. It was one of those utterly unremarkable fading structures of indeterminate age in which the sweat work of governing the country was done.

The impending assault involved two ministers who sat on the Joint Intelligence Committee. Their heads were now poking through the door, side by side, bespectacled faces scanning the room until they spotted their target. Once an image of television's Two Ronnies had sidled into his head, M could not dislodge it. As they strode forward, however, there was nothing comedic about their expressions.

'Miles,' the older one greeted him. 'Sir Andrew' prefaced the man's surname and those two words were in perfect harmony with his distinguished face and silver mane.

The other, Bixton, tipped his head, whose fleshy dome reflected light from the dusty chandelier. He was breathing hard. In fact, they both were.

M didn't invite them to do so but they sat anyway, upon the Edwardian sofa across from the tea tray. He longed to remove a cheroot from his attaché case and chew on it but decided against the prop.

'We'll come straight to the point,' Sir Andrew said.

'We know you have to get back to the security conference,' Bixton interjected.

'We've just been with the foreign secretary. He's in the Chamber at the moment.'

That explained their heaving chests. They couldn't have driven up from the House of Commons, since Whitehall, from Horse Guards Avenue to just past King Charles Street, had been sealed, like a submarine about to dive, so that the security conference might meet, well, securely.

'Incident Twenty?' M asked.

'Just so,' Bixton said. 'We're trying to track down the DG of Six, as well, but this bloody conference . . . ' He was new to Joint Intelligence and appeared suddenly to realise perhaps he shouldn't be quite so bluntly birching the rears of those who paid him.

' . . . is bloody disruptive,' M grumbled, filling in. He had no problem whipping anyone or anything when it was deserved.

Sir Andrew took over. He said, 'Defence Intelligence and GCHQ are reporting a swell of SIGINT in Afghanistan over the past six hours.'

'General consensus is that it's to do with Incident Twenty.'

M asked, 'Anything specific to Hydt — Noah — or thousands of deaths? Niall Dunne? Army bases in March? Improvised explosive devices? Engineers in Dubai? Rubbish and recycling facilities in Cape Town?' M read every signal that crossed his desk or arrived in his mobile phone.

'We can't tell, can we?' Bixton answered. 'The Doughnut hasn't broken the codes yet.' GCHQ's headquarters in Cheltenham was built in the shape of a fat ring. 'The encryption packages are brand spanking new. Which has stymied everyone.'

'SIGINT is cyclical over there,' M muttered dismissively. He had been very, very senior at MI6 and had earned a reputation for unparalleled skill at mining intelligence and, more important, *refining* it into something useful.

'True,' Sir Andrew agreed. 'Rather too coincidental, though, that all these calls and emails have popped up just now, the day before Incident Twenty, wouldn't you think?'

Not necessarily.

He continued, 'And nobody's turned up *anything* that specifically links Hydt to the threat.'

'Nobody' translated to '007'.

M looked at his wristwatch, which had been his son's, a soldier with the Royal Regiment of Fusiliers. The security meeting was set to resume in a half hour. He was exhausted and Friday, tomorrow, would be an even longer session, culminating in a tiresome dinner followed by a speech by the home secretary.

Sir Andrew noted the less-than-subtle glance at the battered timepiece: 'Long story short, Miles, the JIC is of the opinion that this Severan Hydt fellow in South Africa's a diversion. Maybe he's involved but he's not a key player in Incident Twenty. Five and Six's people think the real actors are in Afghanistan and that's where the attack will happen: military or aid workers, contractors.'

Of course, that was what they would *say* — whatever they actually *thought*. The adventure in Kabul had cost billions of pounds and far too many lives; the more evil that could be found there to justify the incursion, the better. M had been aware of this from the beginning of the Incident Twenty operation.

'Now, Bond — '

'He's good, we know that,' Bixton interrupted, eyeing the chocolate biscuits M had asked not to be brought with the tea but had arrived anyway.

Sir Andrew frowned.

'It's just that he hasn't actually found much,' Bixton went on. 'Unless there've been details that haven't yet circulated.'

M said nothing, merely regarding both men with equal frost.

Sir Andrew said, 'Bond *is* a star, of course. So the thinking is that it would be good for everybody if he deployed to Kabul post haste. Tonight, if you could make that work. Put him in a hot zone along with a couple of dozen of Six's premier-league lads. We'll tap the CIA too. We don't mind spreading the glory.'

And the blame, thought M, if they get it wrong.

Bixton said, 'Makes sense. Bond was stationed in Afghanistan.'

M said, 'Incident Twenty's supposed to happen tomorrow. It'll take him all night to get to Kabul. How can he stop anything happening?'

'The thinking is . . . ' Sir Andrew fell silent, realising, M supposed, that he'd repeated his own irritating verbal filler. 'We aren't sure it *can* be stopped.'

Silence washed in unpleasantly, like a tide polluted with hospital waste.

'Our approach would be for your man and the others to head up a post-mortem analysis team. Try to find out for certain who was behind it. Put together a response proposal. Bond could even head it up.'

M knew, of course, what was happening here: the Two Ronnies were offering the ODG a face-saving measure. Your organisation could be a star ninety-five per cent of the time, but if you erred even once, with a big loss, you might appear at the office on Monday morning and find your whole outfit disbanded or, worse, turned into a vetting agency.

And the Overseas Development Group was on

thin ice to start with, hosting as it did the 00 Section, to which many people objected. To stumble on Incident Twenty would be a big stumble indeed. By getting Bond to Afghanistan forthwith, at least the ODG would have a player in the game, even if he arrived on the pitch a bit late.

M said evenly, 'Your point is noted, gentlemen. Let me make some phone calls.'

Bixton beamed. But Sir Andrew hadn't quite finished. His persistence, infused with shrewdness, was one of the reasons M believed that future audiences with him might take place at 10 Downing Street. 'Bond will be all-hands-on-deck?'

The threat implicit in the question was that if 007 remained in South Africa in defiance of M's orders, Sir Andrew's protection of Bond, M and the ODG would cease.

The irony in giving an agent like 007 *carte blanche* was that he was *supposed* to exercise it and act as he saw fit — which sometimes meant he would *not* be on deck with all of the other hands. You can't have it both ways, M reflected. 'As I said, I'll make some calls.'

'Good. We'd better be off.'

As they departed, M stood up and went through the french doors on to the balcony, where he noted a Metropolitan Police Specialist Protection officer, armed with a machine gun. After an examination of and a nod to the new arrival on his turf, the man returned to looking down over the street, thirty feet below. 'All quiet?' M asked.

385

'Yes, sir.'

M walked to the far end of the balcony and lit a cheroot, sucking the smoke in deep. The streets were eerily quiet. The barricades were not just the tubular metal fences you saw outside Parliament; they were cement blocks, four feet high, solid enough to stop a speeding car. The pavements were patrolled by armed guards and M noted several snipers on the roofs of nearby buildings. He gazed absently down Richmond Terrace towards Victoria Embankment.

He took out his mobile and called Moneypenny.

Only a single ring before she answered. 'Yes, sir?'

'I need to talk to the chief of staff.'

'He's popped down to the canteen. I'll connect you.'

As he waited, M squinted and gave a gruff laugh. At the intersection, near the barricade, there was a large lorry and a few men were dragging bins to and from it. They were employees of Severan Hydt's company, Green Way International. He realised he'd been watching them for the past few minutes yet not actually noticing them. They'd been invisible.

'Tanner here, sir.'

The dustmen vanished from M's thoughts. He plucked the cheroot from between his teeth and said evenly, 'Bill, I need to talk to you about 007.'

50

Guided by sat-nav, Bond made his way through central Cape Town, past businesses and residences. He found himself in an area of small, brightly coloured houses, blue, pink, red and yellow, tucked under Signal Hill. The narrow streets were largely cobbled. It reminded him of villages in the Caribbean, with the difference that here careful Arabic designs patterned many homes. He passed a quiet mosque.

It was six thirty on this cool Thursday evening and he was en route to Bheka Jordaan's house.

Friend or foe . . .

He wound the car through the uneven streets and parked nearby. She met him at the door and greeted him with an unsmiling nod. She had shed her work clothing and wore blue jeans and a close-fitting dark red cardigan. Her shiny black hair hung loose and he was taken by the rich aura of lilac scent from a recent shampooing. 'This is an interesting area,' he said. 'Nice.'

'It's called Bo-Kaap. It used to be very poor, mostly Muslim, immigrants from Malaysia. I moved here with . . . well, with someone years ago. It was poorer then. Now the place is becoming very chic. There used to be only bicycles parked outside. Now it's Toyotas but soon it'll be Mercedes. I don't like that. I'd rather it was as it used to be. But it's my home. Besides, my sisters and I take turns to have

Ugogo living with us, and they're close so it's convenient.'

'Ugogo?' Bond asked.

'It means 'grandmother'. Our mother's mother. My parents live in Pietermaritzburg, in KwaZulu-Natal, some way east of here.'

Bond recalled the antique map in her office.

'So we look after Ugogo. That's the Zulu way.'

She didn't invite him in, so, on the porch, Bond gave her an account of his trip to Green Way. 'I need the film in this developed.' He handed her the inhaler. 'It's eight-millimetre, ISO is twelve hundred. Can you sort it?'

'Me? Not your MI6 associate?' she asked acerbically.

Bond felt no need to defend Gregory Lamb. 'I trust him but he raided my minibar of two hundred rands' worth of drink. I'd like somebody with a clear head to handle it. Developing film can be tricky.'

'I'll take care of it.'

'Now, Hydt has some associates coming into town tonight. There's a meeting at the Green Way plant tomorrow morning.' He thought back to what Dunne had said. 'They're arriving at about seven. Can you find out their names?'

'Do you know the airlines?'

'No, but Dunne's meeting them.'

'We'll put a stake-out in place. Kwalene is good at that. He jokes, but he's very good.'

He certainly is. Discreet, too, Bond reflected.

A woman's voice called from inside.

Jordaan turned her head. '*Ize balulekile.*'

Some more Zulu words were exchanged.

Jordaan's face was still. 'Will you come in? So Ugogo can see you're not someone in a gang. I've told her it's no one. But she worries.'

No one?

Bond followed her into the small flat, which was tidy and nicely furnished. Prints, hangings and photos decorated the walls.

The elderly woman who'd spoken to Jordaan was sitting at a large dining table set with two places. The meal had largely concluded. She was very frail. Bond recognised her as the woman in many of the pictures in Jordaan's office. She wore a loose orange and brown frock and slippers. Her grey hair was short. She started to rise.

'No, please,' Bond said.

She stood anyway and, hunched, shuffled forward to shake his hand with a firm, dry grip.

'You are the Englishman Bheka spoke of. You don't look so bad to me.'

Jordaan glared at her.

The older woman introduced herself: 'I'm Mbali.'

'James.'

'I am going to rest. Bheka, give him some food. He's too thin.'

'No, I must be going.'

'You are hungry. I saw how you looked at the *bobotie*. It tastes even better than it looks.'

Bond smiled. He *had* been looking at the pot on the stove.

'My granddaughter is a very good cook. You will like it. And you will have some Zulu beer. Have you ever had any?'

'I've had Birkenhead and Gilroy's.'

'No, Zulu beer is the best.' Mbali shot a look at her granddaughter. 'Give him some beer and he will have some food too. Bring him a plate of *bobotie*. And *sambal* sauce.' She looked critically at Bond. 'You like spice?'

'I do, yes.'

'Good.'

Exasperated, Jordaan said, 'Ugogo, he said he has to be going.'

'He said that because of you. Give him some beer and some food. Look how thin he is!'

'Honestly, Ugogo.'

'That's my granddaughter. A mind of her own.'

The old woman picked up a ceramic crock of beer and walked into a bedroom. The door closed.

'Is she well?' Bond asked.

'Cancer.'

'I'm sorry.'

'She's doing better than expected. She's ninety-seven.'

Bond was surprised. 'I would have thought she was in her seventies.'

As if afraid of the silence that might engender the need for conversation, Jordaan strode to a battered CD player and loaded a disc. A woman's low voice, buoyed by hip-hop rhythms, burst from the speakers. Bond saw the CD cover: Thandiswa Mazwai.

'Sit down,' Jordaan said, gesturing at the table.

'No, it's all right.'

'What do you mean, no, it's all right?'

'You don't have to feed me.'

Jordaan said shortly, 'If Ugogo learns I haven't offered you any beer or *bobotie*, she won't be happy.' She produced a clay pot with a rattan lid and poured some frothy pinkish liquid into a glass.

'So that's Zulu beer?'

'Yes.'

'Homemade?'

'Zulu beer is always homemade. It takes three days to brew and you drink it while it's still fermenting.'

Bond sipped. It was sour yet sweet and seemed low in alcohol.

Jordaan then served him a plate of *bobotie* and spooned on some reddish sauce. It was a bit like shepherd's pie, with egg instead of potato on top, but better than any pie Bond had ever had in England. The thick sauce was well flavoured and indeed spicy.

'You're not joining me?' Bond nodded towards an empty chair. Jordaan was standing, leaning against the sink, arms folded across her voluptuous chest.

'I've finished eating,' she said, the words clipped. She remained where she was.

Friend or foe . . .

He finished the food. 'I must say you're quite talented — a clever policewoman who also makes marvellous beer and,' a nod at the cooking pot, '*bobotie*. If I'm pronouncing that right.'

He received no response. Did he insult her with every remark he made?

391

Bond tamped down his irritation and found himself regarding the many photographs of the family on the walls and mantelpiece. 'Your grandmother must have seen a great deal of history in the making.'

Glancing affectionately at the bedroom door, she said, 'Ugogo *is* South Africa. Her uncle was wounded at the battle of Kambula, fighting the British — a few months after the battle I told you about, Isandlwana. She was born just a few years after the Union of South Africa was formed from the Cape and Natal provinces. She was relocated under apartheid's Group Areas Act in the fifties. And she was wounded in a protest in 1960.'

'What happened?'

'The Sharpeville Massacre. She was among those protesting against the *dompas* — the 'dumb pass', it was called. Under apartheid people were legally classified as white, black, coloured or Indian.'

Bond recalled Gregory Lamb's comments.

'Blacks had to carry a passbook signed by their employer allowing them to be in a white area. It was humiliating, it was horrible. There was a peaceful protest but the police fired on the demonstrators. Nearly seventy people were killed. Ugogo was shot. Her leg. That's why she limps.'

Jordaan hesitated and at last poured herself some beer, then sipped. 'Ugogo gave me my name. That is, she told my parents what they would call me and they did. One usually does what Ugogo says.'

' 'Bheka',' Bond said.

'In Zulu it means 'one who watches over people'.'

'A protector. So you were destined to become a policewoman.' Bond was quite enjoying the music.

'Ugogo is the old South Africa. I'm the new. A mix of Zulu and Afrikaner. They call us a rainbow country, yes, but look at a rainbow and you still see different colours, all separate. We need to become like me, blended together. It will be a long time before that happens. But it will.' She glanced coolly at Bond. 'Then we'll be able to dislike people for who they really are. Not for the colour of their skin.'

Bond returned her gaze evenly and said, 'Thank you for the food and the beer. I should be going.'

She walked with him to the door. He stepped outside.

Which was when he caught his first clear glimpse of the man who'd pursued him from Dubai. The man in the blue jacket and the gold earring, the man who had killed Yusuf Nasad and had very nearly killed Felix Leiter.

He was standing across the road, in the shadows of an old building covered with Arabic scrolls and mosaics.

'What is it?' Jordaan asked.

'A hostile.'

The man had a mobile but wasn't making a call; he was taking a picture of Bond with Jordaan — proof that Bond was working with the police.

Bond snapped, 'Get your weapon and stay inside with your grandmother.'

He sprinted hard across the street as the man fled up a narrow alley leading towards Signal Hill, through the deepening dusk.

51

The man had a ten-yard lead, but Bond began closing the distance as they pounded up the alley. Angry cats and scrawny dogs fled, a child with round Malaysian features stepped out of a door into Bond's path and was instantly jerked back by a parental hand.

He was nearly fifteen feet from the assailant when operational instinct kicked in. Bond realised that the man might have prepared a trap to aid his escape. He glanced down. Yes! The attacker had strung a piece of wire across the alley, a foot off the ground, nearly invisible in the darkness. The man himself had known where it was — a shard of broken crockery marked the spot — and had stepped over it smoothly. Bond wasn't able to stop in time but he could prepare himself for the fall.

He twisted his shoulder forward and when his own momentum swept his legs out from under him, he half somersaulted on to the ground. He landed hard and lay dazed for a moment, cursing himself for letting the man get away.

Except that he wasn't escaping.

The wire hadn't been intended to hinder pursuit but to render Bond vulnerable.

In an instant the man was on him, exuding the stench of beer, stale cigarette smoke and unwashed flesh, and ripping Bond's Walther from the holster. Bond launched himself upwards, gripping the man's right arm in a lock and twisting his wrist until the weapon fell to the ground. The attacker kicked the gun, which flew far from Bond's reach. Gasping, Bond kept hold of the man's right arm and dodged vicious blows from his other fist.

He glanced back, wondering if Bheka Jordaan had ignored his advice and come after him, armed with her own weapon. The empty alley gaped at him.

Now his assailant eased back to deliver a forehead blow. But, as Bond twisted to avoid it, the man rolled away, in a virtual backward somersault, like a gymnast. It was a brilliant feint. Bond recalled Felix Leiter's words.

Man, the SOB knows some martial arts crap . . .

Then Bond was on his feet, facing the man, who stood in a fighter's stance, a knife in his hand, blade protruding downwards, sharp edge facing out. His left hand, open and palm down, floated distractingly, ready to grab Bond's clothing and pull him in to be stabbed to death.

On the balls of his feet, Bond circled.

Ever since his days at Fettes in Edinburgh, he had practised various types of close combat, but the ODG taught its agents a rare style of unarmed fighting, borrowed from a former (or not so former) enemy — the Russians. An ancient martial art of the Cossacks, *systema* had been updated by the Spetsnaz, the special forces branch of GRU military intelligence.

Systema practitioners rarely use their fists. Open palms, elbows and knees are the main

396

weapons. The goal, though, is to strike as infrequently as possible. Rather, you tire out your adversary, then catch him in a come-on or take-down hold on the shoulder, wrist, arm or ankle. The best *systema* fighters never come into contact with their opponent at all . . . until the final moment, when the exhausted attacker is largely defenceless. Then the victor takes him to the ground and drops a knee into his chest or throat.

Instinctively falling into *systema* choreography, Bond now dodged the man's assault.

Evade, evade, evade . . . Use his energy against him.

Bond was largely successful but twice the knife blade swept inches from his face.

The man moved in fast, swinging his massive hands, testing Bond, who stepped aside, sizing up his opponent's strengths (he was very muscular and experienced in hand-to-hand combat and was psychologically prepared to kill) and his weaknesses (alcohol and smoking seemed to be taking their toll).

The man grew frustrated at Bond's defence. Now he gripped the knife for thrusting and began to move in, almost desperate. He was grinning demonically, sweating despite the chill in the air.

Presenting a vulnerable target, his lower back, Bond stepped towards his Walther. But the move was a feint. And even before the man lunged, Bond reared back, pushed the knife blade away with his forearm and delivered a fierce open-palm slap to the man's left ear. He cupped his hand as he made contact and felt the pressure that would damage if not burst the attacker's ear drum. The man howled in pain, infuriated, and lunged carelessly. Bond easily lifted the knife arm away and up, then stepped in, gripping the wrist in both hands, a solid compliance hold, and bent backwards until the knife fell to the ground. He assessed the assailant's strength and his mad determination. He made a decision . . . and he twisted further until the wrist cracked.

The man cried out and sank to his knees, then dropped into a sitting position, face pale. His head lolled to the side and Bond kicked the knife away. He frisked the man carefully and took a small automatic pistol from his pocket, along with a roll of duct tape. A pistol? Why didn't he just shoot me? Bond wondered.

He slipped the gun into his pocket and collected his Walther. He grabbed the man's phone — to whom had he texted the photo of him and Jordaan? If it had been to Dunne alone, could Bond find and incapacitate the Irishman before he reported to Hydt?

He scrolled through the call and text logs. Thank God, he had sent nothing. He'd simply been videoing Bond.

What was the point of that?

Then he had his answer.

'*Jebi ti!*' his attacker spat.

The Balkan obscenity explained everything.

Bond went through the man's papers and confirmed he was with the JSO, the Serbian paramilitary group. His name was Nicholas Rathko.

He was moaning now, cradling his arm. 'You let my brother die! You abandoned him! He was your partner on that assignment. You *never* abandon your partner.'

Rathko's brother had been the younger of the BIA agents with Bond on Sunday night near Novi Sad.

My brother, he smokes all time he is out on operations. Looks more normal than not smoking in Serbia . . .

Bond knew now how the man had found him in Dubai. To secure the BIA's co-operation in Serbia, the ODG and Six had given the senior security people in Belgrade Bond's real name and mission. After his brother had died, Rathko and his comrades at the JSO would have put together a full-scale operation to find Bond, using contacts through NATO and Six. They'd learnt Bond was bound for Dubai. Of course, Bond now realised, it had been *Rathko*, not Osborne-Smith, who'd been making those subtle inquiries at MI6 about Bond's plans earlier in the week. Among Rathko's papers he now found authorisation for a flight by military jet from Belgrade to Dubai. Which explained how he'd beaten Bond to the emirate. A local mercenary, the documents revealed, had put an untraceable car — the black Toyota — at the JSO agent's disposal.

And the purpose?

Probably not arrest and rendition. Rathko had most likely been planning to video Bond confessing or apologising — or perhaps to record his torture and death.

'You call yourself Nicholas or Nick?' Bond asked, crouching.

'*Yebie se,*' was the only response.

'Listen to me. I'm sorry your brother lost his life. But he had no business being in the BIA. He was careless and he wouldn't follow orders. He was the reason we lost the target.'

'He was young.'

'That's no excuse. It wouldn't be an excuse for me and it wasn't an excuse for you when you were with Arkan's Tigers.'

'He was only a boy.' Tears glistened in the man's eyes, whether from the pain of the broken wrist or the sorrow he felt for his dead brother, Bond couldn't tell.

Bond looked down the alleyway and saw Bheka Jordaan and some SAPS officers sprinting towards him. He bent down, picked up the man's knife and sliced through the trip wire.

He squatted beside the Serb. 'We'll get you to a doctor.'

Then he heard a woman's voice call sharply, 'Stop!'

He glanced at Bheka Jordaan. 'It's all right. I have his weapons.'

But then he realised that her pistol was aimed at himself. He frowned and stood up.

'Leave him alone!' she snapped.

Two SAPS officers stepped between Bond and Rathko. One hesitated, then carefully took the knife from his hand.

'He's a Serbian intelligence agent. He was trying to kill me. He's the one who murdered that CIA asset in Dubai the other day.'

'That doesn't mean you can cut his throat.' Her dark eyes were narrow with anger.

'What are you talking about?'

'You are in my country. You will obey the law!' The other officers were staring at him, Bond saw, some angrily. He glanced at Jordaan and stepped away, gesturing to her to follow.

Jordaan did so and when they were out of earshot, she continued harshly, 'You won. He was down, he wasn't a threat. Why were you going to kill him?'

'I wasn't,' he said.

'I don't believe you. You told me to stay in the house with my grandmother. You didn't ask me to call my officers because you didn't want witnesses while you tortured and killed him.'

'I assumed you'd call for back-up. I didn't want you to leave your grandmother in case he wasn't working alone.'

But Jordaan wasn't listening. She raged, 'You come here, to our country, with that double-0 number of yours. Oh, I know all about what you do!'

Finally Bond understood the source of her anger with him. It had nothing to do with any attempted flirtation, nothing to do with the fact that he represented the oppressive male. She despised his shameless disregard for the law: the Level 1 missions — assassinations — for the ODG.

He stepped forward and said in a low murmur, barely able to control his anger, 'In a few instances when there's been no other way to protect my country, yes, I've taken a life. And

401

only if I've been ordered to. I don't do it because I want to. I don't enjoy it. I do it to save people who deserve to be saved. You may call it a sin — but it's a necessary sin.'

'There was no need to kill him,' she spat back.

'I wasn't going to.'

'The knife . . . I saw — '

'He left a trap. The trip wire.' He gestured. 'I cut it so nobody would fall. As for him,' he nodded towards the Serb, 'I was just telling him we'd get him to a doctor. Ask him. I rarely take someone to hospital when I'm about to murder them.' He turned and pushed past the two police officers blocking his way. His eyes defied them to try and stop him. Without looking back, he called, 'I'll need that film developed as soon as possible. And the IDs of everyone coming to Hydt's tomorrow.' He strode away from them down the alley.

Soon he was in the Subaru, streaking past the colourful houses of Bo-Kaap, driving far faster than was safe through the winding, picturesque streets.

52

A restaurant featuring local cuisine beckoned and James Bond, still angry from his run-in with Bheka Jordaan, decided he needed a strong drink.

He'd enjoyed the stew at Jordaan's house but the portion was rather small, as if doled out with the intent that the diner finish quickly and depart. Bond now ordered a hearty meal of *sosaties* — grilled meat skewers — with yellow rice and *marog* spinach (having politely declined an offer to try the house speciality of *mopane* worms). He downed two vodka martinis with the food, then returned to the Table Mountain Hotel.

Bond had a shower, dried himself and dressed. There was a knock on the door. A porter delivered a large envelope. Whatever else, Jordaan had not let her personal view that he was a coldblooded serial killer interfere with the job. Inside he found black-and-white prints of the images he'd taken with the inhaler camera. Some were blurred and others had missed their mark but he had managed a clear series of what he was most interested in: the door to Research and Development at Green Way and its alarm and locking mechanisms. Jordaan had also been professional enough to provide a flash drive of the scanned pictures, and his anger diminished further. He loaded them on to his laptop, encrypted them and sent them to Sanu Hirani, with a set of instructions.

Thirty seconds after he'd hit send, he received a message back. We never sleep.

He smiled, and texted an acknowledgement.

A few minutes later he took a call from Bill Tanner in London.

'I was just about to ring you,' Bond said.

'James . . . ' Tanner sounded grave. There was a problem.

'Go ahead.'

'There's a bit of a flap on here. Whitehall's come round to thinking that Incident Twenty doesn't have much of a connection with South Africa.'

'What?'

'They think Hydt's a diversion. The killings in Incident Twenty are going to be in Afghanistan, aid workers or contractors, they reckon. The Intelligence Committee voted to pull you out and send you to Kabul — since, frankly, you haven't found much of anything concrete where you are.'

Bond's heart was pounding. 'Bill, I'm convinced the key — '

'Hold on,' Tanner interrupted. 'I'm just telling you what they wanted. But M dug his heels in and insisted you stay. It turned into Trafalgar, big and loud. We all went to the foreign secretary and pitched the case. There's some talk the PM was involved, though I can't confirm that. Anyway, M won. You're to stay in place. And you'll be interested to know there was a witness for the defence — in your support.'

'Who?'

'Your new friend Percy.'

'Osborne-Smith?' Bond nearly laughed.

'He said if you had a lead you ought to be allowed to follow it up.'

'Did he now? I'll buy him a pint when all this is over. You too.'

'Well, things aren't as rosy as they seem,' Tanner said glumly. 'The old man put the ODG's reputation on the line to keep you there. *Your* reputation too. If it turns out Hydt *is* a diversion, there'll be repercussions. Serious ones.'

Was the very future of the ODG riding on his success?

Politics, Bond reflected cynically. He said, 'I'm sure Hydt's behind it.'

'And M's going with that judgement.' Tanner asked what his next steps would be.

'I'll be at Hydt's plant tomorrow morning. Depending on what I find, I'm going to have to move fast, and communications could be a problem. If I can't learn anything by late afternoon, I'll get Bheka Jordaan to raid the place, interrogate the hell out of Hydt and Dunne and find out what's planned for tomorrow night.'

'All right, James. Keep me informed. I'll brief M. He'll be in that security meeting all day.'

'Night, Bill. And thank him for me.'

After they had rung off, he poured a generous amount of Crown Royal into a crystal glass, added two ice cubes and turned off the lights. He flung wide the curtains, sat on the sofa and gazed out over the snowflake lights on the harbour. A massive British-flag cruise ship was easing up to the dock.

His phone trilled and he glanced at the screen. 'Philly.' He took another sip of the fragrant whisky.

'Are you in the middle of dinner?'

'It's après-cocktail cocktail hour here.'

'You are a man after my own heart.' As she said this, Bond's eyes happened to be on the bed he'd shared last night with Felicity Willing. Philly continued, 'I didn't know if you wanted more updates on the Steel Cartridge operation . . .'

He sat forward. 'Yes, please. What've you found?'

'Something interesting, I think. Seems the whole point of the operation wasn't to kill just *any* of our agents and contractors. The Russians were killing their moles within MI6 and the CIA.'

Bond felt something detonate inside him. He put his glass down.

'With the fall of the Soviet Union, the Kremlin wanted to solidify ties with the West. It would've been awkward politically if their doubles were exposed. So active KGB agents killed the most successful moles in Six and the CIA and made the murders look like accidents — but left a steel cartridge at the scene as a warning to the others to keep quiet. That's all I know at this point.'

My God, Bond thought. His father . . . his father had been a double — a *traitor?*

'Are you still there?'

'Yes — just a bit distracted by what's going on here. But that's good work, Philly. I'll be incommunicado for most of tomorrow but text me or

406

email what you find.'

'I will. Take care of yourself, James. I worry.'

They rang off.

Bond lifted the cold crystal glass, wet with condensation, and pressed it against his forehead. He now scrolled mentally through his family's past, trying to find clues about Andrew Bond that might shed light on this appalling theory. Bond had been quite fond of his father, who was a collector of stamps and photographs of cars. He'd owned several vehicles but took more pleasure in repairing and cleaning them than in fast driving. When older, Bond had asked his aunt about the man. Charmian had thought for a moment and said, 'He was a good man, of course. Solid, dependable. A rock. But quiet. Andrew was never one to stand out.'

Qualities of the best covert intelligence agents.

Could he have been a mole for the Russians?

Another jarring thought: his father's duplicity — if the story were true — had resulted in the death of his wife, Bond's mother, too.

Not just the Russians but his father's betrayal had orphaned young Bond.

He started as his phone buzzed with an incoming text.

Late night getting ready for food shipments.
Just left office. Interested in some company?
Felicity.

James Bond hesitated a moment. Then he typed Yes.

Ten minutes later, after slipping his Walther

under the bed beneath a towel, he heard a soft knock. He opened the door and let in Felicity Willing. Any doubt he might have had about whether or not they would pick up where they left off yesterday was dashed when she flung her arms around him and kissed him hard. He smelt her perfume, radiating from behind her ear, and she tasted of mint.

'I'm a mess,' she said, laughing. She wore a blue cotton shirt, tucked into designer jeans, which were crumpled and dusty.

'I won't hear of it,' he said and kissed her again.

'You're sitting in the dark, Gene,' she said. And for the first time in the operation he was jarred by the reminder of his Afrikaner cover.

'I like the view.'

They stepped apart and in the dim light from outside Bond took in her face and thought it as intensely sensual as last night, but she was clearly tired. He supposed the logistics of marshalling the largest shipment of food ever to arrive on the African continent were daunting, to say the least.

'Here.' A wine bottle appeared from her shoulder bag — vintage Three Cape Ladies, a red blend from Muldersvlei on the Cape. Bond knew its reputation. He took out the cork and poured. They sat on the sofa and sipped.

'Wonderful,' he said.

She worked her boots off. Bond slipped his arm around her shoulders and struggled to put aside thoughts of his father.

Felicity slumped, and rested her head against him. On the horizon there were even more ships than there had been last night. 'Our food ships. Look at them all,' she said. 'You hear so many bad things about people but that's not the complete truth. There's a lot of good out there. You can't always count on it, it's never certain, but at least — '

Bond interrupted, 'At least someone's . . . *willing* to help.'

She laughed. 'You nearly made me spill my wine, Gene. I could've ruined my shirt.'

'I have a solution.'

'Stop drinking the wine?' She pouted playfully. 'But it's so nice.'

'Another solution, a better one.' He kissed her and slowly began to undo the buttons of the garment.

★　★　★

An hour later, they lay in bed, on their sides, Bond behind Felicity. His arm was curled around her and his hand cupped her breast. Her fingers were entwined in his.

Unlike last night, however, in the after-moment, Bond was wholly awake.

His mind was racing furiously, past all assortment of topics. Exactly how much was the future of the ODG resting on him? What secrets did the Research and Development department of Green Way hold? What exactly was Hydt's goal with Gehenna and how could Bond craft a suitable countermeasure?

Purpose . . . response.

And what of his father?

'You're thinking about something serious,' Felicity said drowsily.

'What makes you say that?'

'Women know.'

'I'm thinking how beautiful you are.'

She lifted his hand to her face and gently bit his finger. 'The first lie you've told me.'

'My job,' he said.

'Then I'll forgive you. It's the same with me. Co-ordinating the help on the docks, paying the pilots' fees, working on the ship charters and lorry leases, the trade unions.' Her voice took on the edge he'd heard before, as she said, 'And then *your* speciality. We've already had two attempted break-ins at the dock. And no food has even been offloaded yet. Odd.' Silence for a moment. Then: 'Gene?'

Bond knew something significant was coming. He grew alert and receptive. The intimacy of bodies comes prepacked with an intimacy of mind and spirit, and you ought not seek the first if you're unwilling to take delivery of the second. 'Yes?'

She said evenly, 'I have a feeling there's more to your work than you've told me. No, don't say anything. I don't know how you feel but if it turns out we can keep seeing each other, if . . .' She trailed off.

'Go on,' he whispered.

'If it turns out we see each other again, do you think that maybe you could change just a bit? I mean, if you do go to some dark places, could you promise me not to go to the . . . worst?' He felt the tension that rippled through her. 'Oh, I

410

don't know what I'm saying. Ignore me, Gene.'

Although she was speaking to a security expert-cum-mercenary soldier from Durban, in a way she was also talking to him, James Bond, a 00 Section agent.

And, ironically, he took her acknowledgement that she could live with a certain degree of darkness in Theron as indication that she might accept Bond as he was.

He whispered, 'I think that's very possible.'

She kissed his hand. 'Don't say any more. That's all I wanted to hear. Now, I have an idea. I don't know what your plans are for this weekend . . . '

Neither do I, Bond thought sourly.

' . . . but we'll have finished the food shipments tomorrow night. There's an inn I know in Franschhoek — have you been to that area?'

'No.'

'It's the most beautiful spot on the Western Cape. A wine district. The restaurant has a Michelin star and the most romantic deck in the world, overlooking the hills. Come with me on Saturday?'

'I'd love to,' he said and kissed her hair.

'You really mean that?' The tough warrior who seemed so at ease fighting the world's agropolies now sounded vulnerable and unsure.

'Yes, I do.'

In five minutes she was asleep.

Bond, however, remained awake, staring out at the lights of the harbour. His thoughts were no longer on his father's possible betrayal, nor on his promise to Felicity Willing to consider changing his darkest nature nor on the anticipation of the time they might spend together this weekend. No, James Bond was focusing on one thing only: the indistinct faces of those, somewhere in the world, whose lives — despite Whitehall's belief — he knew that he alone could save.

Friday
DOWN TO GEHENNA

53

At eight forty a.m. Bond steered his dusty, mud-spattered Subaru into the Cape Town SAPS headquarters car park. He killed the engine, climbed out and entered the building, where he found Bheka Jordaan, Gregory Lamb and Kwalene Nkosi in her office.

Bond greeted them with a nod. Lamb responded with a look that bespoke intrigue, Nkosi with an energetic smile.

Jordaan said, 'Regarding Hydt's newly arrived associates, we've identified them.' She spun her laptop and clicked on a slide-show. The first photos depicted a large man with a round ebony face. He wore a brash gold and silver shirt, designer sunglasses and voluminous brown slacks.

'Charles Mathebula. He's a black diamond from Joburg.'

Lamb explained: 'From the new wealthy class in South Africa. Some of them become rich overnight in ways that aren't quite transparent, if you get my drift.'

'And some,' Jordaan added frostily, 'became wealthy by hard work. Mathebula owns businesses that seem to be legitimate — shipping and transport. He was on the borderline with some arms deliveries a few years ago, true, but there was no evidence of wrongdoing.' A tap of a key and another picture appeared. 'Now, this is David Huang.' He was slim and smiled at the camera. 'His daughter posted the snapshot on her Facebook page. Stupid girl . . . though good for us.'

'A known mobster?'

Nkosi qualified, 'A *suspected* mobster. Singapore. Mostly money-laundering. Possibly human trafficking.'

Another face appeared. Jordaan tapped her computer screen. 'The German — Hans Eberhard. He came in on Wednesday. Mining interests, diamonds primarily. Industrial grade but some jewellery.' A good-looking blond man was pictured leaving the airport. He was wearing a well-cut light suit, a shirt without a tie. 'He's been suspected of various crimes but he's technically clean.'

Bond studied the photos of the men.

Eberhard.

Huang.

Mathebula.

He memorised the names.

Frowning, Jordaan said, 'I don't understand why Hydt needs partners, though. He's got money enough to fund Gehenna himself, I should think.'

Bond had already considered this. 'Two reasons, most likely. Gehenna must be expensive. He'd want outside money so that if he's ever audited he doesn't have to explain huge liabilities on the books. But, more important, he doesn't have a criminal background or network. Whatever Gehenna's about, he'll need the contacts that people like these three can offer.'

'Yes,' Jordaan allowed. 'That makes sense.'

Bond looked at Lamb. 'Sanu Hirani in Q

416

Branch texted me this morning. He said you had something for me.'

'Ah, yes — sorry.' The Six agent handed him an envelope.

Bond peered inside and then pocketed it. 'I'm going out to the plant now. Once I'm inside I'll try to find out what Incident Twenty is, who's at risk and where. I'll get word out as soon as I can. But we need a fall-back plan.' If they hadn't heard from him by four p.m., Jordaan should order tactical officers to raid the plant, detain Hydt, Dunne and the partners and seize the contents of the Research and Development department. 'This will give us — or you, if I'm no longer in the game — five or six hours to interrogate them and find out what Incident Twenty's all about.'

'A raid?' Jordaan was frowning. 'I can't do that.'

'Why not?'

'I've told you. Unless I have reasonable belief that a crime is occurring at Green Way, or a magistrate's order, there's nothing I can do.'

Damn the woman. 'This isn't about preserving his rights for a fair trial. This is about saving thousands of people — possibly many South Africans.'

'I can do nothing without a warrant and there's no evidence to present to the court to get one. No justification to act.'

'If I don't turn up by four, you can assume he's killed me.'

'Obviously I hope that doesn't happen, Commander, but your absence doesn't equal cause.'

'I've told you he's willing to dig up the graves

of massacre victims and turn them into building materials. What more do you want?'

'Evidence of a crime somewhere in the plant.' Her jaw was set and her eyes black granite. It was clear she wouldn't yield.

Bond said sharply, 'Then let's hope to God I can find the answer. For the sake of several thousand innocent people.' He nodded to Nkosi and Lamb and, ignoring Jordaan, left the office. He strode downstairs to his car, dropped into the driver's seat and fired up the engine.

'James, wait!' Turning, he saw Bheka Jordaan walking towards him. 'Please, wait.'

Bond thought about speeding away but instead he rolled the window down.

'Yesterday,' she said, bending down, close to him, 'the Serbian?'

'Yes?'

'I spoke to him. He told me what you'd said — that you were going to get him to a doctor.'

Bond nodded.

After a breath, the policewoman added, 'I was making assumptions. I . . . sometimes I do that. I judge first. I try not to but it's hard for me to stop. I wanted to apologise.'

'Accepted,' he said.

'About a raid at Green Way, though? You must understand. Under apartheid the old police, the SAP and their Criminal Investigation Department, did terrible things. Now everyone watches *us*, the new police, to make sure we don't do the same. An illegal raid, arbitrary arrests and interrogations . . . that's what the old regime did. We cannot do the same. We must be *better* than the people who came before us.' Her face taut with determination, she said, 'I'll fight side by side with you if the law permits, but without cause, without a warrant, there's nothing I can do. I'm sorry.'

Much of the training of 00 Section agents in the Group was psychological and part of that arduous instruction was to instil within them the belief that they were different, that they were allowed to — no, *required* to — operate outside the law. A Level 1 project order, authorising assassination, had to be, to James Bond, just another aspect of his job, no different from taking pictures of secret installations or planting misinformation in the press.

As M had put it, Bond had to have *carte blanche* to do whatever was required to fulfil his mission.

We protect the Realm . . . by any means necessary.

That was part of Bond's fabric — indeed, he couldn't do his job without it — and he had to remind himself continually that Bheka Jordaan and the other hard-working law enforcers of the world were one hundred per cent right in respecting the rules. It was *he* who was the outlier.

He said, not unkindly, 'I do understand, Captain. And whatever happens, it's been quite an experience working with you.'

Her response was a smile, faint and fleeting but, Bond judged, honest — the first time that such an expression had warmed her beautiful face in his presence.

54

Bond skidded the Subaru into the car park outside the fortress of Green Way International and braked to a stop.

Several limousines were lined up close to the gate.

REDUCE, REUSE, RECYCLE

A few people were milling about. Bond recognised the German businessman, Hans Eberhard, in a beige suit and white shoes. He was talking to Niall Dunne, who stood still as a Japanese fighting fish. The breeze ruffled his blond fringe. Eberhard was finishing a cigarette. Perhaps Hydt didn't allow anyone to smoke inside the plant, which seemed ironic; the outside air was bleached with haze and vapours from the power plant and the methane that was being burnt.

Bond waved to Dunne, who acknowledged him with a blank nod and continued his conversation with the German. Then Dunne pulled his phone off his belt and read a text or email. He whispered something to Eberhard, then stepped away to make a call. On the pretence of using his own phone, Bond loaded the eavesdropping app and lifted it to his ear, rolling down the passenger window of his car and aiming it in the direction of the Irishman. He stared ahead and mouthed to himself so that

Dunne would not guess a microphone was pointed his way.

The Irishman's conversation was one-sided but Bond heard him say, ' . . . outside with Hans. He wanted a smoke . . . I know.'

He was probably speaking to Hydt.

Dunne continued, 'We're on schedule. I just had an email. The lorry left March for York. Should be there any minute. The device is already armed.'

So, this was Incident Twenty! The attack would take place in York.

'The target's confirmed. Detonation's still scheduled for ten thirty, their time.'

Dismayed, Bond noted the time of the attack. They'd assumed ten thirty at night but every time Dunne had referred to a time he'd used the twenty-four-hour clock. Had it been half past ten in the evening he would have said, 'Twenty-two thirty.'

Dunne looked at Bond's car and said into the phone, 'Theron's here . . . Right, then.' He disconnected and called to Eberhard that the meeting would start soon. Then he turned to Bond. He seemed impatient.

Bond dialled a number. Please, he whispered silently. Answer.

Then: 'Osborne-Smith.'

Thank God. 'Percy. It's James Bond. Listen carefully. I have about sixty seconds. I've got the answer to Incident Twenty. You'll have to move fast. Mobilise a team. SOCA, Five, local police. The bomb's in York.'

'York?'

421

'Hydt's people're driving the device in a lorry from March to York. It's going to detonate later this morning. I don't know where they'll plant it. Maybe a sporting event — there was that reference to 'course', so try the racecourse. Or somewhere there's a big crowd. Check all the CCTVs in and around March, get the number plates of as many lorries as you can. Then compare them to the plates of any lorries arriving in York about now. You need to — '

'Hold on there, Bond,' Osborne-Smith said coolly. 'It has nothing to do with March or Yorkshire.'

Bond noted the use of his last name and the imperious tone in Osborne-Smith's voice. 'What are you talking about?'

Dunne gestured to him. Bond nodded, struggling to smile amiably.

'Did you know Hydt's companies reclaim dangerous materials?'

'Well, yes. But — '

'Remember I told you he was digging tunnels for some fancy new rubbish collection system under London, including around Whitehall?' Osborne-Smith sounded like a barrister before a witness.

Bond was sweating now. 'But that's not what this is about.'

Dunne was acting increasingly impatient, his eyes focusing on Bond.

'I beg to differ,' Osborne-Smith said prissily. 'One of the tunnels isn't far from the security meeting today in Richmond Terrace. Your boss, mine, senior CIA, Six, Joint Intelligence

422

Committee — it's a veritable *Who's Who* of the security world. Hydt was going to release something nasty that his hazardous-materials operation had recovered. Kill everybody. His people have been hauling bins in and out of the tunnels and buildings near Whitehall for the past several days. Nobody's thought to check them out.'

Bond said evenly, 'Percy, that's not what's going on. He's not going to use Green Way people directly for the attack. It's too obvious. He'd be implicated himself.'

'Then how do you explain our little find in the tunnels? Radiation.'

'How much?' Bond asked bluntly.

A pause. Osborne-Smith replied in his petulant lisp, 'About four millirems.'

'That's *nothing*, Percy.' All O Branch agents were well versed in nuclear exposure statistics. 'Every human being on earth gets hit with sixty millirems from cosmic rays alone each year. Add an X-ray or two and you're up to two hundred. A dirty bomb's going to leave more trace than four.'

Ignoring him, Osborne-Smith said brightly, 'Now, about York, you misheard. It must be the Duke of York pub or the theatre in London. Could be a staging area. We'll check it. In the event, I cancelled the security meeting, moved everyone to secure locations. Bond, I've been thinking about what makes Hydt tick ever since I saw he was living in Canning Town and you told me all about his obsession with thousand-year-old dead bodies. He revels in decay, cities crumbling.'

Dunne was now walking slowly forward, making directly for the Subaru.

Bond said, 'I know, Percy, but — '

'What better way to promote social decay than to take down the security apparatus of half the Western powers?'

'Dammit, fine. Do what you want in London. But have SOCA or some teams from Five follow up in York.'

'We don't have the manpower, do we? Can't spare a soul. Maybe this afternoon but for now, afraid not. Nothing's going to happen till tonight, anyway.'

Bond explained that the time of the operation had been moved forward.

A chuckle. 'Your Irishman prefers the twenty-four-hour clock, does he? . . . Bit fine-tuned, that. No, we'll stick with my plan.'

This was why Osborne-Smith had backed M's stand to have Bond remain in South Africa; he hadn't in fact believed Bond was on to anything. He had simply wanted to steal the thunder. Bond disconnected and started to dial Bill Tanner.

But Dunne was at the door, yanking it open. 'Come on, Theron. You're keeping your new boss waiting. You know the drill. Leave the phone and the gun in the car.'

'I thought I'd check them in with your smiling concierge.'

If it came down to a fight, he hoped to be able to pick up his weapon and to communicate with the outside world.

But Dunne said, 'Not today.'

Bond didn't argue. He secured his phone and the Walther in the car's glove box, joined Dunne and locked the car with the key fob.

As he once again endured the rituals at the security post, Bond happened to glance at a clock on the wall. It was nearly eight a.m. in York. He had just over two and a half hours to find out where the bomb was planted.

55

The Green Way lobby was deserted. Bond supposed Hydt — or, more likely, Dunne — had arranged for the staff to have the day off so that the meeting and the Gehenna plan's maiden voyage could go forward without interruption.

Severan Hydt strode up the hall, greeting Bond warmly. He was in good spirits, ebullient even. His dark eyes shone. 'Theron!'

Bond shook his hand.

'I'll want you to make a presentation to my associates about the killing-fields project. It'll be their money too that'll fund it. Now, you don't need to do anything formal. Just outline on a map where the major graves are, how many corpses roughly are in each one, how long they've been in the ground and what you think your clients will be willing to pay. Oh, by the way, one or two of my partners are in lines of work similar to yours. You might know each other.'

The alarming thought now occurred to Bond that these men might wonder the opposite: why they had *not* heard of the ruthless Durban-based mercenary Gene Theron, who'd seeded the African earth with so many bodies.

As they walked through the Green Way building, Bond asked where he could work, hoping that Hydt might take him to Research and Development, now that he was a trusted partner.

426

'We have an office for you.' But the man led him past the R&D department to a large, windowless room. Inside were a few chairs, a work table and a desk. He'd been provided with office supplies like yellow pads and pens, dozens of detailed maps of Africa and an intercom but no phone. Corkboards on the walls displayed copies of the pictures that Bond had delivered of the decaying bodies. He wondered where the originals were.

In Hydt's bedroom?

The Rag-and-bone Man asked pleasantly, 'Will this do?'

'Fine. A computer would be helpful.'

'I could arrange that — for word processing and printing. No Internet access, of course.'

'No?'

'We're concerned about hacking and security. But for now, don't worry about writing anything up formally. Handwritten notes are enough.'

Bond maintained a calm façade as he noted the clock. It was now eight twenty in York. Just over two hours to go. 'Well, I'd better get down to it.'

'We'll be up the hall in the main conference room. Go to the end and turn left. Number nine hundred. Join us whenever you like, but make sure you're there before half twelve. We'll have something on television I think you'll find interesting.'

Ten thirty York time.

After Hydt had gone, Bond bent over the map and drew circles around some of the areas he'd arbitrarily picked as battle zones when he and

Hydt had met at the Lodge Club. He jotted a few numbers — signifying the body counts — then bundled up the maps, a yellow pad and some pens. He stepped into the corridor, which was empty. Orienting himself, Bond went back to Research and Development.

Tradecraft dictates that simpler is usually the best approach, even in a black bag operation like this.

Accordingly Bond knocked on the door.

Mr Hydt asked me to find some papers for him . . . Sorry to bother you, I'll just be a moment . . .

He was prepared to rush the person who opened the door and use a take-down hold on wrist or arm to overpower them. Prepared for an armed guard too — indeed, hoping for one, so he could relieve the man of his weapon.

But there was no answer. These staff had apparently been given the day off, too.

Bond fell back on plan two, which was somewhat less simple. Last night he had uploaded to Sanu Hirani the digital pictures he'd taken of the security door to Research and Development. The head of Q Branch had reported that the lock was virtually impregnable. It would take hours to hack. He and his team would try to think up another solution.

Shortly thereafter Bond had received word that Hirani had sent Gregory Lamb to scrounge another tool of the trade. He'd be delivering it that morning, along with written instructions on how to open the door. This was what the MI6 agent had handed to Bond in Bheka Jordaan's office.

Bond now checked behind him once more, then went to work. From his inside jacket pocket he took out what Lamb had provided: a length of 200-pound-test fishing line, nylon that wouldn't be picked up by the Green Way metal detector. Bond now fed one end through the small gap at the top of the door and continued until it had reached the floor on the other side. He ripped a strip of the cardboard backing from the pad of yellow paper and tore it, fashioning a J shape — a rudimentary hook. This he slipped through the bottom gap until he managed to snag the fishing line and pull it out.

He executed a triple surgeon's knot to fix the ends together. He now had a loop that encircled the door from top to bottom. Using a pen, he made this into a huge tourniquet and began to tighten it.

The nylon strand grew increasingly taut . . . compressing the exit bar on the other side of the door. Finally, as Hirani had said would 'most likely' happen, the door clicked open, as if an employee on the inside had pushed the bar to let himself out. For the sake of fire safety, there could be no number pad lock release on the inside.

Bond stepped into the dim room, unwound the tourniquet and pocketed the evidence of his intrusion. Closing the door till it latched, he swept the lights on and glanced around the laboratory, looking for phones, radios or weapons. None. There were a dozen computers, desk- and laptop models, but the three he booted up were password protected. He didn't waste time on the others.

429

Discouragingly, the desks and work tables were covered with thousands of documents and file folders, and none was conveniently labelled 'Gehenna'.

He ploughed through reams of blueprints, technical diagrams, specification sheets, schematic drawings. Some had to do with weapons and security systems, others with vehicles. None answered the vital questions of who was in danger in York and where exactly was the bomb?

Then, at last, he found a folder marked 'Serbia' and ripped it open, scanning the documents.

Bond froze, hardly able to believe what he was seeing.

In front of him there were photographs of the tables in the morgue at the old British Army hospital in March. Sitting on one was a weapon that theoretically didn't exist. The explosive device was unofficially dubbed the 'Cutter'. MI6 and the CIA suspected the Serbian government was developing it but local assets hadn't found any proof that it had actually been built. The Cutter was a hypervelocity anti-personnel weapon that used regular explosives enhanced with solid rocket fuel to fire hundreds of small titanium blades at close to three thousand miles an hour.

The Cutter was so horrific that, even though it was only rumoured to be in development, it had already been condemned by the UN and human rights organisations. Serbia adamantly denied that it was building one and nobody — even the best-connected arms dealers — had ever seen such a device.

How the hell had Hydt come by it?

Bond continued through the files, finding elaborate engineering diagrams and blueprints, along with instructions on machining the blades that were the weapons' shrapnel and on programming the arming system, all written in Serbian, with English translations. This explained it; Hydt had *made* one. He had somehow come into possession of these plans and had ordered his engineers to build one of the damn things. The bits of titanium Bond had found in the Fens army base were shavings from the deadly blades.

And the train in Serbia — this explained the mystery of the dangerous chemical; it had had nothing to do with Dunne's mission there. He probably hadn't even known about the poison. The purpose of his trip to Novi Sad had been to steal some of the titanium on the train to use it in the device — there had been two wagons of scrap metal behind the locomotive. *Those* had been his target. Dunne's rucksack hadn't contained weapons or bombs to blow open the chemical drums on rail car three; the bag had been *empty* when Dunne arrived. He'd filled it with unique titanium scraps and taken them back to March to make the Cutter.

The Irishman had arranged the derailment to make it look like an accident so no one would realise the metal had been stolen.

But how had Dunne and Hydt got hold of the plans? The Serbs would have done all they could to keep the blueprints and specifications secret.

Bond found the answer a moment later in a memo from the Dubai engineer Mahdi al-Fulan, dated a year ago.

Severan:

I have looked into your request to see if it is possible to fabricate a system that will reconstruct shredded classified documents. I'm afraid with modern shredders the answer is no. But I would propose this: I can create an electric eye system that serves as a safety device to prevent injuries when someone tries to reach into a document shredder. In fact, though, it would double as a hyper-speed optical scanner. When the documents are fed into the system, the scanner reads all the information on them before they are shredded. The data can be stored on a 3- or 4-terabyte hard drive hidden somewhere in the shredder and uploaded via a secure mobile or satellite link, or even physically retrieved when your employees replace the blades or clean the units.

I further recommend that you make and offer to your clients shredders that are so efficient they literally turn their documents to dust, so that you will instil confidence in them to hire you to destroy even the most sensitive materials.

In addition, I have a plan for a similar device that would extract data from hard drives before they are destroyed. I believe it's possible to create a machine that would break apart laptop or desktop computers, optically identify the hard drive and route it to a special station where the drive would be temporarily connected to a processor in the destruction machine. Classified information *could be copied before the drives were wiped and crushed.*

He recalled his tour of Green Way and Hydt's excitement about the automated computer destruction devices.

In a few years that will be my most lucrative operation.

Bond read on. The document-shredder scanners were already in use in every city where Green Way had a base, including at top-secret Serbian military facilities and weapons contractors outside Belgrade.

Other memos detailed plans to capture less classified but still valuable documents, using special teams of Green Way refuse collectors to gather the rubbish of targeted individuals, bring it to special locations and sort through it for personal and sensitive information.

Bond noted the value of this: he found copies of credit-card receipts, some intact, others reconstructed from simple document shredders. One bill, for instance, was from a hotel outside Pretoria. The card holder had the title 'Right Honourable'. Notes attached to it warned that the man's extramarital affair would be made public if he didn't agree to a list of demands an opposing politician was making. So, such items would be the 'special materials' Bond had seen being shipped here in Green Way lorries.

There were also pages upon pages of what seemed to be phone numbers, along with many other digits, screen names, pass codes and excerpts of emails and text messages. E-waste.

Of course, workers in Silicon Row were looking through phones and computers, extracting electronic serial numbers for mobiles, passwords, banking information, texts, records of instant messages and who knew what else?

But the immediate question, of course: where exactly was the Cutter going to be detonated?

He flipped through the notes again. None of the information he'd found gave him a clue as to the location of the York bomb, which would explode in a little over an hour. Leaning forward over a work table, staring at the diagram of the device, his temples throbbed.

Think, he told himself furiously.

Think . . .

For some minutes, nothing occurred to him. Then he had an idea. What was Severan Hydt doing? Assembling valuable information from scraps and fragments.

Do the same, Bond told himself. Put the pieces of the puzzle together.

And what scraps do I have?

- *The target is in York.*
- *One message contained the words 'term' and '£5 million'.*
- *Hydt is willing to cause mass destruction to divert attention from the real crime he intends to commit, as with the derailment in Serbia.*
- *The Cutter was hidden somewhere near March and has just been driven to York.*
- *He's being paid for the attack, not acting out of ideology.*
- *He could have used any explosive device but*

434

he's gone to great trouble to build a Cutter with actual Serbian military designations, a weapon not available on the general arms market.
- *Thousands of people will die.*
- *The blast must have a radius of 100 feet minimum.*
- *The Cutter is to be detonated at a specific time, ten thirty a.m.*
- *The attack has something to do with a 'course', a road or other route.*

But rearrange these ragged bits as he might, Bond saw only unrelated scraps.

Well, keep at it, he raged. He focused again on each shred. He picked it up mentally and placed it somewhere else.

One possibility became clear: if Hydt and Dunne had recreated a Cutter, the forensic teams doing post-blast analysis would find the military designations and believe the Serbian government or army was behind it since the devices weren't yet available on the black market. Hydt had done this to shift attention away from the real perpetrators: himself and whoever had paid him millions of pounds. It would be a misdirection — just like the planned train crash.

That meant there were two targets: the apparent one would have some connection to Serbia and, to the public and police, would be the purpose of the attack. But the real victim would be someone else caught in the blast, an apparent bystander. No one would ever know that he or she was the person Hydt and his client really wanted to die . . . and *that* death would be the one that harmed British interests.

Who? A government official in York? A scientist? And, goddamn it, where specifically would the attack take place?

Bond played with the confetti of information once more.

Nothing . . .

But then, in his mind, he heard a resounding tap. 'Term' had ended up next to 'course'.

What if the former didn't refer to a clause in a contract but a period in the academic year? And 'course' was just that — a course of study?

That made some sense. A large institution, thousands of students.

But where?

The best Bond could come up with was an institution at which there was a course, a lecture, a rally, a museum exhibit or the like involving Serbia, at half past ten this morning. This suggested a university.

Did his reassembled theory hold up?

There was no time left for speculation. He glanced at the digital clock on the wall, which advanced another minute.

In York it was nine forty.

56

Carrying the killing-fields map, Bond walked casually down a corridor.

A guard with a massive bullet-shaped head eyed him suspiciously. The man was unarmed, Bond saw to his disappointment; neither did he have a radio. He asked the guard for directions to Hydt's conference room. The man pointed it out.

Bond started to walk away, then turned back as if he'd just remembered something. 'Oh, I need to ask Ms Barnes about lunch. Do you know where she is?'

The guard hesitated, then pointed to another corridor. 'Her office is down there. The double doors on the left. Number one oh eight. You will knock first.'

Bond moved off in the direction indicated. In a few minutes he arrived and glanced back. No one was in the corridor. He knocked on the door. 'Jessica, it's Gene. I need to talk to you.'

There was a pause. She'd said she'd be here but she might be ill or have felt too tired to come in, notwithstanding her 'short leash'.

Then, the click of a lock. The door opened and he stepped inside. Jessica Barnes, alone, blinked in surprise. 'Gene. What's the matter?'

He swung the door shut and his eyes fell on her mobile phone, lying on her desk.

She sensed immediately what was happening.

Her dark eyes wide, she went to the desk, grabbed the mobile and backed away from him. 'You . . . ' She shook her head. 'You're a policeman. You're after him. I should've known.'

'Listen to me.'

'Oh, I get it now. Yesterday, in the car . . . you were, what do the Brits say? Chatting me up? To get on my good side.'

Bond said, 'In forty-five minutes Severan's going to kill a lot of people.'

'Impossible.'

'It's true. Thousands are at risk. He's going to blow up a university in England.'

'I don't believe you! He'd never do that.' But she hadn't sounded convinced. She'd probably seen too many of Hydt's pictures to deny her partner's obsession with death and decay.

Bond said, 'He's selling secrets and blackmailing and killing people because of what he reconstructs from their rubbish.' He stepped forward, his hand out for the phone. 'Please.'

She backed further away, shaking her head. Just outside the open window there was a puddle from a recent storm. She thrust her hand out and held the mobile over it. 'Stop!'

Bond did. 'I'm running out of time. Please help me.'

Interminable seconds passed. Finally her narrow shoulders slumped. She said, 'He has a dark side. I used to think it involved just pictures of . . . well, terrible pictures. His sick love of decay. But I've always suspected there was more. Something worse. In his heart he doesn't want to be just a witness to destruction. He wants to *cause* it.' She stepped away from the window and handed him the phone.

He took it. 'Thank you.'

Just then the door flew open. The guard who'd given Bond directions stood there. 'What is this? There are no phones for visitors here.'

Bond said, 'I have an emergency at home. There's an illness in my family. I wanted to see about it. I asked to borrow Ms Barnes's mobile and she was kind enough to say yes.'

'That's right,' she confirmed.

'Well, I think I will take it.'

'I think you won't,' Bond replied.

There was a heavy pause. The man launched himself at Bond, who tossed the phone on to the desk and went into a *systema* defence position. The fight began.

The man had three or four stones on Bond and he was talented — very talented. He'd studied kick-boxing and *aikido*. Bond could counter his moves but it took a lot of effort, and manoeuvring was difficult because the office, though large, was cluttered with furniture. At one point the massive guard backed up fast, slamming into Jessica, who screamed and fell to the floor. She lay stunned.

For sixty seconds or so they sparred fiercely, Bond realising that *systema's* evasive moves would not be enough. His opponent was strong and showed no sign of tiring.

His eyes focused and fierce, the man judged angles and distances and came in with a kick — or so it seemed. The move was a feint. Bond had anticipated this, though, and when the huge man twisted away, Bond delivered a powerful thrust of his elbow into his kidney, a blow that would not only be excruciatingly painful but could permanently damage the organ.

But, Bond realised too late, the guard had feinted again; he'd taken the hit intentionally so that now he could do as he'd planned and launch himself sideways towards the table where the phone lay. He grabbed the Nokia, snapped it in half and flung the pieces out of the window. One skipped across the surface of the water before it sank.

By the time the man righted himself, however, Bond was on him. He dropped *systema* and went into a classic boxer's stance, swung a left fist into his opponent's solar plexus, doubling him over, then drew back his right and brought it arching down to a spot below and behind the man's ear. The strike was perfectly aimed. The guard shivered and went down, unconscious. He wouldn't be out for long, though, even with a solid hit like that. Bond quickly trussed him with lamp cord and gagged him with napkins from a breakfast tray.

As he did so he turned to Jessica, who was getting to her feet. 'Are you all right?' he asked.

'Yes,' she whispered breathlessly. She ran to the window. 'The phone is gone. What are we going to do? There aren't any others. Only Severan and Niall have one. And he's closed the switchboard today because the employees are off.'

Bond said, 'Turn round. I'm going to tie you up. It'll be tight — we have to make them believe

440

you didn't try to help me.'

She held her hands behind her back, and he bound her wrists. 'I'm sorry. I tried.'

'Sssh,' Bond whispered. 'I know you did. If someone comes in, tell them you don't know where I went. Just act scared.'

'I won't have to act,' she said. Then: 'Gene . . . '

He glanced at her.

'My mother and I prayed before every one of my beauty contests. I won a lot. We must've prayed pretty well. I'll pray for you now.'

57

Bond was hurrying down the dim corridor, passing photographs of the reclaimed land that Hydt's workers had turned into Elysian Fields, the beautiful gardens covering Green Way's landfills to the east.

It was nine fifty-five in York. The detonation would take place in thirty-five minutes.

He had to get out of the plant immediately. He was sure there'd be an armoury of some kind, probably near the front security post. That was where he was headed now, walking steadily, head down, carrying the maps and the yellow pad. He was about fifty yards from the entrance, thinking tactically. Three men at the security post in front. Was the rear door guarded too? Presumably it was; although there were no employees in the business office, Bond had seen workers through-out the grounds. Three guards had been there yesterday. How many other security personnel would be present? Had any of the visitors handed weapons in, or had they all been told to leave them in their cars? Maybe —

'There you are, sir!'

The voice startled him. Two beefy guards appeared and walked in front of him, barring his way. Their faces revealed no emotion. Bond wondered if they'd discovered Jessica and the man he'd trussed up. Apparently not. 'Mr Theron, Mr Hydt is looking for you. You were not in your office so he sent us to bring you to the conference room.'

The smaller one regarded him with eyes as hard as a black beetle's carapace.

There was nothing for it but to go with them. They arrived at the conference room a few minutes later. The larger guard knocked on the door. Dunne opened it, examined Bond with a neutral face and beckoned the men inside. Hydt's three partners sat around a table. The huge dark-suited security man who'd escorted Bond into the plant yesterday stood near the door, arms crossed.

Hydt called, with the excitement he'd exhibited earlier, 'Theron! How have you been getting on?'

'Very well. But I've not quite finished. I'd say I need another fifteen or twenty minutes.' He glanced at the door.

But Hydt was like a child. 'Yes, yes, but first let me introduce you to the people you'll be working with. I've told them about you and they're eager to meet you. I have about ten investors altogether but these are the three main ones.'

As introductions were made, Bond wondered if anyone of the three would be suspicious that they had not heard of Mr Theron. But Mathebula, Eberhard and Huang were distracted by the day's business and, contrary to Hydt's comment, apart from brief nods they ignored him.

It was five past ten in York.

Bond tried to leave. But Hydt said, 'No, stay.'

He nodded at the TV, which Dunne had turned on to Sky News in London. He lowered the volume.

'You'll want to see this, our first project. Let me tell you what's going on here.' Hydt sat down and explained to Bond what he already knew: that Gehenna was about the reconstruction or scanning of classified material, for sale, extortion and blackmail.

Bond lifted an eyebrow, pretending to be impressed. Another glance at the exits. He decided he could hardly bolt for the door; the huge security man in the black suit was inches from it.

'So you see, Theron, I was not quite honest with you the other day when I described the Green Way document-shredding operation. But that was before we had our little test with the Winchester rifle. I apologise.'

Bond shrugged it off and measured distances and assessed the strength of the enemy. His conclusions were not good.

With his long, yellowing nails, Hydt raked at his beard. 'I'm sure you're curious about what's happening today. I started Gehenna merely to steal and sell classified information. But then I grasped there was a more lucrative . . . and, for me, more *satisfying* use for resurrected secrets. They could be used as weapons. To kill, to destroy.

'Some months ago I met with the head of a drug company I'd been selling reconstructed trade secrets to — R and K Pharmaceuticals, in Raleigh, North Carolina. He was pleased with that but he had another proposition for me, something a bit more extreme. He told me of a brilliant researcher, a professor in York, who was developing a new cancer drug. When it came to market, my client's company would go out of business. He was willing to pay millions to make sure that the researcher died and his office was destroyed. That was when Gehenna truly blossomed.'

Hydt then confirmed Bond's other deductions — about using a prototype of a Serbian bomb they'd constructed from reassembled plans and blueprints that people in Hydt's Belgrade subsidiary had managed to piece together. This would make it appear that the intended target was another professor at the same university in York — a man who'd testified at the International Criminal Tribunal for the former Yugoslavia. He was teaching a course in Balkan history in the room next to the cancer researcher's. Everyone would think that the Slav was the intended target.

Bond glanced at the time on the TV programme crawl. It was ten fifteen in England.

He had to get out now. 'Brilliant, absolutely brilliant,' he said. 'But let me get my notes so I can tell you all about my idea.'

'Stay and watch the festivities.' A nod towards the television. Dunne turned the volume up. Hydt said to Bond, 'We were originally going to detonate the device at ten thirty in England, but since we've got confirmation that both classes are in session, I think we can do it now. Besides,' Hydt confessed, 'I'm rather eager to see if our device works.'

Before Bond could react, Hydt had dialled a number on his phone. He looked at the screen. 'Well, the signal's gone through. We shall see.'

Silent, everyone turned to stare at the television. A recorded item about the royal family was in progress. A few minutes later the screen went blank, then flashed to a stark red-and-black logo.

BREAKING NEWS

The screen went to a smartly dressed South-Asian woman sitting at a desk in the newsroom. Her voice was shaking as she read the story. 'We're interrupting this programme to report that there has been an explosion in York. Apparently a car bomb . . . the authorities are saying a car bomb has detonated and destroyed a large part of a university building . . . We're just learning . . . yes, the building is on the grounds of Yorkshire-Bradford University . . . We have a report that lectures were in progress at the time of the explosion and the rooms nearest the bomb were thought to be full . . . No one has yet claimed responsibility.'

Bond's breath hissed through his set teeth as he stared at the screen. But Severan Hydt's eyes shone in triumph. And everyone else in the room applauded as heartily as if their favourite striker had just scored a goal at the World Cup.

58

Five minutes later, a local news crew had arrived and was beaming pictures of the tragedy to the world. The video footage showed a half-destroyed building, smoke, glass and wreckage covering the ground, rescue workers running, dozens of police cars and fire engines pulling up. The crawler said, 'Massive explosion at university in York.'

In this era we've become inured to terrible images on television. Scenes appalling to an eyewitness are somehow tame when observed in two dimensions on the medium that brings us *Dr Who* and advertisements for Ford Mondeos and M&S fashions.

But this picture of tragedy — a university building in ruins, enveloped by smoke and dust, and people standing about, confused, helpless — was gripping beyond words. It would have been impossible for anybody in the rooms closest to the bomb to survive.

Bond could only stare at the screen.

Hydt did, too, but he, of course, was enraptured. His three partners were chatting among themselves, boisterous, as one might expect of people who had made millions of pounds in a thousandth of a second.

The presenter now reported that the bomb had been loaded with metal shards, like razor blades, which had shot out at thousands of miles per hour. The explosive had ripped apart most of the lecture theatres and the teaching staff's offices on the ground and first floors.

The presenter reported that a newspaper in Hungary had just found a letter, left in its reception area, from a group of Serbian military officers claiming responsibility. The university, the note stated, was 'harbouring and giving succour' to a professor described as 'a traitor to the Serbian people and his race'.

Hydt said, 'That was our doing too. We collected some Serbian army letterhead from a rubbish bin. That's what the statement's printed on.' He glanced at Dunne, and Bond understood that the Irishman had incorporated this fillip into the master blueprint.

The man who thinks of everything . . .

Hydt said, 'Now, we need to plan a celebratory lunch.'

Bond glanced once more at the screen and started to make for the door.

Just then, though, the presenter cocked her head and said, 'We have a new development in York.' She sounded confused. She was touching her earpiece, listening. 'Yorkshire Police Chief Superintendent Phil Pelham is about to make a statement. We'll go live to him now.'

The camera showed a harried middle-aged man in police uniform but without hat or jacket standing in front of a fire engine. A dozen microphones were being thrust towards him. He cleared his throat. 'At approximately ten fifteen a.m. today an explosive device detonated on the grounds of Yorkshire-Bradford University. Although property damage was extensive, it appears that there were no fatalities and only half a dozen minor injuries.'

The three partners had fallen silent. Niall Dunne's blue eyes twitched with uncharacteristic emotion.

Frowning deeply, Hydt inhaled a rasping breath.

'About ten minutes before the explosion, authorities received word that a bomb had been planted in or around a university in York. Certain additional facts suggested that Yorkshire-Bradford might be the target but as a precaution all educational institutions in the city were evacuated, according to plans put into effect by officials after the Seven-Seven attacks in London.

'The injuries — and again I stress they were minor — were sustained mostly by staff, who remained after the students had gone to make certain the evacuation was complete. In addition, one professor — a medical researcher who was lecturing in the hall nearest the bomb — was slightly injured retrieving files from his office just before the explosion.

'We are aware that a Serbian group is claiming credit for the attack and I can assure you that police here in Yorkshire, the Metropolitan Police in London and Security Service investigators are giving this attack the highest priority — '

With the silent tap of a button, Hydt blackened the screen.

'One of your people there?' Huang snapped. 'He had a change of heart and warned them!'

'You said we could trust everyone!' the German observed coldly, glaring at Hydt.

The partnership was fraying.

Hydt's eyes slipped to Dunne, on whose face the fractional emotion was gone; the Irishman was concentrating — an engineer calmly analysing a malfunction. As the partners argued heatedly among themselves Bond took the chance to move to the door.

He was halfway to freedom when it burst open. A security guard squinted at him and pointed a finger. 'Him. He's the one.'

'What?' Hydt demanded.

'We found Chenzira and Miss Barnes tied up in her room. He'd been knocked unconscious but as he came to he saw that man reach into Miss Barnes's purse and take something out. A small radio, he thought. That man spoke to someone on it.'

Hydt frowned, trying to make sense of this. Yet the look on Dunne's face revealed that he'd almost been expecting a betrayal from Gene Theron. At a glance from the engineer, the massive security man in the black suit drew his gun and pointed it directly at Bond's chest.

59

So the guard in Jessica's office had woken sooner than Bond had anticipated . . . and had seen what had happened after he'd tied her up: he had retrieved from her handbag the other items Gregory Lamb had delivered, along with the inhaler, yesterday morning.

The reason Bond had asked Jessica such insensitive questions when they were parked near her house yesterday was to upset, distract and, ideally, to make her cry so that he could take her handbag to find a tissue . . . and to slip into a side pocket the items Sanu Hirani had provided yesterday via Lamb. Among them was the miniature satellite phone, the size of a thick pen. Since the double fence around Green Way made it impossible to hide the instrument in the grass or bushes just inside the perimeter and since Bond knew Jessica was coming back today, he'd decided to hide it in her bag, knowing she'd walk through the metal detector undisturbed.

'Give it to me,' Hydt ordered.

Bond reached into his pocket and dug it out. Hydt examined it, then dropped and crushed it beneath his heel. 'Who are you? Who are you working for?'

Bond shook his head.

No longer calm, Hydt gazed at the angry faces of his partners, who were asking furiously what steps had been taken to shield their identities.

They wanted their mobile phones. Mathebula demanded his gun.

Dunne studied Bond in the way he might a misfiring engine. He spoke softly, as if to himself: '*You* had to be the one in Serbia. And at the army base in March.' His brow beneath the blond fringe furrowed. 'How did you escape? . . . *How?*' He didn't seem to want an answer; he wasn't speaking to anyone but himself. 'And Midlands Disposal wasn't involved. That was a cover for your surveillance there. Then here, the killing fields . . . ' His voice ebbed. A look approaching admiration tinted his face, as perhaps he decided Bond was an engineer in his own right, a man who also drafted clever blueprints.

He said to Hydt, 'He has contacts in the UK — it's the only way they could have evacuated the university in time. He's with some British security agency. But he would've been working with somebody here. London will have to call Pretoria, though, and we've got enough people in our pocket to stall for a time.' He said to one of the guards, 'Get the remaining workers out of the plant. Keep only security. Hit the toxic-spill alarm. Marshal everyone into the car park. That'll jam things up nicely if SAPS or NIA decides to pay us a visit.'

The guard walked to an intercom and gave the instructions. An alarm blared and an announcement rattled from the public-address system in various languages.

'And him?' Huang asked, nodding to Bond.

'Oh,' Dunne said matter of factly, as if it were

understood. He looked at the security man. 'Kill him and get the body into a furnace.'

The huge man was equally blasé as he stepped forward, aiming his Glock pistol with care.

'Please, no!' Bond cried and lifted a hand imploringly.

A natural gesture under the circumstances.

So the guard was surprised by the swirling black razor knife that Bond had pitched towards his face. This was the final item in Hirani's CARE package, hidden in Jessica's bag.

Bond had not been able to adjust his distance for knife throwing, at which he was not particularly proficient anyway, but he'd flung it more as a distraction. The security man, though, swatted away the spiralling weapon and the honed edge cut his hand deeply. Before he recovered or anyone else could react, Bond moved in, twisted his wrist back and relieved him of his gun, which he fired into the guard's fat leg, to make sure that the weapon was ready to shoot and to disable him further. As Dunne and the other armed guard drew their weapons and began firing, Bond rolled through the door.

The corridor was empty. Slamming the door shut, he sprinted twenty yards and took cover behind, ironically, a green recycling bin.

The door to the conference room opened cautiously. The second armed guard eased out, narrow eyes scanning. Bond saw no reason to kill the young man so he shot him near the elbow. He dropped to the floor, screaming.

Bond knew they would have called for back-up so he stood up and continued his flight. As he ran he dropped out the magazine and glanced at it. Ten rounds left. Nine millimetre, 110 grain, full-metal jacket. Light rounds, and with the copper jacketing they'd have less stopping power than a hollow point but they'd shoot flat and fast.

He shoved the magazine back in.

Ten rounds.

Always count . . .

But before he got far, there was a huge snap near his head and the nearly simultaneous boom of a rifle from a side corridor. He saw two men in security-guard khaki approaching, holding Bushmaster assault rifles. Bond fired twice, missing, but giving himself enough cover to kick in the door to the office beside him and run into the cluttered workspace. No one was inside. A fusillade from the .223 slugs tore up the jamb, wall and door.

Eight rounds left.

The two guards seemed to know what they were about — ex-army, he guessed. Deafened by the shots, he couldn't hear voices, but from the shadows in the corridor, he got the impression that the men had joined up with others, perhaps Dunne among them. He sensed, too, they were about to make a dynamic entry, all of them at once, fanning out, going high and low, right and left. Bond would have no chance against a formation like that.

The shadows moved closer.

Only one move was possible and not a very clever or subtle one. Bond flung a chair through the window and leapt after it, sprawling on the ground six feet below. He landed hard, but with nothing sprained or broken, and sprinted into the Green Way facility, now deserted of workers.

Again he turned towards his pursuers and dropped to the ground, under cover of a detached bulldozer blade sitting near Resurrection Row. He aimed back at the window and a nearby door.

Eight rounds left, eight rounds, eight . . .

He put a bit of pressure on the sensitive trigger, waiting, waiting. Controlling his breathing as best he could.

But the guards weren't going to fall for a trap. The shattered window remained empty. That meant they were heading outside by other exits. Their intention, of course, was to flank him. Which they now did — and very effectively too. At the south end of the building Dunne and two Green Way guards sprinted to cover behind some lorries.

Instinctively Bond glanced the other way and saw the two guards who'd fired on him in the corridor. They were moving in from the north. They too went to cover, behind a yellow-and-green digger.

The bulldozer blade protected him from assault only from the west, and the hostiles weren't coming from that direction but from the poles. Bond rolled away just as one of the men started to fire from the north — the Bushmaster was a short but frighteningly accurate weapon. The bullets thudded into the ground and clanged loudly against the bulldozer's yoke and Bond was pelted with searing shards of lead and copper from the fracturing slugs.

With Bond pinned down by the two in the north, the other team, Dunne leading, moved in closer from the opposite direction. Bond lifted his head slightly to scan for a target. But before he could paint one of his attackers, they moved on, finding cover among the many piles of rubbish, oil drums and equipment. Bond scanned again but couldn't spot them.

Suddenly earth exploded all around him as both groups caught him in a crossfire, the slugs finding homes closer and closer to where he huddled in a dip in the ground. The men to the north vanished behind a low hill, presumably intending to crest it, where they'd have a perfect vantage-point from which to snipe at him.

Bond had to leave his position immediately. He turned and crawled as quickly as he could through grass and weeds, east, deeper into the grounds, feeling the chill of absolute vulnerability. The hill was behind him and to the left and he knew the two shooters would soon be at the top, targeting him.

He tried to picture their progress. Fifteen feet from the top, ten, five? Bond imagined them easing slowly up to the hillock, then aiming at him.

Now, he told himself.

But he waited five harrowing seconds more, just to be sure. It seemed like hours. He then rolled on to his back and lifted his pistol over his feet.

One guard was indeed standing on top of the rise, painting a target, his partner crouching beside him.

Bond squeezed the trigger once, then shifted his aim to the right and fired again.

The standing man gripped his chest and went down hard, tumbling to the base of the hill. The Bushmaster slid after him. The other guard had rolled away, unhurt.

Six rounds left. Six.

Four hostiles remaining.

As Dunne and the others peppered his location with rounds, Bond rolled between oil drums in a tall stand of grass, studying his surroundings. His only chance of escape was through the front entrance, a hundred feet away. The pedestrian walkway was open. But a lot of unprotected ground separated him from it. Dunne and his two guards would have a good shooting position, as would the remaining guard still at the top of the hill to the north. He could —

A rapid barrage erupted. Bond kept his face pressed into the dusty ground until there was a pause. Surveying the scene and the positions of the shooters, he rose fast and started to sprint to an anaemic tree — at its foot there was some decent cover: oil drums and the carcasses of engines and transmissions. He ran flat out. But halfway to his destination he stopped abruptly and spun round. One of the guards with Dunne assumed he was going to continue running and had stood tall, leading with his rifle to fire in front of Bond so the bullets would meet him a few yards further on. It hadn't occurred to him that Bond was running solely to force a target to present; the double tap of Bond's 9-millimetre

457

rounds took the guard down. As the others ducked, he kept running and made it to the tree, then beyond that to a small mound of rubbish. Fifty feet from the gate. A series of shots from Dunne's position forced him to roll into a patch of low vegetation.

Four rounds.

Three hostiles.

He could make it to the gate in ten seconds but that would mean five of full exposure.

He didn't have much choice, though. He would soon be flanked. But then, looking for the enemy, he saw movement through a gap in two tall piles of construction debris. Low on the ground, barely visible through stands of grass, three heads were close together. The surviving guard from the north had joined Dunne and the man with him. They didn't notice they were exposed to Bond and seemed to be whispering urgently, as if planning their strategy.

All three men were in his field of fire.

It wasn't an impossible shot by any means, though with the light rounds and an unfamiliar gun, Bond was at a disadvantage.

Still, he couldn't let the opportunity pass. He had to act now. At any moment they'd realise they were vulnerable and go to cover.

Lying prone, Bond aimed the boxy pistol. In competitive shooting, you're never conscious of pulling the trigger. Accuracy is about controlling your breathing and keeping your arm and body completely still, with the sights of your weapon resting steadily on the target. Your trigger finger slowly tightens until the gun discharges, seemingly of its own accord; the most talented shooters are always somewhat surprised when their weapons fire.

Under these circumstances, the second and third shots would have to come more quickly, of course. But the first was meant for Dunne, and Bond was going to be sure he didn't miss.

And he didn't.

One powerful crack, then two others in succession.

In shooting, as in golf, you usually know the instant the missile leaves your control whether you've aimed well or badly. And the fast, shiny rounds struck exactly where they were aimed, as Bond had known they would.

Except, he now realised to his dismay, accuracy wasn't the issue. He'd hit what he'd aimed at, which turned out not to be his enemies at all, but a large piece of shiny chrome that one of the men — the Irishman, of course — must have found in a nearby skip and set up at an angle to reflect their images and draw Bond's fire. The reflective metal tumbled to the ground.

Dammit . . .

The man who thinks of everything . . .

Instantly the men split up, as Dunne would have instructed, and moved into position, now that Bond had helpfully revealed his exact location.

Two ran to Bond's right, to secure the gate, and Dunne to the left.

One round left. One round.

They didn't know he was nearly out of ammunition, though they soon would.

He was trapped, his only cover a low pile of cardboard and books. They were moving in a circle round him, Dunne in one direction, the other two guards together in another. Soon he'd be in a crossfire again, with no effective protection.

He decided his only chance was to give them a reason not to kill him. He'd tell them he had information to help them get away or offer them a huge sum of money. Anything to stall. He called, 'I'm out!' then stood, flinging the gun away, lifting his hands.

The two guards to the right peered out. Seeing that he was unarmed, they cautiously came closer, crouching. 'Don't move!' one called. 'Keep your hands in the air.' Their muzzles were aimed directly at him.

Then, from nearby, a voice said, 'What the hell are you doing? We don't need a bloody prisoner. Kill him.' The intonation was, of course, Irish.

60

The guards looked at each other and apparently decided to share the glory of murdering the man who had brought down Gehenna and killed several of their fellow workers.

They both raised their black weapons to their shoulders.

But just as Bond was about to dive to the ground in a hopeless bid to avoid the slugs, there was a crash behind him. A white van had ploughed through the gate, sending chain-link and razor wire flying. Now the vehicle skidded to a stop and the doors opened. A tall man in a suit, wearing body armour under his jacket, leapt out and began firing at the two guards.

It was Kwalene Nkosi, nervous and tense, but standing his ground.

The guards returned fire, though only to cover their retreat east, deeper into the Green Way facility. They disappeared into the brush. Bond glimpsed Dunne, who was surveying the situation calmly. He turned and sprinted in the same direction as the guards.

Bond picked up the weapon he'd been using and ran to the police vehicle. Bheka Jordaan climbed out and stood beside Nkosi, who was looking around for more targets. Gregory Lamb peered out and stepped cautiously to the ground. He carried a large 1911 Colt .45.

461

'You decided to come to the party after all,' Bond said to her.

'I thought it wouldn't hurt to drive here with some other officers. While we were waiting nearby up the road I heard gunshots. I suspected poaching, which is a crime. That was sufficient cause to enter the premises.'

She didn't seem to be joking. He wondered if she had prepared the lines for her superiors. If so, she needed to work on her delivery, Bond decided.

Jordaan said, 'I brought a small team with me. Sergeant Mbalula and some other officers are securing the main building.'

Bond told her, 'Hydt's in there — or was. His three partners too. I'd assume they're armed by now. There'll be other guards.' He explained where the hostiles had been and gave a rough geography of the headquarters. Jessica's office, too. He added that the older woman had helped him; she would not be a threat.

At a nod from the captain, Nkosi, keeping low, started for the building.

Jordaan sighed. 'We had trouble getting back-up. Hydt's being protected by somebody in Pretoria. But I called a friend in the Recces — our special-forces brigade. A team is on its way. They aren't so much concerned about politics; they look for any excuse to fight. But it'll be twenty or thirty minutes before they arrive.'

Suddenly Gregory Lamb stiffened. Crouching low, he lumbered south, towards a stand of trees. 'I'll flank them.'

Flank them? Flank *who*?

462

'Wait,' Bond shouted. 'There's nobody there. Go with Kwalene! Secure Hydt.'

But the big man seemed not to have heard and plodded over the ground like an elderly Cape buffalo, disappearing into the brush. What the hell was he doing?

Just then a few rounds peppered the ground near them. Bond and Jordaan dropped to the ground. He forgot about Lamb and looked for a target.

Several hundred yards away Dunne and the two men with him had regrouped and paused in their retreat, firing back at their pursuers. Bullets hit near the van but caused no damage or injury. The three men vanished behind piles of rubbish on the edge of Disappearance Row, the seagull population thinning as the birds fled from the gunfire.

Bond jumped into the driver's seat of the van. In the back, he was pleased to see half a dozen large containers of ammunition. He started the engine. Jordaan ran to the passenger side. 'I'm coming with you,' she said.

'Better if I do this myself.' He suddenly recalled Philly Maidenstone's recitation of Kipling's verse, which he'd decided was not a bad battle cry.

Down to Gehenna or up to the throne, He travels the fastest who travels alone . . .

But Jordaan jumped into the seat beside him and slammed the door. 'I said I'd fight by your side if it was legal to do so. Now it is. So go! They're getting away.'

Bond hesitated only a moment, then slammed

the van into first and they bounded off down the dirt roads that gridded the huge complex, past Silicon Row, Resurrection Row, the power plants.

And rubbish, of course — millions of tons of it: paper, carrier bags, bits of dull and shiny metal, fragments of ceramic and food scraps, over which the eerie canopy of frantic seagulls was reassembling.

It was hard driving as they swerved around earth-moving equipment, skips and bales of refuse awaiting burial, but at least the winding route gave Dunne and the two guards no easy target. The three men turned and fired sporadically but were concentrating mostly on escaping.

On her radio Jordaan called in and reported where they were and whom they were pursuing. The special-forces team would not arrive for at least another thirty minutes, Bond heard the dispatcher tell her.

Just as Dunne and the other men reached the fence separating the filthy sprawl of the plant from the reclaimed area, one guard spun around and fired an entire magazine their way. The rounds pounded the front grille and tyres. The van jerked sideways, out of control, and ploughed head first into a pile of paper bales. The air bags deployed and Bond and Jordaan sat stunned.

Seeing that their enemy was down, Dunne and the other guards began firing in earnest.

Amid the sound of bullets slamming into sheet metal, Bond and Jordaan rolled out of the shuddering vehicle and into a ditch. 'You injured?' he asked.

'No. I . . . It's so loud!' Her voice quivered but her eyes told Bond she was successfully fighting down her fear.

From beneath the wing of the van, Bond had a good shot at one of their adversaries and, lying prone, he aimed with the automatic.

One round left.

He squeezed the trigger — but the instant the firing pin hit primer, the man ducked. He was gone when the bullet arrived.

Bond grabbed an ammunition box and ripped off the lid. It contained only .223 rounds, for rifles. The second held the same. In fact, they all did. There were no 9mm pistol rounds. He sighed and looked through the van. 'Do you have anything that'll shoot these?' He gestured at the wealth of useless bullets.

'No assault rifles. All I have is this.' She drew her own weapon. 'Here, you take it.'

The pistol was a Colt Python, a .357-calibre magnum — powerful and boasting a tight cylinder lock-up and superb pull. A good weapon. But it was a revolver, holding only six rounds.

No, he corrected when he checked. Jordaan was a conservative gun owner and kept the chamber under the hammer empty. 'Speed-loader? Loose rounds?'

'No.'

So, they had five bullets against three adversaries with semiautomatic weapons. 'You've never heard of Glocks?' he muttered, slipping the

465

empty one into his back waistband and weighing the Colt in his palm.

'I investigate crimes,' she replied coolly. 'I don't have much occasion to shoot people.'

Though when those rare instances *do* arise, he thought angrily, it would be helpful to have the right tool. He said, 'You go back. Just keep to cover.'

She was looking steadily into his eyes, sweat beading at her temples, where her luxurious black hair frothed. 'If you're going after them I'm coming with you.'

'Without a weapon, there's nothing you can do.'

Jordaan glanced to where Dunne and the others had disappeared. 'They have a number of guns and we only have one. That's not fair. We must take one away from them.'

Well, maybe Captain Bheka Jordaan had a sense of humour, after all.

They shared a smile and in her fierce eyes Bond saw the reflection of orange flames from the burning methane. It was a striking image.

Crouching, they slipped into Elysian Fields, using a dense garden of fine-needled fynbos varieties, watsonias, grasses, jacaranda and King Protea as cover. There were kigelia trees too, and some young baobabs. Even in the late autumn, much of the foliage was in full colour, thanks to the Western Cape climate. A brace of guinea fowl observed them with some irritation and continued on their awkward way. Their gait reminded Bond of Niall Dunne's.

He and Jordaan were seventy-five yards into

the park when the assault began. The trio had been moving away but it seemed that they had done so merely to lure Bond and the SAPS officer further into the wilderness . . . and a trap. The men had split up. One of the guards dropped on to a hillock of soft green ground cover and laid down suppressing fire while the other — Dunne, too, possibly, though Bond couldn't see him — crashed through the tall grasses towards them.

Bond had a good shot and took it, but the guard went to cover the instant Bond fired. He missed again. Slow down, he told himself.

Four rounds left. Four.

Jordaan and Bond scrabbled into a dip near a small field filled with succulents and a pond that would probably be home to stately koi, come the spring. They looked up, over the grass veld, scanning for targets. Then what seemed to be a thousand shots, though it was probably more like forty or fifty, rained down on them, striking close, shattering rock and spraying water.

The two men in khaki, probably desperate and frustrated at their delayed escape, tried a bold assault, charging Bond and Jordaan from different directions. Bond fired twice at the man coming at them from the left, hitting the man's rifle and left arm. The guard cried out in pain and dropped the weapon, which tumbled to the bottom of the hill. Bond saw that, though the man's forearm was injured, he'd drawn a pistol with his right hand and was otherwise capable of fighting. The second guard made a run to cover and Bond fired fast, tapping him somewhere on his thigh, but that wound too seemed superficial. He vanished into the brush.

One round, one round.

Where was Dunne?

Sneaking up behind them?

Then silence again, though silence filled with ringing in their ears and the internal bass of heartbeats. Jordaan was shivering. Bond eyed the Bushmaster, the rifle that the injured guard had dropped. It lay around ten yards away.

He studied the scene around them carefully, the landscape, the plants, the trees.

Then he noted tall grasses swaying fifty or sixty yards distant; the two guards, invisible in the thick foliage, were moving in, keeping some distance between them. In a minute or two they'd be on top of Bond and Jordaan. He might take one out with his last bullet but the other guard would be successful.

'James,' Jordaan whispered, squeezing his arm. 'I'll lead them off — I'll go that way.' She pointed to a plain covered with low grass. 'If you fire, you can hit one and the other may take cover. That'll give you a chance to get to the rifle.'

'It's suicide,' he whispered back. 'You'd be completely exposed.'

'You really *must* stop your incessant flirting, James.'

He smiled. 'Listen. If anybody's going to be a hero, it's me. I'm going to head towards them. When I tell you, go for the Bushmaster.' He pointed to the black rifle lying in the dust. 'You're qualified to use it?'

468

She nodded.

The guards moved closer. Thirty yards now.

Bond whispered, 'Stay low until I tell you. Get ready.'

The guards were making their way cautiously through the tall grass. Bond surveyed the landscape again, took a deep breath, then rose calmly and walked towards them, his pistol pointed down at his side. He raised his left hand.

'James, no!' Jordaan whispered.

Bond did not respond. He called to the men, 'I want to talk to you. If you help me get the names of the other people involved, you'll receive a reward. There'll be no charges against you. You understand?'

The two guards, about ten paces apart, stopped. They were confused. They saw that he couldn't hit them both before the other shot him, yet he was walking slowly in their direction, calm, not lifting his pistol.

'Do you understand? The reward is fifty thousand rand.'

They stared at each other, nodding a little too enthusiastically. Bond knew they were not seriously considering his offer; they were thinking they might draw him closer before they fired. They faced him.

And as they did so the powerful gun in Bond's hand barked once, still pointed downward, letting go its final bullet into the ground. As the guards crouched, startled, Bond sprinted to his left, putting a row of trees between him and the guards.

They glanced at each other, then ran forward

to where they had a better view of Bond, who dived behind a hill as their Bushmasters began to clatter.

It was then that the entire world exploded.

The muzzle flashes from the men's rifles ignited the methane spewing from the fake tree root, transporting the gas from the landfill beneath them to Green Way's burn off facilities. Bond had ruptured it with his last bullet.

The men now vanished in a tidal wave of flame, a roiling thunderhead. The guards and the ground they'd stood on were simply gone, the fire widening as panicked birds fled into the air, the trees and brush bursting into flames as if they were soaked in incendiary accelerant.

Twenty feet away Jordaan rose unsteadily. She started towards the Bushmaster. But Bond ran to her, shouting, 'Change of plan. Forget it!'

'What should we do?'

They were thrown to the ground as another mushroom cloud of flame erupted not far away. The roar was so loud Bond had to press his lips against her sumptuous hair to make himself heard. 'Might be a good idea to leave.'

61

'You are making a terrible mistake!'

Severan Hydt's voice was low with threat but a very different state of mind was revealed in the expression on his long, bearded face: horror at the destruction of his empire, both physical, from the fires in the distance, and legal, from the special-forces troops and police descending on the grounds and office.

There was nothing imperious about him now.

Hydt, in handcuffs, and Jordaan, Nkosi and Bond were standing amid a cluster of bulldozers and lorries in the open area between the office and Resurrection Row. They were near the spot where Bond would have been killed . . . if not for Bheka Jordaan's dramatic arrival to arrest the 'poachers'.

Sergeant Mbalula handed Bond his Walther, extra clips and mobile phone from the Subaru.

'Thank you, Sergeant.'

SAPS officers and South African special forces roamed through the facility, looking for more suspects and collecting evidence. In the distance, fire crews were struggling — and it was a struggle — to put out the methane fires, as the western edge of Elysian Fields became just another outpost of hell.

Apparently the corrupt politicians in Pretoria, the ones in Hydt's pocket, had not been so very high up, after all. Senior officials stepped in quickly and ordered their arrest and full back-up for Jordaan's operation in Cape Town. Additional officers were sent to seize Green Way's offices in all South African cities.

Medics scurried about here too, attending to the wounded, which included only Hydt's security staff.

Hydt's three partners were in custody, Huang, Eberhard and Mathebula. It was not clear yet what their crimes were but that would be established soon. At the very least they had all smuggled firearms into the country, justifying their arrest.

Four of the surviving guards were in custody and most of the hundred or so Green Way employees who'd been milling about in the car park had been detained, pending questioning.

Dunne had escaped. Special-forces officers had found evidence of a motorcycle, which had apparently been hidden under a tarp covered with straw. Of course, the Irishman would have kept his lifeboat ready.

Severan Hydt persisted, 'I'm innocent! You're persecuting me because I'm British. And white. You're prejudiced.'

Jordaan could not ignore this. 'Prejudiced? I've arrested six black men, four whites and an Asian. If that's not a rainbow, I don't know what is.'

The reality of the disaster kept coming home to him. His eyes swivelled away from the fires and began taking in the rest of the grounds. He was probably looking for Dunne. He would be lost without his engineer.

He glanced at Bond, then said to Jordaan, his

voice laced with desperation, 'What sort of arrangement could we work out? I'm very wealthy.'

'That's fortunate,' she said. 'Your legal bills will be quite high.'

'I'm not trying to bribe you.'

'I should hope not. That's a very serious offence.' She then said matter-of-factly, 'I want to know where Niall Dunne has gone. If you tell me, I'll let the prosecution know that you helped me find him.'

'I can give you the address of his flat here — '

'I've already sent officers there. Tell me some other places he might go to.'

'Yes . . . I'm sure I can think of something.'

Bond noticed Gregory Lamb approaching from a deserted part of the grounds, carrying his large pistol as if he'd never fired a weapon. Bond left Jordaan and Hydt standing together between rows of pallets containing empty oil drums and joined Lamb near a battered skip.

'Ah, Bond,' the Six agent said, breathing heavily and sweating despite the chilly autumn air. His face was streaked with dirt and there was a tear in the sleeve of his jacket.

'You caught one?' Bond nodded at the slash, caused, it seemed, by a bullet. The assailant had been close; powder burns surrounded the rent.

'Didn't do any damage, thankfully. Except to my favourite gabardine.'

He was lucky. An inch to the left and the slug would have shattered his upper arm.

'What happened to the guys you went after?' Bond asked. 'I never saw them.'

'Got away, sorry to say. They split up. I knew

they were trying to circle back on me but I went after one of them anyway. That's how I got my Lord Nelson here.' He touched his sleeve. 'But dammit, they knew the lie of the land and I didn't. I got a piece of one of them, though.'

'Do you want to follow the blood trail?'

He blinked. 'Oh. I did. But it vanished.'

Bond lost interest in the adventurer's excursion into the bush and moved aside to call London. He was just punching in the number when, a few yards away, he heard a series of loud cracks he recognised instantly as powerful bullets finding a target, followed by the booms of a distant rifle's report.

Bond spun round, his hand going for his Walther as he scanned the grounds. But he saw no sign of the shooter — only his victim: Bheka Jordaan, her chest and face a mass of blood, clawed at the air as she stumbled backwards and rolled into a muddy ditch.

62

'No!' Bond cried.

His inclination was to run to her aid. But the amount of blood, bone and tissue he'd seen told him she could not have survived the devastating shots.

No . . .

Bond thought of Ugogo, of the fiery orange gleam in Jordaan's eye as they'd taken on the two guards in Elysian Fields, the faint smile.

They have a number of guns and we only have one. That's not fair. We must take one away from them . . .

'Captain!' Nkosi cried, from his position behind a skip nearby. Other SAPS officers were firing randomly now.

'Hold your fire!' Bond shouted. 'No blind shooting. Guard the visible perimeter, look for muzzle flashes.'

The special forces were more restrained, watching for targets from good cover positions.

So the engineer *did* have an escape plan for his beloved boss. *That's* what Hydt had been looking for. Dunne would keep the officers pinned down while Hydt fled, probably to where the other security guards were waiting in the woods nearby with a car or perhaps even a helicopter hidden on the grounds. Hydt had not started his sprint to freedom yet, though; he'd still be hiding between the rows of pallets where

Jordaan had been questioning him. He'd be waiting for more covering fire.

Crouching, Bond began to make his way there. Any minute now, the man would make a run for the brush, protected by Dunne and perhaps other loyal guards.

And James Bond was not going to let that happen.

He heard Gregory Lamb whisper, 'Is it safe?' but couldn't see him. He realised the man had dived into a full skip.

Bond had to move. Even if it meant exposing himself to Dunne's fine marksmanship, he wouldn't let Hydt escape. Bheka Jordaan would not have died in vain.

He sprinted into the shadowy space between the tall pallets of oil drums to secure Hydt, his gun raised.

And froze. Severan Hydt was not about to escape anywhere. The Rag-and-bone Man, the visionary king of decay, the lord of entropy, lay on his back, two bullet wounds in his chest, a third in his forehead. A significant part of the back of his skull was missing.

Bond slipped his gun away. Around him the tactical forces began to rise. One called that the sniper had left his shooting position and vanished into the bush.

Then a harsh sound behind him, a woman's voice: '*Sihlama!*'

Bond spun around to see Bheka Jordaan crawling from the ditch, wiping her face and spitting blood. She was unharmed.

Either Dunne had missed completely or his

476

boss had been his intended target. The gore on Jordaan was Hydt's — it had spattered her as she stood beside him.

Bond pulled her to cover behind the oil drums, smelling the sickly copper scent of blood. 'Dunne's still out there somewhere.'

Nkosi called, 'You are okay, Captain?'

'Yes, yes,' she said dismissively. 'What about Hydt?'

'He's dead,' Bond said.

'*Masende!*' she snapped.

This brought a smile to Nkosi's face.

Jordaan tugged her shirt off — underneath she wore body armour over a black cotton vest — and wiped her face, neck and hair with it.

A call came in from officers on the ridge that the perimeter was clear. Dunne, of course, would have had no interest in staying; he'd accomplished what he needed to.

Bond regarded the body once more. He decided that the tight grouping of the shots meant that Hydt had indeed been the intended target. Of course, this made sense; Dunne had had to kill the man to make sure he told the police nothing about him. Now he recalled several glances that Dunne had cast towards Hydt over the past few days, dark looks, hinting at . . . what? Irritation, resentment? Almost jealousy, it seemed. Perhaps there was something else behind the murder of the Rag-and-bone Man, something personal.

Whatever the reason, he'd certainly done a typically proficient job.

Jordaan hurried into the office building. Ten

minutes later she emerged. She'd found a shower or tap somewhere; her face and hair were damp but more or less blood-free. She was furious at herself. 'I lost my prisoner. I should have guarded him better. I never thought — '

A ghastly wail interrupted her. Someone was speeding forward, 'No, no, no . . . '

Jessica Barnes was running towards Hydt's body. She flung herself to the ground, oblivious to the grotesque wounds, and cradled her dead lover.

Bond stepped forward, gripped her narrow, quivering shoulders and helped her up. 'No, Jessica. Come over here with me.' Bond led her to cover behind a bulldozer. Bheka Jordaan joined them.

'He's dead, he's dead . . . ' Jessica pressed her head against Bond's shoulder.

Bheka Jordaan lifted her handcuffs out of their holster. 'She tried to help me,' Bond reminded her. 'She didn't know what Hydt was doing. I'm sure of it.'

Jordaan put the cuffs away. 'We'll drive her down to the station, take a statement. I don't think we'll have to pursue it beyond that.'

Bond detached himself from Jessica. He took her by the shoulders. 'Thank you for helping me. I know it was hard.'

She breathed in deeply. Then, calmer, she asked, 'Who did it? Who shot him?'

'Dunne.'

She didn't seem surprised. 'I never liked him. Severan was passionate, impulsive. He never thought things through. Niall realised that and

478

seduced him with all his planning and his intelligence. I didn't think he could be trusted. But I never had the courage to say anything.' She closed her eyes momentarily.

'You did a good job with the praying,' Bond told her.

'Too good,' she whispered.

On Jessica's cheek and neck were stark patches of Hydt's blood. It was the first time, Bond realised, that he'd seen any colour on her. He looked her in the eye. 'I know some people who can help you when you get back to London. They'll be in touch. I'll see to it.'

'Thank you,' Jessica murmured.

A policewoman led her away.

Bond was startled by a man's voice nearby: 'Is it clear?'

He frowned, unable to see the speaker. Then he understood. Gregory Lamb was still in the skip. 'It's clear.'

The agent scrambled out of his hiding-place.

'Mind the blood,' Bond told Lamb, as he nearly stepped in some.

'Oh, my God!' he muttered and looked as if he was going to be sick.

Ignoring him, Bond said to Jordaan, 'I need to know how extensive Gehenna is. Can you get your officers to collect all the files and computers in Research and Development? And I'll need your computer-crimes outfit to crack the passwords.'

'Yes, of course. We'll have them brought to the SAPS office. You can review them there.'

Nkosi said, 'I'll do it, Commander.'

479

Bond thanked him. The man's round face seemed less wry and irrepressible than earlier. Bond supposed this had been his first firefight. He'd be changed forever by the incident but, from what Bond was seeing, the change would not diminish but rather would enhance the young officer. Nkosi gestured toward some SAPS Forensic Science Service officers and led them inside the building.

Bond glanced at Jordaan. 'Can I ask you a question?'

She turned to him.

'What did you say? After you climbed out of the ditch, you said something.'

With her particular complexion, she might or might not have been blushing. 'Don't tell Ugogo.'

'I won't.'

'The first was Zulu for . . . I guess you'd say, in English, 'crap'.'

'I have some variations on that myself. And the other word?'

She squinted. 'That, I think, I will not tell you, James.'

'Why not?'

'Because it refers to a certain part of the male anatomy . . . and I do not think it wise to encourage you in that regard.'

63

Late afternoon, the sun beginning to dip in the north-west, James Bond drove from the Table Mountain Hotel, where he'd showered and changed, to Cape Town's central police station.

As he entered and made for Jordaan's office he noticed several pairs of eyes staring at him. The expressions were no longer curious, he sensed, as had been the case upon his first visit here, several days ago, but admiring. Perhaps the story of his role in foiling Severan Hydt's plan had circulated. Or the tale of how he'd taken out two adversaries and blown up a landfill with a single bullet, no mean accomplishment. (The fire, Bond had learnt, was largely extinguished — to his immense relief. He would not have wanted to be known as the man who had burnt a sizeable area of Cape Town to its sandstone foundation.)

He was met by Bheka Jordaan in the hall. She'd taken another shower to clean off the remnants of Severan Hydt and had changed into dark trousers and a yellow shirt, bright and cheerful, perhaps an antidote to the horror of the events at Green Way.

She gestured him into her office. They sat together in chairs before her desk. 'Dunne's managed to get to Mozambique. Government security spotted him there but he got lost in some unsavoury part of Maputo — which, frankly, is most of the city. I called some

481

colleagues in Pretoria, in Financial Intelligence, the Special Investigations Unit and the Banking Risk Information Centre. They checked his accounts — under a warrant, of course. Yesterday afternoon two hundred thousand pounds were wired into a Swiss account of Dunne's. Half an hour ago he transferred it to dozens of anonymous online accounts. He can access it from anywhere so we have no idea where he intends to go.'

Bond's expression of disgust closely matched hers.

'If he surfaces or leaves Mozambique, their security people will let me know. But until then he's out of our reach.'

It was then that Nkosi appeared, pushing a large cart filled with boxes — the documents and laptop computers from the Green Way Research and Development department.

The warrant officer and Bond followed Jordaan to an empty office where Nkosi put the boxes on the floor around the desk. Bond started to lift off a lid, but Jordaan said quickly, 'Put these on. I won't have you ruining evidence.' She handed him blue latex gloves.

Bond gave a wry laugh but took them. Jordaan and Nkosi left him to the job. Before he opened the boxes, though, he placed a call to Bill Tanner.

'James,' the chief of staff said. 'We've got the signals. Sounds like all hell's broken loose down there.'

Bond laughed at his choice of words and explained in detail about the shootout at Green Way, Hydt's fate and Dunne's escape. He explained too about the drug company president who had hired Hydt; Tanner would ask the FBI in Washington to open an investigation of their own and arrest the man.

Bond said, 'I need a rendition team to capture Dunne — if we can find out where he is. Any of our double-one agents nearby?'

Tanner sighed. 'I'll see what I can do, James, but I don't have a lot of people to spare, not with the situation in eastern Sudan. We're helping the FCO and the marines with security. I might be able to get you some special forces — SAS or SBS? Would that suit?'

'Fine. I'm going to look through everything we've collected from Hydt's headquarters. I'll call back when I've finished and brief M.'

They rang off and Bond started to lay out the Gehenna documents on the large desk in the office Jordaan had provided. He hesitated. Then, feeling ridiculous, he slipped on the blue gloves, deciding that at least they would provide an amusing story for his friend Ronnie Vallance of the Yard. Vallance often said that Bond would make a terrible detective-inspector, given his preference for beating up or shooting perpetrators, rather than marshalling evidence to see them in the dock.

He leafed through the documents for almost an hour. Finally, when he felt well enough informed to discuss the situation he telephoned London again.

M said gruffly, 'It's a nightmare here, 007. That fool in Division Three pushed a very big button. Got all of Whitehall closed up. Downing

483

Street too. If there's anything that plays badly with the tabloids, it's an international security meeting being cancelled because of a bloody security alert.'

'Was it groundless?' Bond had been convinced that York was the site of the attack but that didn't mean London wasn't at some risk, as he'd told Tanner during his satellite call from Jessica Barnes's office.

'Nothing. Green Way had its legitimate side, of course. The company's engineers were working with the police to make sure the refuse-removal tunnels around Whitehall were safe. No dangerous radiation, no explosives, no Guy Fawkes. There was a spike in Afghan SIGINT traffic, but that was because we and the CIA descended on the place last Monday. And everybody was wondering what the hell we were doing there.'

'And Osborne-Smith?'

'Inconsequential.'

Bond didn't know whether the word referred to the man himself or meant that his fate was not worth discussing.

'Now, what's been going on down there, 007? I want details.'

Bond explained first about Hydt's death and the arrest of his three main partners. He also described Dunne's escape and Bond's plan to execute the Level 2 project order from Sunday, which was still valid, for the Irishman's rendition when they found him.

Then Bond detailed Gehenna — Hydt's stealing and assembling classified information — the blackmail and extortion, adding the cities

484

where most of his efforts had taken place: 'London, Moscow, Paris, Tokyo, New York and Mumbai, and there are smaller operations in Belgrade, Washington, Taipei and Sydney.'

There was silence for a moment and Bond imagined M chomping on his cheroot as he took it all in. The man said, 'Damn clever, putting all that together from rubbish.'

'Hydt said nobody ever sees dustmen and it's true. They're invisible. They're everywhere and yet you look right through them.'

M gave a rare chuckle. 'I happened to be thinking much the same myself yesterday.' Then he grew serious. 'What're your recommendations, 007?'

'I'd get our embassy people and Six to roll up all the Green Way operations as fast as they can before the actors start disappearing. Freeze their assets and trace all incoming monies. That'll lead us to the rest of the Gehenna clients.'

'Hmm,' M said, his voice uncharacteristically light. 'I suppose we *could*.'

What was the old man thinking?

'Though I'm not sure we should be too hasty. Let's arrest the principals in all the locations, yes, but what do you think about getting some double-one agents into their offices and keeping Gehenna going a bit longer in some places, 007? I'd love to see what GRS Aerospace outside Moscow throws away. And I wonder what the Pakistani consulate in Mumbai is shredding. Be interesting to find out. We'd have to pull in some favours with the press to stop them reporting what Hydt was really up to. I'll have the

485

misinformation chaps at Six leak word that he was mixed up with organised crime or some such. We'll keep it vague. Word will get out at some point but by then we'll have scooped up some valuable finds.'

The old fox. Bond laughed to himself. So the ODG was going into the recycling business. 'Brilliant, sir.'

'Get all the details to Bill Tanner and we'll go from there.' M paused, then barked, 'Osborne-bloody-Smith has brought traffic in London to a complete standstill. It'll take me ages to get home. I've *never* understood why they couldn't run the M4 all the way in to Earl's Court.'

The line went dead.

64

James Bond found Felicity Willing's business card and called her at her office to break the news that one of her donors was a criminal . . . and had died in an operation to arrest him.

But she'd heard. Already reporters had been on to her and asked for a statement, in light of the fact that Green Way was heavily involved with the Mafia and the Camorra (Bond reflected that the grass did not grow beneath the feet of the 'misinformation chaps at Six').

Felicity was furious that some journalists were suggesting she'd known there was something disreputable about him but that she'd been happy to take his donations anyway. 'How the bloody hell could they ask that, Gene? For heaven's sake, Hydt gave us fifty or sixty thousand pounds a year, which was generous but nothing compared to what a lot of people donate. I'd drop anyone in an instant if I thought they were up to something illegal.' Her voice softened. 'But you're all right, aren't you?'

'I wasn't even there when they raided the place. The police rang me and asked a few questions. That's all. Hell of a shock, though.'

'I'm sure it was.'

Bond asked how the deliveries were going. She told him that the tonnage was even higher than had been pledged. Distribution was already under way to ten different countries in sub-Saharan Africa. There was enough food to keep hundreds of thousands of people fed for months.

Bond congratulated her, then said, 'You're not too busy for Franschhoek?'

'If you think you're getting out of our weekend in the country, Gene, you'd better think again.'

They made plans to meet in the morning. He reminded himself to find someone to wash and polish the Subaru, for which he'd formed some affection, despite the flashy colour and the largely cosmetic spoiler on the boot.

After they'd disconnected, he sat back, relishing the cheer in her voice. Relishing, too, the memory of the time they'd spent together. And thinking of the future.

If you do go to some dark places, could you promise me not to go to the . . . worst?

Smiling, he flicked her card, then put it away and pulled on the gloves once more to continue ploughing through the documents and computers, jotting notes about Green Way's offices and the Gehenna operation for M and Bill Tanner. He laboured for an hour or so until he decided it was time for a drink.

He stretched luxuriously.

He then paused and slowly lowered his arms. At that moment he had felt a jolt deep within him. He knew the sensation. It arose occasionally in the world of espionage, that great landscape of subtext where so little is as it seems. Often the source for such an unsettling stab was a suspicion that a basic assumption had been wrong, perhaps disastrously so.

Staring at his notes, he heard himself breathing fast, his lips dry. His heartbeat quickened.

Bond flipped through hundreds of documents again, then grabbed his mobile and emailed Philly Maidenstone a priority request. As he waited for her reply he rose and paced in the small office, his mind inundated with thoughts, hovering and swooping like the frantic seagulls over Disappearance Row at Green Way.

When Philly responded he snatched up his mobile and read the message, sitting back slowly in the uncomfortable chair.

A shadow fell over him. He looked up and found Bheka Jordaan standing there. She was saying, 'James, I brought you some coffee. In a proper mug.' It was decorated with the smiling faces of the players from Bafana Bafana in all their football finest.

When he said nothing and didn't take it, she set it down. 'James?'

Bond knew his face betrayed the alarm burning within him. After a moment he whispered, 'I think I got it wrong.'

'What do you mean?'

'Everything. About Gehenna, about Incident Twenty.'

'Tell me.'

Bond sat forward. 'The original intelligence we had was that someone named Noah was involved in the event today — the event that would result in all those deaths.'

'Yes.' She sat next to him. 'Severan Hydt.'

Bond shook his head. He waved at the boxes

of documents from Green Way. 'But I've been through nearly every damn piece of paper and most of the mobiles and computers. There isn't a single reference to Noah in any of it. And in all my meetings with Hydt and Dunne there was no reference to the name. If that *was* his nickname, why didn't it turn up in *something*? An idea occurred to me so I contacted an associate at MI6. She knows computers rather well. Are you familiar with metadata?'

Jordaan said, 'Information embedded in computer files. We convicted a government minister of corruption because of it.'

He nodded at his phone. 'My colleague looked at the half-dozen Internet references we found that mentioned Hydt's nickname was Noah. The metadata in every one of them showed they were written and uploaded this week.'

'Just like *we* uploaded data about Gene Theron to create your cover.'

'Exactly. The real Noah did that to keep us focused on Hydt. Which means Incident Twenty — the thousands of deaths — *wasn't* the bombing in York. Gehenna and Incident Twenty are two entirely different plans. Something else is going to happen. And soon — tonight. That's what the original email said. Those people, whoever they are, are still at risk.'

Despite the success at Green Way, he was back to the vital questions once more: who was his enemy and what was his purpose?

Until he answered those enquiries, he couldn't form a response. Yet he had to. There was little time left.

confirm incident friday night, 20th, estimated initial casualties in the thousands . . .

'James?'

Fragments of facts, memories and theories spiralled through his mind. Once again, as he'd done in the bowels of Green Way's research facility, he began to assemble all the bits of information he possessed, trying to put back together the shredded blueprint of Incident Twenty. He rose and, hands clasped behind his back, bent forward, as he looked over the papers and notes covering the desk.

Jordaan had fallen silent.

Finally he whispered, 'Gregory Lamb.'

She frowned. 'What about him?'

Bond didn't answer immediately. He sat down again. 'I'll need your help.'

'Of course.'

65

'What's the matter, Gene? You said it was urgent.'

They were alone in Felicity Willing's office at the charity in downtown Cape Town, not far from the club where they'd met at the auction on Wednesday night. Bond had interrupted a meeting involving a dozen men and women, aid workers instrumental in the food deliveries, and asked to see her alone. He now swung her door closed. 'I'm hoping you can help me. There aren't many people in Cape Town I can trust.'

'Of course.' They sat on her cheap sofa. In black jeans and a white shirt, Felicity moved closer to Bond. Their knees touched. She seemed even more tired than yesterday. He recalled she'd left his room before dawn.

'First, I have to confess something to you. And, well, it may affect our plans for Franschhoek — it may affect a lot of plans.'

Frowning, she nodded.

'And I have to ask you to keep this to yourself. That's very important.'

Her keen eyes probed his face. 'Of course. But tell me, please. You're making me nervous.'

'I'm not who I said I was. From time to time I do some work for the British government.'

A whisper: 'You're a . . . spy?'

He laughed. 'No, nothing as grand as that. The title is security and integrity analyst. Usually it's as boring as can be.'

'But you're one of the good guys?'

'You could put it like that.'

Felicity lowered her head to his shoulder. 'When you said you were a security consultant, in Africa that usually means a mercenary. You said you weren't but I didn't quite believe it.'

'It was a cover. I was investigating Hydt.'

Her face flooded with relief. 'And I was asking if you could change a little bit. And . . . now you've changed *completely* from who I thought you were. A hundred and eighty degrees.'

Bond said wryly, 'How often does a man do that?'

She smiled briefly. 'That means . . . you're not Gene? And you're not from Durban?'

'No. I live in London.' And discarding the faint Afrikaans accent, he extended his hand. 'My name's James. It's good to meet you, Miss Willing. Are you going to throw me out?'

She hesitated only briefly, then flung her arms around him, laughing. She sat back. 'But you said you needed my help.'

'I wouldn't involve you if there was any other way but I've run out of time. Thousands of lives are at stake.'

'My God! What can I do?'

'Do you know anything about Gregory Lamb?'

'Lamb?' Felicity's sharp eyebrows drew together. 'He comes over as a rather high roller so I've approached him for donations several times. He always said he'd give us something but he never did. He's rather a queer man. A boor.' She laughed. 'B-O-O-R. Not Afrikaner.'

'I have to tell you he's a bit more than that.'

'We heard rumours that he was in the pay of somebody. Though I can't imagine anybody taking him seriously as a spy.'

'I think that's an act. He plays the fool to put people at ease around him so they don't suspect he's up to some pretty rough business. Now, you've been down at the docks for the past few days, right?'

'Yes, quite a bit.'

'Did you hear anything about a big ship charter that Lamb's putting together tonight?'

'I did, but I don't know any details.'

Bond was silent for a moment. Then: 'Have you ever heard anyone refer to Lamb as Noah?'

Felicity thought about it. 'I can't say for certain but . . . wait, yes, I think so. A nickname somebody once used for him. Because of the shipping business. But what did you mean when you said, 'Thousands of lives are at stake'?'

'I'm not sure exactly what he has in mind. My guess is he's going to use the cargo ship to sink a cruise liner, a British one.'

'My God, no! But why on earth would he do that?'

'With Lamb, it has to be money. Hired by Islamists, warlords or pirates. I'll know more soon. We've tapped his phone. He's meeting somebody in an hour or so at a deserted hotel south of town, the Sixth Apostle Inn. I'll be there to find out what he's up to.'

Felicity said, 'But . . . James, why do you have to go? Why not call the police and have him arrested?'

Bond hesitated. 'I can't really use the police for this.'

'Because of your job,' she asked evenly, 'as a 'security analyst'?'

He paused. 'Yes.'

'I see.' Felicity Willing nodded. Then she leant forward fast and kissed him full on the lips. 'In answer to your question, whatever you do, James, whatever you're *going* to do, it won't affect our plans for Franschhoek one bit. Or our plans for anything else, as far as I'm concerned.'

66

In May the sun sets in Cape Town around half past five. As Bond sped south on Victoria Road the scenery grew surreal, bathed in a glorious sunset. Then dusk descended, streaked by slashes of purple cloud over the turbulent Atlantic.

He'd left Table Mountain behind, Lion's Head too, and was now motoring parallel to the solemn craggy rock formations of the Twelve Apostles mountain chain to his left, dotted with grasses, fynbos and splashes of protea. Defiant cluster pines sprouted in incongruous places.

Half an hour after leaving Felicity Willing's office, he spotted the turning to the Sixth Apostle Inn, to the left, east. Two signs marked the drive: the name of the place in peeling, faded paint, and below that, brighter and newer, a warning about construction in progress, prohibiting trespass.

Bond skidded the Subaru into the entrance, doused the lights and proceeded slowly along a lengthy winding drive, gravel grinding under the tyres. It led directly towards the imposing face of the Apostle ridge, which rose a hundred or more feet behind the building.

Before him was the inn, shabby and desperately in need of the promised reconstruction, though he supposed it had once been *the* place for a holiday or to romance your mistress from London or Hong Kong. The rambling one-storey structure was set amid extensive gardens, now overgrown and gone to seed.

Bond drove round to the back and into the weed-filled car park. He hid the Subaru in a stand of brush and tall grass, climbed out and looked towards the darkened caravan used by the construction crews. He swept his torch over it. There were no signs of occupation. Then, drawing his Walther, he made his way silently to the inn.

The front door was unlocked and he walked inside, smelling mould, new concrete and paint. At the end of the lobby, the front desk had no counter. To the right he found sitting rooms and a library, to the left a large breakfast room and lounge, with french windows facing north, offering a view of the gardens and above them the Twelve Apostles, still faintly visible in the dusk. Inside this room the construction workers had left their drill presses, table saws and various other tools, all chained and padlocked. Behind that area there was a passage to the kitchen. Bond noticed switches for both work and overhead lights but he kept the place dark.

Tiny animal feet skittered beneath the floorboards and in the walls.

Bond sat down in a corner of the breakfast room, on a workman's tool kit. There was nothing to do but wait until the enemy appeared.

Bond thought of Lieutenant Colonel Bill Tanner, who had said to him not long after he joined ODG, 'Listen, 007, most of your job is going to involve waiting. I hope you're a patient man.'

He wasn't. But if his mission called for waiting, he waited.

Sooner than he had expected, a fragment of light hit the wall and he rose to look out of one of the front windows. A car bounded towards the inn, then stopped in the undergrowth near the front door.

Someone emerged from the vehicle. Bond's eyes narrowed. It was Felicity Willing. She was clutching her belly.

Holstering his gun, Bond pushed through the front door and ran towards her. 'Felicity!'

She struggled forward but fell to the gravel. 'James, help me! I'm . . . Help me! I'm hurt.'

As he approached he saw a red stain on the front of her shirt. Her fingers, too, were bloodied. He dropped to his knees and cradled her. 'What happened?'

'I went to . . . I went to check on a shipment at the docks. There was a man there,' she gasped. 'He pulled out a gun and shot me! He didn't say anything — just shot me and ran. I made it back into the car and drove here. You have to help me!'

'The police? Why didn't you — '

'He *was* a policeman, James.'

'*What?*'

'I saw a badge on his belt.'

Bond lifted her and carried her into the breakfast room, laying her gently on some dust sheets that were stacked against the wall. 'I'll find a bandage,' he murmured. Then he said angrily, 'This is my fault. I should have worked it out! *You*'re the target of Incident Twenty.

Lamb's not after a cruise liner; it's the food ships. He was hired by one of those agribusiness companies in America and Europe you were telling me about to kill you and destroy the food. He must've paid someone in the police to help him.'

'Don't let me die!'

'You'll be fine. I'll get some bandages and call Bheka. We can trust her.'

He started towards the kitchen.

'No,' Felicity said. Her voice was eerily calm and steady.

Bond stopped. He turned.

'Throw your mobile away, James.'

He was staring at her sharp green eyes, focused on him like a predator's. In her hand was his own weapon, the Walther PPS.

He slapped his holster, from which she'd slipped the gun as he'd whisked her inside.

'The phone,' she repeated. 'Don't touch the screen. Just hold it by the side and toss it into the corner of the room.'

He did as she instructed.

'I'm sorry,' she said. 'I'm so sorry.'

And James Bond believed that, in some very tiny part of her heart, she was.

67

'What's that?' James asked, gesturing at her blouse.

It was blood, of course. Real blood. Hers. Felicity still felt the sting in the back of her hand where she'd pricked a vein with a safety-pin. It had bled sufficiently to stain her shirt and make a credible appearance of a bullet wound.

She didn't answer him. But the agent's eyes noted her bruised hand and revealed that he'd deduced as much. 'There was no cop on the dock.'

'I lied, didn't I? Sit down. On the floor.'

When he had done so, Felicity worked the slide of the Walther, which ejected one round but made sure one was in the chamber, ready to fire. 'I know you're trained to disarm people. I've killed before and it has no effect on me. It's not essential that you stay alive so I'm happy to shoot you now if you make any move.'

Her voice, though, almost caught on 'happy'. What the hell is the matter with you? she asked herself angrily. 'Put them on.' She tossed handcuffs towards his lap.

He caught them. Good reflexes, she noted. She stepped back three feet or so.

Felicity smelt the pleasant scent from where he'd gripped her a moment ago. It would be soap or shampoo from the hotel. He was not an aftershave sort of man.

The anger again. Damn him!

'The cuffs,' she repeated.

A hesitation, then he ratcheted them on to his wrists. 'So? Explain.'

'Tighter.'

He squeezed the mechanism. She was satisfied.

'Who exactly do you work for?' she asked.

'An outfit in London. We'll have to leave it at that. So, you're working with Lamb?'

She gave a laugh. 'With that fat sweaty fool? No. Whatever he's coming here for, it has nothing to do with my project tonight. It's probably some ridiculous business venture he has in mind. Maybe buying this place. I was lying when I told you I'd heard him referred to as Noah.'

'Then what are you doing here?'

'I'm here because I'm sure you've briefed your bosses in London that Lamb's your main suspect.'

A flicker in his eyes confirmed this.

'What Captain Jordaan and her moderately competent officers will find in the morning here is a fight to the death. You and the traitor who was going to bomb a cruise liner, Gregory Lamb, and anybody he was meeting here. You found them and there was a gun fight. Everybody died. There'll be loose ends but, on the whole, the matter will go away. Or, at least, go away from me.'

'Leaving you free to do whatever it is you're doing. But I don't understand. Who the hell is Noah?'

'It's not a who, James, it's a what. N-O-A-H.'

Confusion in his handsome face. Then under-standing dawned. 'My God . . . your group is the International Organisation Against Hunger. IOAH. At the fundraiser you said you'd recently expanded to make it international in scope. Which meant that it used to be National Organisation Against Hunger. NOAH.'

She nodded.

Frowning, he mused, 'In the text we inter-cepted last weekend, 'noah' was typed all lower case. Everything else in the message was too. I just assumed it was a name.'

'We were careless there. It hasn't been NOAH for a while, but it was the original name and we still refer to it like that.'

'We? Who sent that message?'

'Niall Dunne. He's *my* associate, not Hydt's. He's just on loan.'

'Yours?'

'Been working together for a few years now.'

'And how did you get with Hydt?'

'Niall and I work with a lot of warlords and dictators in sub-Saharan Africa. Nine, ten months ago Niall heard about Hydt's plan, this Gehenna, through some of them. It was pretty far-fetched, but there was a good chance of a decent return on investment. I gave Dunne ten million to put into the pot. He told Hydt it was from an anonymous businessman. A condition for the money was that Dunne himself worked with Hydt to oversee how it was spent.'

'Yes,' Bond said, 'he mentioned other inves-tors. So Hydt knew nothing about you?'

'Nothing at all. And it turned out that Severan was delighted to use Dunne as a tactical planner. Gehenna wouldn't have got nearly so far without him.'

'The man who thinks of everything.'

'Yes, he was rather proud that Hydt described him like that.'

James said, 'There was another reason Dunne stayed close to Hydt, though, right? He was your escape plan, a possible diversion.'

Felicity said, 'If somebody got suspicious — just as you did — we'd sacrifice Hydt. Make him the fall-guy so nobody would look any further. That was why Dunne convinced Hydt that the bombing in York should happen today.'

'You'd just sacrifice ten million dollars?'

'Good insurance is expensive.'

'I always wondered why Hydt kept going with his plan — after I turned up in Serbia and in March. I was careful to cover my tracks but he accepted me a lot more readily here, as Gene Theron, than I would have. That was because Dunne kept telling him I was safe.'

She nodded. 'Severan always listened to Niall Dunne.'

'So it was Dunne who planted the reference on the Internet to Hydt's nickname being Noah. And that he used to build his own boats in Bristol.'

'That's right.' Her anger and disappointment blossomed again. 'But dammit! Why didn't you let it go when you should have — after Hydt was dead?'

He was looking at her coldly. 'And then what?

503

You'd wait for me to fall asleep next to you . . . and cut my throat?'

She snapped, 'I hoped you were who you claimed to be, a mercenary from Durban. That was why I kept on at you last night, asking if you could change — giving you the chance to confess you really were a killer. I thought things might . . . ' Her voice trickled to silence.

'Work out between us?' His lips tightened. 'If it matters, I thought so too.'

Ironic, Felicity thought. She was bitterly disappointed that he had turned out to be one of the good guys. He must be equally disappointed to discover that she was not at all what he'd thought.

'So what are you doing tonight? What is the project we've been calling Incident Twenty?' he asked, shifting on the floor. The cuffs jingled.

Keeping the gun trained on him, she said, 'You know about world conflict?'

'I listen to the BBC,' he responded drily.

'When I was a banker in the City my clients sometimes invested in companies in trouble spots of the world. I got to know those regions. The one thing I noticed was that in every single conflict zone, hunger was a critical factor. Those who were hungry were desperate. You could get them to do anything if you promised them food — switch political loyalties, fight, kill civilians, overthrow dictatorships or democracies. Anything. It occurred to me that hunger could be used as a weapon. So that's what I became — an arms dealer, you could say.'

'You're a hunger broker.'

Well put, Felicity thought.

Smiling coolly, she continued, 'The IOAH controls thirty-two per cent of the food aid coming into the country. We'll soon be doing the same in various Latin-American countries, India, South East Asia. If, say, a warlord in the Central African Republic wants to get into power and he pays me what I ask, I'll make sure his soldiers and the people supporting him get all the food they need and his opponent's followers get nothing.'

He blinked in surprise. 'Sudan. *That's* what's happening tonight — war in Sudan.'

'Exactly. I've been working with the central authority in Khartoum. The president doesn't want the Eastern Alliance to break away and form a secular state. The regime in the east plans to solidify their ties to the UK and shift their oil sales there rather than to China. But Khartoum's not strong enough to subdue the east without assistance. So it's paying me to supply food to Eritrea, Uganda and Ethiopia. Their troops will invade simultaneously with the central forces. The Eastern Alliance won't stand a chance.'

'So the thousands of deaths in the message we intercepted — that's the body count of the initial invasion tonight.'

'That's right. I had to guarantee a certain loss of life of Eastern Alliance troops. If the number is more than two thousand, I get a bonus.'

'The adverse impact on Britain? That the oil's going to Beijing, not to us?'

A nod. 'The Chinese helped Khartoum pay my bill.'

'When does the fighting start?'

'In about an hour and a half. As soon as the food planes are in the air and the ships are in international waters, the invasion of eastern Sudan begins.' Felicity looked at her demure Baume & Mercier watch. She supposed Gregory Lamb would arrive soon. 'Now, I need to broker something else: your co-operation.'

He laughed coldly.

'If you don't, your friend Bheka Jordaan will die. Simple as that. I have many friends throughout Africa who are quite skilled at killing and happy to put those talents to work.'

She was pleased to see how this troubled him. Felicity Willing always enjoyed finding people's weaknesses.

'What do you want?' he asked.

'You send a message to your superiors that you've confirmed Gregory Lamb is behind an attempted cruise-ship bombing. You've managed to stop the plot and you'll be meeting with him soon.'

'You know I can't do that.'

'We're negotiating for the life of your friend. Come on, James, be a proper hero. You're going to die anyway.'

He turned his eyes to her and repeated, 'I really thought it might work out between us.'

A shiver ran down Felicity Willing's spine.

But then Bond's eyes grew stony and he snapped, 'Okay, that's enough. We have to move fast.'

She frowned. What was he talking about?

He added, 'Try to use non-lethal force on her . . . if you can.'

'Oh, Christ, no,' Felicity whispered.

A tidal wave of light — the overheads — came on and, as she started to turn towards the sound of running feet, the Walther was ripped out of her hand. She was slammed on to her belly by two people, one of whom knelt hard in the small of her back and secured her hands expertly behind her with handcuffs.

Felicity heard a crisp voice, a woman's: 'In accordance with Section Thirty-five of the Constitution of South Africa, 1996, you have the right to remain silent and to be advised that any statements made to your arresting officers can be used as evidence in trial against you.'

68

'No!' Felicity Willing gasped, her face a mask of disbelief. Then the word was repeated in rage, nearly a scream.

James Bond looked down at the petite woman sitting on the floor in about the same place that he had been a moment before. She shouted, 'You knew! You son of a bitch, you knew! You never suspected Lamb at all!'

'I lied, didn't I?' he said coldly, throwing the words back at her.

Bheka Jordaan was also gazing down unemotionally, assessing her prisoner.

Bond was rubbing his wrists, from which the cuffs had been removed. Gregory Lamb was nearby, on his mobile. Lamb and Jordaan had arrived before Bond to plant microphones and monitor the conversation, in case Felicity took the bait. They'd hidden in the workers' caravan; Bond's flash of the torch earlier had verified they were invisible and alerted them that he was going inside. He hadn't wanted to use radio transmissions.

Jordaan's phone rang and she answered it. She listened, jotting information in her notebook, then said, 'My people have raided Ms Willing's office. We've got the landing locations of all the planes and the routes of the ships delivering the food.'

Gregory Lamb looked over her notes and

relayed the information into his phone. While the man did not instil confidence as an intelligence agent, apparently he indeed had his contacts and he was using them now.

'You can't do this!' Felicity wailed. 'You don't understand!'

Bond and Jordaan ignored her and stared at Lamb. Finally he disconnected. 'There's an American carrier off the coast. They've launched fighters to intercept the food planes. And RAF and South African attack helicopters are on their way to turn the ships.'

Bond thanked the big sweating man for his efforts. He'd never suspected Lamb — whose odd behaviour stemmed from the fact that he was essentially a coward. He admitted that he'd disappeared during the action at the Green Way plant to hide in the bushes, though stopped short of confessing he'd shot through his own sleeve. But Bond had thought him the perfect bait to lay before his suspect, Felicity Willing.

Bheka Jordaan took a call too. 'Back-up's going to be a little delayed — bad accident on Victoria Road. But Kwalene says they should be here in twenty or thirty minutes.'

Bond looked down at Felicity. Even now, sitting on the filthy floor of this decrepit construction site, she radiated defiance, a caged, angry lioness.

'How . . . how did you know?' she asked.

They could hear the soothing yet powerful sound of the Atlantic crashing on the rocks, birds calling, a far-off car horn bleating. This place wasn't far from the centre of Cape Town but the city seemed a universe away.

'A number of things made me wonder,' Bond told her. 'The first was Dunne himself. Why the mysterious funds transfer to his account yesterday, *before* Gehenna? That suggested Dunne had another partner. And so did another intercept we caught, mentioning that if Hydt was out of the picture, there were other partners who could proceed with the project. Who had that been sent to? One explanation was that it was somebody entirely independent of Gehenna.

'Then I remembered Dunne travelled to India, Indonesia and the Caribbean. At the fundraiser you said your charity had opened offices in Mumbai, Jakarta and Port-au-Prince. Bit of a coincidence, that. Both you and Dunne had connections in London and Cape Town and you'd both had a presence in South Africa *before* Hydt opened the Green Way office here.

'And I made the NOAH connection on my own,' Bond continued. When he was in SAPS headquarters he'd found himself staring at her card. IOAH. He'd suddenly realised there was merely one letter difference. 'I checked company records in Pretoria and found the group's original name. So when you told me you'd heard Lamb referred to as Noah, I knew you were lying. That confirmed your guilt. But we still needed to trick you into telling us what you knew and what Incident Twenty was.' He regarded her coldly. 'I didn't have time for aggressive interrogation.'

Purpose . . . response.

Not knowing Felicity's goal, this deception

510

had been the best response he could put together.

Felicity eased herself towards the wall. The movement was accompanied by a glance out of the window.

Suddenly several thoughts coalesced in Bond's mind: the shift of her eyes, the 'accident' blocking Victoria Road, Dunne's genius for planning and the car horn, which had sounded about three minutes earlier. It had been a signal, of course, and Felicity had been counting down since it had blared in the distance.

'Incoming!' Bond cried and launched himself into Bheka Jordaan.

The two of them and Lamb tumbled to the floor as bullets crashed through the windows, filling the room with shards of glistening confetti.

69

Bond, Lamb and Jordaan took cover as best they could, which wasn't easy because the entire north wall of the room was exposed. Table saws and the rest of the construction equipment provided some protection but they were still vulnerable, since the work lights and overheads gave the sniper a perfect view of the rooms.

Felicity hunkered down further.

'How many men does Dunne have with him?' Bond snapped to her.

She didn't answer.

He aimed close to her leg and fired a deafening shot, which spat splinters of wood into her face and chest. She screamed. 'Just him for now,' she whispered quickly. 'He's got some other people on the way. Listen, just let me go and — '

'Shut up!'

So, Bond reflected, Dunne had used part of his money to bribe security forces in Mozambique to lie that he'd been spotted in the country while he had remained here to back up Felicity. And to hire mercenaries to extract them, if necessary.

Bond glanced round the breakfast room and the nearby lobby. There was simply no way to get to cover. Aiming carefully, he shot out the work lights but the overheads were still bright and too numerous to take out. They gave Dunne a perfect view of the interior. Bond rose but was rewarded with two close shots. He'd seen no target. There was some moonlight but the glare inside rendered outdoors black. He could tell Dunne was shooting from high ground, on the Apostles range. Yet the Irishman could be anywhere up there.

A moment or two passed, then more bullets crashed into the room, striking bags of plaster. The dust rose and Bond and Jordaan coughed. Bond noted that the angle of those shots had been different; Dunne was working his way into a position from which he could begin to pick them off.

'The lights,' Lamb called. 'We've got to get them out.'

The switch, however, was in the passage to the kitchen and to get to it one of them would have to run past a series of glass doors and windows, presenting a perfect target to Dunne.

Bond tried but he was in the most vulnerable position and the instant he rose slugs slammed into a pillar and the tools beside him. He fell back to the floor.

'I'll go,' said Bheka Jordaan. She was gauging distances to the light switch, Bond saw. 'I'm closest. I think I can make it. Did I tell you, James, I was a star rugby player at university? I moved very quickly.'

'No,' Bond said firmly. 'It's suicide. We'll wait for your officers.'

'They won't be here in time. He'll be in position to kill us all in a few minutes. James, rugby is a wonderful game. Have you ever

513

played?' She laughed. 'No, of course not. I can't see you on a team.'

His smile matched hers.

'You're better placed to give covering fire,' Bond said. 'That big Colt of yours'll scare the hell out of him. I'm going on three. One . . . two — '

Suddenly a voice called, 'Oh, please!'

Bond looked toward Lamb, who continued, 'Those countdown scenes in movies are such dreadful clichés. Nonsense. In real life nobody counts. You just stand up and go!'

Which was exactly what Lamb now did. He leapt to his meaty legs and lumbered towards the light switch. Bond and Jordaan both aimed into the blackness and fired covering rounds. They had no idea where Dunne was and it was unlikely that their slugs went anywhere near him, yet whether they did or not, the rounds didn't deter the Irishman from firing a spot-on burst when Lamb was ten feet from the switch. The bullets shattered the windows beside him and found their target. A spray of the agent's blood painted the floor and wall and he lurched forward, collapsed and lay still.

'No,' Jordaan cried. 'Oh, no.'

The casualty must have given Dunne some confidence because the next shots were even closer to their mark. Finally Bond had to abandon his position. He crawled back to where Jordaan crouched behind a table saw, its blade dented by Dunne's .223 rounds.

Bond and the policewoman now pressed against each other. The black slits of windows

514

glared at them. There was nowhere else to go. A bullet snapped over Bond's head — it broke the sound barrier inches from his ear.

He felt, but couldn't see, Dunne moving in for the kill.

Felicity said, 'I can stop this. Just let me go. I'll call him. Give me a phone.'

A muzzle flash, and Bond shoved Jordaan's head down as the wall beside them exploded. The slug actually tugged at the strands beside her ear. She gasped and pressed against him, shivering. The smell of burning hair wafted around them.

Felicity said, 'Nobody'll know you let me escape. Give me a phone. I'll call Dunne.'

'Oh, go to hell, bitch!' came a voice from across the room and, staggering to his feet, gripping his bloody chest, Lamb rose and charged to the far wall. He swept his hand down on the light switch as he dropped once more to the floor. The inn went dark.

Instantly Bond was on his feet, kicking out one of the side doors. He plunged into the brush to pursue his prey.

Thinking: four rounds left, one more magazine.

★ ★ ★

Bond was sprinting through the brush that led to the base of the steep cliff, the Twelve Apostles ridge. He ran in an S pattern as Dunne fired towards him. The moon wasn't full but there was light to shoot by, yet none of the slugs hit closer than three or four feet from him.

Finally the Irishman stopped targeting Bond — he must have assumed he'd hit him or that he'd fled to find help. Dunne's goal, of course, wasn't necessarily to kill his victims, but simply to keep them contained until his associates arrived. How soon would that be?

Bond huddled against a large rock. The night was now freezing cold and a wind had come up. Dunne would be about a hundred feet directly above him. His sniper's eyrie was an outcrop of rock with a perfect view of the inn, the approaches to it . . . and of Bond himself in the moonlight, had Dunne simply leant over and looked.

Then a powerful torch was signalling from the rocks above. Bond turned to where it was pointed. Offshore a boat churned towards the beach. The mercenaries, of course.

He wondered how many were on board and what they were armed with. In ten minutes the vessel would land and he and Bheka Jordaan would be overrun — Dunne would have made sure that Victoria Road remained impassable for longer than that. Still, he pulled out his phone and texted Kwalene Nkosi about the impending beach landing.

Bond looked back up the mountain face.

Only two approaches would lead him to Dunne. To the right, the south, there was a series of steep but smooth traverses — narrow footpaths for hikers — that led from the back of the Sixth Apostle Inn past the outcrop where Dunne lay. But if Bond went that way, he'd be exposed to Dunne's gunfire along much of the path; there was no cover.

The other option was to assault the castle directly: to climb straight up a craggy but steep rock face, one hundred vertical feet.

He studied this possible route.

Four years nearly to the day after his parents had died, fifteen-year-old James Bond had decided he'd had enough of the nightmares and fears that reared up when he looked at mountains or rock walls — even, say, the impressive but tame foundation of Edinburgh Castle as seen from the Castle Terrace car park. He'd talked a master at Fettes into setting up a climbing club, which made regular trips to the Highlands for the members to learn the sport.

It took two weeks, but the dragon of fear had died and Bond added rock climbing to his repertoire of outdoor activities. He now holstered the Walther and looked up, reiterating to himself the basic rules: use only enough strength for a sufficient grip, no more; use your legs to support your body, your arms for balance and shifting weight; keep your body close to the rock face; use momentum to peak at the dead point.

And so, with no ropes, no gloves, no chalk and in leather shoes — quite stylish but a fool's footwear on a damp face like this — Bond began his ascent.

70

Niall Dunne was making his way down the face of the Twelve Apostles ridge, along the hiking trails that led to the inn. His Beretta pistol in hand, he carefully stayed out of sight of the man who'd masqueraded so cleverly as Gene Theron — the man Felicity had told him an hour or so ago was a British agent, first name James.

Although he couldn't see him any longer, Dunne had spotted the man a few minutes ago ascending the rock cliff. James had taken the bait and was assaulting the citadel — while Dunne had slipped out of the back door, so to speak, and was moving carefully down the traverses. In five minutes he'd be at the inn, while the British agent would be fully occupied on the cliff face.

All according to the blueprint . . . well, the *revised* blueprint.

Now there was nothing for it but to get out of the country, fast and forever. Though not alone, of course. He would leave with the person he admired most in the world, the person he loved, the person who was the engine of all his fantasies.

His boss, Felicity Willing.

This is Niall. He's brilliant. He's my draughtsman . . .

She'd described him thus several years ago. His face had warmed with pleasure when he'd heard the words and now he carried them in his memory, like a lock of her hair, just as he carried the memory of their first job together, when she was a City investment banker and had hired him to inspect some works installations her client was lending money to complete. Dunne had rejected the shoddy job, saving her and the client millions. She'd taken him to dinner and he'd had too much wine and prattled on about how morality had no place in combat or business or, bloody hell, in *anything*. The beautiful woman had agreed. My God, he'd thought, here's somebody who doesn't care that my feet go in different directions, that I'm built out of spare parts, that I can't tell a joke or turn on the charm to save my life.

Felicity was his perfect match at detachment. Her passion for making money was identical to his for creating efficient machines.

They'd ended up in her luxurious flat in Knightsbridge and made love. It had been, without question, the best night of his life.

They had begun to work together more frequently, making the transition into jobs that were, well, not to put too fine a point on it, a bit more profitable and a lot less legitimate than taking a percentage of a revolving credit construction loan.

The jobs had become bolder, darker and more lucrative, but the other thing — between them — well, that had changed . . . as he'd supposed all along it would. She didn't, she finally confessed, think of him in *that* way. The night they were together, yes, it had been wonderful and she was sorely tempted, but she was worried

519

that it would ruin their astonishing intellectual — no, *spiritual* — connection. Besides, she'd been hurt before, very badly. She was a bird with a broken wing that hadn't yet mended. Could they simply remain partners and friends, oh, please? You can be my draughtsman . . .

The story rang a bit hollow but he had chosen to believe her, as one will do when a lover spins a tale less painful than the truth.

But their business soared with success — an embezzlement here, some extortion there — and Dunne bided his time, because he believed that Felicity would come round. He made it seem that he, too, was over the romance. He managed to keep his obsession for her buried, as hidden and as explosive as a VS-50 land mine.

Now, though, everything had changed. They were soon to be together.

Niall Dunne believed this in his soul.

Because he was going to win her love by saving her. Against all the odds, he'd save her. He'd spirit her away to safety on Madagascar, where he'd created an enclave for them to live very comfortably.

As he approached the inn, Dunne was recalling that James had caught out Hydt with his comment about Isandlwana — the Zulu massacre in the 1800s. Now he was thinking of the *second* battle that day in January, the one at Rorke's Drift. There, a force of four thousand Zulus had attacked a small outpost and hospital manned by about 130 British soldiers. As impossible as it seemed, the British had successfully defended it, suffering minimal casualties.

What was significant about the battle to Niall Dunne, though, was the commander of the British troops, Lieutenant John Chard. He was with the Corps of Royal Engineers — a sapper, like Dunne. Chard had come up with a blueprint for the defence against overwhelming odds and executed it brilliantly. He'd earned the Victoria Cross. Niall Dunne was now about to win a decoration of his own — the heart of Felicity Willing.

Moving slowly through the autumn evening, he now arrived at the inn, staying well out of sight of the rock face and the British spy.

He considered his plan. He knew the fat agent was dead or dying. He remembered what he'd seen of the breakfast or dining room through the rifle scope before the man, irritatingly, had turned off the lights. The only other officer in the inn seemed to be the SAPS woman. He could easily take her — he would fling something through the window to distract her, then kill her and get Felicity out.

The two of them would sprint to the beach for the extraction, then speed to the helicopter that would take them to freedom in Madagascar.

Together . . .

He stepped silently to a window of the Sixth Apostle Inn. Looking in carefully, Dunne saw the British agent he'd shot, lying on the floor. His eyes were open, glazed in death.

Felicity sat on the floor nearby, her hands cuffed behind her, breathing hard.

Dunne was shaken by the sight of his love being so ill-treated. More anger. This time it did not go away. Then he heard the policewoman, in the kitchen, make a call on her radio and ask about back-up. 'Well, how long is it going to be?' she snapped.

Probably some time, Dunne reflected. His associates had overturned a large lorry and set it on fire. Victoria Road was completely blocked.

Dunne slipped round the back of the hotel into the car park, overgrown and filled with weeds and rubbish, and went to the kitchen door. His gun before him, he eased it open without a sound. He heard the clatter of the radio, a transmission about a fire engine.

Good, he thought. The SAPS officer was concentrating on the radio call. He'd take her from behind.

He stepped further inside and moved down a narrow corridor to the kitchen. He could —

But the kitchen was empty. On a counter sat the radio, the staticky voice rambling on and on. He realised that these were just random transmissions from SAPS's central emergency dispatch, about fires, robberies, noise complaints.

The radio was set to scan mode, not communications.

Why had she done that?

This couldn't be a trap to lure him inside. James wouldn't possibly know that he'd left the sniper's nest and was here. He stepped to the window and gazed up at the rock face, where he could see the man climbing slowly.

His heart stuttered. No . . . The vague form was exactly where it had been ten minutes ago.

And Dunne realised that what he'd glanced at earlier on the rock face might not have been the spy at all, but perhaps his jacket, draped over a rock and moving in the breeze.

No, no . . .

Then a man's voice said, in a smooth British accent, 'Drop your weapon. Don't turn round or you'll be shot.'

Dunne's shoulders slumped. He remained staring out at the Twelve Apostles ridge. He gave a brief laugh. 'Logic told me you'd climb to the sniper's nest. I was so certain.'

The spy replied, 'And logic told me you'd bluff and come here. I just climbed high enough to leave my jacket in case you looked.'

Dunne glanced over his shoulder. The SAPS officer was standing beside the spy. Both were armed. Dunne could see the man's cold eyes. The South African officer was just as determined. Through the doorway, in the lobby, Dunne could also see Felicity Willing, his boss, his love, straining to look into the kitchen. Felicity called, 'What's going on in there? Somebody answer me!'

My draughtsman . . .

The British agent said harshly, 'I won't tell you again. In five seconds I'll shoot into your arms.'

There was no blueprint for this. And for once the inarguable logic of engineering and the science of mechanics failed Niall Dunne. He was suddenly amused, thinking that this would be perhaps the first wholly irrational decision he'd ever made. But did that mean it wouldn't succeed?

Pure faith sometimes worked, he'd been told.

He leapt sideways on his long legs, dropping into a crouch, spinning about and aiming toward the woman officer first, his pistol rising.

Shattering the stillness, several guns sang, voices similar but differently pitched, in harmonies low and high.

71

The ambulances and SAPS cars were arriving. A Recces special-forces helicopter was hovering over the vessel containing the mercenaries who'd come to collect Dunne and Felicity. Glaring spotlights pointed downwards, as did the barrels of two 20mm cannon. One short burst over the bow was enough to force the occupants to surrender.

An unmarked police car screeched up amid a cloud of dust, directly in front of the hotel. Kwalene Nkosi leapt out and nodded to Bond. Other officers joined them. Bond recognised some from the raid earlier today at the Green Way plant.

Bheka Jordaan assisted Felicity Willing to her feet. She asked, 'Is Dunne dead?'

He was. Bond and Jordaan had fired simultaneously before the muzzle of his Beretta could rise to the threat position. He'd died a moment later, blue eyes as flat in death as they had been in life, though his last glance had been towards the room where Felicity sat, not at the pair who had shot him.

'Yes,' Jordaan said. 'I'm sorry.' She spoke this with some sympathy, apparently having assumed a personal as well as professional connection between the two.

'You're sorry,' Felicity responded cynically. 'What good is he to me dead?'

Bond understood that she wasn't mourning the loss of a partner but of a bargaining chip.

Felicity Wilful . . .

'Listen to me. You have no idea what you're up against,' she muttered to Jordaan. 'I'm the Queen of Food Aid. I'm the one saving the starving babies. You may as well give up your badge right now if you try to arrest me. And if *that* doesn't impress you, remember my partners. You've cost some very dangerous people millions and millions of dollars today. Here's my offer. I'll close down my operation here. I'll move elsewhere. You'll be safe. I guarantee it.

'If you don't agree, you won't live out the month. Neither will your family. And don't think you're going to throw me into a secret prison somewhere. If there's even a hint that the SAPS treated a suspect illegally, the press and the courts'll crucify you.'

'You're not going to be arrested,' Bond told her.

'Good.'

'The story everybody will hear is that you're fleeing the country after embezzling five million dollars from the IOAH treasury. Your partners aren't going to be interested in revenge on Captain Jordaan or anybody else. They'll be interested in finding you . . . and their money.'

In reality, she'd be whisked off to a black site for extensive 'discussions'.

'You can't do that!' she raged, her green eyes fiery.

At that moment a black van pulled up. Two

uniformed men got out and walked up to Bond. He recognised on their sleeves the chevron of the British Special Boat Service, depicting a sword over a motto Bond had always liked: 'By Strength and Guile'.

This was the rendition team Bill Tanner had arranged.

One saluted. 'Commander.'

The civilian Bond nodded. 'Here's the package.' A glance at Felicity Willing.

'What?' the lioness cried. 'No!'

He said to the soldiers, 'I'm authorising you to execute an ODG Level Two project order dated Sunday last.'

'Yes, sir. We have the paperwork. We'll handle it from here.'

They led her away, struggling. She disappeared into their van, which sped down the gravel drive.

Bond turned back to Bheka Jordaan. But she was walking briskly to her car. Without looking back she climbed in, started the engine and drove away.

He walked up to Kwalene Nkosi and handed over Dunne's Beretta. 'And there's a rifle up there, Warrant Officer. You'll want to get it down.' He pointed out the general area where Dunne had been sniping.

'Yes indeed — my family and I hike here many weekends. I know the Apostles well. I'll collect it.'

Bond's eyes were on Jordaan's car, the tail lights receding. 'She left rather quickly. She wasn't upset about the rendition, was she? Our embassy contacted your government. A magistrate in Bloemfontein approved the plan.'

'No, no,' the officer said. 'Tonight Captain Jordaan has to take her *ugogo* to her sister's house. She is never late, not when it involves her grandmother.'

Nkosi was watching closely as Bond stared after Jordaan's car. He laughed. 'That woman is something, is she not?'

'She is indeed. Well, goodnight, Warrant Officer. You must get in touch if you're ever in London.'

'I will do that, Commander Bond. I am not, I think, such a great actor, after all. But I do love my theatre. Perhaps we could go to the West End and attend a play.'

'Perhaps we could.'

A traditional handshake followed, Bond pressing firmly, keeping the three-part rhythm smooth and, most important, making sure that he did not release his grip too soon.

72

James Bond was sitting outside, in a corner of the terrace restaurant at the Table Mountain Hotel.

Calor gas heaters glowed overhead, sending down a cascade of warmth. The scent of propane was curiously appealing in the cool night air.

He held a heavy crystal glass containing Baker's bourbon, on ice. The spirit had the same DNA as the Basil Hayden's but was of higher proof; accordingly he swirled it to allow the cubes to mellow the impact, though he wasn't sure he wanted much mellowing, not after this evening.

Finally he took a long sip and glanced at the tables nearby, all of them occupied by couples. Hands caressed hands, knees pressed against knees, while secrets and promises were whispered on wine-scented breath. Veils of silky hair swirled as women tilted their heads to hear their companions' soft words.

Bond thought of Franschhoek and Felicity Willing.

What would Saturday's agenda have been? Was she planning to tell Gene Theron, ruthless mercenary, about her career as a hunger broker and recruit him to join her?

And, if she had been the woman *he* had at first believed, the saviour of Africa, would he have confessed to her that he was an operational agent for the British government?

But speculation irritated James Bond — it was a waste of time — and he was relieved when his mobile buzzed.

'Bill.'

'So here's the overall position, James,' Tanner said. 'The troops in the countries surrounding eastern Sudan have stood down. Khartoum issued a statement that the West has once again 'interfered with the democratic process of a sovereign nation, in an attempt to spread feudalism throughout the region'.'

'Feudalism?' Bond asked, chuckling.

'I suspect the writer meant to say 'imperialism' but got muddled. Don't see why Khartoum can't just use Google to find a decent press agent like everyone else.'

'And the Chinese? They've been deprived of quite a lot of discount petrol.'

'They're hardly in a position to complain since they were partly responsible for what would have been a very unpleasant war. But the regional government in the Eastern Alliance are over the moon. Their governor let slip to the PM that they're voting to separate from Khartoum next year and hold democratic elections. They want long-term economic connections with us and America.'

'And they have a lot of oil.'

Tanner said, 'Gushers, James, positive gushers. Now, nearly all the food that Felicity Willing was doling out is on its way back to Cape Town. The World Food Programme is going to oversee distribution. It's a good outfit. They'll send it to places that need it.' He then said, 'Sorry to hear about Lamb.'

'Walked into the line of fire to save us. He ought to get a posthumous commendation for it.'

'I'll give Vauxhall Cross a bell and let them know. Now, sorry, James, but I need you back by Monday. Something's heating up in Malaysia. There's a Tokyo connection.'

'Odd combination.'

'Indeed.'

'I'll be in at nine.'

'Ten'll do. You've had a rather busy week.'

They rang off and Bond had enough time for one sip of whiskey before the phone vibrated once more. He peered at the screen.

On the third buzz he hit answer.

'Philly.'

'James, I've been reading the signals. My God — are you all right?'

'Yes. A bit of a rough day but it looks like we got everything sorted.'

'You are the master of the understatement. So Gehenna and Incident Twenty were entirely different? I wouldn't have thought it. How did you suss it all out?'

'Correlation of analysis and, of course, you need to think three-dimensionally,' Bond said gravely.

A pause. Then Philly Maidenstone asked, 'You're winding me up, aren't you, James?'

'I suppose I am.'

A faint trickle of laughter. 'Now, I'm sure you're knackered and need to get some rest but I found one more piece of the Steel Cartridge

531

puzzle. If you're interested.'

Relax, he told himself.

But he couldn't. Had his father been a traitor or not?

'I've got the identity of the KGB mole inside Six, the one who was murdered.'

'I see.' He inhaled slowly. 'Who was he?'

'Hold on a second . . . where is it now? I *did* have it.'

Agony. He struggled to stay calm.

Then she said, 'Ah, here we go. His cover name was Robert Witherspoon. Recruited by a KGB handler when he was at Cambridge. He was shoved in front of a tube train at Piccadilly Circus by a KGB active-measures agent in 1988.'

Bond closed his eyes. Andrew Bond had not been at Cambridge. And he and his wife had died in 1990, on a mountain in France. His father had been no traitor. Neither had he been a spy.

Philly continued, 'But I also found that *another* MI6 freelance operator was killed as part of Steel Cartridge, not a double — considered quite a superstar agent, apparently, working counterintelligence, tracking down moles in Six and the CIA.'

Bond swirled this around in his mind, like the whiskey in his glass. He said, 'Do you know anything about his death?'

'Pretty hush-hush. But I do know it occurred around 1990, somewhere in France or Italy. It was disguised as an accident, too, and a steel cartridge was left at the scene as a warning to other agents.'

A wry smile crossed Bond's lips. So maybe his father *had* been a spy after all — though not a

532

traitor. At least, not to his country. But, Bond reflected, had he been a traitor to his family and to his son? Hadn't Andrew been foolhardy in taking young James along when he was meeting enemy agents he was trying to trick?

'But one thing, James. You said 'his death'.'

'How's that?'

'The Six counter-intelligence op who was killed in '90 — you said 'his'. A signal in the archives suggested the agent was a woman.'

My God, Bond thought. No . . . His *mother* a spy? Monique Delacroix Bond? Impossible. But she *was* a freelance photojournalist, which was a frequently used nonofficial cover for agents. And she was by far the more adventurous of his parents; it was she who had encouraged her husband to take up rock climbing and skiing. Bond also recalled her polite but firm refusal to let young James accompany her on photographic assignments.

A mother, of course, would never endanger her child, whatever tradecraft recommended.

Bond didn't know the recruitment requirements back then but presumably the fact that she was Swiss-born would not have been an obstacle to her working as a contract op.

There was more research to do, of course, to confirm the suspicion. And, if it was true, he would find out who had ordered the killing and who had carried it out. But that was for Bond alone to pursue. He said, 'Thanks, Philly. I think that's all I need. You've been a star. You deserve an OBE.'

'A Selfridges gift voucher will do . . . I'll stock

up when they have Bollywood week in the food hall.'

Ah, another instance of their similar interests. 'In that case, better yet, I'll take you to a curry house I know in Brick Lane. The best in London. They're not fully licensed but we can bring a bottle of one of those Bordeaux you were talking about. A week on Saturday, how's that?'

She paused, consulting her diary, Bond guessed. 'Yes, James, that'll be great.'

He imagined her again: the abundant red hair, the sparkling golden-green eyes, the rustling as she crossed her legs.

Then she added, 'And you'll have to bring a date.'

The whiskey stopped halfway to his lips. 'Of course,' Bond said automatically.

'You and yours, Tim and me. It'll be such great fun.'

'Tim. Your fiancé.'

'You might've heard we went through a bad patch. But he turned down a chance of a big job overseas to stay in London.'

'Good man. Came to his senses.'

'It's hardly his fault for considering it. I'm not easy to live with. But we decided to see if we could make it work. We have history together. Oh, do let's try for Saturday. You and Tim can talk cars and motorbikes. He knows quite a lot about them. More than I do, even.'

She was talking quickly — too quickly. Ophelia Maidenstone was savvy, in addition to being clever, of course, and she was fully aware of what had happened between them at the

534

restaurant last Monday. She'd sensed the very real connection they'd had and would be thinking even now that something might have developed . . . had the past not intruded.

The past, Bond reflected wryly: Severan Hydt's passion.

And his nemesis.

He said sincerely, 'I'm very glad for you, Philly.'

'Thank you, James,' she said, a dash of emotion in her voice.

'But listen, I won't have you spending your life wheeling babies around Clapham in a pram. You're the best liaison officer we've ever had and I'm insisting on using you on every assignment I possibly can.'

'I'll be there for you, James. Whenever and wherever you want me.'

Under the circumstances, probably not the best choice of words, he reflected, smiling to himself. 'I have to go, Philly. I'll ring you next week for the post-mortem on Incident Twenty.'

They disconnected.

Bond ordered another drink. When it arrived, he drank half as he looked out over the harbour, though he was not seeing much of its spectacular beauty. And his distraction had nothing — well, little — to do with Ophelia Maidenstone's repaired engagement.

No, his thoughts dealt with a more primal theme.

His mother, a spy . . .

Suddenly a voice intruded on his turbulent musings. 'I'm late. I'm sorry.'

James Bond turned to Bheka Jordaan, sitting down across from him. 'She's well, Ugogo?'

'Oh, yes, but at my sister's she made us all watch a *'Sgudi 'Snaysi* rerun.'

Bond lifted an eyebrow.

'A Zulu-language sitcom from some years ago.'

It was warm under the terrace's heater and Jordaan slipped off her navy-blue jacket. Her red shirt had short sleeves and he could see that she had not used make-up on her arm. The scar inflicted by her former co-workers was quite prominent. He wondered why she was not concealing it tonight.

Jordaan regarded him carefully. 'I was surprised you accepted my invitation to dinner. I am paying, by the way.'

'That's not necessary.'

Frowning, she said, 'I didn't assume it was.'

Bond said, 'Thank you, then.'

'I wasn't sure I'd ask you. I actually debated for some time. I'm not a person who debates much. I usually decide rather quickly, as I think I've told you.' She paused and looked away. 'I'm sorry your date in the wine country didn't work out.'

'Well, all things considered, I'd rather be here with you than in Franschhoek.'

'I should think so. I'm a difficult woman but not a mass murderer.' She added ominously, 'But you should not flirt with me . . . Ah, don't deny it! I remember very well your look in the airport the day you arrived.'

'I flirt a lot less than you think I do.

Psychologists have a term for that. It's called projecting. You project your feelings on to me.'

'That remark in itself is flirtatious!'

Bond laughed and gestured the sommelier forward. He displayed the bottle of the South African sparkling wine Bond had ordered to be brought when his companion arrived. The man opened it.

Bond tasted it and nodded approval. Then he said to Jordaan, 'You'll like this. A Graham Beck Cuvée Clive. Chardonnay and Pinot Noir. The 2003 vintage. It's from Robertson, the Western Cape.'

Jordaan gave one of her rare laughs. 'Here I've been lecturing you about South Africa, but it seems you know a few things yourself.'

'This wine's as good as anything you'll get in Reims.'

'Where is that?'

'France — where champagne is made. East of Paris. A beautiful place. You'd enjoy it.'

'I'm sure it's lovely but apparently there's no need to go there if our wine is as good as theirs.'

Her logic was unassailable. They tilted their glasses towards each other. '*Khotso*,' she said. 'Peace.'

'*Khotso*.'

They sipped and sat for some moments in silence. He was surprisingly comfortable in the company of this 'difficult woman'.

She set her glass down. 'May I ask?'

'Please,' Bond responded.

'When Gregory Lamb and I were in the caravan at the Sixth Apostle, recording your conversation with Felicity Willing, you said to her that you'd hoped it might work out between you two. Was that true?'

'Yes.'

'Then I'm sorry. I've had some bad luck too when it comes to relationships. I know what it's like when the heart turns against you. But we're resilient creatures.'

'We are indeed. Against all odds.'

Her eyes slipped away and she stared at the harbour for a time.

Bond said, 'It was my bullet that killed him, you know — Niall Dunne, I mean.'

Startled, she began, 'How did you know I was . . . ?' Her voice faded.

'Was that the first time you'd shot someone?'

'Yes, it was. But how can you be sure it was your bullet?'

'I'd decided at that range to make my target vector a head shot. Dunne had one wound in his forehead and one in the torso. The head shot was mine. It was fatal. The lower wound, yours, was superficial.'

'You're sure it was your shot in his head?'

'Yes.'

'Why?'

'In that shooting scenario I wouldn't't've missed,' Bond said simply.

Jordaan was silent for a moment. Then she said, 'I suppose I'll have to believe you. Anyone who uses the phrases 'target vector' and 'shooting scenario' surely would know where his bullets went.'

Earlier, Bond thought, she might have said this

with derision — a reference to his violent nature and flagrant disregard for the rule of law — but now she was simply making an observation.

They sat back and chatted for a time, about her family and his life in London, his travels.

Night was cloaking the city now, a kind autumn evening of the sort that graces this part of the southern hemisphere, and the vista sparkled with fixed lights on land and floating lights on vessels. Stars, too, except in the black voids nearby — where the king and prince of Cape Town's rock formations blocked out the sky: Table Mountain and Lion's Head.

The plaintive baritone call of a horn reached up to them from the harbour.

Bond wondered if its source was one of the ships delivering food.

Or perhaps it was from a tour boat bringing people back from the prison museum on nearby Robben Island where people like Nelson Mandela, Kgalema Motlanthe and Jacob Zuma — all of whom had become presidents of South Africa — had been locked away for so many hard years during apartheid.

Or maybe the horn was from a cruise ship preparing to depart for other ports of call, summoning tired passengers, carrying bags of clingfilm-wrapped biltong, pinotage wine and ANC black, green and yellow tea towels, along with their tourist impressions of this complicated country.

Bond gestured to the waiter, who proffered menus. As the policewoman took one, her wounded arm brushed his elbow briefly. And they shared a smile, which was slightly less brief.

Yet despite the personal truth-and-reconciliation occurring between them at the moment, Bond knew that, when dinner concluded, he would put her into a taxi to take her to Bo-Kaap, and return to his room to pack for his flight to London tomorrow morning.

He knew this, as Kwalene Nkosi would say, without doubt.

Oh, the idea of a woman who was perfectly attuned to him, with whom he could share all secrets — could share his life — appealed to James Bond and had proved comforting and sustaining in the past. But in the end, he now realised, such a woman, indeed *any* woman, could occupy but a small role in the peculiar reality in which he lived. After all, he was a man whose purpose found him constantly on the move, from place to place, and his survival and peace of mind required that this transit be fast, relentlessly fast, so that he might overtake prey and outpace pursuer.

And, if he correctly recalled the poem Philly Maidenstone had so elegantly quoted, travelling fast meant travelling forever alone.

GLOSSARY

AIVD: Algemene Inlichtingen- en Veiligheidsdienst. The Netherlands security service, focusing on intelligence gathering and combating internal, non-military threats.

BIA: Bezbednosno-informativna Agencija. The Serbian foreign intelligence and internal security agency.

CIA: Central Intelligence Agency. The main foreign intelligence gathering and espionage organisation of the United States. Ian Fleming reportedly played a role in the founding of the CIA. During the Second World War, he penned an extensive memo on creating and running an espionage operation for General William 'Wild Bill' Donovan, head of America's Office of Strategic Services. Donovan was instrumental in the formation of OSS's successor, the CIA.

COBRA: Cabinet Office Briefing Room A. A senior-level crisis-response committee in the United Kingdom, usually headed by the prime minister or other high-ranking government official and composed of individuals whose jobs are relevant to a particular threat facing the nation. Although the name usually includes, in the media at least, a reference to Conference Room A in the main Cabinet Office building in Whitehall, it could convene in any meeting room.

541

CCID: Crime Combating and Investigation Division of the South African Police Service (see below): The major investigative unit. It specialises primarily in serious crimes, such as murder, rape and terrorism.

DI: Defence Intelligence. The British military's intelligence operation.

Division Three: A fictional security organ of the British government based in Thames House. Loosely affiliated with the Security Service (see below), Division Three engages in tactical and operational missions within the UK's borders to investigate and neutralise threats.

FBI: Federal Bureau of Investigation. The main domestic security agency in the United States, responsible for investigating criminal activities within the borders, and certain threats to the United States and its citizens abroad.

Five: Informal reference to MI5, the Security Service (see below).

FO or FCO: The Foreign and Commonwealth Office. The main diplomatic and foreign policy agency of the United Kingdom, headed by the foreign secretary, who is a senior member of the cabinet.

FSB: Federal'naya Sluzhba Bezopasnosti Rossiyskoy Federatsii. The domestic security agency within Russia. Similar to the FBI (see above) and the

Security Service (see below). Formerly the KGB (see below) performed this function.

GCHQ: Government Communications Headquarters. The government agency in the United Kingdom that collects and analyses foreign signals intelligence. Similar to the NSA (see below) in America. Also referred to as the Doughnut, because of the shape of the main building, which is located in Cheltenham.

GRU: Glavnoye Razvedyvatel'noye Upravleniye. The Russian military intelligence organisation.

KGB: Komitet Gosudarstvennoy Bezopasnosti. The Soviet foreign intelligence and domestic security organisation until 1991, when it was replaced by the SVR (see below) for foreign intelligence and the FSB (see above) for internal intelligence and security.

Metropolitan Police Service: The police force whose jurisdiction is Greater London (excluding the City of London, which has its own police). Known informally as the Met, Scotland Yard or the Yard.

MI5: The Security Service (see below).

MI6: The Secret Intelligence Service (see below).

MoD: Ministry of Defence. The organisation within the United Kingdom overseeing the armed forces.

NIA: National Intelligence Agency. The domestic security agency of South Africa, like MI5 (see above) or the FBI (see above).

NSA: National Security Agency. The government agency in the United States that collects and analyses foreign signals and related intelligence, from mobile phones, computers and the like. It is the American version of the UK's GCHQ (see above), with which it shares facilities both in England and the US.

ODG: Overseas Development Group. A covert operational unit of British security operating largely independently but ultimately under the control of the UK's FCO (see above). Its purpose is to identify and eliminate threats to the country by extraordinary means. The fictional ODG operates from an office building near Regent's Park, London. James Bond is an agent with the 00 Section of O (Operations) Branch of the ODG. Its director-general is known as M.

SAPS: South African Police Service. The main domestic police operation serving South Africa. Its efforts range from street patrol to major crime.

SAS: Special Air Service. The British Army's special forces unit. It was formed during the Second World War.

SBS: Special Boat Service. The Royal Navy's special forces unit. It was formed during the Second World War.

Security Service: The domestic security agency in the United Kingdom, responsible for investigating both foreign threats and criminal activities within the borders. It corresponds to the FBI (see above) in the United States, though it is primarily an investigative and surveillance operation — unlike the FBI, it has no authority to make arrests. Known informally as MI5 or Five.

SIS: Secret Intelligence Service. The foreign intelligence gathering and espionage agency of the United Kingdom. It corresponds to the CIA in the United States. Known informally as MI6 or Six.

SOCA: Serious Organised Crime Agency. The law-enforcement organisation within the United Kingdom responsible for investigating major criminal activity inside the borders. Its agents and officers have the power of arrest.

Spetznaz: Voyska Spetsialnogo Naznacheniya. A general reference to special forces in the Russian intelligence community and the military. Known informally as Spetznaz.

SVR: Sluzhba Vneshney Razvedk. The Russian foreign intelligence gathering and espionage agency. Formerly the KGB (see above) performed this function.

ACKNOWLEDGEMENTS

All novels are to some extent collaborative efforts, and this one more so than most. I wish to express my deep appreciation to the following for so tirelessly assisting to make sure this project got off the ground and that it grew into the best book it could be: Sophie Baker, Francesca Best, Felicity Blunt, Jessica Craig, Sarah Fairbairn, Cathy Gleason, Jonathan Karp, Sarah Knight, Victoria Marini, Carolyn Mays, Zoe Pagnamenta, Betsy Robbins, Deborah Schneider, Simon Trewin, Corinne Turner and my friends in the Fleming family. Special thanks go to the copyeditor of all copyeditors, Hazel Orme, as well as Vivienne Schuster, whose inspired title graces the novel.

Finally, thanks to the operatives of my own Overseas Development Group: Will and Tina Anderson, Jane Davis, Julie Deaver, Jenna Dolan and, of course, Madelyn Warcholik.

And for readers thinking that Cape Town's Table Mountain Hotel I mention in the book sounds familiar, that's because its inspiration is the Cape Grace, which is just as lovely but is not — to my knowledge — populated by any spies.

We do hope that you have enjoyed reading this large print book.

Did you know that all of our titles are available for purchase?

We publish a wide range of high quality large print books including:
Romances, Mysteries, Classics
General Fiction
Non Fiction and Westerns

Special interest titles available in large print are:
The Little Oxford Dictionary
Music Book
Song Book
Hymn Book
Service Book

Also available from us courtesy of Oxford University Press:
Young Readers' Dictionary
(large print edition)
Young Readers' Thesaurus
(large print edition)

For further information or a free brochure, please contact us at:
Ulverscroft Large Print Books Ltd.,
The Green, Bradgate Road, Anstey,
Leicester, LE7 7FU, England.
Tel: (00 44) **0116 236 4325**
Fax: (00 44) **0116 234 0205**

Other titles published by
The House of Ulverscroft:

EDGE

Jeffery Deaver

In Washington, D.C., when Henry Loving targets police detective Ryan Kessler, the investigator and his family are immediately put under government protection. Loving is a ruthless 'lifter', hired to extract information from his victims. And he uses whatever means necessary, including kidnapping, torturing or killing their family. Corte is assigned to guard the Kesslers; an uncompromising officer devoted to protecting his charges. A brilliant game strategist, he knows how brutal the lifter can be — six years earlier, Loving killed someone close to him. The situation escalates into a deadly battle of wits between protector and lifter. But as the lifter closes in on his prey, will Corte protect his charges, or expose them to a killer in the name of personal revenge . . . ?